I0677017

longing
to Be

OTHER BOOKS BY THE AUTHOR

Last Goodbye

Longing to Be

LAUREL OSTIGUY

Copyright © 2016 by Laurel Ostiguy

All rights reserved.

Visit my website at www.facebook.com/AuthorLaurelOstiguy

http://twitter.com/authorlaurelo

Email: authorlaurelo@gmail.com

Cover Designer: RBA Designs | Romantic Book Affairs

Cover model: Haley Jorden

Photographer: Lindee Robinson Photography

Editor and Interior Designer: Jovana Shirley, Unforeseen Editing, www.unforeseenediting.com

No part of this book may be reproduced or transmitted in any form or by any means, electronic or mechanical, including photocopying, recording, or by any information storage and retrieval system without the written permission of the author, except for the use of brief quotations in a book review.

This book is a work of fiction. Names, characters, places, and incidents either are products of the author's imagination or are used fictitiously. Any resemblance to actual persons, living or dead, events, or locales is entirely coincidental.

ISBN-13: 978-0692833483

Acknowledgments

To my family and friends—Thank you for supporting me these past few years. The outpouring of support cannot be thanked adequately here, but you have truly been unbelievable to me. I owe any and all success to you.

To all of those who read *Last Goodbye*, my sincere thank you for taking a chance on me. Please consider leaving a review on Goodreads or retail sites, like Amazon.

Thank you Jovana, Letitia, Kate, Carol, Lindee, Catherine Milos, and Mila for your continued guidance, feedback, and help.

To Jeff—Thank you for all your love.

To Connor and Brennan—Knowing how proud you have been of me through this journey has made every moment worth it.

One

THE HAMPTONS' OWN
AUBREY VAN TOUSEN

MAY 20, 1995

"Bree, senorita, time to wake up," Claudia says softly as she touches my arm.

Claudia has been my unofficial alarm clock for the better part of my childhood. I groan slightly as I turn to face her.

"You don't want to be late for your own graduation," she says in her thick Spanish accent.

"I know," I say as I open my eyes and peer up at her.

I love Claudia. She has been good to me throughout the better part of my childhood. My father hired her years ago to clean our house, but within a few months, my parents decided that we could not function without her. I have to believe it was because she always went the extra mile. Like bringing in fresh flowers to fill the vase in the front foyer or how she would leave a chocolate on my bed after she made it. My personal favorite: she would tuck a note in my bag each and every day with some kind reminder of what I had scheduled the next day, or had to bring to school. She'd add a Spanish word at the bottom and what it meant in English. So, they asked her to live with us and manage our household. She has done much more than that. Sometimes, I think she is one of the only people in my life who I can be myself around. I've never told her that, but I get the sense that she knows it.

See, growing up in Hampton Bays in Southampton, New York, I've kind of been expected to act a certain way, dress in all the best clothes, and be friends with the kids in my town who are, for all intents and purposes, exactly like me. This is one of the many reasons I am beyond excited to be leaving for college in a few months.

Onondaga State University was my first choice. The campus is breathtaking and the marketing program is top-notch. I toured many schools, but since the moment I told my father I wanted to study marketing, OSU has continued to remain in the conversation. It is an elite school, and, since my visit to the campus last year, I simply cannot envision myself anywhere else. I *could* go anywhere since money is not a factor whatsoever. Therefore, like most of my high school friends, I appeased my parents and applied to seven schools. They have instilled in me to keep my options open, but when it comes to college, there is no other choice.

Reluctantly, and under the careful stare of Claudia, I drag my tired body out of bed and head into my bathroom. I turn on the shower, and then I go over to the sink and put toothpaste on my toothbrush.

"I hung your dress in your closet!" Claudia yells to me.

"Thank you," I reply with a mouthful of peppermint foam.

"I'll be back in a few minutes," she states.

Then, my bedroom door closes.

I undress and get into the shower. I wash my hair, shave my legs, and scrub my body. I towel off and then wrap my hair in a towel before twisting it on top of my head.

My bra and panties are hanging on the back of the bathroom door. I never ask her to do this, but she does it every day. I've never had the heart to tell her that I don't want her to do it. I know she takes such pride in how she cares for me. Every time I leave the house, she smiles brightly at me and tells me how wonderful I look.

When I was seven years old, I came down the stairs with tears in my eyes, feeling like I didn't look pretty, and Claudia was waiting at the bottom of the stairs, smiling from ear to ear.

"Oh, Aubrey, you are—what's wrong?"

"I don't want to go to school."

"Oh, cariño. Por qué?" She asked me why.

"Because," I said as I fumbled with my dress.

She knelt down in front of me. She reached up around her neck and pulled off the gorgeous pink-and-gold scarf she had on and quickly whisked it around my neck. She hugged me tightly and then turned me toward the mirror in the foyer. The smile that erupted across her face was infectious, and I smiled in return. I had her scarf, and something about having it made me feel warm inside.

Then, she whispered in my ear, "You'd look beautiful in a paper bag." She laughed.

Consequently, here I am, at eighteen, still having Claudia lay out my clothes for me.

I lean over the mirror and pull open my makeup drawer. I inspect my skin before I put on my moisturizer.

As a model, I've been told by agents and photographers, "Be cocky, or no one will believe you are worth their time."

In many ways, while modeling has brought me some fame and acknowledgment, it has also made me incredibly hyperaware of my appearance.

After I put on my makeup, accentuating my large brown eyes, I dry my long brunette hair.

Claudia comes in the bathroom, holding up my light-blue dress. "Come."

She takes the dress off the hanger. I step into it and hold up my hair as she zippers up the back. I love this dress. I smooth down the material and inspect it. It fits perfectly, and I am happy she chose this for me today.

As I turn around to thank her, I notice her eyes are misty.

She wipes away a tear. "Look at you, such a magnificent woman you have become. I am so proud of you."

"Oh, Claudia," I gush.

In some way, with me graduating, a sudden urgency pulses through me, as though the years we have spent together, have not nearly been long enough. I can see in her eyes that she feels the same way.

"Here," she beckons to me as she reaches into her pocket. She pulls out a small jewelry box.

"No, Claudia, I can't."

"It's a gift for your graduation. Please."

I take the box from her and open it. Inside, I find a lovely necklace.

"It's an Indalo!" she exclaims as I take it out.

It is a stick figure with an arch over the head from one hand to the other, like it's holding a rainbow.

"An Indalo?"

"Yes, it is a magical symbol. I can remember, as a little girl, it was customary to paint the Indalo symbol on the fronts of houses and businesses to protect them from evil. To carry the charm is only beneficial if it has been presented as a gift. And, now, as you leave your home, this will protect you, too, my precious Aubrey."

She reaches for me and pulls me into her. She strokes my hair. Then, she whispers, *"Fue un placer verte crecer. Mantente fiel a ti mismo, y nunca te equivocarás."* It was a pleasure to see you grow. Stay true to yourself, and you will never go wrong.

I catch most of what she relayed to me, but I presume that it would lose its true meaning if I asked her to say it in English. She says it with such love and care that I know, she meant it. I put the necklace on with Claudia's help.

"Bree!" My mother yells. "Come on, darling." My mother's tone is impatient.

I glance at Claudia one last time and smile at her. I hate that she isn't coming to my graduation, but then again, I know she'll be here, waiting for me when I return. I have to accept it. The help doesn't come to graduations.

"Coming, Mother!" I yell back as I slip on my nude Jimmy Choo high heels.

I grab my cap and gown, which Claudia also laid out for me, and I leave my room. I tuck the necklace she gave me into the front of my dress. I want it to be our little secret. I get the sense that my mother is a bit jealous of my connection with Claudia. But I know, no matter what my parents have in store for me as a graduation present, it will pale in comparison to what Claudia gave me. My mother doesn't understand that, sometimes, meaningful possessions are far better than expensive ones.

I rush down our staircase and see my parents are waiting at the bottom for me. My father places his hand over his heart as we lock eyes.

My father and I have a much better relationship than my mother and I do. It's not that I necessarily love my father more, but I sense he understands me a little better and actually listens to me when I talk. My mother, conversely, is more concerned with my modeling career and being kind of a stage mom instead of really understanding what my dreams are. I plan to make my mark in this world—and not by being on the cover of a magazine. Not that I have an issue with being on a cover, but after I graduate, I want to work my way to being the first woman chief marketing officer at a large technology firm. I want to change the digital structure of the future. I know this would make my father very proud.

"Bree, sweetheart, you look stunning," my father says.

"Thanks, Dad. You look handsome."

It's hard not to look good in a thousand-dollar suit. I lean in and give him a big hug.

"Let me see you," my mother says. She reaches up and puts her thumb and forefinger on my chin. She turns my head from side to side, inspecting me.

I catch my mother's eyes and plead with her to stop. She makes me second-guess myself; she always has. She notices.

"You look wonderful!" she exclaims. Then, she gently kisses me on the cheek.

"Thank you," I say in a hushed voice.

"Claudia, we are leaving!" my mother yells.

But Claudia is already standing at the top of the stairs. She must have seen the awkward encounter between my mother and me. I glance up and wave slightly to her before following my parents toward the garage.

"One last thing before we go." My father pauses as he opens the door to the oversize garage.

He holds it open as I walk past him. There, parked next to my father's Range Rover, is a brand-new navy-blue Mercedes GLC300 SUV.

"Happy graduation," he says.

"Yes, happy graduation, darling," my mother adds.

"Daddy, this is amazing, but it's too much, honestly," I say as I approach the car.

It is a gorgeous machine and more than any person my age should have.

"You like it?" he asks.

"Yes, of course. But what did you do with my Jeep?"

I love my Jeep. Driving the Jeep makes me feel free, down to earth, and untouchable. I know it sounds silly, but with the roof off and my hair blowing in the breeze, it always takes me away. Helps me escape the reality that is my life. The reality that my mother would rather have an eighteen-year-old drive a Mercedes than a Jeep. She has told me she didn't like me driving the Jeep. I'm betting this was her idea.

"Don't worry, darling; you can still use the Jeep for the beach, but this is a more grown-up car," my mother says.

Grown-up car? I wouldn't exactly consider myself a full-fledged grown-up.

I suppose, with the way they see me in photos, working as a model, I probably appear to be much older than I actually am.

"Thank you. Thank you, both. Really, it's…"

"You can drive it later, honey. We need to leave," my mom says as she climbs into my father's car.

"Yes, of course." I get into the backseat. I'm used to my mother cutting me off mid-sentence, but it still stings when she does it.

My father pulls into the parking lot of Hampton Bays High School. The sea of luxury cars spread out before us is something I'm all-too used to by now since half of my friends' parents drive these cars. That is why I prefer my Jeep. My father knows this, and I'm now convinced the Mercedes was solely my mother's idea

"Have either of you spoken to Andrew?" I ask.

My brother, Andrew, is seven years older than me and lives in California. He is a lawyer and barely visits anymore. Can't say I blame him. It's a long flight. In all honesty, what's there to come back to? I think our age difference is part of the reason we don't seem to have much in common, but I always look forward to him being home.

"He should be arriving by six. He was very sorry he couldn't be here sooner," my father replies.

"I know," I say. "He called me this morning."

I'm disappointed he won't make it to my graduation, but at least he is coming home on the same day.

My parents walk me through the main doors of the high school.

"See you after," my father says to me.

"Don't forget to smile," my mother chimes in.

"Okay. Bye."

They approach the double doors and go into the auditorium. I mosey down the hallway, toward the back of the school where they told us all to meet to line up for the ceremony.

"Pretty dress, bitch," someone says snidely.

It's not a compliment, but I am used to this by now.

I whip around and see none other than my so-called best friend, Joss, standing there. Her real name is Jill, but she hates that name, so she goes by Joss. I've known her pretty much my whole life, so by default, she is kind of my best friend. But, deep, deep, deep down in a place I don't like to think about, I secretly hate her. I secretly hate all my friends here.

"Hi, Joss. I know. Isn't this dress awesome?" I toss my hair to the side and smile at her.

"Check these out," she says as she pushes back her perfect blonde hair to show me her gigantic diamond earrings.

"Wow. A grad present, I assume?"

"Of course."

"Cool," I say.

She pulls me by the arm. "Come on, you're going to make us late."

We hurry toward the restless group of graduates gathered ahead.

Our classmates are all lined up. Joss and I find our group of friends settled somewhere in the middle. In the gym, we have our marching orders as to where each of us needs to be seated.

"Joss, babe, you are hot," Dashiell remarks. He eyes her up and down.

Dashiell and Joss have been together since sophomore year and have basically ruled the school as the *It* couple. They were homecoming king and queen our senior year, junior prom king and queen, and voted Best Couple in the yearbook our junior and senior years. I find them terribly annoying, but I have a feeling most people do; they just don't have the balls to say it. Much like me.

"Thank you, baby," Joss coos as she snuggles up next to him.

He is tall with blond hair and pale blue eyes. They have continuously reminded me of Ken and Barbie, but I would never tell them that to their faces.

"Bree, how goes it?"

"Good. You know, ready for the big day to finally be over," I say with of a laugh.

"I hear you," Dashiell says.

"Hey, Bree. You coming to the party tonight?" Asher says.

Asher is best friends with Dashiell. That's why we are constantly around each other. To me, he appears to be unaffected by his environment, which I've admired about him. He has long, thick dark hair, doesn't care what kind of clothes he wears, and never, ever talks about his parents' money—which, around here, is unheard of. He's not my type, but something about him appeals to me. I imagine, if I'd ever had a high school boyfriend, I would have wanted it to be him. I think I could have tolerated him for extended periods of time. But it felt too cliquey to me to date Asher while Joss and Dashiell were dating, too.

"Well, Andrew is coming home tonight, so I might come by later."

"She'll be there," Joss interjects.

I roll my eyes at Asher, and he laughs. She is bossy, and we've had to put up with it over the years.

"Come on, Class of 1995. Put your caps and gowns on," Mr. Jenkins, our principal, announces as he passes by.

Joss makes a face at me. I can't help but giggle. She hates being told what to do, no matter where it comes from.

The ceremony is relatively painless. Our valedictorian, Danielle Hassle, gives an intriguing speech.

She is a pretty quiet girl who keeps to herself. It is rare to see her at parties or school events. She talks mostly about how little it matters what happens today when it is our future we need to worry about. I'm paraphrasing, but I kind of get where she is going with her speech. Worrying about what others thought was exactly how I lived my high school days and why I can't wait to get the hell out.

As I stare ahead and watch Danielle, I realize that she was nice to me, but I'm deducing she wouldn't say the same in return. It's sort of a product of the crowd I run with. At a young age, I knew that, if I didn't play along with the mean crowd, I'd be nothing but a target for my entire life. In many ways, I guess I acted like Joss, so she wouldn't make me a target, like I saw her do to others countless times, including Danielle. I blame Joss for most of the people who hate me. It's easier than acknowledging I'm an asshole, too.

After the ceremony, we go outside to meet our families by the large oak tree on the side of the high school. It is a tradition for groups to gather there for photos after graduation.

"Bree, Bree!" Nelly yells.

I turn to see her hurrying toward me.

"Hi, Nelly." I give her a hug.

"Where, oh where, is that gorgeous brother of yours?" she asks.

Nelly has been in love with my brother for the better part of her teenage years. It's sad because he's hardly paid any attention to her.

"Coming home tonight."

Her eyes fly open. "Please say you'll bring him to Dashiell's party."

"I'll ask him, for you," I say sarcastically.

Nelly rolls her beautiful eyes at me and laughs.

Nelly is my better friend, only Joss doesn't know that. Joss and Nelly don't really get along, and when I get caught in the middle, it usually means that Joss wins, and Nelly pays the price. I hate it because, deep down, I know the only reason Joss doesn't like Nelly is because other people do. It's a no-win situation for Nelly and one more reason I secretly hate Joss.

I know, I know; it's a terrible thing to say about a friend, but honestly, she doesn't know how to be a friend, and sometimes, in life, it is better to go along to get along.

"Here comes the sovereign," Nelly says under her breath, forcing a huge smile across her face.

Joss and Dashiell approach like the king and queen of graduation.

"Hello, Nelly," Joss says.

Nelly leans in to give her a hug, and Joss gently pats her on the back with one hand.

"Congratulations, Joss," she says. "You too, Dashiell."

Now, Dashiell, on the other hand—and in my humble opinion—is infatuated with Nelly, only he would never admit it. But I see the way he stares at her; it's painfully obvious to me. Nelly is a nicer and slightly prettier version of Joss. Her blonde hair is perfectly flowing. Her lips are pouty, and hers eyes sparkle when she gazes at you. Maybe because Joss always has that bitch expression on her face, it makes her seem less attractive in spite of her lovely appearance.

"Come on, kids," Joss's mother hollers. "Get in front of the tree, so we can get a picture of the Class of 1995!"

"Mother, we are not kids," Joss barks at her.

"Okay, dear," she says as she shuffles us along.

I see my mother and father and wave slightly. My father pulls out his camera and starts snapping away as we try to corral ourselves under the tree.

I note Asher moving to stand next to me as we settle in for photographs. He slightly drapes his arm around my waist. It is the kind of attention I need to make me smile during these dreadful pictures.

Finally, our parents finish, and I quickly remove my cap and gown before anyone can protest.

"I'll see you all later," I say to everyone.

As I head over to my parents, I get the usual *good-bye*s and *see you later*s as I walk off. I approach my parents. The smile that grows across my father's face is electric.

"Bree, I am very proud of you, my straight-A student. You've made us so happy." He beams.

"Thanks, Daddy," I reply as he hugs me.

Once he lets me go, I hand him my diploma and smile at him.

"Yes, honey, you looked wonderful up there," my mom says softly.

"Thanks, Mom."

She gives me a hug, which surprises me since she doesn't often show her affection.

"Your mother and I have a reservation at Catch. We thought we'd take you there before Andrew comes home," my father says.

Catch is my favorite seafood restaurant and impossible to get into, but my father knows the owner. My father dabbles in the restaurant business from time to time. Although I have a hard time in keeping up with his latest ventures, I know he's made a lot of connections along the way.

"Oh, wonderful." I follow them toward our car.

I turn around to gaze at the high school, and my parents drift further away from where I stand. I am no longer a high school student. I am finally going to get out of this place. I smile to myself. I am almost there. In only a few months, I will be at Onondaga State University.

Two

PRELUDE TO AN ENCOUNTER

"Where's the graduate?" my brother yells as he enters the front foyer.

I am sitting in the den with my father. We're watching tennis, which I've come to love doing with my father, as he scours over some paperwork. The den is my favorite room. The walls are enclosed in shelves that reach all the way to the ceiling. Thousands of books are in the room, and a ladder runs around the room on a track. I can remember coming in here as a kid and climbing all over the shelves, much to my mother's chagrin. My father's desk sits in front of floor-to-ceiling windows overlooking the backyard garden, which is probably why the garden is my second favorite place. In the center of the room, are two dark brown leather chairs and a leather couch facing a large glass coffee table. The TV comes up from inside the mantel above the fireplace.

"In here!" I yell.

I hear my brother drop his suitcase on the floor and approach the den. He comes in, holding a bouquet of bright pink tulips. My favorite.

"Bree," he says with a huge smile. "Congratulations, sis."

I get up from the couch and run over to him. "Are these guilt flowers?" I say with a sly smile.

"Yes." He hands them to me and gives me a big hug, lifting me.

"Put me down, you Neanderthal," I squeal, but not before hugging him tightly in return.

He reluctantly lowers me to the ground. "Looking good, kid."

"And you are very tan," I say.

My brother is the definition of handsome. At six foot three inches with thick dark hair and strong features, including striking light-brown eyes, he carries himself with confidence. My whole life, I've caught more than Nelly looking his way. Yet he still remains single and seems to love every minute of it.

"Andrew, how was your flight?" my father asks.

"Great, Dad." Andrew walks over to my father and kisses him on top of his head.

My father reaches up and pats his arm.

"Where is Mother?"

"Not sure. Maybe in the pool?"

"Yes, she said she was going for a swim."

"Great. I'll go say hello," he says with a smile.

"Before you do, can I ask a favor?" I ask.

"Sure," my brother says, rolling his eyes.

"Can you stop by Dashiell's party tonight, to say hello?"

"Since I missed your graduation, yes, I will," he says with a grin. "But it'll be later. I have plans to see Dean before he heads back to Connecticut tonight."

"Dean's in town?" my father asks.

Dean was my brother's closest friend in high school and has become quite the real estate developer in Connecticut.

"Yes, on business, but he has to head back first thing in the morning."

"Ah, great. Well, tell him we say hello," my father adds.

"Will do." Then, he turns back toward me. "When are you leaving for the party, sis?"

I glance at the grandfather clock. "Probably in an hour. I'm going up to get ready now."

"Okay, I'll see you later then," he says. He kisses me on the cheek.

I turn and leave the room to put my flowers in a vase, but Claudia is already standing in the foyer, holding a vase with water.

"Lovely flowers," she says.

I smile at her and then whisper, "You keep them. You know, I can never manage to keep even the most gorgeous flowers from wilting within a day in my care."

I place them in the vase. She smiles brightly as she inhales their scent.

"Of course."

"I'm going to go change for the party," I announce as I start walking up the stairs.

She smiles at me, which means she has already laid out my clothes.

By the time I arrive at Dashiell's house, the driveway is littered with cars. I park my new Mercedes at the very end of the driveway and walk the quarter of a mile or so to the tent that is set up on his parents' property.

Dashiell has been my friend for a long time. Long before Joss started dating him. We spent most of our summer vacations at summer camps and passed the days sailing and swimming when we were young. He used to be much less affected by the money as a kid than he is now. It was as if he woke up one day and realized exactly how much money his parents had. He has sort of become a real dipshit, which always saddens me because I remember the sweet boy I used to play with on the beach. Our fathers have been business partners on a few real estate projects in the city, and our mothers work together on most of the charities in town. In many ways, we remain connected.

His family owns more property than half of the people in this town. His father inherited multiple properties by the time he was thirty years old, and much to everyone's surprise, his father kept them all. He turned three into a local restaurant, a hotel, and a golf course. On his family land, he built two homes and turned the last two properties into gardens, both of which are adjacent to the homes, making the homes seem even bigger. Dashiell is set to inherit half of it; the other half will go to his sister.

It's a wonder why Dashiell is even going away to college. I personally think it's because he wants to party and can afford to go and hang out for four years.

The DJ is encouraging people to come and dance as I near the tent. I don't recognize anyone from school at first until I catch Joss and Dashiell sitting in king and queen chairs at the end of the tent, as though they were glaring down on their royal subjects, judging and plotting their evil revenge on those who had not kissed their majestic rings.

I take a deep breath. It's not as though I don't belong here; it's that I don't *want* to be here. I don't want to do any of this anymore. I want to get to college already.

"Hi!" I say with my fakest smile.

Joss jumps up and comes over to give me a big hug. "Where have you been, bitch?" she exclaims.

"You know, waiting for Andrew to get home."

Dashiell slowly gets up. "What's up?" he says with a half-smile.

"Cool party," I remark.

"Yeah, cool. Food is over there, drinks at the bar, and the DJ plays until I tell them to stop, you know," he says almost incoherently.

"Let's mingle." Joss grabs my arm. She pulls me over toward the drinks. "What do you want?" she asks as she pours herself a drink.

"Club soda for now."

If I didn't specify *for now*, she'd be all over me for not drinking. They like to drink and get sloshed. I like to sit and have a glass of wine. Huge difference.

"Here," she sighs. "God, I'm, like, so high right now; it's crazy." She smiles this wicked grin.

"High? High on what?" *Jesus Christ*, I think. *You have to be high right now? How am I going to get through this night? I am not in the mood to babysit.*

"Dashiell's maid had some Xanax or something, so we took some."

"Xanax? You know that will only make you tired," I scoff.

I know this because my mother once had to take it, and she said she hated how tired it made her.

"Whatever. I feel great, and if you want one, I'll get you one."

"Maybe later," I lie.

"Cool. Mingle?"

Before I can answer, she is halfway across the tent and headed right toward some of our other friends. I notice Nelly and head in that direction as well. I'd best save her before Joss gets in one of her moods and lashes out at her.

"Nelly!" I say.

Thank God for Nelly. She makes me feel like there is still hope that I might have one friend to come out of high school after all is said and done.

"Hey, girl. Looking good," she says sincerely.

"Thanks. You, too!" I smooth down my silk camisole and tweed skirt.

"Some party, huh?"

"Yeah, you'd think he graduated at the top of our class," I reply with a smirk.

"I know, but I'm sure his parents know he's a moron."

"Who's a moron?" Joss pipes up.

Thankfully, it is not light enough to see Nelly's cheeks turn a fiery pink.

"Our landscaper. He left the tractor running in the garage and nearly set it on fire." I, myself, am even amazed at how quickly I can come up with a believable lie.

"Idiot. My father would have fired his ass, like, yesterday," she hisses.

"I know, right?" Nelly adds.

Joss turns and stares at her. It's painfully awkward for all of us as Joss's eyes lock in for too long.

I try to break up this conversation by asking, "Anyway, you guys seen Asher?"

"Yeah. Heard he's inside, playing some stupid video game."

"Cool," I say.

"Hey, your brother coming?" Nelly asks with hopeful wide eyes.

"Yeah, but later." I try to hide the sly grin.

"He is still gorgeous, right?"

"Tan."

"Oh, shit. Ugh, you're so lucky."

"Nelly, gross. That's, like, her brother. What the hell is wrong with you?" Joss barks.

"Yeah, I mean, he *is* my brother. Why would I think he is hot? Isn't that completely gross and taboo?" I say with another smile.

I have to play along with Joss, or she'll pounce on me. Nelly knows this game—or I should say the dynamics between the three of us. I often feel guilty for flipping on Nelly, but she knows I like her far better. I am just playing along.

"Right. Jesus, you guys know what I mean," she says in an attempt to stick up for herself.

"Sure, incest." Joss flips her hair and turns her back to us.

"Hey, let's go dance or something." I turn to Nelly.

With hunched shoulders, she moves past me and toward the dance floor.

We dance for a good hour, enjoying the crowd of people, the music, and the sense of freedom that comes with losing yourself in the moment. It is probably the best I've felt all day.

I notice Dashiell watching us dance, and I can't help but wonder what he is thinking, being so obvious and all. He is totally checking Nelly out. Practically licking his lips. Maybe he doesn't care anymore. Maybe he thinks, because it is his party, he can do whatever he wants. He comes out on the dance floor and grabs Nelly by the waist. He starts grinding with her, like some sexed-up '90s MTV video. I'll never comprehend why he's behaving like this. Drunk and stupid is no way to act at a party. Not with Joss around the corner.

I step back and watch as Dashiell and Nelly fall into this incredible rhythm of moving, shaking, and grinding. It even makes me blush. I swear, by the way they hold on to one another, they truly believe not a soul is left at this party. I try to catch Nelly's eye, but she is not paying attention to me anymore.

Not wanting to be an accomplice any more than I already am, I slowly make my way off the dance floor. I slip past some of our friends before Joss notices that her boyfriend and friend are embarrassing her. They should know better than to mess with her. This is entirely on them.

I stroll into Dashiell's house. A handful of people are lingering in the living and dining room areas. I make my way to the basement in the hopes that some of the guys will be hanging out there, playing video games. This way, I can at least have an alibi if I'm asked to testify at the murder trial of Dashiell and Nelly.

"Hello?" I call out as I make my way down the stairs to the lavish finished basement.

"Yep," I hear someone call back with little enthusiasm.

I enter the massive playroom and see a few guys sitting on the leather couches, eyes glued to the television, as their thumbs beat down on the controls in their hands.

"Bree, what's up?" Asher says as he glances up at me. He smiles wide.

"Hey. Thought I might find you down here." I return an equally kind smile.

"Seeking solitude?" he asks.

"Yeah, something like that."

He knows me too well. Asher and I often find ourselves wanting seclusion at parties, away from all the drama.

"Hey, guys," I say to the other two kids. I think they are both juniors. I recognize one of them from the lacrosse team.

They both mumble something and barely notice me, which I am fine with.

"Have a seat," Asher says as he moves over on the couch.

"Sure. Why not?"

"What's going on up at the party?"

Now, Asher can appreciate the dynamic that is our lives here in the Hamptons. Nothing seems to surprise or faze him, so I lay it out for him.

"So, Joss and Dashiell took Xanax and are all high and stuff, only I don't think they realize they'll both be out," I say as I glance at my watch, "in about an hour. Joss has set her claws deep into Nelly over some stupid remark she made about my brother. And, for some reason, Dashiell has decided that tonight is the night to grind on Nelly on the dance floor. It's like he's been harboring feelings for her since the dawn of time. Well, I scrammed from the scene and am taking refuge down here, as not to be some kind of accomplice in what I am sure will be an epic blowup."

"We gotta see this," one of the other kids says.

The two kids drop their remotes and fly up the stairs, as if they'd heard Michael Jordan himself was at the party.

"Jesus, what the hell?" Asher yells after them. "Have some freaking class!"

"Is it something I said?" I say with a smile.

"Right? Jesus. Amateurs," he scoffs. He puts down his control and turns off the television. "Lots of bullshit going on up there?"

"Yeah, typical party drama." I sigh and stare ahead at the television.

Now, I could use a drink. I get up and go over to the bar where I pour myself a glass of red wine. I walk back over to Asher and sit down next to him. I notice him slide closer to me on the couch. This is not entirely uncommon, considering how often we have hung out over the years. He puts his hands behind his head and turns to glance at me.

"I need to unwind before I can go back up there."

"I hear you." His voice is soft, different almost.

"You okay?"

"Who me?" he says as he leans forward. He takes a sip of his drink and winces as he swallows. "Yeah, you know me. I go with the flow."

"Yeah, I kind of wish I hadn't gone with the flow so much in high school, to be honest." I can't believe I'm even saying this to him, but what the hell? I think he of all people will get where I'm coming from.

I take another sip and feel my shoulders relax. He places his arm around me and gently rubs my shoulder.

"Relax, girl. You're too stressed."

"Is it that obvious?"

"Yeah. I mean, totally." He laughs and continues to massage my tense shoulder.

It feels good, and I start to close my eyes.

"Bree, you ready to go to college?" he asks.

It isn't necessarily what he asks me that makes me pause; it is how he says it—with a seductive tone that seems out of place for him.

I open my eyes. "Yeah, obviously. I'm excited to get out of here; that's for sure."

He stops rubbing my neck and puts his hand on my leg.

"You?"

"Yep. I'm always ready." He tucks a piece of hair behind his ear.

More so today, I notice how attractive his hair is, long and thick, with slightly rust-colored highlights throughout.

"Always ready. You? Mr. Laid-Back himself?"

"Hey, of course." As he slides over more, so does his hand, up my leg.

I stare at his hand.

He gazes longingly at me and smiles kindly. "You're so gorgeous, Bree. You know that?"

I smile but don't answer. He reaches up and brushes a strand of my hair back.

"How about a little kiss for your friend Asher?" he asks with a wicked grin.

I have wondered what it would be like to kiss him. Therefore, I figured, why not? We're friends, and we're also moving halfway across the country from one another in two months. It couldn't be more perfect.

I smile. "Sure."

He leans in, and as he does, his hand goes further up my leg, to the top of my thigh. He kisses me; it is soft and sweet.

He draws back. "See? Friends, easy."

"Yeah, friends, easy." I laugh. I can taste the hard alcohol he must be drinking.

He leans in again—only this time, he pushes me back on the couch.

"What's up, Asher?"

"Nothing, babe. You are hot tonight; that's all." He starts to kiss me again.

It must be the alcohol because he's never been so forward with me—ever.

I kiss him back and run my hand through his hair. As we kiss, I feel my body calming. It's been a while since I've had a good, friendly make-out session.

Jesus, has it really been a year since I last kissed someone? I think.

But then he starts to aggressively pull up my shirt.

I push his hand away. "Slow down, Asher. Jesus."

"Sorry, sorry," he mumbles as he starts kissing my neck.

We kiss more, and then he tries again to raise my shirt, his fingers fumbling wildly.

"Asher, stop it. What happened to just making out?"

"Come on. You need to get ready for college," he says in an uncharacteristically harsh tone.

"What the hell does that mean?" I attempt to shove him to no avail.

"You know, you rich Hamptons bitches need to give it up. Don't be like them, Bree. They are all so stiff."

"Stiff!" I say as I try to push him off.

With all my might, I slip out from under him and crash on the floor. "Screw you, Asher!" I say as I clumsily scramble to my feet.

"Come on back, and we will," he says with a maniacal laugh.

I narrow my eyes at him. "Not funny, Asher, and so not cool." I smooth my camisole and tuck it back in.

"Whatever. Can't you handle a little fun?" He laughs as he lies there on the couch, like some god I am supposed to give myself to.

"I suppose I could if I thought you were worth it." I turn on my heel with tears in my eyes.

I'm painfully surprised that my own friend would treat me with such little care. I hardly think making out should automatically equate to screwing on a couch.

When I get to the stairs, I hear him chuckle and yell, "Stiff!"

My skin crawls, and I want to punch a hole in the wall. But instead, I march up the stairs and straight out of the house, heading toward my car.

As if I needed a reason to be done with high school. Well, I got another one. I am ready. Ready to leave this place behind and all the *friends* I hate.

It must be about one in the morning when my brother creeps into my room.

"Bree? Jesus, you all right?" he asks.

"Yeah. Why? What time is it?"

"Not sure, but I went to the party, and they said you left without telling anyone. Everything okay?"

"Yeah, sorry. Asher was being such an asshole. I'm just done with all that drama." *My so-called friend. What a jerk he turned out to be. Ugh.*

"I hear you. Sounds like there was lots of it, too. Joss made a scene and then ended up hooking up with your friend Asher, and Nelly hooked up with Dashiell. I got the hell out of there once I found out you weren't there."

There is a hatred that swarms inside me. "Good Lord! Seriously? Guess he was determined to get it from someone. They all were."

"Yeah. Crazy stuff."

"Wow, I am even happier I left." *Happy? No. Pissed off. Yes. Needed to get the hell out of there. Unequivocally.*

"You sure you are okay, Bree? Need me to kick Asher's ass before I head back to California?"

"Thanks for the offer, but he's not worth your time." *Not worth anything to me anymore.*

"Well, I'm always here for you, no matter what."

"I sure have missed you." I grasp his hand.

"You, too. But I'm excited for you. It's time, Bree, for you to get out of this town. Experience life outside this bubble we have both lived in."

"It absolutely is," I respond, with total conviction.

Three

WELCOME TO COLLEGE

I must say, I did an exceptional job of avoiding my *friends* this summer. Thankfully, I had a few modeling jobs lined up that kept me away for weeks at a time.

My friend Miguel is a photographer and asked me to be a part of his exhibit, subsequently I spent a few weeks working with him at different locations throughout the city.

The jobs I usually get are print for advertisements. These tend to pay better because they are considered commercial. Agents want to see fresh and interesting photographs that grab their attention, not the same generic shots that they are bombarded with fifty times a day. It's a cutthroat business. Thankfully, I've been doing this for a long time, and because of my experience, I have landed with large companies like PepsiCo, CoverGirl, and *Seventeen Magazine*.

I care about my career as a model, but it pales in contrast to what my friends have done.

Last year, Dashiell spent an entire winter in Colorado, training alongside Olympic athletes because his father paid for it. I mean, he missed an entire semester to go skiing, and no one seemed to care. He came back with what he said was a lifetime pass to any Olympics he wanted. Seriously.

Then, there is Joss. She spent that summer in Milan, helping fashion designers with the next season's line. But what's worse is, she came home with samples worth thousands of dollars. They were some of the most fine-looking pieces of clothing I had ever seen. Half of them, she never wears.

Around town, modeling, believe it or not, is simply not as glamorous.

Your anonymity becomes, in its own way, your selling point because the merchandise takes precedence. So, for many of these jobs, it takes me a few days to shoot, and then a month or so later, I'll see myself on some random magazine, billboard, or bus in the city. No one knows who I am, but it gives me a sense of accomplishment. Silly, I know, but at least I'm spending my own money and not my father's, contrary to what most would believe.

The other weeks that I didn't have work, my father let me tag along with him to the city and mill around his office. I mostly did little odds and ends for him, but in reality, I spent a lot of the time shopping and going out to lunch. He didn't need me around, but I get the feeling, since I'm leaving for school soon, he wanted me close by.

Joss and Asher started dating after the blowup at Dashiell's party, and much to my surprise, Dashiell and Nelly started dating. I thought Nelly had better taste, but dating Dashiell was the ultimate slap in the face for Joss. After the years of torment Joss bestowed upon Nelly, it was well deserved.

Being the odd man out made it easy for me to step aside and let them have their drama-filled summer. I got away, unharmed and unaffected. I saw them from time to time, but you know, young lust leaves little room for a third wheel.

But, now, as I lie in bed and stare up at the ceiling on my last night before college, I can't help but have mixed emotions. Tomorrow, I will be on my own and away from here. I sure will miss my father, Claudia, my mother, and of course, the amenities that go along with living in a mansion. Aside from all that, I am ready to make new friends and start a new life.

Claudia wakes me. "Bree, time to wake," she says sweetly.

I roll over to see her standing in my room, a sad expression upon her face.

I rub my eyes and sit up. "Claudia, what is it?"

She smooths down her dress and stares at her fingers; her face is drawn and sad. I get out of bed and stand before her. I reach for her hand.

"I-I am going to miss having you around this house," she says.

"Me, too. I will miss you; you know that."

I try to smile to make her smile, but then it hits me. I am going to miss her terribly. She has been my sounding board. Whenever I thought no one else, especially my friends, even cared, Claudia has always genuinely cared about me.

"Of course. Please make sure to call me and tell me how your time at college is." She smiles slightly.

"I will, and you can call me, too, whenever you want."

"I packed your stuff. If you are missing anything at school, I'll be sure to overnight it and get it right to you."

"Thank you, Claudia." I lean in and give her a hug. *How am I going to survive without her?*

"Now, you'd better hurry. I laid out your clothes. Your father and mother are eating breakfast. You've a long ride ahead of you."

"Tell them I'll be down in thirty minutes, ready to go."

"Yes, Bree." She smiles and starts to turn but stops. She reaches her arms around me and gives me a big squeeze with a slight kiss on the cheek, something she has never done before.

I am about to tell her how much I love her, but she turns and leaves my room, closing the door behind her.

"Thank you, Claudia, for…everything," I whisper.

I slip into the chair at my desk and pen her a note, much like she used to do for me.

> *Dear Claudia,*
>
> *I hope you know just how much I will miss you. I am, in part, who I am, deep down inside, because of you.*
>
> *Love always,*
>
> *Bree*

After I am done getting dressed, I leave the note on my bed.

I am downstairs in a little over half an hour. My father and mother are already waiting for me in their car. The car is jam-packed with all kinds of items for my room, but many things—like the new mattress, the refrigerator, and the extra dresser my mom insisted I get—are being delivered this afternoon, hence the tight travel schedule we are on.

My father paid for me to have a double room to myself. The single rooms are smaller, and I would have been fine with it, but he wanted me to have a larger room to myself. Sometimes, I don't bother to argue.

My father also requested that I get an on-campus parking pass. One hefty donation to the school, and, voilà, a parking pass arrived at my house. Although I didn't mind the idea of having a car at school, I'd much rather have my Jeep. It's less flashy. But I almost feel obligated to bring the Mercedes. My mother made a comment to me about putting gas in the

Mercedes and the Jeep in the garage. I got her point. Therefore, I'm taking the Mercedes.

My parents help me carry all my belongings into Willis Hall. The mattress, refrigerator, and dresser are all delivered on time and pass my father's inspection. I am anxious to unpack and settle in, but I even surprise myself at how emotional I get when my parents finally say that they are heading back home.

"Be good, darling," my mother says.

"Of course," I say with tears in my eyes.

My father, on the other hand, gives me a huge hug and squeezes me so tight that I let out a groan. He pulls back, and I notice he is crying.

"Dad, please don't. You'll make me cry." My heart pounds in my chest, and my stomach churns. I can't decide if I'll cry or throw up. I'm nervous they are leaving, and I'm nervous about being alone.

"Just promise me, you'll be safe and always be smart about your environment."

"Yes, Daddy. I promise you. Besides, this place compared to New York City? Piece of cake."

I lean in again to hug him, and this time, my mother joins in, wrapping her arms around us both.

"I love you," I say to them. My heart is filled to its maximum capacity.

"We love you, darling, so very much," My father adds.

"Would you like me to walk you out?" I ask.

"No, honey. Stay here and unpack," my mother responds, fighting back her tears.

"Okay, I will." My lip quivers. I wipe a tear from my eye.

My mom and dad head toward my door, and within a moment, they are gone. The strangest sensation washes over me. I still feel so young, yet to be left on my own seems unnatural. I am wishing even more I had insisted on having a roommate. It would be great not to be alone right now.

I spend a good hour unpacking. Lucky for me, Claudia is an incredible packer, and it takes me no time at all to empty the boxes. When I get to the last one, I open it, only to find another box. It's a little smaller than a shoebox, and it's wrapped. I take it out. A small card is attached to it.

Longing to Be

I'M SURE YOU'LL NEED THIS.

LOVE,

CLAUDIA

The anticipation is killing me. I tear off the wrapping paper. I laugh out loud when I realize that she bought me an alarm clock.

Of course I'll need this, I think, *because I no longer have you.*

I plug it in next to my bed and set the time. I can't help but smile as I think of her.

With my room now in order and my stomach rumbling, I decide to venture out and see what I can find at the Student Union. I grab my student ID and my water bottle and put them both in my brand-new Burberry messenger bag that I bought in the city.

I take the stairs down to the main lobby, which is naturally packed with students and parents trying to move into the dorm. I am eager to get out of this mess. I push open the heavy glass door and go out into an absolutely gorgeous summer day. The sun feels incredible on my skin as I make my way toward the Union.

The campus is packed with students milling about. The old brick buildings are bursting with activity as I mosey past them and closer to the center of campus. I fight my way into the busy student center. Once inside the Union, I wander around the bookstore to check out what kinds of things they have before I grab something to eat.

The bookstore is exactly how I remembered it from my campus tour in April, only much more congested. I thumb through some textbooks in the Marketing section and peruse the OSU sweatshirts and T-shirts, but surprisingly, I don't feel like shopping, which is rare for me. I finally decide on buying a few snacks for my room, an address book, some stamps, and stationery.

I go to the coffee shop in the Union and order a bagel and green tea to go. I push open the door to the Union and fumble with my bag, trying to get my wallet back inside.

"Nice bag," I hear a feminine voice say.

I see a girl standing in front of me. "Thanks. It's Burberry."

"I know," she says.

Uh, a girl who knows her stuff? Most people don't know a Burberry from a Coach bag. I eye her up and down for a moment. She is well put together. I notice her watch; it's sporty but expensive.

"Bree," I finally say.

"Missy."

"Nice to meet you. You a freshman?" I ask.

"Yeah, I live in Simmons Hall, other side of campus."

"I live in Willis. First year, too."

"Cool. Where are you from?"

Probably the question I dread the most or love the most, depending on my audience. This time, I dread it, only because I want to make friends of my own accord, not because I have money. Or should I say, my parents' money.

"Hamptons, in New York."

I see her eyes get wide.

"I know where that is."

"You?"

"Connecticut."

A guy approaches us and hands Missy a flyer.

"You girls seem like you'd be up for a dope party tonight!" he says.

"Really? You don't say?" Missy answers with an edge.

I like it.

He turns to me and hands me one as well. "Back-to-school party at one forty-two North Adams Street," he says as he points in the direction of my dorm. "You'll miss a good time if you don't go. Only five bucks to get in." He turns and walks away.

Missy smiles at me. "What do you think?"

"I mean, I'll go if you go since you're the only person I've met so far," I say with a slight chuckle.

"Yeah, why not? See if other girls in your dorm want to go, and I'll do the same! Safety in numbers." She smiles.

"Sounds good."

"Good. Let's meet right back here, say, at eight, and we can all head over."

"Perfect. It was nice meeting you."

"You, too, Bree. See you later."

I go back to my room to eat and call Claudia. I want to call her before my parents get home because I'd like to get the chance to speak with her.

She picks up on the first ring. "Van Tousen estate."

"Claudia, it's me."

"Ah, Miss Bree. *Senorita*, how are you?"

"Wonderful. Thank you so much for the alarm clock. It made me laugh because I was wondering how I was going to get up every day without you around."

"Glad you like it. You know I try to be funny." She laughs.

"You are."

"Tell me what you have done so far in your first few hours."

"Well, I've already unpacked, thanks to your incredible organization."

"You're welcome."

"And I just went to the Union to get a few things for my room and something to eat."

"Oh, good, you are eating."

"Yes, and I met a friend, a girl named Missy. We were invited to a party tonight."

"Please be safe."

"Of course. We are going as a group."

"*Genial*," she says in Spanish.

"Yes, it is great." I laugh. I know she is worried about me by her tone, so I have to let her know that I'm being smart. "Going as a group is the only way to go."

"Okay. Now, do you need anything else?"

"No, thank you. I will call you soon. Tell my parents I called and that I'm doing *genial*."

"Of course. *Adios*." I can hear her smile as she speaks, and I echo the sentiment.

"Bye, Claudia." I put the receiver down and whisper, "You're the best."

I hem and haw over my outfit for the next hour. Finally, I decide on navy-blue shorts and a white lace tank top. Once I get dressed, the necklace Claudia gave me seems to clash with my outfit. It stands out too much. I like it better when I can keep it close to me. I can tell when she gave it to me, the way she held her hand over her heart that she meant it to be kept close to mine. I pause, and then after consideration, I take it off and hang it on my jewelry stand.

Since my floor is quiet and I have yet to see another living soul, I decide to leave and go to meet Missy at the Union.

She is already waiting there with two other girls from her dorm.

"Hey, Bree. This is Rachel and Lizzy."

"Hey. Nice to meet you."

"You, too," they say in unison.

We basically find our way to the party by simply following the hordes of students marching in the general direction of North Adams Street. The girls chat mostly about where they are from and why they picked OSU. By the time we get to the party, it is around eight thirty. There are two guys standing by the back door. We each pay five dollars to get in, and then we walk down the stairs and into the basement.

The basement is absolutely packed, and we are hardly able to move through the crowd. The music is exceptionally loud, making it almost impossible to hear anyone talk. Missy nods her head toward the back room, and we follow her to the bar.

Missy cozies up to the bar and orders our drinks.

I grab the red Solo cup from Missy's hand and take a sip. It doesn't necessarily taste bad, mostly like Kool-Aid—not that there was a lot of Kool-Aid in my house, but this is sweet and red nonetheless.

I realize quickly that I have very little in common with Lizzy. She speaks mostly about hunting on her family's property and what kind of meat she likes to eat. Honestly, it's a disgusting conversation to witness. Listening to her talk about killing animals is a bit too primitive for my taste. Rachel, in contrast, seems pretty cool. She is tall and pretty with long, curly blonde hair. She converses with me about how she makes her own soaps and candles at her studio in Vermont and spends her time with her family making clothes and jewelry to sell. She's interesting, like no one I've met before.

We stand by the bar for one more drink until we start to mingle and move around. Rachel starts chatting with a group of people near the entrance to upstairs. The music is terribly deafening that we decide to move upstairs to the main level where it will be easier to try to carry on a conversation.

Missy and I sit on a couch in the living room with a group of kids we do not know.

"Where are Lizzy and Rachel? I thought they were coming up," I ask.

"I think she said they were going to grab a few more drinks and then meet us up here."

"I see."

"Holy shit! Mark!"

Quickly, a guy turns his head. "Wow. Hey, uh...Missy, right?"

"Yeah, I was two grades below you," she says with a huge smile.

I can see why she's smiling; the guy is cute. Piercing blue eyes. Not chubby but stocky, with a dynamic smile.

"Right. Awesome. So, you're a freshman?"

"Sure am."

"Great. Welcome to OSU."

I can see her beaming from ear to ear. She is smitten.

"Thanks!"

"Your friend?"

"Hey, I'm Bree."

He barely pays any mind to me but sort of nods in my direction. I know I'm wasting my breath but whatever.

"Nice to meet you. This your first party?"

"Yes. So exciting to be here," Missy gushes. She moves her seat over one and starts rambling on with Mark.

I occasionally chime in, but it seems I am witnessing the beginning of a hook-up.

"Let's go get us another drink from the bar," she says.

"Sure." He stands.

Before I can join, she says, "I'll be right back, Bree."

Taking the hint, I say, "Okay, sure."

Not too long after, a guy enters the room and sits down next to me on the couch. He is a little bigger than average, has spiked short hair, and is wearing an Onondaga State T-shirt.

"Hey, how goes it?"

"Good. You?" I say.

"Good, good. What year are you?"

"Freshman. You?"

"Junior. I play lacrosse."

"Wow. Good for you."

He slightly reminds me of Asher—lacrosse player, sort of laid-back—only he has short hair.

"What dorm are you in?"

"Willis."

"Cool. My girlfriend lives in Willis."

"Oh, yeah?"

"Yeah, but she's a sophomore."

"Cool," I say, only I don't really mean it. I am bored, painfully bored.

"Yeah, she's a biology major."

Great. Not sure why you think I even care. You have a girlfriend. Shouldn't you be hanging with her?

"You from around here? I mean, New York State or?" he asks.

"Um, yeah."

"Me, too. Where about?"

Crap. Why does everyone need to know this?

"Hamptons."

"Oh, fancy."

"You?"

"Troy."

"Cool."

I wait on the couch for Missy to return. Half an hour later, I excuse myself and go into the basement to find her. I search the basement and never find her or Lizzy or Rachel. I start to feel my desire for another drink plummet, so I decide to leave.

I go up the basement stairs and open the back door. To be honest, the music is so resounding that my ears are ringing when I step outside. The two guys who were taking money when we came in are standing near the door, smoking cigarettes. It's a relief to be out in the quiet, fresh air.

"Have a great night," one says.

"Thanks." I pass them and through the backyard, toward the road.

Then, someone yells.

"Hey, Hamptons!"

I turn and see the lacrosse player I was chatting with moments before jog toward me.

"Yeah?" I say.

"You leaving, too?" he asks.

"Yes, it would appear so," I say sarcastically. *Why won't this guy just go away?*

"Well, I'm heading to my girlfriend's. You said you lived in the same dorm as her, so I'll walk with you." He pauses. "You know, you shouldn't be walking alone. Rule number one on campus."

I know, I know, I think. *I should have found Missy and walked home with her. Safety in numbers.*

I roll my eyes ever so slightly. He is acting all macho, like I am some damsel in distress who can't walk home alone for ten minutes. I have done this a hundred times in far more grandiose places than a college campus. *And, besides, if he is some big-shot athlete, why is he not out with his team or his girlfriend? Instead, he's making sure I get home safe. I mean, really, why does he even care?*

"Ah"—he laughs as we pass by a few parties—"I see you don't know the shortcuts yet. Come on. I take my girlfriend this way to her place," he says. "We'll be home in a flash." He smiles kindly at me.

"Why would I know any shortcuts?" I don't think he catches my cynicism.

He gestures in the opposite direction from the main road him and I were on before —at least I think that was the road we were on. But I can't remember.

"If you say so."

"I do. I've been on this campus far longer than you. Trust me that way is the long way home."

I think about not following him. I even pause in the middle of the street, but he never turns or signals toward me in the least. He seems harmless. I know he is on the lacrosse team, and he has a girlfriend. Who knows? Maybe his girl and I will end up being friends or something.

I start to trail him. I can't wait to get home and get into bed, so I welcome a shortcut through campus. It has been a very long and emotional day for me, and I know what I need is a good night's sleep.

We meander for a few minutes down the sidewalk. We seem to be walking further from my dormitory, although, I have no real sense of direction on campus yet. We continue toward a path that runs behind one of the buildings. I can see the glow of the streetlights on campus ahead. I long to be in my room. The few drinks I had are now making me sleepy.

"Ladies first," he says as he pulls back the branches from a tree that shades the path.

"Sure," I say halfheartedly.

He chuckles.

An unfamiliar emotion comes over me. One I can't place in the moment. *Could this be raw fear?* My skin unexpectedly prickles, despite the August heat. I realize that there is no path ahead. I am trapped in an area with no obvious exit. The trees and bushes seem like they are closing in on me. I'm suffocating, and I am surrounded. I see no way out. It is in this moment I realize that this is not a good situation.

Before I can turn, his arm grabs me around my waist. My heart pumps blood at a rate it is not supposed to, nor can my body handle it. He squeezes hard. I go to scream, but he covers my mouth and nose with his other hand. I can't breathe. My lungs burn as the life begins to fade within me, draining from my once naïve soul.

Then, he whispers with hatred brewing in his voice, "Don't scream, or I will hurt you."

I am even more frightened as my eyes flash wide.

He slowly spins me around, still holding his hand over my mouth. "Don't scream."

I shake my head. But I know my eyes are telling him that I cannot be trusted because I do want to scream. I need to scream. I notice how dark and empty his eyes appear. He couldn't care less that he is scaring the crap out of me. In fact, I see the grin form across his face, and I know he is enjoying this. Anyone who would get pleasure from this is pure evil.

He releases his hand and kisses me. Hard and aggressive, bumping my lip with his teeth as he does. I taste blood.

He takes his other hand off my body and places it behind my neck, forcing my face into his, but I refuse to kiss him. Then, he starts to move his hand up my tank top, trying to pull it off. I panic and start to fight. Something in me tells me to fight or else I will undoubtedly suffer the consequences. Therefore, I do. I start to punch and scratch at him, doing everything in my power to get him to stop.

But the harder I fight, the more he seems to try. Finally, he pushes me on the ground. I land hard on the dirt path, pain shooting up my tailbone. I go to cry out, but he jumps on top of me, forcing his heavy body on mine. He kisses me again and again, but I reject him, violently moving my head from side to side, doing anything to avoid contact with him.

"You rich little bitch," he growls.

This angers me even more. He thinks he knows me because I told him I was from the Hamptons. *Asshole.* I try punching his smug face, but he just laughs as I struggle to land even one blow. I continue to fight as he holds my free arm while I try to hit him with the other. My arm gets heavy as I'm aggressively swinging it, desperate to land a single punch. I'm scared to death, but I know, if I don't fight this guy off, I'll undeniably pay the price. And what that means for me exactly, I'm terrified to find out.

Then, he props up off me and starts to pull down my shorts. I freeze completely. My head is spinning. Everything around me stops moving, and my life until this very moment flashes before me. I am lying in the dirt on my first night of college with this horrible human being. It has all come to this.

No one knows where I am. No one is going to come and save me.

My breathing is heavy, and my heart might burst within my chest.

I close my eyes.

"What? No fight left in you?" he says harshly.

I don't move. I can't. My body and mind are equally paralyzed by fear.

He slaps me across the face. A pain I've never endured screams out. *My face. My future.*

He laughs.

I can't speak. A tear falls down my cheek.

Then, he slaps me again and again. His last strike jerks my head to the side. I know he is getting off from hurting me.

And it does. It hurts like hell, yet I am totally emotionless.

Then, without warning, he stands up. My heart leaps into my throat, as I know something terrible is coming. But I can't get my legs to move, to try to run. My body remains still. The blood from my lip runs down my chin, and my cheek burns. I am too afraid to even think about what is coming next.

I slowly open my eyes. He's now leaning over me, and his chest heaves as he draws in another breath.

"*Please.*" My voice barely cracks.

"You're too stiff to screw," he barks.

Stiff, I think. It brings me back to that night with Asher, my so-called friend. He treated me like a worthless piece of meat to take for his own desire.

And, now, here I find myself again.

I try to cover my face from his stare, but just to add insult to injury, he sneers at me before he spits on me, his saliva landing somewhere on my body. Then, he wipes his mouth and quickly turns, disappearing through the bushes, as a group of rowdy students start yelling somewhere in the distance. Before I can truly comprehend what is happening, he is gone, just like that, back into the night, a horrid nightmare escaping back into civilization.

My adrenaline kicks in, and I scramble to my feet. More than anything, I fear that he will change his mind and return. I pull back the bushes and peer out toward the street. Unfortunately, I see no one in sight. I know I need to run. I run as quickly as I can, back the way I came with Missy hours earlier.

I sprint down the street. As I pump my arms, I notice they are scratched and bleeding. I dodge behind a building and end up near the Student Union. I know my dorm is close, and I have to make it there without seeing anyone. I pick up my stride and hustle toward the building. As I am about to come onto the main part of campus, I literally bump right into a man carrying coffee, spilling it everywhere.

"Oh my God!" I scream.

"Oh Lord, are you okay?" he winces as he tries to wipe the coffee off his shirt while still holding the cup.

"I'm terribly sorry," I say, barely able to catch my breath.

"Why are you in such a hurry, young lady?" he asks me.

His eyes grow enormous and they tell me everything I need to know. I look terrible.

"Jesus, are you all right? What happened to you?"

He moves toward me. Alarmed, I stumble backward.

"Are you okay?" he asks again when I don't speak.

He motions toward his lip. I reach my hand up and touch my lips. I can feel the blood wetting my fingertips.

"Yes, yes," I say as I begin to cry.

The man tries to come closer, but I put my hand up in protest. I can't be around anyone, let alone a man.

"Hey, hey…I'm a police officer. I can help you."

"No, please, I just want to go home," I say, my voice shaking.

I don't want anyone to know. I am horrified, embarrassed, ashamed, disappointed, and on and on and on and on.

Please don't make me talk right now.

"Can you tell me what happened?"

The radio on his hip starts squawking at him. As he glances down, I take it as my chance to run, so I do.

"Wait! Please let me help you!" he yells after me.

But it is too late. I am running full speed toward Willis.

I am almost home.

I run up to my room, shielding my face as I do, but thankfully, I see no one in the stairwell at this hour of the night.

I get into my room and go right over to the dresser before fearfully gazing into the mirror. My lip is cut and bleeding, my cheek is bright red from where he slapped me, my hair is tangled and wild, and the scrapes on my arms are only surface scratches. I tear off my clothes and throw them into the trash, never to be worn again.

I notice my necklace swinging on the jewelry stand, and my anger rises within me. I'm angry with myself for being stupid and shallow. I quickly grab the necklace and put it back on.

Then, I put on my robe and hurry back down the hallway to take my first shower at college. As I step into the slightly wet communal shower, I start to cry.

This is my first experience at college? This sucks. This more than sucks.

Four

HELPING MYSELF

It is Sunday morning, and I know my mother will be at church and then lunching with her friends. I call my father on his office line.

"Daddy?" I say, trying hard not to cry.

"Bree, sweetheart!"

"Sorry, I have a sore throat." I know he'll catch the strain in my voice, so I have to make up something.

"Sorry, honey. Drink some orange juice. How is college?"

"It's only been a day, Daddy, but so far, so good," I lie.

I didn't sleep last night. I lay curled up on the corner of my bed, staring at the locked door, out of fear he'd find where I lived. He had said his girlfriend lived in my dorm. As a result, I watched the door all night, making sure no one came inside.

"Great. What is going on?"

I take a deep breath. I spent the entire night thinking about what I could tell my father to convince him that I needed to leave school.

"Um, well, I was hoping I could ask you for a favor."

"Of course," he says.

"I got a call from Miguel yesterday, and they need me to come back for a few days, Daddy, to reshoot some of the photos for his collection. He needs to have them submitted no later than Friday, or he won't get credit for the show. I know what you are going to say, but please, he has been so good to me, and I just know if I don't do this, I might never get another opportunity from him again."

I hear him let out a deep sigh, and before he can protest, I continue, "I promise, I will only be gone for a few days."

"Bree, you're in college now."

"I know this, but it's just the first few days. It's not like I'd be missing major exams. In reality, it's perfect because it's just the beginning."

"Huh. What will your mother say?"

"Well, I was kind of hoping that we could keep this between us, for now."

"Bree." He pauses. "Only if you promise not to stay a day longer than Friday."

"Done. Thank you, thank you, thank you, Daddy."

"Okay, call me when you get there."

"I will. I love you."

"Love you, too."

I feel terrible about lying to my father, but I had to. I can't tell anyone about last night. No one can ever know. I'm too ashamed that I was so stupid—and on my first night of college, no less.

I pack a bag, put on my dark Prada sunglasses, and close my door. I drive about twenty minutes to my appointment with a plastic surgeon. I am concerned that my lip might need a stitch, and considering I model for a living, it's best that I get a medical professional's opinion.

Leaving my sunglasses on, I enter the surgeon's office and hand the woman behind the desk my insurance information. I notice my hand trembles.

"Yes, Aubrey, the doctor will be right with you."

I take a seat in the waiting area, and gratefully, I am called right away.

I follow the nurse to the room.

"Please take a seat there," she says, pointing to a table. "And can you please remove your glasses?"

Reluctantly, I take them off. She turns to me, and I see her eyes are wide.

I swallow hard. "I fell," I say quickly.

"I can see that, you poor thing." She gives me this sympathetic expression that makes me feel worse, only I know she doesn't mean to make me feel bad.

"Yes, I want to know if my lip needs a stitch."

"Okay, let me get your vitals, and the doctor will be right in. Dr. Tamburino is an excellent surgeon."

"Thank you," I say to her.

A few moments pass, and then Dr. Tamburino knocks on the door and enters.

"Ms. Van Tousen, I'm Dr. Tamburino," she says as she comes in and shakes my hand.

I am thankful Dr. Tamburino is a female. I know I would not be very comfortable right now with a male doctor.

"Hello, Doctor."

"I hear you had a bit of an accident. Let me take a gander." She washes her hands and then comes over toward me. "My, my, seems like you took quite a spill," she says as she reaches up and moves my head from side to side.

This reminds me of my mother inspecting me. I sigh.

"Yes, silly me. New dorm room, came home late, and tripped over my roommate's boxes. She felt terrible," I lie.

"Good news is, the bruising around your eye should subside within the week. I highly recommend icing it a few times a day for twenty minutes. I can give you some excellent cream to put on your bruise, and we offer makeup that can cover it up very well. I can put a new type of adhesive glue on your lip to keep it closed and prevent it from splitting once it starts to heal. A stitch might scar, therefore the glue is the better option for you."

"Okay, great. That sounds good to me."

Thirty minutes later, I leave the office with a bag full of supplies. I drive about twenty minutes, slightly southwest of Syracuse, to check into the Swoonstone Inn & Spa in the village of Skaneateles, New York. Luckily, I have my own money from modeling, so I'm able to afford all of this without putting it on my father's credit card.

The woman behind the check-in desk speaks softly as I approach, "Checking in?"

"Yes, Van Tousen."

"Ah, yes, Ms. Van Tousen. We have you for four nights, correct?"

"Yes."

"Great. Would you like to book your spa treatments now or check in to your room?"

"I'd like to check in, and then I'll call for my services. Thank you."

"Of course. We have a lovely room for you overlooking the pond and bridge."

"Thank you."

"Our restaurant is open until ten this evening, and it opens every morning at six."

"Wonderful." I take my keys and information and grab my bag.

She points me in the direction of my room, and I am able to find it with no problem.

She is right; the room is gorgeous with white linen bedding and pale blue walls. A seating area is near the large sliding door, and the windows give a perfect view of the pond and bridge. It is breathtaking, to say the least.

Swiftly, my spirits rise. That is, until I remember why I am here.

I unpack my bag, hanging my summer dresses and long-sleeved shirts in the closet and putting the rest of my items in the dresser. I keep my shawl out and wrap it around me. I approach the sliding glass door and open it, leaving the screen door closed so that the breeze can come in.

It is a glorious day, only I don't think I can enjoy it. I survey the beautiful grounds in front of me and notice a woman sitting by herself in a wooden lounge chair beneath a red oak tree. She is striking, like a glamorous actress from the 1950s, with her large black sunglasses, vibrant red lips, and her hair flawlessly pinned at the sides and back. She is perfectly poised while reading a book.

She suddenly glances up and catches me watching her. She lowers her glasses and waves slightly at me. Embarrassed that I have been caught, I hurriedly close the curtains. I wait a moment and then peek out from behind them. Thankfully, she has gone back to reading her book.

I go over to the bed, pull back the covers, get in, and close my eyes. My dreams, once filled with fun and enjoyable activities, are now full of horrible thoughts. I am paralyzed by the darkness growing in front of me. I try desperately to sleep, but I toss and turn for hours until I finally drift off, succumbing to exhaustion.

I'm in the woods. Wandering, not knowing how to get to my dorm. Quickly and without warning, I feel a presence behind me.

"Hello?" I call out.

I hear a laugh. Then, two hands push me hard, and I land on the ground. A man with a dark face leers at me. Before I can respond, he jumps on me.

"Want me to mess up your face?" he growls.

He beats me with repeated slaps to my face. He laughs as he does so and then spits on me as I try to shield my face from his evil pounding.

His lips distort and darken as he yells at me, "You stiff bitch!"

As I discover the energy to push him off, he suddenly disappears, and Asher replaces him. We're lying on the couch, and he's forcing himself on me, baiting me into kissing him.

"Come on, friend, kiss me." He laughs.

Then, I'm back on the ground, in the dirt. Asher's kissing me, and I'm desperate to break free, only he doesn't leave this time. He stays and has his way with me.

My heart stops beating, and the pressure in my chest begins to burn. I can no longer breathe. I can no longer feel anything. My innocence, my virtue, is gone, as I'm humiliated and tortured by two men who care nothing for me. All they care about is degrading me and teaching me a lesson. One I'll never forget. They'll make sure of it.

I wake up in a cold sweat.

Screaming.

It's nearly dark.

I reach for my watch that I placed on the dresser. It is after six thirty. My stomach rumbles as I swing my legs over the side of my bed. My body aches as my feet hit the floor. I didn't realize just how much the other night had physically taken out of me. My muscles mimic the same sensation I have after running for miles along the wet sand of the beach. Only this ache is not welcome.

I decide to freshen up in the bathroom before dinner. I inspect my face in the mirror. Dr. Tamburino told me not to get my face wet for at least twelve hours after the sealant on my lip dried. It does appear better but not nearly good enough for me. I put on the makeup the doctor gave me since I won't be able to wear sunglasses in the restaurant.

I go to the closet to take out a long-sleeved shirt. I put it on over my head and then pull down the sleeves to cover the scratches on my arms. I slip into my jeans and flat shoes, grab my bag and book, and force myself to head to the restaurant. If I don't get out of this room and get used to a routine, I'm afraid my mind will become even darker, and I'm not willing to let myself sink lower.

I have to be strong. I have to.

Hardly anyone is in the restaurant. The hostess seats me outside at a small table adjacent to the pond. Once I sit, she hands me the menu. Immediately, a young waitress comes over to me and asks what I'd like, so I order. Eager to eat, I pick at the crackers on the table.

I stare out at the pond, and I can't help but think about what I will miss back at school. Tomorrow is the first day of classes, and I'm disappointed that I'll be absent my first day. I have always been excited to attend college. I want to get my degree and make my own contribution in life, much like my brother has. I don't just want to inherit money.

But my attacker has taken that away from me. I can't be there. I can't let anyone see me with these cuts and bruises. They would know what happened to me. Worse, what if *he* sees me and tells his friends about me, makes fun of me? I don't want a reputation as a stupid freshman. My whole life, I've cared about what others think. As a model, all that matters is others' opinions of how you appear, act, and perform. I wish so badly that I could turn this part of me off. But it has been so ingrained in me, it's almost impossible to change.

But isn't that what he wanted?

He wanted to change me…for the worse.

"Hello," a soft voice says.

It startles me. I turn my head and notice the woman from under the tree. She sits down at a table near mine. She is also alone.

"Hello," I say.

"What is your name, dear?"

"Bree," I say.

"Bree? Is that a family name?"

"Well, no, my real name is Aubrey."

"Lovely," she says.

"Thank you." I smile, and as I do, my lip pulls. It hurts terribly, and I reach up to touch my cut, hoping it doesn't bleed.

"Are you okay, dear?"

"Yes, I'm fine," I say.

"Eva. My name is Eva."

"Nice to meet you."

The waitress returns with my salmon salad and places it in front of me. I pick up my fork and knife, and my hands tremble as I start to eat. I'm so hungry that I can't even worry about appearing rude to her. I notice she glances away, which I appreciate. I open my marketing textbook and continue reading in anticipation of what I'll miss during my first week. I figure, at a minimum, I can at least keep up with school since I do plan on returning once my face heals.

As soon as I'm done eating, I sign the bill, charging it to my room, and quietly get up from the table. As I exit, I glance briefly at Eva, and she smiles at me.

In my room, I undress. I open the sliding door and let the warm breeze fill the space. I put on my pajamas and go into the bathroom to wash up before I retire.

I pull my hair up in a bun on top of my head. I have a lot of hair, and I don't like to sleep with it down because it gets too tangled.

I wrench back the covers and climb into bed. It's soft and comfortable, and a welcome sensation comes over me. My body relaxes as I lean back on my pillows. I place my watch next to me on the nightstand. I open up my textbook and continue reading as I anxiously wait for sleep to come.

I'm in the basement at Dashiell's house. I am trying desperately to find the stairs, but I can't. It's cloudy in here, like there was a fire, only there is no smell of smoke. I'm waving my hands in front of me in an attempt to find an exit, a door, a window, or something where I can escape.

I hear a noise, a snicker of some kind.

I yell, "Hello?"

Then the laughter gets louder.

I ask, "Who is there?"

They don't answer.

My heart quickens, and I swallow hard. "Hello?" I say again.

No answer.

I continue searching through the darkness. I'm moving slowly, like I'm walking in mud. I trip on something and fall on a table. I cut my lip. I see blood on my fingertips. I am bleeding badly. My lip is throbbing. I need to get out of here.

"Don't cry, baby," a man's voice says.

"Who is that?" I ask.

I sense a disturbance in the darkness. My skin prickles as I try to change my direction, yet I'm fearful that I'll trip again. I am frozen. I want to cry, but I can't. I sluggishly travel in the opposite direction, and no sooner do I step when something flies and strikes me directly in the cheek. My face burns and stings. I reach up to touch it and feel blood running down my face.

"Stop hurting me!" I yell.

"I don't want to," he says.

"Please," I beg.

Abruptly, his arms wrap around me. I struggle to get free.

"Don't scream," he says.

He puts his hand over my mouth. The cuts sting from the sweat on his hand.

He spins me around and pushes me to the ground. I hit the floor in Dashiell's basement, and suddenly, the lights come on.

I'm no longer in the basement. I'm outside in the woods.

"Asher!" I yell.

"See? You should have let me have you. Now, look at you," he says. "You look disgusting!"

"What?" I say as I scramble to my feet.

He thrusts a mirror at me. My face is now covered in blood, and my eyes and lips are swollen to almost an unrecognizable state. It can't be me. I attempt to scream, but I have no voice. He throws the mirror on the ground, smashing it into a thousand pieces.

I want to scream, but I can't. He pushes me back down on the glass. The shards enter my skin. He climbs on top of me, and I start to fight. I attempt to punch and kick, but my limbs feel like they are made of cement.

"Stop it!" My words come bursting out of me. I have my voice back. "Stop it!"

"Stop it!" My eyes fly open.

There is daylight in the room as the curtains billow from the morning breeze. My body is soaked in sweat. I reach my hands up and touch my face. There is no blood. My lip is still sealed and only slightly swollen, and I can see out of both of my eyes. My heart is beating rapidly. I swing my legs over the side of the bed and try to calm myself by taking deep breaths.

I had another nightmare.

Will I ever be able to sleep soundly again?

I grab my watch and see it's almost eight. I slowly stand and head into the bathroom. I turn on the shower and let the water warm up. I glance in the mirror, half-expecting my face to be mutilated, half-expecting it to appear better than it did yesterday. I'm surprised to find my appearance is the same, not any improvement.

I disrobe and step into the hot shower. I clean myself and wash my hair. Then, I step out and towel off. I dress in shorts and a T-shirt.

I call the front desk.

"Good morning, Ms. Van Tousen."

"Good morning."

"How can I help you?"

"Yes, I'd like to book the steam room for today."

"Great. What time?"

"Ten."

"Of course. You can access the pool and other amenities at any time before your appointment and afterward as well."

"Wonderful. Thank you."

"Have a good day."

I need to relax; that's why I'm here. I am making my own therapy and praying that it will work. I have three more days. That is all I'm allowing myself, and then I'm going back to school. No matter what.

I find myself in this situation because I wanted to be independent and prove myself to my family. I am a Van Tousen, and we are capable of anything.

But, unfortunately for me, I want to be closer to home, and I can't. I must fight my way through this.

Five

AN UNDESIRABLE CONNECTION

I spent almost the entire day yesterday in the spa. I consumed time in the sauna and steam room, and I got a manicure and pedicure. Being in the company of women chatting about their social calendars somehow brought me comfort. For just a moment, I forgot about my own problems.

I reluctantly went back to my room and ordered room service for dinner. Somewhere in between ordering food and it showing up at my door, I had a meltdown and sobbed uncontrollably.

I am alone and isolated in my room. I'm not sure I am going to make it one more minute in this place. I seem to have little energy to get dressed or shower or do anything. It doesn't help that it is raining hard. I stand in the window, my expression reflecting on the glass pane.

I am not myself. I know it, and I have to accept the fact that I am different, that I feel different, despite how badly I want to be better. The scratches on my arms are fading, but they are still noticeable. I touch my lip, and I start to cry again.

"Why, Bree? Why did you have to be so stupid that night?"

An anger I have never experienced before brews inside me.

The rain continues to beat down on the ground below, the noise loud and unwelcoming in my ears. I want to yell, but I can't. My mood darkens, and I'm petrified as to where it might take me. I need something to put me out of my misery.

I call down to the front desk to ask if they have anything over the counter that I can take to sleep.

"Like a sleeping pill?" the woman asks.

Ashamed for some reason, I respond quietly, "Yes, I can't sleep."

"No, unfortunately, we do not; however, we do offer an herbal tea that will indeed help you sleep," she said.

"Thank you. I'd like that," I say.

Will it help with my nightmares? I think. *Probably not.*

I drink the tea after it is sent to my room, and within an hour, I am fast asleep.

I wake up crying again. My nightmares are somewhere in between an attack on campus and me falling and unable to run away from the faceless man chasing me through the woods. My heartbeat fills my chest with heavy thuds, one after another after another after another.

I sit on the edge of my bed, staring at the curtains as the material wafts into my room. The sunlight is tempting me to enjoy the day, but instead, I have a cold sweat and am drenched from head to toe.

I will myself to take a shower. I know all too well that, once I stop showering, I will definitely be on a downward trajectory toward darkness. At least, if I shower and somewhat continue to care for myself, then I won't succumb to the pessimism.

I remember reading this book in my high school psychology class about how to recognize the signs of depression after a tragedy and having the courage to heal.

I need to keep going. I have to keep going. It is imperative that I come out of this on the other side—the other side being college and the rest of my life.

I dress after my shower and pull my hair back in a bun. I am hungry, starving in fact.

I grab my bag and book and head down to the restaurant.

"Good morning," the hostess says with an eager smile.

"Good morning," I mutter. "May I please sit outside?" I ask.

"Of course. This way."

I follow her to a table; it's the exact table I sat at before. Once the waitress comes over, I order a green tea, fruit, yogurt, and a scone.

"Yes, of course. I'll be right back with your tea," she says.

"Thank you."

I turn and gaze out at the pond. It's like a Claude Monet painting with all the lily pads floating on top. The rain left the grounds particularly lush today. I only wish I could enjoy the wilderness more. Unfortunately, right now, it reminds of a few nights ago in the woods. My body shudders.

The waitress brings me my tea and the scone. "Your yogurt and fruit will be right out."

"Thank you."

The scone is warm and smells delicious. I don't even bother with butter. I just break it open and eat it.

She returns with the rest of my breakfast.

I eat and glance up at the pond while sipping my tea, trying more than anything not to think about that I am missing my first day of college. This is not how I envisioned my college experience beginning, not at all.

I finish and sign the bill, charging it to my room. Then, I exit the restaurant and head toward the concierge desk.

"How may I help you?"

"I'd like to take the meditation class."

"Great. Your room number?"

"Thirty-two."

"Okay Ms. Van Tousen."

"Wonderful. Thank you."

I walk out toward the large back porch, which leads to the lawn. I'm eager to see more of this stunning property and try to settle my mind in the process. I stroll over to the pond and watch a woman meditating on a yoga mat in front of it. She seems in tune with herself and unaware of her surroundings. I make a mental note of this and wonder if I might need to incorporate some yoga into my ten-cent self-therapy that I seem to be creating on the fly.

I watch the fish swim effortlessly and find myself eager to be that free again. I approach the edge and lean in to watch them closer. It reminds me of the massive aquarium my father has in his office in the city.

I start to think of my father. I lied to him. I feel terrible about it, but I had to. If I had told him what had happened to me on my first night, he'd have pulled me right out of school. Probably would have had a helicopter come and pick me up to literally hoist me out of the dorm and whisk me back to my bubble in the Hamptons. I can't tell him—ever. It's for the best.

Something terrible transpired, and I have to accept that, but that doesn't mean *he* gets to win. That horrible guy will not be the reason I am no longer in college. I refuse to give him that kind of control over my life.

I notice white anemone flowers growing near the pond. They are my other favorite flower, like the tulips, because I find them to be an unpredictable choice, and I like that. My father typically gets anemone flowers for me. He once told me that, in Greek, it means daughter of the wind, and similar to the meaning, I might tend to go whichever way the breeze will take me.

I approach the lovely flowers, pick one, and put it in my hair.

I wander throughout the grounds, enjoying the sun on my skin, until I notice my shoulders are beginning to burn. I need to take shelter although I have no interest in going inside. I notice the large red oak tree and think it might be comforting to sit under there and read my book. I approach the tree.

The woman I spoke with yesterday is sitting under the tree, poised perfectly again, reading her book. She is like a goddess, dressed in a long flowing linen dress with a bright pink shawl draped over her shoulders, her lipstick matching the striking pink hue. Her hair is down and curled slightly, much less formal than her hair before. Yet she still dons the wide catlike black sunglasses, despite being covered by the shade. She appears to be in her late sixties, and from what I can tell, she thinks of herself as thirty-something and appears to be comfortable with herself.

I turn to walk away.

"Please, won't you join me?" she says.

My cheeks flush. Not wanting to insult her, I say, "I shouldn't. You seem to be enjoying the solitude."

"Yes, of course. That's why we are all here. But that doesn't mean we can't enjoy it together."

I'm torn.

She motions to the lounge chair next to her and smiles wide.

"Thank you," I say. "I appreciate the offer."

I walk over and place my bag on the end of the chair. Then, I slide into the chair. It's comfortable. I take out my book and turn to the last page I remember reading. I notice she opens her book as well. I am relieved.

About fifteen minutes later, a waitress comes by to take drink orders.

"Ms. Simmons, a drink?"

"Yes, I'll have an iced green tea. Thank you, Danielle."

"And you?"

"Thank you. I'll have water."

"I'll be right back."

Ms. Simmons must come here a lot if they know her name, I think.

I decide to speak. "Do you recommend I do anything in particular while I'm staying here?" I ask.

"Yes, get lots of massages and rest."

"Massages, I can do," I say softly. Although the thought of someone touching me is nothing I want to welcome right now.

She puts her book down. "Are you in school, dear?" she asks.

"Yes, I'm a student at OSU."

"What year?"

"First year."

She pauses. "Hasn't school already started?"

"Yes," I respond.

"I see."

Danielle brings back our drinks and places them on the table between us.

"Thank you, Danielle. Please put these on my account, and when you have a moment, please bring us some of that delicious apricot preserves and some scones."

"Of course, Ms. Simmons."

"Do they give you time off during your first week of school?" she asks with a playful grin.

It surprisingly puts me at ease.

I think about how I want to respond as I take a sip of my water with cucumber. It tastes refreshing and light. I peer over at her as she eagerly stares at me. I recognize that I can play this one of two ways. One, I can lie right through my teeth and tell this woman, this stranger, anything I want, and she'll never be the wiser. Or, two, I can answer her questions truthfully and see where the conversation takes me.

"I don't get any time off from school." I pause and then turn slightly in my chair toward her. "No one knows I'm even here."

She does not react, nor does she seem surprised by my confession. "I see," she says. "And you want it this way?"

"Yes."

"Well then, I shall keep your secret."

"Thank you."

"But I get the sense you don't have a lot of secrets."

How in the hell does she know this? I think. "No, I typically don't."

"Yes, me, too. I find it keeps the mind and body free. Do you plan to return to school?"

"Yes, of course," I say. "I just needed to…" I stop.

She holds on to see if I'm going to continue. When I don't, she asks, "Are you in some kind of trouble, Aubrey?"

"Bree. And no," I say quickly. "No, Ms. Simmons, I am not."

"Eva. Please call me Eva. Okay, because if you are…well, I am willing to help if I can."

"But why? Why would you want to help me?" I ask.

"Because," she begins, "isn't that what people do for people?"

"Yes. I suppose."

"Well, as I'm sure you can imagine by my age, someone has helped me, and, well, I wouldn't be where I am today without a little support from time to time."

She is right. Everyone needs help at some point in their life. I only wish I'd had aid a few nights ago, but I also understand that no one knew I needed it. My thoughts dive toward darkness as I think of *him* again. His face flashes across my memory bank, and I shudder.

"Aubrey?"

I'm pulled back to reality, and I am grateful to be here.

Danielle approaches with our scones and apricot preserves.

"Thank you, Danielle."

"Yes, thank you," I say.

"I brought you each a glass of champagne as you ladies seem like you are enjoying each other's company quite nicely," she says.

I am surprised by this for a few reasons. One, they know I am not of age to drink, and two, I didn't think our conversation appeared to be celebratory.

"Ah, yes, thank you, Danielle," Eva says with a smile.

Danielle hands each of us a glass, sets the food on the table, and leaves.

"I am assuming you are underage?"

"Yes, I am, but I have drunk before at social functions with my family."

"I see. And where is home for you?"

"Hamptons."

"Lovely. I've been several times. It's beautiful there."

"Yes, it certainly is."

"Well then, cheers to the Hamptons, finding help, and healing."

"Cheers," I say.

I raise my glass, but an overwhelming sense of sadness washes over me. Eva has no idea what she is dealing with, and I'm sorry she has run into someone like me. Someone in the midst of a crisis.

I take a sip. The champagne is delicious, and I welcome it. I put the glass back down and stare out toward the stunning landscape as a breeze catches us under the tree, allowing the warm air to surround us.

"What will you be studying at school?" she asks.

"Marketing with a minor in business."

"Smart. A universal degree yet specific enough."

"Did you go to college?"

"Yes, I did. The University of California, Berkeley."

Wow, impressive.

"Did you like it?"

"Yes. In fact, I was in a sorority."

Really? I think.

I'm not sure what I thought exactly, but I can't picture her in a sorority—at least, not one like those of today. The heavy drinking and hobnobbing with fraternities doesn't seem to be her forte.

"Well, that must have been fun. I mean, was it fun?"

"It sure was. There were social functions, women's rights marches, and all sorts of other political movements."

"Sounds much more interesting than today."

"Well, each year, a class of young students holds an opportunity to help mold and change our future. This has gone on since the beginning. You'll see; you and your friends will find something to fight for to make a change for the better."

If she only knew.

I gaze out and let out a deep sigh. But, quickly, I realize I need to snap back into the conversation I'm having.

"So, California. Is that where you are from originally?"

"No, New Jersey."

"Great. Not too far from here."

"No, not at all."

I take another sip of my champagne and notice my body is beginning to unwind. I needed this today. I glance at my watch and notice it is almost noon.

"You have an appointment?" she asks.

"Yes, I am taking a meditation class."

"Excellent. If you get Maria, then you are definitely in for a treat, but everyone here is fabulous."

"Yes, the services I've had thus far have been wonderful. I'm sure this will be as well."

"Well," she says before she finishes her champagne, "I have a few appointments myself this afternoon." She starts to get up, and I can't help but be disappointed that she is leaving. "It would be wonderful if you would join me for dinner this evening."

Pleasantly surprised by her invitation, I answer, "I'd like that." *I'd really like some company*, I think.

"Great. Let's say six, so we can enjoy the sunset."

"Wonderful. Thank you."

"Enjoy the rest of your day, Aubrey," she says with sincerity.

I watch her as she sashays away from me. Her mannerisms can only be described as elegant. The way she moves, it's as though she is royalty. I find her intriguing. She has this air about her that tells me she too has escaped the realities of her life on occasion. Just like I am now. I'm truly excited about having dinner with her.

My mediation class was heavenly, and I feel wonderful as I shower and dress for dinner. I decide to wear a navy-blue cotton dress and sandals for my dinner date with Eva. It is the only decent outfit I brought, and I should wear it tonight because I get the sense that she will mirror a million dollars.

I spend a little more time on my makeup. The bruise around my eye is getting better, and my lip is healing. Although, as I apply makeup, I find it hard to lock eyes with myself. Covering up the bruise in many ways is like covering up what happened.

I inspect myself one last time before I head down to the lobby.

"Ms. Van Tousen," a woman calls.

"Yes?" I say as I turn to see who is speaking.

"Ms. Simmons is waiting for you. This way, please."

I follow her as she leads me toward the lobby, through the kitchen, and out to the side of the main building toward an old barn. She takes me through the barn, which is filled with furniture that I assume they use for outdoor wedding and events. As we approach the other side of the barn, she opens one large wood door. I can see a patio off the back, and on it is an enormous wood table with a linen tablecloth with stunning anemone flowers in small vases gathered in the middle. Hanging from the tree branches above is an antique chandelier. The table is set so exquisitely, like nothing I have ever seen. It's quaint and simple yet truly elegant. I'm used to over the top, expensive, and quite honestly, at times, gaudy. This is much more my style.

She is standing on the edge of the patio, gazing out over the rolling hills. As I approach, I note she is wearing a long green skirt and a crisp white shirt, her sleeves rolled up. Her arms are filled with gold and green bracelets. A pair of green emerald earrings adorns her ears, and her hair is impeccably pinned back. As she parallels a model, I feel terribly underdressed.

"Eva," I say quietly.

She turns. "Aubrey, thank you for coming."

"No, thank you. This is lovely. But what is all of this? I mean, how did you get to be back here?"

She politely ignores my questions and waves over the waitress who has been standing quietly near the barn.

"Would you care for a drink? Perhaps some champagne or a rosé?"

"Rosé, please," I say.

"Of course."

The waitress nods, and within a moment, she returns with two glasses. She hands one to me and then the other to Eva.

"I bought this property back in 1959 after I won an Academy Award for Best Actress in a role I played opposite Cary Grant."

My jaw drops slightly at her admission.

"I needed a place to get away, a dwelling I could create that would, in fact, be a refuge for rest and relaxation for all those who would need solitude and to get away from their problems in life."

A chill runs up my spine. I'm silent.

"I think that is why you are here, and I want to help."

The tears start to sting my eyes. I blink hard. Thankfully, she is not paying attention.

Finally, I speak, "Yes, but how did you know?"

She turns to me. "Oh, dear," she says as she gently touches my face, "your face. You don't strike me as the clumsy type, and judging by your appearance, I'd say your face is important to you, no?"

I nod. She releases her hand.

"But, I, um…I thought I was doing a better job of…"

She waits. Then, she says, "Well, you can't hide your screams, my darling, and I've been worried about you since the first day you arrived."

My screams. Oh my God, she has heard me scream.

My eyes get wide.

"Come, please sit."

I follow her, too speechless to say anything. She sits at the head of the table, and I take a seat on her left, so I can face the hills.

The waitress reels out a large metal bin on wheels; it is a transportable bar. She opens the chest. The coolness escapes as she pulls out two perfectly plated salads. She puts one in front of each of us.

"I took the liberty of asking my chef to make something off the menu, special for us. I hope you like it."

"Yes, thank you. This is more than I could have ever expected."

"That's all for now, Samantha. Please tell Roberto thank you."

"Of course," Samantha says before she leaves.

"Now, please eat and drink, my dear. I want you to be relaxed and renewed when you leave here."

"I'm trying," I say, which even surprises me.

"I can see that. But, in order to move forward, you must release what is holding you back."

"I don't know how to do that."

"Well, you can start by saying what is on your mind right now."

"Okay, well…" I think about why I'm here. Why I'm really here. "I'm angry."

"Angry, okay. Angry at what?"

"Him." I can't believe I'm telling her this.

"Okay, why?"

"Because he did this to me," I say, pointing at my face.

For some reason, telling a stranger feels much easier than someone who knows me and already has their mind made up as to the person I am.

I hesitate and then say, "He tried to take something from me that you don't just take from someone. It's mine to give, and he had no right to force himself on me." I start to cry.

She watches me for a moment and then hands me a napkin.

"I know, Aubrey. You are right to feel that way."

"But how do I make it stop? How do I go back to school and risk having him recognize me or making fun of me, like he did, so he can humiliate me all over again?"

"You can't. You will have to be stronger, and I'm here to tell you, you'll need to be. You'll need to be one step ahead if you want to get your life back. You can't hide out forever; you can't let him win twice."

"But how do I forget?"

"You don't forget, Aubrey. You learn and move forward." She breaks for a moment, and I can tell she is choosing her words carefully. "I once loved a very cruel man. He took so much from me, more than I ever realized until it was almost too late. I let him keep taking from me until I barely recognized myself anymore.

"I see a lot of me in you. You seem to be strong and ambitious, and you have more to offer than you have been allowed to give. Now is your time, Aubrey. Don't wait as long as I did."

"But my dreams—"

"I know. Your dreams will just take time to fulfill. What I learned through self-therapy was that, in time, this will not hurt as much as it does today. That is a fact, and if you believe it, then each day will be a little better for you."

A tear falls down my cheek. "Why are you being so kind to me?"

"You are a guest in my home," she says with such confidence and truth that I believe I am a guest in her home, not a paying customer at a spa.

"Thank you, Eva, for everything."

"Of course. Now, when you go back to school, you'll need to focus on your studies. Trust me, an education is what is most important. Modeling, acting, and entertainment are not guarantees, and in many cases, they cannot predict a successful future. However, a degree can."

I shake my head.

She picks up her glass and raises it to me. "To new beginnings, Aubrey."

I cheer with her and smile. It's a small smile, but it is a start.

"Now, I don't normally let my underage guests drink, but you seem like a smart girl, and I think you have earned a glass of wine. This is from my private collection. Enjoy, my dear."

"Thank you."

"You're welcome. Now, you must eat. Roberto is the best chef, and I'm sure what he has prepared for us will be superb."

We eat and laugh for a few hours. The only light now surrounding us is the chandelier above and the candles on the table. It is breathtaking, and I don't want this night to end.

But, sadly, it does.

"I have a long day tomorrow, and I must retire," she says.

"Of course. Thank you again," I say as I place my napkin on the table. I rise and find her standing in front of me, her arms spread out. I can't help myself, and I hug her. To be touched by someone who was a stranger mere days ago and feel so relaxed in her arms now is new to me. New to me on many levels.

"Come," she says as she lets go of me.

I follow her through the barn, which is dimly lit, and back into the kitchen.

Once in the lobby, she smiles at me. "Good night, Aubrey."

"Good night."

I wake in the morning, drenched in sweat from another night of terrible memories that raced through my mind. I stroll over to the sliding door and pull back the curtain, hoping to see Eva sitting under the tree, reading.

She is not.

I shower and pack my clothes in my bag. I see a slip under my door. I pick it up. The only thing I have been charged for is my room; everything else, she's comped for me. My cheeks flush. She is being too kind. I cannot accept this.

I gather all my belongings, take a deep breath, and exit out my door. All in all, my time spent here went far better than expected. I believe I have Eva to thank for that. I am eager to see her and thank her for everything.

I approach the concierge desk.

"Yes, Ms. Van Tousen, how can I help?"

"I was hoping to speak with Eva."

"I'm sorry. Eva has left. Is there something I can help you with?"

"No. When will she be back?"

"Not for quite some time, I'm afraid."

"Oh," I say sadly.

"But she left you this," she says as she retrieves a package from under the desk.

"Okay. Thank you." I take the package and put it in my bag.

"Did you enjoy your stay?" she asks.

"Yes. Please thank Eva for me, for everything."

I slowly exit out of the double doors and reluctantly walk to my car. I turn after placing my bag in the back, hoping to catch sight of the beautiful Eva before I depart. Sadly, I do not see her, but I wave slightly just in case she is watching.

 Six

IN CONTROL

The hours I wasted driving around and shopping did nothing for me. I am sad and alone again. My depression starts to creep back toward the surface as I see the entrance for campus up ahead. A myriad of emotions washes over me.

No one even knows I was gone. No one at this school is aware of my existence. I'm that girl—the loner with no friends—and worse, I've put myself a week behind. But I had to. I had to leave.

The fight within me battles on as I park my car in the student lot.

I exhale as I approach my dormitory. I key into the front door and head directly toward my room.

My room. I have no memory of it since I literally spent less than twenty-four hours in here. It is unwelcoming, to say the least.

Before I close my door, someone in the hallway says, "Oh, there *is* someone in that room. Weird. Thought it was empty."

"Me, too," another voice responds.

I sink down onto my bed. I take the package Eva left for me, and with a heavy heart, I open it. Inside, I find a small leather journal with an anemone flower pressed inside and a business card for Dr. Claire Leo, a psychiatrist in North Syracuse. On the inside cover, I find a note she penned.

Dear Aubrey,

Never let what happens to you in your life change you for the worse, only for the better.

Sincerely,

Eva

My eyes fill up with tears as I read the business card again.

Also inside is a VHS tape. A movie starring Eva with Cary Grant, titled *A Love to Remember.* My excitement rises as my fingers tremble to open the case. I put the tape in, turn on my television, and sit back on my bed as I watch in amazement.

Watching Eva on TV is almost overwhelming. She is fabulous, gorgeous, and very talented. I am grateful to have met her. My connection to her was so strong that I am yearning to be near her. I am longing to be near Claudia, my father, and even my mother. I am isolated and alone in this double room that I have all to myself.

I glance at the clock. It's eight, and I decide the best thing I can do is go to bed. I have classes in the morning, and I need to be ready.

Great, I think. *A full day of classes and kissing my professors' asses to look forward to.*

I get in the shower early. I see a few girls who must be in my wing and just smile at them. They smile back.

Back in my room, I take extra time doing my makeup and covering up what is left of the cut on my lip and the slight bruise on my cheek. I am satisfied with the results of my handiwork when I'm done.

I snatch my bag, student ID, and books, and then I head to the Union to buy a bagel and coffee before class.

I sit in the café and sip on my coffee, trying desperately to blend in, like I've been here before, like this is not my first day. I'm aching to be me again. Just Bree, a typical freshman student excited about starting her academic career, but instead, I'm more nervous about whether or not *he* is here, in the same building—or worse, in one of my classes.

I enter my Advanced Marketing class. I received such high marks in high school that it was recommended I start in the advanced class. Naturally, I accepted. The marketing department is in a lecture hall on the south end of campus in the Draper building. Unfortunately for me, my next class is on the opposite side of campus. That's one of the joys of combining an advanced schedule with the standard freshman courses.

I take a seat near the front. When the professor calls out names, I notice he is surprised when I say I am present.

Once class is finished, I decide it is best to approach him and introduce myself.

"Professor Gilford? Hello, I'm Bree Van Tousen," I say, extending my hand.

He takes my hand and briefly shakes it. "Yes, Bree, nice of you to join us," he says.

"Yes, I am hoping you got my message that I left?"

"Yes, I did, and I hope all is taken care of now."

"Yes, thank you, and again, sorry I had to leave school suddenly, but I did read the first two chapters while I was gone."

"Great, but we started with chapter fifteen."

Surprised, I say, "Do you have notes or—"

"No, but you can work with Assistant Professor Cooper. He has office hours from six to eight this evening, here in the building, room three forty-eight."

"Okay, great. I will do that." I smile as I head toward the door. "See you next week," I say as I push open the exit.

I hurry across campus to my second class, psychology.

I'm anxious to see who is in each class. Thankfully, no one of interest is in my psychology class.

My last class of the day is calculus. I am less than thrilled about it, but I know it is required. I walk into class and take the last empty seat. The girl next to me smiles at me. She is attractive with a short brown bob hairstyle and very striking hazel eyes.

"Hello," she says.

"Hey."

"I'm Laura. Nice to meet you."

"You as well."

"You just get to school?"

"No, I had to leave for work," I whisper, hoping she'll let it be and not ask me about where I have been.

"Work? Wow, must be exciting work."

Before I can respond, Professor Smith coming bounding in, and in a booming voice, he says, "Welcome again, math lovers!"

Oh, God, I think, *what a cheeseball.*

Thus far, in all my classes, by what each professor has spoken about, I am pleased to find that I'll be able to catch up to the rest of the students in no time at all. This class being no different, as it finally ends.

"I'm heading over to the cafeteria. Would you care to join me?" she says.

Surprised by this, I stumble over my answer. "Sure, I suppose."

I see her eyes get wide, and I realize how rude that might have seemed.

"Okay," Laura says softly.

I haven't been to the cafeteria yet, so it will be great not to go alone or eat another bagel from the Union.

I walk with her out the door.

"What kind of work do you do?" she asks me.

"I model."

"Wow. Well, that is cool."

"Yes, I needed to reshoot some images for a photographer."

"Ah, I see. So, where are you from?"

This again! "Hamptons," I say.

I see her eyes get wide again. She swallows hard.

"Cool."

"You?"

"Stockbridge, Massachusetts. It's a small town. You've probably never heard of it."

"No, sorry."

"No worries, but anyway, I hope you don't mind, but I usually meet my floor mates for lunch around this time. They are a great group of girls."

"Floor mates?"

"Yes, people who live on the same floor as me."

"Oh, sorry. I have yet to meet anyone on my floor yet."

"You got a single?"

"Well, not exactly."

"A big room all to yourself? Lucky you."

I smile slightly but don't answer.

I enter the cafeteria alongside her and wander slowly through the line, nose turned up high in the air. This food smells atrocious, but I will force myself to get used to it.

I order a sandwich, and then as I turn to speak with Laura, I halt. My heart beats hard within my chest. I am having difficulty swallowing, like pressure is being applied around my throat. I notice a guy standing near the drink station with spiked brown hair and a slightly muscular build.

It's him, I think. *Oh my God, it's him.*

My skin is alert with goose bumps, and I quickly catch my breath. Before he can turn to see me, I drop my plate on the counter and hurry out of the cafeteria, bumping into a few people, but I can't even speak to say I'm sorry.

I know it's him. I'm positive. I just know it.

I run back to my dorm. I close the door to my room and lock it. From behind my shades, I glance out toward campus to see if he followed me. Then, I go back over to my door and listen for the sound of him to arrive outside my very door. I stand there for over an hour, frozen and unable to move an inch.

By nightfall, I'm so hungry that I eat what snacks I have stashed in my room while I watch Eva's movie again. I should be studying, but I can't pull myself away from her movie.

It's a love story, a very sad one because they don't end up together in the end, despite her attempt to find him halfway around the world, but regardless, I watch it again and again. The scene where she cries is tragically beautiful. By watching her and from what she told me about her life, I get the sense that it wasn't a stretch for her to cry like that. I believe it came all too easy for her.

I cry along with her.

Finally, I glance at the clock. It's already six forty five, and I fear, if I don't unglue myself from my bed, Assistant Professor Cooper might think no one is coming to his office hours and leave. That would not be good for me.

I put on a pair of jeans, a gray top, and my leather jacket. I peruse myself in the mirror and undoubtedly appear like I have been crying, but I don't care. I touch up my makeup and brush my hair. I take my bag, ID, keys, and water bottle.

As I walk out of my room and down the hallway, I literally bump into a girl.

"Very sorry!" she says.

"It's okay," I grumble.

"Hey, you must be in room six ten?"

"Yes, I am."

"You have a roommate?"

"No, just me." *Yes, my father paid for me to have my own double room. I know I'm spoiled. I get it*, I think.

"Oh, huh. I'm Melissa."

"Bree."

"Nice to meet you."

"You, too. Hey, I have to run."

"Oh, sure. Of course. Well, I'm down the hallway here, so…" she says, pointing to her room.

"Great."

"Okay, see ya."

I feel worse now as I wander back across campus. *Do I even know how to make friends, or have I just been so tainted by my community that basically told me who my friends were by how much money their parents made? Do I even know how to be a good friend?*

I am surprised by this, but I miss Nelly. I wonder if she likes school, if she is still with Dashiell, and, well, if she even misses me. My guilt is kicking in, and I'm starting to hate that I dissed my so-called friends this summer.

I shake the dark thoughts as best as I can when I open the door to the marketing building. I walk down the hallway, watching the numbers on the door, until I get to room 348. The door is open, and I peer inside.

A young man glances up at me. He has semi short, wavy brown hair that is pushed back off his face. He has strong features, pink cheeks, and striking blue eyes. He is wearing dark-rimmed eyeglasses. He smiles, and I am instantly caught off guard.

"Sorry. Wrong room," I say. I turn to walk away.

"Ms. Van Tousen, I presume?" he says.

I stop. "Um, yes." I turn back toward the door.

He stands. "Please come in," he states. "You can close the door."

I don't say a word as I do as he said even though it makes me uncomfortable to be alone with a man.

"I'm Assistant Professor Cooper."

I am shocked. He cannot be older than twenty-four or twenty-five years old.

"Sorry. I thought I had the wrong office."

"No, this is the right one."

I sit down on the chair across from his desk. I notice there are hardly any pictures or decorations, only books and papers. It's rather drab.

"I hear you missed the first week of class?"

I answer slowly, "Yes, I had some work to do." The cut on my lip pulls as I run my tongue over it. I'm so self-conscious about it, as though anyone who fixates on me must know I was beaten and humiliated on my first night of college.

"What sort of work are you involved in—a charity or something?"

"Charity? No, I am a model. I was modeling." I can't be sure, but it appears by the slight smile he gives me that it is as though he just realized that teaching a model will be easy. We are vapid and have no brains.

"I see, modeling. Well then, let's get right to it, shall we? You read the first two chapters; however, Professor Gilford usually starts from the middle. This way, we can assess the students in the class better and see what they might already know. The first chapters are junk."

Not sure how to respond, I open my textbook to chapter fifteen. I wait patiently as he reviews the chapter and goes over everything I missed in detail. I can tell he is smart—obviously—and much younger than I expected.

About forty minutes later, he is finished. I spoke very little during his diatribe, but diligently took notes. I wouldn't say he dumbed it down for me, but he definitely took his sweet time.

"Well, any questions?" he asks.

"No, I think I've got it."

"Okay then," he says.

He takes his glasses off for a moment and pinches the bridge of his nose. He glances up at me before putting them back on, and I am taken aback by his piercing blue eyes.

I lean down to grab my bag and place my book and notebook inside. "Thank you for your time," I say as I stand.

He peers up at me, and I get a funny sensation in the pit of my stomach.

"Of course," he says politely. "See you in class."

I exit his office and down the hallway. I'm anxious about walking home alone now that it is dark, but I have to. I have no other choice.

I hurry across campus as fast as possible, constantly peering over my shoulder. I hate this.

I finally arrive at my dorm and open the front glass door. I head toward the lounge area to grab a drink before going up to my room when someone calls my name.

"Excuse me, Aubrey?"

This is how I know the person doesn't know me. Anyone who knows me calls me Bree.

I turn. My dormitory monitor is standing in the office located outside of the lounge.

Then, I notice him. I freeze.

"Can we see you for a moment?" she asks.

I swallow hard.

"Um, yes, sure."

I enter the office, and she nods for me to close the door.

"Hello. Not sure if you remember me from your first day, but I'm Brittney, and this is Officer Murphy. We are asking a few questions, and...well, we—I mean, you've been gone for a few days, so if we can just catch up now about some campus security items, that would be great."

"Am I in some kind of trouble?" I ask.

"No," he says. "But I would like to ask you a few questions, if I can?"

"I suppose."

"I wanted to make sure you knew how to report a crime on campus if you ever needed to."

"I guess," I say as bile rises in my throat. Then, I turn into my father. "Is this typical throughout the dorm? I mean, have you approached each and every student on a one-on-one basis?"

I see her cheeks flush.

He clears his throat. "Well, yes, we often approach students and talk about their safety."

"Yes, of course, this is standard, Aubrey," she adds.

"It's Bree," I say coldly. "I see. Okay, well, thank you both for your time, and if you don't need me for anything else, I'm sure you have lots of students to get to tonight." I turn to walk out.

I hurry toward the elevator. I hit the button, and then I see him coming around the corner.

"Bree," he says.

The elevator arrives. I step in, but he puts his hand on the door, keeping it open.

"Yes?"

"One more question."

I just stare at him, waiting for him to ask.

"Here is my card. As an officer, my responsibility is to keep the students on this campus safe."

I take the card. "Is there a question?"

A sad expression grows over his face. "I'm here to help; that's all."

"I don't know what you are talking about," I say as I hit the button for my floor again.

He finally takes the hint and releases his hand. As the elevator door closes, he says, "I never forget a face, Bree."

The only good thing about not having a roommate at this point is that no one can hear my screams at night. I wake again in a cold sweat, heart beating rapidly in my chest. I notice the clock. It's almost eight. I have plenty of time to shower and be ready for my nine thirty class.

I meander to the shower and take my time. I'm depressed after another sleepless night, but I am thankful I have only two classes on Fridays. I forgo the cafeteria yet again and opt for a quick bagel and coffee at the Union before my history class.

My history class is useless. It's like I'm back in high school.

However, my next class is my branding class. It is quite interesting, and I think I'll get something out of it.

But, as soon as my branding class ends, this sadness creeps over me. I wonder—no, more like, I fear what my first real weekend at college will be like. I have no friends, no one to talk to, and nothing to do.

I slowly amble back toward my dorm, hiding myself behind my large black sunglasses. I make my way to the sixth floor, and when I approach my hallway, I am surprised to find a few girls sitting on the floor, almost right outside of my room. My face flushes, and I realize I am uncomfortable with the idea of making new friends.

"Bree, right?" the somewhat heavyset girl asks.

"Um, yes."

"Hi! I'm Casey, and this is Maddie and Melissa."

I recognize the girl I bumped into.

Melissa smiles at me. "Hello again."

"Hello," I say to them.

"Care to join us?" Maddie asks.

I stare at the floor and think for a minute. She expects me to sit on the floor in the hallway. It's probably the same carpet that has been peed on and vomited on for years.

"Let me just put my bag away," I say.

I unlock my door and enter... I contemplate just not going back out and seeing if they even care or notice, but something tells me I could use some kind of a distraction from myself. I put my bag on my desk and return to the hallway. I hesitate as I slide down the wall. In my three-hundred-dollar jeans, I sit on the floor.

"Where are you from?" Casey asks.

"Hamptons, New York. About five hours from here."

"We know where it is," Casey says with a chuckle. "I'm from Georgia. Maddie here is from New York, too, and Melissa is from Texas."

I nod. "Where in New York?"

"Cortland," Maddie says.

"And, wow, Texas? That is so far away. What made you choose this school?"

"Their journalism program," Melissa responds.

"Cool."

"What are you studying?"

"Marketing with a minor in business."

"Excellent. I was just telling them how a girl in my last class was saying there was a huge party tonight. We are thinking about going if you want to join us," Melissa says.

"Really? Huge party?" I say sarcastically. *I've been to massive parties before, and I'm guessing this is not my definition of one.*

I see Casey's eyes get wide.

Melissa stammers, "Yeah. I mean, that's what she said at least."

"I'm sure. Anyway, what kind of a party are we talking about? Fraternity, athlete, off-campus?" I am hoping for not another off-campus party.

"It's definitely off-campus."

Shit.

"She only got invited because she knows one of the guys who lives in the house. She grew up with him, and he told her to invite people."

Okay, now, I feel a bit better since they know someone at the house.

"That's cool, I suppose. When are you guys going?" I ask.

They all stare at each other. It becomes obvious to me that they don't have a leader in the group yet.

If I know nothing else about hanging with girls, I at least know there can only be one alpha. Too many strong personalities can ruin the group dynamic before it's even formed. For example, I let Joss be the leader, knowing that I was both smarter and nicer than her, so it was easy to let her make the calls—or should I say, make her think she made the calls. Nelly understood this. It was a win-win for us. We always came out smelling like roses, no matter what. See, Joss was bitchy enough to take the lead, and we let her. Clearly, these girls here on my floor are not. In fact, if I don't make myself in charge of them, they'll get eaten alive. They don't know it yet, but they just met their queen, and I plan to rule over this tiny section of college. Having experienced a horrible act at this university, I can now protect them and gain back control over my social relationships. Something that *he* stripped from me a week ago.

Thus, my reign commences.

"Why don't you all meet in my room at nine sharp. We can make sure we are not dressed alike or, even worse, dressed poorly?" I add as I glance slightly in Casey's direction.

She doesn't glimpse at me because she doesn't think it's her who dresses badly. *Ugh.*

"Sound good?"

They all just nod at me.

"Great. Now, if you will excuse me, I have a few phone calls to make." I rise to my feet, making sure to dust the dirt from the floor off my jeans and go back into my room. *Always leave them wanting more*, I think as I close my door.

I spend the rest of the afternoon organizing my room, taking another shower, and going back out to the Union to get more snacks and necessities for my room. Then, I decide to grab a coffee and sit in the Union to people-watch. I need to psych myself up to go out to another party. I'm weary of dipping my toes back into the social waters of school, but I know I'll have to eventually. I can't become a recluse.

Somehow, knowing the girls are going with me makes me feel somewhat protected. By making sure they'll want to follow my lead gives me a cushion of support. Safety in numbers, I've always been told, and, boy, I learned it the hard way.

I take a seat at a small table in the back of the lounge area, away from the large fireplace in the middle. I put my coffee and bags down. I am semi-facing the flow of the afternoon traffic of crowds in the Union. I pretend to read my book, peering over the edge of it, as I watch the people go by.

It's amazing just how many people go to school here. I see hundreds of kids aimlessly wandering around, nothing to do, not a care in the world, all just waiting for the weekend to arrive.

I notice a few kids bang on the glass booth of the radio station, startling the DJ, as he talks into the microphone. He politely gives them the middle finger and smiles.

They are probably his dipshit friends, I think.

Then, I notice Assistant Professor Cooper walking in the crowd of students. I don't notice him because he appears older, but because of his hair and those piercing blue eyes. Thankfully, I'm too far away for him to notice me, which is good since I didn't quite get the vibe that he liked me all too much. I raise the book up to shield my face, just in case he does notice me. I watch him go over to the big display board next to the radio station and tack a bright yellow flyer on it. He eyes a few other things on the board before leaving the Union.

I wait for him to be gone before I get up and go over to the board. It is filled with all kinds of requests to join social clubs, student reminders, intramural sports clubs, and fraternity and sorority pledging information. Then, there is his neon flyer.

Seeking a marketing intern for top-ranked marketing program. Only serious applicants apply. Please see Assistant Professor Cooper in the Draper building, room 348.

Why the heck did he not comment about this to me? I just spent, like, an hour with the guy. Is it because I'm a freshman? That shouldn't have prevented him from mentioning it to me. Isn't that a bias or something? Is it because I'm a woman? Oh, that would be even worse.

I sense the steam come out of my ears. He must think I'm a real ditz to not bring it up to me. Well, I'll prove him wrong. And, if this is how they want to market for the internship, by putting a lousy piece of paper on a board filled with fraternity and intramural sports ads, then I think they might need me more than I need them.

I leer around, and when there is no one in the hallway, I take down the ad, fold it, and put it in my pocket. Not that I wouldn't beat out the competition fair and square, but I plan to make my point with said piece of paper when I apply in person on Monday.

Shortly before nine, there is a faint knock on my door.

"Come in!" I yell.

The door opens, and a girl steps in. I instantly recognize her.

"Hello," she says.

"Laura, right?"

"Yes, you're Bree?"

"That's me."

"Wow. Casey and Maddie told me to meet them in this room."

"Does that mean you're on my floor?"

"Yes, I am. Abigail and I live a few doors down from you. Huh, small world," she says with a laugh.

She looks fantastic, I think.

I wouldn't change a thing about her right now, which is a good sign for me. The bright aqua polo shirt she has on suits her well.

"Is she coming, too?"

"No, not tonight."

There's another knock on the door.

"Come in!" I yell again.

Melissa, Casey, and Maddie come waltzing in. I am less than pleased to see Casey wearing a red flannel shirt, mainly because she resembles a lumberjack. I cringe slightly to myself but quickly think on my feet.

"Good. You didn't pick out a scarf yet. Great. I have the perfect one for you," I say as I yank a black scarf off my dresser and drape it around her neck.

She smiles awkwardly at me and says, "Thank you."

"Ah, it's so pretty with the shirt. Very grungy. It's all the rage in the city these days."

"The city?"

"Yeah, New York, the fashion capital of the United States. You know what I'm talking about, right?"

She chuckles, and I can see her cheeks pink.

"Oh course! It's wicked."

"Casey, is Jen coming?" Laura asks.

I have not met Jen yet.

"No, she can't." Then, she mumbles, "Unfortunately."

"Well then, ladies, we ready for tonight? Let's go!"

They follow me toward the door, and I make sure to lock it behind me.

We cross campus in less than ten minutes. We can hear the music thumping as we approach the house. The pulsing bass is almost in unison with the loud beat of my heart as I near the party. I take a deep breath and slowly let it out.

There is a line out the door. I hate lines. I never have to wait in them in the city, so this is new for me.

I impatiently tap my foot as I listen to the boring conversations around me.

Finally, Laura steps up close to me. "I'm sorry if I lost you in the cafeteria the other day."

I'm snapped back to reality. "Oh no, my bad. I remembered I had to pick up a package in the Union," I lie. "And I couldn't find you to tell you I was leaving."

"No worries. Just wanted to say something."

She smiles at me, and it is so genuine and nice that it almost catches me off guard. I'm not used to friends like this.

We finally get in the house and locate the bar near the back.

"Let's take these drinks and head outside," I say.

The massive fenced-in yard is just off the kitchen. I notice the backyard is the place to be as we make our way outside. It is even more crowded than the inside of the house. It is packed with students. The guys throwing the party placed speakers in the windows, facing out into the yard, with Radiohead filling the silence of the night. There is a cool late-September breeze. It is a picture-perfect college party, if there ever was such a thing.

We find a cozy corner near the fence and stand there. I notice all the students, a wave of anxiety washes over me as I conclude that I know no one here. They are all strangers, and any one of these men could be another predator. My heart starts to beat hard, and my breathing quickens. I take a sip of the punch, trying to calm my nerves. I'm not sure why I thought this wouldn't happen. It had to. I'm not over it, and I'm not going to be for quite some time. But I have to start somewhere. I have to get my independence back.

"Are you okay?" Laura asks.

"Yeah. Great party, right?"

I notice a group of guys watching us. They make their way over to us.

"Ladies, welcome to our party," the tall, muscular guys says.

"This is your house?" Casey asks.

"Sure is. If you need anything, just say the word," another one says.

"We mean, anything," the third kid with the Pearl Jam T-shirt says.

"We will, obviously," I say coolly for the group. I'm trying to get them to leave us alone—or should I say, leave me alone.

The only guy who hasn't spoken stares at me and smiles. "Hey, I've seen you before. You a sophomore?" he asks.

"No, first year."

"Nah, then I don't know you from here. You been on TV before or something?"

"Yes," I say.

The entire group turns to me.

"Really?" Melissa says.

"Yes, I have been in some advertisements. Clothing brands mostly and some soft drinks." I decide not to mention the Miss New York Pageant I was in and won.

"Wow, thought you might be a model or something," the guy says. "I'm Sully, by the way." He moves closer to me, nearly pushing his friend out of the way.

"Nice to meet you, Sully. I'm Bree, and this is Mel—"

"Yes, totally nice to meet you girls, too. Why don't the guys here go get you ladies a few more drinks?" he says, never taking his eyes off me. "Tell me more about the stuff you've done."

He's cute and all, so I decide to oblige, knowing that the girls will be right here with me. I give Laura a wide-eyed glance, and I think she gets it.

"Stuff?" I say, sounding offended he called my work stuff on purpose.

"Yeah. Meet any famous people or go anywhere cool?"

"Well, sure. Mostly other models, some actors. Do you know Jason Maxwell?"

"No kidding? I love his movies."

"Yeah, he was cool. I mostly work in New York City. Occasionally, I need to travel." I notice the more I talk, the closer he gets to me.

Thankfully, I see Laura inching over toward me.

"Here, Bree," Laura says as she hands me another drink.

I barely touched my first one, but I take the new one and dump it into my cup anyway. "Thanks."

"You are all first year?" he asks.

"Yes," Casey, who is now next to me, says.

"Well, let me officially welcome you to the best four years of your lives," he says with a cute laugh.

Hardly, I think.

We all raise our cups.

"Now, drink up, ladies. Tonight is sure to be a great night!" He watches me and waits for me to start drinking before he does.

I watch out of the corner of my eye as he gulps down his entire glass.

We stand around, drinking and laughing for almost an hour. The girls seem nice enough. I'm used to getting attention. I don't mind that it is coming from the girls, asking me a lot of questions, and from the guys, eyeing me up and down. I am at ease right now for the first time in weeks. But, unfortunately, it is short-lived.

Sully leans in. "Hey, why don't we go inside to the bar and grab a drink?"

"Sure, I guess," I say.

He takes my hand and starts to lead me away. I pull back.

"Hold on a sec," I say as I approach Laura.

She leans in to me.

I whisper in a firm tone, "You and the girls meet me in the front of the house in twenty minutes. Don't be late." I turn before she can say a word, and I leave with Sully.

He walks me into the house and coyly says, "I am going to grab us two more drinks, and then I have something to show you."

"Okay." I follow him to the bar and watch as he goes behind it and grabs two cups of punch. I reassuringly pat the mace I have hidden in my jacket. It makes me feel safe to have it, but I pray I'll never have to use it.

"This way," he says as he heads toward the back room.

The party is packed as we walk down the hallway. Tons of kids are just hanging out, drinking, laughing, and dancing.

"This here," he says, "is an autographed picture of Jason Maxwell. My dad gave it to me."

I can't help but laugh as I realize how sweet it is that he wanted to show me that, considering I couldn't care less. "So cool."

"Right? Totally cool."

"Yeah, he's wicked awesome. Nice guy to work with."

Lub-dub, lub-dub, lub-dub. My heart beats loudly that I'm almost positive he can hear it.

Being away from the girls makes me more panicky than I anticipated.

He takes my hand and leads me over to the window where he pulls the blinds open. We have a bird's eye view of the entire backyard. The whole party is spread out in front of us. A first look of the shenanigans is happening right in front of our eyes. I see the girls by the fence, still talking to one of the guys from before.

"Wow, do you sit here a lot and just watch?" I release his hand.

"Sometimes, but only if I'm alone."

He puts his arm around my waist and spins me, so I'm facing him. My body tenses.

"I don't need to tell you how hot you are because I get the sense that you're told that a lot," he says.

I say nothing and just smile at him.

I can do this, I can do this, I chant in my head.

I'm nervous as hell.

He's harmless, Bree. Not everyone is out to hurt you.

Then, deliberately, he leans down and kisses me. I think I can handle this. Sort of. He is a decent kisser and seems innocuous. Then, he takes his other hand and brings it behind my head, pulling me closer. I don't like this at all. He's kissing me harder now. I open my eyes a little and see the girls out of the corner of my eye. They start to move in the direction of the house. I let him kiss me once more.

"Hey, Sully." I pull back.

He appears like a lost puppy.

"I need to use the restroom," I say.

"Oh, sure. Yeah, it's just down the hall."

"Great. I'll be right back."

Quietly, I head back down the hallway, passing all the girls in line for the bathroom, and I go toward the front door. I step out and am thrilled to see the girls standing there, waiting for me.

"Ready?" I say.

What they don't know is that my heart is beating hard—out of fear, not raging hormones.

"Yep," they all say.

Laura gives me a peculiar grin. "You okay, Bree?"

I just nod at her and start walking.

We are back in the dorm about ten minutes later. The whole way home, I sensed my adrenaline pumping through my body. I was convinced it was going to make me heave on the street, but thankfully, it didn't.

We say our good nights, and we each go to our respective doors and unlock them. Once I'm inside my room, I lock the door and let out a huge sigh as I lean back up against my door.

"You are in control, Bree," I whisper. "You are in control."

Seven

THE INTERN

It's four in the afternoon, and I walk into the Draper building and toward Assistant Professor Cooper's office. His door is open, and I peek in. He is sitting at his desk and doesn't even notice as I approach and sit down.

"Ms. Van Tousen," he says with a bit of surprise. "Do you have an appointment?"

Irritated at his question, I simply unfold the piece of paper in my hand and say, "No, I'm applying for the internship." I place the paper on his desk.

"I see. Did you take the paper, so no one else would apply?" he says with an edgy chuckle.

He is particularly handsome today, which annoys me even more. I've been around a lot of good-looking men, but there is something about him that is different. Maybe it's his eyes or the way he appears in those glasses. Or is it the fact that I get the indication he couldn't care less about his appearance? There is quality in him that is hard for me to place.

"No, quite the opposite. My reason for taking down the paper was to prove that anyone could have taken it down for a number of reasons, and you might have ended up with zero—how did you define it? Serious applicants. By casting a wider net and advertising to the masses, the probability of getting more candidates is almost a guarantee."

I watch his mouth drop open.

He quickly responds, "How do you propose advertising to the masses?"

"Well, for starters, the radio station is right next door to the bulletin board you put this on. I'm sure a professor at this school could get a few minutes of airtime to talk about the internship and what is required in an applicant. Second, I'd have started searching for people a lot sooner than the second week of school. By now, most kids have their paying jobs lined up. They go for those first to make sure they can even afford this place, therefore an unpaid internship is not exactly jumping out at them. And then, honestly, the very first thing I would have done was told your marketing classes. Or even, for example, told someone who came in during your office hours because they'd read the wrong chapters to start with. Maybe those opportunities would have gotten you more applicants." I exhale.

He pauses and leans back in his chair. He is definitely contemplating his next move. I wait.

"Well, Ms. Van—"

"Bree. You can just call me Bree."

"Well, Bree, I see your point."

Damn it. Does that mean I didn't get the internship? I think.

I start to stand. "Well, thank you for your time, and I will see you in class."

I turn and walk out. Vapor releases through my ears. I am fuming. I blew it. I'll never be chosen now. I didn't close the deal and ask for the job.

I never let anyone know when I feel defeated. When I am not chosen for a modeling job, I typically act like I never wanted it anyway. I plan to do the same today with the internship.

I take my time in getting ready. I put on a nice pair of skintight black pants and a powder-blue silk tank top, and then I wrap a light cotton scarf around my neck. I pull my hair back in a ponytail, and the waves of my thick, dark hair fall on my back. I dab on a nude lip gloss and inspect myself in the mirror before heading out for the day. I'm well put together, so maybe everyone around me will think I actually feel good.

I take a deep breath before I open the door to the Draper building. With my head high, I waltz into class with just a moment to spare, leaving me no time for chitchat. I take my usual seat near the aisle, next to a girl named Mila, and open my notebook.

"Ready for another riveting class?" Mila asks me, with a devilish grin. I find her sarcastic wit, refreshing. I smile at her then turn my attention to the front of the room when Professor Gilford starts to speak.

Out of the corner of my eye, I see Assistant Professor Cooper coming down the opposite aisle. I notice as he walks how defined and muscular he is, probably a runner or swimmer or something. His body is long and athletic. It's obvious that he cares about being in shape. He takes a seat at the desk in the front of the room and starts preparing our handouts. I shift my eyes back to Professor Gilford. I don't want Assistant Professor Cooper to see me peeking at him.

Toward the end of class, Assistant Professor Cooper stands up and approaches the pretty blonde girl in the front of the room. He asks her quietly to pass out the papers.

"Assistant Professor Cooper is now going to explain this assignment to all of you," Professor Gilford says.

My cheeks flush as Assistant Professor Cooper starts to talk, as I'm embarrassed by my last interaction with him.

Once he explains the assignment pertaining to the group project we have to work on throughout the semester, a few students in the class have some questions. He answers them and then pauses, waiting for more feedback, as we all scan the packet in front of us. My feedback would be that I detest group assignments. But I'm pretty sure that is not what they are asking for.

"Okay, well, if there are no more questions on the assignment, we do have one final announcement before we let you go. As many of you know, Professor Gilford and I pick one student each year for an internship in our department. We are pleased to announce that Bree Van Tousen will be our intern this year. Congratulations to Ms.—er, Bree," he says as he motions for me to stand up.

My cheeks have to be bright pink at this point. I can't believe, after the debacle of a conversation we had, he still chose me. I force a smile and act as though I knew all along. I stand slightly and then quickly sit back down.

"Good for you," Mila whispers.

"Thanks," I respond.

"Want to work together on the assignment?" she asks.

"Definitely."

Assistant Professor Cooper clears his throat and the room quiets down. "Okay, if there is nothing else, see you next class,"

I stand and make a split-second decision to just march right out of class. A few students gather around both professors, so I take my chance to just bolt. I need time to think about how I want to play this. But, deep down somewhere I can't find yet, I'm excited that I got the job even though I hardly interviewed for it.

"Bree! Bree, wait up!" someone yells.

I turn and see the blonde girl from the front row approach me.

"Hey, I'm Ashley Duncan." She extends her hand rather forcefully.

"Hi, Ashley," I say, shaking her hand.

"Tell me, Bree, what did you do to get the internship?" Before I can respond, she quickly adds, "I've applied two years in a row and never even been considered." She laughs awkwardly as she fidgets with her hands.

Startled by this and not even sure of the answer myself, I simply say, "I presented my case and let the chips fall, I suppose."

She shakes her head. "Yeah, I suppose presenting your case is how one would get it." She pauses, and then just as I'm about to part ways so that I can get to my next class, she says, "Anyway, I know we have to get a group together for our assignment. You want to work together?"

I wasn't expecting this. "Yes, I think that would be great. Do you have anyone else in mind?"

"Yes, my friend Mallory is in. She's smart, so she'll work well with us."

"The girl I sit next to, Mila is in, too. She's cool."

"Okay, great. Well, good luck in the internship. Nice meeting you." She hurries off in the opposite direction.

"Okay. Nice meeting you," I call after her.

I head to my second class, my thoughts swirling with all sort of crazy thoughts. I got the internship and now I have no idea what that means!

I can't avoid Assistant Professor Cooper for long, so after dinner, I wander back over to the Draper building. I've had a day to think about how I want to approach this.

I walk in to the Draper building, and as I near, I notice that his door is closed. I hear voices, so I decide to wait and take a seat in one of the metal chairs across from his office. As I sit, the chair squeaks loudly, and I notice the voices inside stop. There is silence, and then they start again. A few minutes go by, and then the door opens. I see Ashley exit, and she appears to be flustered.

"Hi, Ashley," I say. "What's going on?" I'm somewhat surprised to see her.

"Hi, Bree. Um, nothing. I'll see you on Tuesday." She hurries off toward the main door.

Her tone seemed sad. Although I hardly know her, it was quite apparent.

Assistant Professor Cooper steps into the doorway. "Bree, come in."

I stand and go into his office.

"Have a seat." He closes the door and then takes a seat at his desk. "How can I help you?"

Really, I think. *No clue why I'm here?*

"I wanted to talk about the internship." *And why Ashley seemed so upset*, I think but dare not ask.

"Yes, of course. Okay?" He seems flustered, too.

He starts searching on his desk for I don't know what.

I try to stay calm. "I didn't know I had gotten the internship until you announced it in class yesterday." I cock my head to the side.

He glances up at me. "Yes, I assumed that." Then, he continues to search on his desk.

"Okay, well, don't you even—I mean, didn't you or Professor Gilford want to at least ask me first, face-to-face?"

"You don't want the internship?" He gives me a look of concern.

I let out a sigh. He notices. I'm frustrated.

"No, I didn't say that."

"Okay, well then, we are glad to have you on board."

I am no longer in the mood to argue. He smiles at me. He knows he's won this battle.

"Can you give me the specifics?" I ask as I take out my notebook.

"Sure. Mondays, Wednesdays, and Thursdays from six to eight. There is an office at the end of the hall where you first came in. You'll share it with other interns from other departments in the building. I'll have your first assignment for you tomorrow."

"Tomorrow?"

"Yes, tomorrow is Wednesday."

"Yes, thank you," I say as I close my notebook. "Well then, I will see you tomorrow at six." I stand and open the door.

"Good night," he says. His voice sounds different, and I can't quite place why, but it makes me turn back toward him. His face seems softer but quickly changes. He looks serious again.

"Good night," I say before walking out the door.

I toss and turn all night. There is a heaviness in my chest as I try to push away my nightmares. But I can't. I see *his* face every time I close my eyes. As a result, I stare at the ceiling. This awareness of loneliness envelops me. I get up and pace my room. It's three in the morning, and my head is so filled with thoughts—like, no matter what I do, I'll never be able to shake them free.

I pace for another fifteen minutes at least although it seems much longer. It's quiet in my room. I listlessly amble over and turn on the radio.

"Linger" by The Cranberries is playing, but I find it terribly sad, so I shut it off.

I switch on a small lamp on my dresser. I aimlessly search through my closet and then start organizing my clothes by color, but I don't like it this way. Then, I reorganize by designer and then by style. Finally, I settle back on designer. I pick my outfit for the day and lay it on my bed. I glance at the clock, and it is only four thirty. I decide to lie down with the light still on and read my marketing textbook.

Finally, my alarm goes off. But I was watching each minute tick by, so as a result, I wasn't the least bit surprised when it beeped.

I take my bath stuff and go down to the showers. The restroom is empty. I am in and out in no time.

Once I dress and get ready, I am out of my room for the rest of the day. I decide yet again to go to the Union and grab a large coffee and bagel. I sit back in my seat, away from the fireplace, and wait for the flood of students to come by, signaling to me that it is almost time for my first class of the day.

Sadly, I sit there for over an hour. I see Melissa, one of my floor mates, pass by. She sees me. I wave slightly.

"Hey, Bree!" she says

"Hey, Melissa."

"Hey, I was thinking about maybe getting some of the girls on our floor together to do a movie night or something."

Normally, I would scoff at the idea. My old friends and I never did movie nights. Seems a little juvenile for college, but maybe it is just the distraction I need.

"Sure. That sounds great. When?"

"Awesome. How about Thursday night or Friday night?"

"Let's do Friday night. My room at eight. I'll get the snacks."

"Sounds good. I'll ask around and see who can come."

"Okay. I'll see you later then."

My day is relatively easy. Nothing exciting about my classes. Nothing exciting about this day in general. I do, however, venture to the cafeteria for dinner. I don't want to be late for the first day of my internship, and I happen to catch a group of my floor mates—Casey, Maddie, and Melissa—walking toward the entrance, so I join them.

"Hey. Early dinner for you, too?" Casey asks.

"Yeah, I need to be somewhere at six. I figured I could sneak in and out before the crowd."

"Cool. This is my roommate, Jen."

"Nice to meet you, Jen." I look her up and down.

She has shoulder-length brown hair and pretty blue eyes, and she wears little makeup. She is attractive in a tomboyish kind of way.

"You, too, Bree. Looks like we are all on the same eating schedule today. We have to study for a test tomorrow, so we want to get to the library early."

"Ugh, a test already?" I say.

"Yeah. Fun, right?" Melissa says as she rolls her eyes.

Thankfully, the cafeteria is almost empty, and we ease in and out of any line we want. Seeing the food, I am no longer hungry, but I force myself to eat a salad and pasta. I'm used to much nicer and higher-quality food, cooked by master chefs, with fresh, local ingredients. OSU's cafeteria food is a far cry from that.

"You guys in for the movie on Friday night?" I ask.

"We sure are." Casey responds.

"Great," I say as I stand. The clock on the wall reads quarter to six. "Hey, come get me for dinner early tomorrow night, too."

I don't give them an opportunity to tell me that they don't plan to go to dinner early. This way, they'll be obligated to go. I can't tell them I'm too afraid to sit alone. They wouldn't understand.

I walk outside and take a deep breath. I usually don't get nervous about the first day on a job, as I've had a million of first days with much higher standards and pressure than an unpaid internship. There is a nagging feeling in my stomach I can't ignore. Maybe it's because, for once, I'm just a nobody with no entourage to pump me up and make me feel special. I'm essentially on my own. I have to use this fear to motivate me. I have to, or I'll crumble.

I arrive at the Draper building and drop my bag in the office that Assistant Professor Cooper told me would be used for the interns. I take another deep breath and walk down the hallway to his office.

I knock slightly. "Hello?" I say as I peer in. "Just want to let you know I am here."

"Yes, great. Come in."

The condition of his office is new to me, much more organized than before. His desk is covered with neat piles of papers. However, he seems somewhat frazzled. He runs his hand through his thick hair. Then, he starts to move a few of the piles off to the side.

"Have a seat, please."

I sit. "Should I grab my notebook?" I ask.

"No. Here, you can use this. Best to keep what you do here and your school work separate."

"Okay. Of course," I say as I take the brand-new book from him. I open it to the first page, and my name and year have already been written on the inside. I smile slightly.

He glances at me. He is wearing a white button-down shirt and a dark blue sports coat. He seems to be more formal than I expect after-hours, but then again, by the way he seems out of sorts, I'm assuming he has not gone home for the day.

I wait for him to speak.

"Your first assignment will involve these essays that my students have written. Here is an outline of the project, and each pile is one class's submission. What I need from you is to read each one and present the top three essays of each class. Keep all your notes and feedback on the essays in the book I have given you, as I will ask you to turn that in on your last day."

"Okay. Do you have a deadline?"

"Yes, two weeks."

"Okay."

"I also ask that you refrain from taking these essays out of the building."

"Understood."

"Okay. That is all for now. When you are done for the evening, you may put them back in my office."

"Okay. Will you still be here at eight?" I can't imagine that he would be.

"Probably, but if I do leave, I'll let you know."

"Okay," I say as I grab one pile. I head back down the hall to my office. About two hours later, I notice him walking by, and a few minutes later, he passes by again. I glance up as he sits down across from me. I'm startled to find that he is now wearing a T-shirt and sweatpants. He is chugging a bottle of water, his brow glistening with sweat.

"No questions?" he asks.

"Did you just work out or something?" I ask.

"About the assignment," he says flatly.

"Oh, yeah. No, nothing thus far," I say as my cheeks fill with heat.

"Really?"

"Yes, the instructions were quite clear," I say with an edge.

"I know. I wrote them."

"Then, why ask?"

Ignoring me he says, "Well, that should do it for your first day. You can return those to my office, and I'll show you where to keep them." He gets up and walks down the hall.

I notice the dark spot of sweat down the middle of his back. Surprisingly, it does not gross me out.

I gather my bag and belongings and then put the pile and notebook in my arms. I follow him down the hall.

"You can leave those completed here and those you still need to read in this file, and your notebook can go here," he says as he points to one of the shelves on the far left wall.

I stack all my papers exactly as I was told. "Okay. Well, I'll see you tomorrow, Professor Cooper."

"Yes, Bree. Thank you. And I went for a bike ride to answer your question."

Startled by his confession, I say "Ah, okay. I can see why you're all sweaty." When the words come out of my mouth, I regret them. "I mean, see you soon."

"Tomorrow," he says with a smirk.

His expression catches me off guard, so I turn and exit the building.

I'm officially in hell. As each night comes upon me, I think this will be the night I sleep. But it has yet to come. I have now been back two weeks at school and am so tired that I don't think I can do this anymore. The only time I have slept was during the movie night with some of my floor mates last Friday. I'm not sure if it was the comfort of having people around that lulled me to sleep for a few hours or if it was the movie they'd picked that couldn't keep my attention. But, either way, I slept through the whole thing.

I slowly make my way to the Draper building, dragging my posh boots across the cement, as I hardly have the energy to pick up my feet. I'm late for my internship, but I'm hoping Assistant Professor Copper won't notice.

He's noticed. When I arrive at my office, my papers and notebook are already waiting for me. I usually go down to his office to pick them up and say hello. I am ten minutes late, and by this subtle sign, I gather he is not happy. I sit at the desk and work. I feel my eyes grow tired. I read the same sentence over and over again. My head starts to feel heavy.

I'm not sure when I sense him standing in the room, but I get this feeling somehow. It startles me, and I wake up.

"You're literally sleeping on the job," he says.

I rub my eyes. "I can explain."

"Finish at least what you remember doing last and see me in my office in ten minutes, please."

I swallow hard. I have no recollection of what I was doing last. I glance down at the essay in front of me, and my cheeks burn with embarrassment. I start reading it from the beginning, giving it my full attention.

A little over ten minutes later, I place the essay in the unread file. I'll need to return to it once I'm a bit more awake. The students at least deserve the best from me when it comes to reviewing their work.

I reluctantly walk down the hall and take a deep breath before I go into his office. He is bent over, untying his shoes. I place my papers back on the shelf.

When I turn toward him, I notice he is not wearing his glasses, and his eyes are remarkable. I blink hard and then stare toward the ground.

"Bree, I'll expect that, if this internship is too much for you, you'll come and have a conversation directly with me or Professor Gilford before you fail at it." He pulls a sweatshirt over his head. He puts his glasses back on.

"Fail at it?" I say quietly.

"Yes."

I can't possibly tell him why I'm not sleeping or why I fell asleep on the job. It's not in my scope to even confide in someone like him. I'm stuck, and I know it. I can't think on my feet right now, but I don't want to lose this opportunity. Moisture fills my eyes. I panic that I'll burst into tears; therefore, I turn and march out, leaving him standing there.

Once outside the building, I hurry across campus. My sadness turns to anger, and I'm mad that he thinks one mistake means I'll fail at the internship. I'm furious. I walk over to my car and drive to the closest drugstore to remedy my situation before it's too late for me.

"I should have done this a long time ago," I mumble to myself as I yank open the door to the pharmacy.

I buy two different kinds of sleep aids and exit quickly.

I park my car back in the student lot and hurry up to my room. I shut the door and get ready for bed. I set my alarm, take the pills, and wait for the effects to take over.

I try to clear my head and think of nothing but happy memories. I think of my father and my mother walking on the beach with me. I think of Claudia as I tightly hold my necklace. Finally, I think of my brother handing me flowers and smiling at me. That is the last thing I remember.

Eight

A PENNY FOR YOUR THOUGHTS

I wake, only to realize that, although I slept okay, I am still living with the pain. I reluctantly climb out of bed and go over to the book Eva had given me. I pull out the business card. I pick up my phone and dial the number Eva wrote on the back.

It rings a few times, and then someone answers, "Hello?" Her voice is kind.

I wasn't prepared to speak, despite the fact that I called. I finally find my voice. "Um, yes, hello. Eva gave me your number."

"Yes, dear, how may I help you?"

"I was hoping I could speak with you about…well, I think I'd be more comfortable not saying it over the phone."

"Of course. What is your name?"

"Bree."

"Okay, Bree. How about this morning? Say ten?"

"Yes. I should come to your office?"

"Yes, I will see you at ten."

After I shower and get dressed, I drive about fifteen minutes to her office, which is on the side entrance of an old Victorian home. I'm deducing she lives in the house by the way the front is decorated for Halloween. I park my car and enter the door with her name etched on the window. There is no one else in the waiting area, which is small with only four chairs. Before I can sit, an older woman with silver hair, dressed conservatively in a white oxford, blue-and-gray scarf, and gray wool pants opens the door.

"Bree, hello. I'm Dr. Leo. Please come in."

I swallow hard as my heart beats forcefully within my chest. "Yes, of course."

I take a seat in the leather chair she points toward.

She opens a bound notebook and takes the cap off her pen. "Bree, tell me, what brings you here today?"

I take a deep breath in. "I haven't been sleeping because I had, um…a situation. I mean, something happened to me." My breath catches in my throat, and I might choke on my own words. I'm suffocating again, like I did that night, and I've feared telling someone, anyone, about what makes me feel this way.

"I see. Can you help me understand what happened to you?"

"I am afraid to say it."

"I understand, and I know it can be scary. Just coming here is a step for you. A big one."

I lower my head as the tears fill my tired eyes. I notice a slight movement, and then I see her hand reach across as she hands me a tissue.

"You are in the safest place possible, Bree. Whatever you tell me is between you and me only. There are no exceptions to that. Consider me, if you will, as an empty box with which you can fill all your thoughts and know it will be sealed and kept private for eternity."

"Private for eternity."

I glance up at her. Her face softens, and she smiles ever so slightly at me. Then, I think of Eva. She must trust this doctor with all her secrets, or she would not have told me to come see her. If she is good enough for Eva's secrets, then somehow, I think she could help me with mine. I need to do something other than what I have been if I'm going to get past this. I want to fall in love, I want to be intimate with someone, I want to be safe on campus, I want to not feel the guilt or anger or whatever this is that I've been battling with for being careless, and I want to truly move on and be myself again.

I dab the corner of my eye and sit up straighter in the chair.

I'm ready to talk, I think. *I have to do this.*

I slowly inhale and then say, "On my first night of school, I went to a party…"

With several more tissues and a few instants where I hyperventilated, I've been able to get through the entire story. I've spent over two hours in her office, and she seems not to even care about the time, which I appreciate.

"I am so ashamed. I am disgusted. I am hurt, and worse, I am so very disappointed that I put myself in that situation. I thought I was so much smarter than how I behaved. There was a moment when I thought I should have turned around and walked in the other direction. Not follow this stranger home. But I did, and I blame myself for not trusting my instincts. I am having a hard time accepting my poor decision."

"These feelings you are having are common and normal, Bree. When it comes to your decisions and choices, you have to release them as part of the healing process."

"I'm scared, Dr. Leo, that I might never heal."

"I wish I had the answer to that, Bree. But you are doing all you can right now to hopefully move toward healing."

Upon further conversation, I leave with a prescription for a mild antidepressant and a sleeping pill that she said was non-habit-forming, but rather would help my body slowly fall to sleep. I also have a standing appointment for every Tuesday for the next six weeks.

As I climb back into my car, I can honestly say, as exhausting as that was, I am looking forward to speaking with her again.

I drive to another drugstore. I choose one closer to her office in the hopes of not running into anyone I know from campus, and I get both prescriptions filled. I hurry back to campus after and quickly run to my next class. I make it with seconds to spare.

I'm finally sleeping. But I've got a new set of problems.

When I went to my marketing class yesterday, Assistant Professor Cooper referred to me as *the intern*, not by my name, and said it in such a way that my skin crawled a bit. He barely glimpsed at me.

Mila, the girl who sits next to me and is also in my group, must have picked up the bad vibe, too, because, at our group meeting for our assignment, she asked, "Do you like the internship?"

"It's okay," I whisper.

"What's it like, working for him?" Mallory says with a smile as she raises her eyebrows.

"Yeah. You like working with him?" Ashley asks.

"Honestly, he's kind of a jerk."

I think Ashley mumbles something in agreement, but before I can ask her to repeat it, he calls my name. I turn to find him right behind me. Thankfully, he seems unaffected, but he always does when it comes to me.

"Bree, I won't be available tonight. You can come and get your papers from my office." His eyes look toward the ground.

"Okay. Now?"

He nods awkwardly at my group and then says, "Ladies, I assume your team project is going well?"

Ashley glances down at her notebook and starts to scribble something.

"Yeah, so far, it's going great," Mallory responds.

I see her nudge Ashley's notepad.

Ashley peers up, and her cheeks seem flushed to me. "Yes, Professor, we are all doing *just dandy*." Her tone sounds sarcastic, but I can't be sure. Seems out of place for the simple question he asked.

"I can follow you to your office and grab those papers," I say, trying to break up the weird atmosphere.

"Yes, please do."

"I'll be right back," I say to them.

Then, I follow him to the hallway. He never says a word to me.

Finally, I say, "I shouldn't leave with these, correct?"

"I know I said for you not to, but…I don't have another option right now." He seems agitated as he runs his hand through his hair. He lets out a long sigh. I'm about to ask if something is wrong, he quickly adds, "That's all for right now. Let's get back to class."

"Okay," I say slightly under my breath as I take my items off the shelf. I can sense his eyes watching me.

I stand in front of him now. My cheeks redden as I anticipate what he might say next to me. He opens his mouth slightly and then closes it.

"Professor—" I say softly.

"We should go," he remarks firmly.

I pause, giving him an opportunity to maybe explain the hostility I'm sensing, but he doesn't, so I turn and leave.

I can't help but think, *I am passing everything that has to do with school, but I'm failing at my relationship with Assistant Professor Cooper. Am I to blame for that?*

Gratefully, today is Friday, and I only have my calculus class left before the weekend.

I sit next to Laura in class again. Mercifully, class flies by. We both stand to leave.

"Hey, ready for the weekend?" I ask.

"Yes, I can't wait. What are you doing?"

"Not sure yet. Hoping to go to a party or maybe a football game or something. You?"

"I have to go home this weekend. Kind of a last-minute trip, but I need to take care of a few things at home."

"I hear you."

"I know my roommate is around. I'm sure she'd go with you. We haven't been socializing a lot."

"Oh, sure. Sounds good."

"Yeah, let me see if she is back in our room. I'll introduce you."

I am not in the mood to make new friends today, but since I am only three doors down from Laura, it's hard to avoid them. We enter our dorm and move at a snail's pace down the hall to their room. Laura opens the door, but no one is inside.

"She'll be here any minute. I'm just going to throw some laundry in a bag."

"Sure. Do what you have to do," I say as I start to pick at my nail polish. *I'm overdue for a manicure. Maybe I'll go tonight.*

"Laura!" a voice says. A girl with long blonde hair, slightly tan skin, and these enormous navy eyes comes waltzing in the room.

"Abigail, hi! Um, this is Bree."

"Hello," she says with the sweetest voice.

I'm taken aback by her beauty. She is alarmingly attractive. I can't believe she lives right on the same floor as me, and I had no idea.

"Nice to meet you."

"You, too. You live on our floor?" she asks.

"Yes. I had business to attend to in the first week, but I'm back now. On this floor."

Yes, I am sort of marking my territory. If there is one thing I've learned, pretty and nice tend to win. I've got the pretty down, but not always the pleasant. I can tell by how her cheeks turn bright pink when she eyes me that she is super kind, too.

"Yes, Bree and I are in the same calculus class."

"Ugh, so boring," I add.

She reluctantly smiles at me. "Laura, I wanted to say good-bye before I went to my afternoon classes."

"Thanks, Abigail. I'll see you on Sunday night. I'm bringing a few things home to wash that I borrowed of yours."

"That is very sweet of you." She goes over to Laura and gives her a hug.

I am immediately jealous of their friendship. If I had a roommate, we could borrow each other's things, talk, and hang out. I spend every night alone in my room. It's like solitary confinement.

"Laura, I'll walk you out. I'm going to grab a water from the vending machine," I say.

"Sure, sounds good. Bye, Abigail."

"Bye. See you later," she says as we leave together.

We get into the elevator.

"Your roommate seems cool."

"Abigail? Yeah, she is so smart, considerate, and—"

"That's great," I add. I think I've heard enough about how perfect she is. "Call me when you get back on Sunday, and we can hang out," I say as we step off the elevator.

She is surprised by my request, but I press on, "Cool. Have a great weekend, Laura. Safe trip!"

"You, too. Hope you have fun!"

I enter the common area and get a bottled water. On my way back up to my room, I decide to stop and see if Melissa is home. I knock twice.

Someone yells, "Coming!"

Melissa opens the door.

"Hey!"

She gives me a surprised expression. "Oh, hey, Bree! What's up?"

"Nothing. Can I come in?"

"Of course."

"Thanks," I say.

The room is modest, to say the least. The comforter on her bed is homemade and a tad worn. She has little, if anything, as far as decorations, just a few lamps and an alarm clock. On the wall, she has a few posters of some country singers I've never even heard of.

She walks over to the desk area. "Have a seat," she says as she pulls out a chair.

"I was wondering if you had plans tonight."

"Plans? No, I don't."

"Well, I'm dying to go to this place for a manicure and pedicure. Want to come with me?"

She is almost shocked. She painstakingly eyes her fingers and then wiggles her toes in her flip-flops. "Um, sure. I've never had a—"

"You've never had a manicure? Please, do not tell me it's true." *Never? Really?*

"Yes. Well, my mom painted my nails for prom."

"For God's sake, I insist you come with me. I'll make our appointments."

"Sounds like fun," she says, her eyes as wide as saucers.

"Okay. Change out of your gym clothes."

"I'm not in my gym clothes."

"Oh, really?" *Oops, could have fooled me.*

"Yes, really."

"Okay, then change into something casual, but not gym clothes-like, and I'll go make the appointments. We can find a place to eat dinner later if you want to."

I leave the room, shaking my head. *What kind of girl has never pampered herself? Isn't that what being a girl is all about?*

I suppose my floor mates do need my guidance after all. This has, unbeknownst to them, given me a new purpose, one that I can focus on. All of them need to live a little more, even the beautiful ones.

Melissa and I head toward the parking lot. Thankfully, she is wearing gray pants and a navy tank top. Her outfit is much more suitable.

"I knocked on Abigail's door. I know Laura is away this weekend, but she wasn't home."

"Right. Yes, well, too bad," I say although my tone would say otherwise.

"Yeah, I thought so, too."

"I just met her."

"Yeah, she is so sweet—"

"She is very pretty."

We approach my car.

"You have a car here? I assumed we'd be taking a car obviously, but I thought freshmen weren't really allowed to have a vehicle."

"We're not really, but a donation to the school from my father seemed to do the trick."

She whistles.

"Wow, impressive ride."

"Thanks. It was my graduation present."

"Boy, you must have graduated at the top of your class."

"Something like that," I say with a slight laugh.

We get in my car and head east toward Main Street and then directly onto the highway.

"What does your daddy do?" she asks.

I notice her Southern accent is decidedly stronger when she says *daddy*.

"My father is an entrepreneur in New York City. He owns a few buildings and was once a lawyer."

"Wow, my daddy is a football coach. Man, does he love it, and I guess, I love it, too."

"I was thinking about going to the game tomorrow. We should go. I hear our team is really good."

"Sounds great. Yes, they are awesome, and tomorrow is supposed to be a fantastic day. We don't have autumn in Texas, so this weather has been a real treat."

"Well, you're about to get another treat, too. This nail salon is ranked as one of the best in the area."

"Exciting." She smiles wide.

We drive for another ten minutes and then pull into the salon. It's relatively quiet for a Friday evening. We pick out our colors, and then we go over to the pedicure chairs. Melissa watches everything I do and follows me to the letter.

"I don't know what I'm doing," she whispers as she rolls up her pant leg.

"Just watch me." I make deliberate moves, so she is more comfortable. I want her to enjoy this.

As we soak our feet in the tubs, a calming sensation washes over me. This is what I needed to start my weekend.

"This is fabulous," she says.

"Yes, it is. I used to hate getting my nails done. I've been doing it since I was a kid."

"Really?"

"Yes, I used to compete in beauty pageants, therefore it was a necessity, not an enjoyable girls' trip like this." I see her smile. It must be because I said it was a girls' trip.

"Ever win?"

I smirk at her. I can't help the competitiveness that has been ingrained in me since I was a child. Win pageants, win modeling jobs…competition, competition, competition. It's starting to wear me down.

"Yes, of course," I mumble.

"What was that like?"

"Thrilling, at first. You get to meet tons of interesting people and travel to other states and pageants, but then it gets old kind of fast."

"It sounds exhausting."

"Tell me, what was it like, growing up in Texas?"

Her eyes light up. "Well, I live in a real small town where football is everything to everybody. My daddy is pretty well known in Texas. He has the highest winning record for any high school coach in the state. He's been in state parades and all that stuff. My mom has written a couple of children's books, which is why I'm interested in journalism, I surmise. I have an older brother who played football at Ole Miss and now lives in Louisiana. He's real smart, too. He's an orthopedic surgeon, mostly working on big-time athletes and the like."

"Has he ever operated on anyone famous?"

"Yeah, a couple of football players, and he once reconstructed the shoulder of a guy who got into this terrible motorbike accident. He's a professional rider, so you know my brother is now into that 'cause he's around it so much."

"Motorbiking?"

"Yeah, you know, competitive bike racing?"

"Didn't know there was such a thing."

"You have got to get out more," she says with a wink.

It makes me smile.

"Right, of course. I'll get right into the bike-racing scene," I say.

Over an hour later, we are finally drying our nails under the hand dryers. I am tired.

"Want to pick up some food near campus and eat in my room?" I ask.

"Sure, that sounds great."

We head back to campus and stop at a sandwich shop near our dormitory. We both get salads and drinks.

I park my car back in the student lot. We get out and within a few minutes are back to our dorm. It is so quiet in the dorm on a Friday night. Almost everyone is out.

We enter my room, and when she turns her back, I take a sleeping pill. By the time we are done eating, I'm hoping I'll be sleepy enough to just go to bed. We sit at the desks and eat while gazing out the window at the campus. It's so peaceful at night with the lampposts lighting the tree-lined brick walkways. It is such a stunning and well-maintained campus. I haven't had much time to appreciate its beauty because, unfortunately, nighttime on campus has given me a terrible feeling.

I shudder, and my thoughts become gloomy again.

Now, as I view the spectacularly lit campus, I think about *him*. He is out there somewhere, awaiting his next prey. *How many women has he assaulted since my first night? How many victims has he terrorized? Should I report this now? Was I stupid not to tell the officer that very night? Did I miss my window?* That eats away at me even more. I can't help how I feel.

"Bree? Did you hear me?"

I snap out of my thoughts. "What? I'm sorry."

"I asked if you liked your salad."

"What? Salad? Yes, it's fine."

I can tell by the way she is staring at me that my expression is dark. Her eyes widen as she leans back in the chair.

"Okay. Well, hey, it's a bit late for me, and I think I'll hit the hay."

"Sure, of course." My eyes are getting heavy.

She stands up and throws her empty salad container in the trash. I notice mine is almost completely untouched. I don't remember even taking one bite. Then, I notice her hands are on my arms, and slowly, I'm being pulled up, like I am floating on a cloud. She smiles at me.

"Sorry, I'm tired for some reason."

"Don't worry. I'll lock your door." She guides me over toward my bed.

I try to kick off my shoes, but to no avail. She reaches down and pulls them off. I think I smile back at her. My head lowers softly onto my pillow. Then, there is darkness.

I never turned off my alarm from the week; consequently, it goes off at eight. I am still dressed in my clothes from the night before. I have no recollection of the evening, but as I start to sit up, I notice my hands and the manicure. Piece by piece, thoughts start to come back to me.

My head is groggy, but at least I slept. I undress, put on my robe, and head for the shower.

On my way back from the bathroom, my towel piled on my head, I run into Melissa. I am slightly embarrassed.

That is, until she speaks, "Hey, sleepyhead. You sure were tired!"

"I know. Sorry."

"Don't be. Hey, I'm running out to get some breakfast. Seems like you could use—"

"Latte. I need a latte."

"Okay, one latte coming up."

She leaves as I open my door. I take my time dressing and putting on my makeup. I put the blow-dryer on high and dry my hair as I aimlessly stare in the mirror.

I never hear Melissa knock, so when I'm done, I open my door. I find her sitting in the hallway across from my room, drinking her coffee and eating a bagel.

"Have a seat!" she says. "I knocked, but the blow-dryer was on."

"Well, thanks." I reluctantly sit on the floor across from her.

She hands me my latte.

I take a long-awaited sip. "Thanks for this."

"Welcome."

"How is it outside this morning?"

"Wonderful. Going to be a nice day."

"Good."

"Well, still want to go down to the football game?"

I take another sip of my latte. I think I remember committing to going. "I suppose I could. I don't really have any other plans for the afternoon."

"Well," she says with a smile, "don't let me stop you from doing anything better."

I peer up from my latte. She doesn't take her eyes off of me. It's as though she is challenging me, but in a friendly sort of way.

"Has anyone hung out with you for two whole days in a row?" I ask.

She laughs. "It's been a while."

Something about her laugh makes me laugh along with her. Then, a door clicks open, and we both glance down the hallway. Abigail steps out into the hall. She is even more striking than when I met her the other day. Her hair is perfect, long, and flowing, and it reminds me of silk ribbons hanging down in curls. She smiles at us both, as though the sound of laughter were enough to make her happy. She approaches, and I can't help but notice her eyes, how they remind me of the ocean outside my window back home. Something is mysterious and endless about them. There is a story behind her eyes, one that she has yet to discover. I can feel it.

"Hello," she says.

I can smell her perfume as she gets closer. It's light and crisp. I inhale, trying to place the scent. It is hibiscus or daffodils or something I have come across in the garden outside my father's office.

"Hi, Abigail," Melissa says.

"Hello," I say.

"What are you guys doing?" Abigail asks.

"Nothing. Just talking about last night."

She blushes for some reason. "Oh," she says.

"Yes, we are going to go down to the football game. Want to go with us?"

"Sure, that sounds like fun."

I glance at her and then scrutinize my appearance and my outfit. I know I can't go to the game like this. She looks far better than I do.

"Great. Well, I'm going to get ready, and we can leave in, like, forty-five minutes." I stand up.

"I thought you already got ready?" Melissa says.

"Oh, Melissa, please. I'm not ready," I say as I enter my room. "I'll get you guys when I'm done."

My hair is flat, not flowing like Abigail's, so I take my wide, round brush and start twisting the brush around my hair while blasting it with quick heat from the dryer, creating my own waves. Once I'm done with that, I change into something new, a bit nicer than what I had on, and decide to put on open-toed sandals to show off my new pedicure. I dab on more lip gloss and spray on a little more perfume.

I realize the game is going to start soon, so I take one last glance at myself before I step out into the hallway and call for the girls.

A minute later, they both step out, and I can tell by the way they eye me that I've nailed it.

"Ready?"

"Yes, we're ready," Melissa says.

We stroll down to Menton Field, and I chat a little with Abigail, but she seems to be put off by the fact that I am a model. She wants to be a veterinarian, so in reality, we are on opposite sides of the spectrum. This makes me feel a little better, although, I'm not exactly sure why.

We enter the stadium. The game is packed, but we luckily find a place on the bleachers. Throughout the game, Melissa talks incessantly about football.

I can't help but watch the incredibly in-shape boys on the field and think to myself that, if I landed a guy like that, I'd never have to worry about something happening to me again. It suddenly hits me. A big football player could be my boyfriend and protect me from anyone at the school. Plus, the football players at OSU are so beloved, it's sickening. They are revered as heroes who walk among us. I'll be in the right crowd, and be forever untouchable. Money can't buy that. I'd not only have one of them, but I'd also have the whole team watching out for me. My mind is made up as I watch them fight and tackle each other. I'll have to set my sights on a player and go for it. It should be easy for me...I think.

The crowd is totally into the game, and they keep yelling and chanting for the quarterback. I think his name is Ryan or something, but the crowd has not stopped screaming his name. Melissa keeps yammering on about how, statistically, he's accomplishing something amazing. I don't know. I'm not paying any attention to what she is saying. At least when I glance over at Abigail, she seems to be about as interested in all this football nonsense as I am.

"Penny for your thoughts," Melissa asks as the crowd starts to disperse and the players run off the field and into the field house.

I smile and then say, "I have got to get me one of those football players. Yummy."

"Come on, let's go," she says with a laugh.

I follow them out of the gate and see Abigail wave to someone. Two guys standing near the fence, watching us, as we approach.

"Hey, Webber!" she says. "These are my floor mates, Bree and Melissa."

These guys are total geeks. Immediately, I'm disinterested in anything they have to say.

"Hi," I mumble.

"Hey, this is Logan. So, hey, Abigail, we are thinking of going to a party at The Ridge. My roommate invited us. Will you come with us?" Webber says.

"What's The Ridge?" Abigail asks.

"The football house."

"Football house? Wait, who is your roommate?" I ask, suddenly engrossed in what he has to say.

"Nathan Ryan—you know, the quarterback?"

"Really? You live at The Ridge?" I ask.

"No, we are both first-year students."

"What dorm do you live in?" I'll have to be sure to find my way around the dorm and maybe casually bump into some football players.

"Well, I can't say. The school won't allow." He chuckles as though he thinks he is being funny.

I glare at him.

Then, Abigail pipes up, "Sure, we can go if you want some company."

"Sure, sounds fine to me," I say halfheartedly. I have to play this cool. I can't seem too eager to land a football player.

The whole way over there, I'm painfully examining myself. Times like this is when I hate my overanalyzing nature. When I have to get ready for a photo shoot or job, it comes in handy to be critical, but not for social situations. I wish I could relax and not care what people think, but I can't. I'm jittery, and I know it. Years of modeling will do that to you. You notice things about yourself that others wouldn't think twice of. Like, does my nail polish match or clash with my outfit? Or worse, is it chipped? I notice a chip on my newly painted toes, and I want to run screaming. This is a problem…and I'm fully aware of it.

As we ascend upon the house, I can hear people talking in the backyard, and from the sounds of it, a lot of people are at this party.

My suspicions are reaffirmed when we near the old Victorian-style house. A man is standing by the side gate with a clipboard in his hand. He is terribly intimidating by the way his massive arms are folded over his chest, giving us an unwelcoming stare.

I let Webber talk first since he was the one invited, but I'll speak up if I need to. I've gotten myself into all kinds of parties in the Hamptons. Ones with much more security than some guy and a clipboard at a football house.

"Can I help you?" he asks in a devastatingly deep voice.

"Um, yes," Webber says with a shaky voice.

"You girls with these guys?" he asks.

"Sort of," I chime in.

I give him one of my best smiles. Surely, he will not be able to resist.

"Okay, what's your name?" he says to Webber.

"Webber."

Without even glancing at his clipboard, he says, "Nope, no Webber on the list. How can I help you guys?"

"Never mind." Webber turns.

I watch him start to walk away. I'm appalled by how easily he gave up.

"Well, his roommate said he was putting him on the list," Abigail interjects.

I can see she is trying, albeit poorly, to defend her friend.

"Who is your roommate?" he asks.

"Nathan Ryan."

"Spidey?"

I see Webber turn slightly, cheeks bright red.

"Yeah."

"Well, why didn't you say so? I'm Junior. Come on in. You gotta be so proud of your boy. He had one of the best games in school history!" He puts his arm around Webber's shoulders, but then, he glances at me. "Are you sure you are only sort of with these guys? Because I don't have any of your names on the list, only Spidey and Logan here."

"Could you make an exception for us?" Melissa asks.

I continue to smile, hoping he'll say yes.

Finally, he glances back at Abigail. "You know what, ladies? Today is your lucky day because it's Nathan's night to celebrate, and he should have his friends here. Let me get your names."

"Thank you so much. I'm Abigail. This is Melissa and Bree," she says politely.

I give her a quick glimpse. She doesn't appear to flinch in the situation. Beautiful, smart, and not easily persuaded. She just might be the one to watch on my floor.

We enter the party after Junior marks each of our hands with a black X. Like a centipede, Webber maneuvers us through the crowd that has gathered in the back. It clears up in the middle, but then there is a vast line for the food—which smells fantastic, I might add.

It reminds me of the clambakes we used to have on the beach right outside my house. All our friends and family used to come and spend hours on the beach, eating, swimming, and tasting some of the freshest and finest foods around. I loved those days on the coast and long for them again.

As I think about home and start missing it, I realize I'm too nervous to eat, so I watch my friends as they meander through the line and fill their plates with some of the best food I've seen in weeks.

We grab a table on the other side where hardly anybody is sitting. It's such a rookie move. We should be sitting on the other side, near the action, not stuffing our faces over here. I survey the crowd and realize this is mostly an alumni-and-player type party. There are not as many students as I expected there to be. It makes a little more sense as to why Junior was so adamant about the list. By the appearances of the food and people here, this is definitely an invitation-only kind of party.

I'm exactly where I need to be, I conclude.

Too nervous to sit, I look around to see if I know anyone to try to get away from these guys. Then, I spot her—the girl from my psychology class. She has these curls running down her back, and during class, I trace them with my eyes to keep myself busy. I'd recognize that head of hair anywhere as I am now intimately aware of each curl attached to her skull.

I turn to my floor mates and watch for a second as they sit there like they are waiting to be picked for a middle school dance. Pathetic.

I feel nothing as I quickly say, "I'll be back later. I see a friend of mine from class." I don't even give one of them the chance to respond as I turn on my heel and saunter to the other side of the party.

I approach, coyly pretending that I am happening upon her. "Jessica?" I say sweetly.

I notice she is sitting with football players as they all glance up. Handsome ones, I might add.

"Bree?" she says, eyeing me up and down. "Is that you?"

"Of course it's me."

"What are you doing here?" she asks.

"Obviously invited," I say, flipping my hair to the side. I smile at the table.

"Really?" one of the players asks.

Another one says to me, "Curious, who invited you?"

"Nathan Ryan's roommate."

The guy across from Jessica now glances up at me. I'm immediately taken aback by how gorgeous he is. Dark hair that is slicked back, gray eyes, and this incredible smile that forms across his face. I swallow hard, and I sense my cheeks turn pink.

"Really?" he says. "Mind telling me if he is here?"

"Yes, over there," I say as I point back across the yard.

He immediately gets up, and without a word, he strides across the lawn. I notice Jessica scowl at me.

"Have a seat," one of the players says as he slides down on the bench.

"Was it something I said?" I ask half-jokingly to Jessica.

"That," she says through gritted teeth, "*was* Nathan Ryan."

"Oh," I say, feeling foolish that I didn't know who the star quarterback was.

He is incredibly hot, and that was before I knew he was a football player. He could be a win-win for me.

The guy next to me is cute, too, but not like Nathan. "You all play?" I ask him.

"Yeah, we all play." He glances at me and gives me a sexy smile. "You sticking around for the after-party?"

Another chimes in, "More like the real party."

Now, I'm intrigued. "Tell me about this after-party."

I can see the guy next to me smile.

"I'm Jason, by the way," he says as he extends his hand to me.

I shake it and notice how large his hand is.

He continues, "And this is Marcus and Troy. Jackson is our coordinator. You know Jessica. And, I'm sorry, what is your name again?" He turns to the girl sitting next to Jessica.

I barely acknowledge the girl next to Jessica because she has been glowering at me since I approached over ten minutes ago.

"Kelly."

"Oh, yeah, and Kelly." When he says her name, he rolls his eyes. I try not to snicker, but it's too funny not to.

"Nice to meet you all."

We talk at the table for about twenty minutes when I notice this boy approaching the table. He is so big that he makes Junior appear like a twelve-year-old. He has shocking blond hair. It's long and hangs down past his chin. It surprisingly suits him. He has to be at least six foot five. He's massive, and I can tell he has these silver-colored eyes. They seem to sparkle as he nears. I find myself sitting back because his demeanor is so harsh and forward, like he's been shot from a cannon.

"Can you guys believe that freaking game?" he says, high-fiving Jason.

"Awesome game, dude," Marcus says.

"You, too, Captain," he says as he high-fives Marcus.

"Yeah, two touchdowns. Not bad, Tank," Troy says.

"Right, I—I mean, *we* were awesome. We killed them! They should be embarrassed to even call themselves a Division One school."

I notice his breathing is rapid, like he can't catch his breath.

He continues, "Speaking of embarrassed, what's up with Ryan? One minute, he's all banged up, and then the next, he's, like, having this killer game. Then, I see him hobbling out like he can't even freaking move his leg. Such a tool move."

Troy laughs, which eggs him on even more.

"Right, Troy? He was like this!"

He starts to act like he's limping badly, only I can tell he's definitely making fun of Nathan, which is strange to me because he is his teammate. Jessica starts to laugh, too. He smiles.

"You at the game, babe?" Tank asks.

"Yeah, of course I was," Jessica says sweetly.

Then, he glances at me, and his eyes get wide. "You, too? Man, where have you girls been hiding?"

I smile faintly and lower my eyes.

"I'll be right back," Jason says abruptly.

"What's his problem?" Tank asks.

"Don't know. Maybe he's pissed he couldn't get in the game, even when Ryan was hurt," Troy adds with little care.

"He might want to get used to it, man," Marcus says.

"What do you mean, get in the game?" I ask.

"He's the backup quarterback," Marcus says to me.

"Oh, and Nathan is hurt?" I ask, confused.

"Well, that's debatable," Tank says. "It's more like he was running around like this." He limps around in a circle and pretends to throw a ball.

It is actually pretty funny, but I try not to laugh.

Marcus stands and whispers in Tank's ear.

Tank smiles wickedly and then peers over at us. "You girls interested in playing a little beer pong with us?"

The sun is starting to fade behind the fence, and the slightest breeze floats over my skin. I feel nervous. Tank isn't quite what I had in mind. He seems more aggressive and overpowering than I'd welcome right now. Marcus and Jason seem nice enough, but I wish Nathan would come back, so I could try to get to know him better. He is so attractive, someone I could get used to gazing at each day. He is majorly on the team and much less antagonistic than the others. I need less aggressive.

Jessica's hand gently touches my leg. Then, she whispers, "Join us. These guys are so much fun." She searches my eyes and then smiles at me.

"Okay, sure."

Tank loudly claps his hands together. "I'm going to go inside and help with the kegs. I'll meet you guys over at the tables in twenty."

I decide now would be a good time to touch up my lip gloss. I stand up from the table. "Do you know where the bathroom is?" I ask Jessica.

"Come with us. We'll show you." She stands and grabs me by the hand.

She pulls me toward the house, and Kelly is close behind.

Once inside the house, I follow her down the hallway and to a bathroom.

She yanks open the door without even knocking and goes inside. "You coming or what?"

Kelly practically pushes me aside and holds open the door for me to come in.

"Come on, come on. Close it, Kelly," Jessica barks.

I squeeze past her before she pulls the door shut.

Jessica starts to pull down her pants to pee. I am trapped and embarrassed.

Then, Jessica says, "You'd better get used to using the bathroom with a bunch of girls. It's the only way to get in and out at these parties."

"Oh, really?" I say sarcastically. "Then, this might be my last party."

Kelly snorts, and it's the first noise she has made. Then, she starts to laugh as she squeezes past me to use the bathroom. I am in some sort of sorority-girl hell. But then again, I have gotten accustomed to dressing and undressing in front of photographers and other models; it kind of comes with the territory. But this, I most definitely did not sign up for.

"I wanted to touch up my lip gloss," I say matter-of-factly. I pull out my bright pink lip gloss and apply a fresh coat to my lips once Jessica is done washing her hands.

"Pretty. Mind if I use it?" Jessica asks.

Actually, I do mind, I think.

But I hand her my expensive lip gloss and cringe inside while she applies it to her pouty lips. She is pretty, no doubt. Much shorter than I am, she is maybe five foot three, and I'm five foot ten. She has that long, dark curly hair I know all too well, naturally pouty lips, and wide eyes with long eyelashes. She must be Italian or Greek or something because her skin coloring is a warm olive color.

Kelly washes her hands.

I wait for them to head toward the door. "I'll meet you guys out there in two, okay?"

"Sure, we'll give you your privacy," Jessica says.

"Thanks."

I lock the door, and I finally have a minute to use the bathroom. I'm in and out in less than three minutes, and they are nowhere to be found in the house, so I head out to the backyard.

Jessica and Kelly are already with some of the players near the beer pong tables. I go over to them. They all seem, I don't know, cocky or forward or something. I can't place it, but it almost instantly turns me off.

I like a little chase. I am used to boys being incredibly aloof due to the amount of money their parents have—basically figuring that, at some point, they'd land a girl seeking wealth—or, on the other hand, boys being obsessed with independent and self-assured girls. Dashiell and Joss are a perfect example. He was almost desperate to crack the code. Like if he could conquer a girl like Joss, he could get anyone. This is probably why I never had a boyfriend in high school. It was completely by choice. I had no interest in letting anyone think they could rule over me. No, thank you.

But I like the attention, too. Who doesn't? I've tried to teeter in between the two—the chase versus attention.

Jason seems to be the friendliest out of them. Well, Marcus, too, but he's older, and he seems like he doesn't have much interest in first-year students. He's nice and all, but by the women surrounding him, I gather he likes them more experienced.

Tank seems the most aggressive of the group. He's kind of loud and demanding, but he's definitely hot. He has a muscular body and a big and distinct appearance. His hair is beautiful, and his eyes truly stand out.

He calls Jessica over. He seems taken with her. "Hey, babe, come here."

Then, I notice Nathan come over.

"Hey, Two," Tank says. "Where have you been all day—talking to reporters, giving interviews?"

My God is Nathan gorgeous. He is tall and lean. His hair is dark, and he has steel-colored eyes that make me shiver. He eyes me for a second and smiles. My knees get weak. Wow. I mean, *wow*. He is beautiful.

"You know," he says bashfully, "standard stuff."

Tank scoffs. "Standard stuff? I suppose, beating the school record is standard stuff. Do you believe this guy?" he says to no one in particular.

To me, the dynamic between them seems odd since they are both such good players, are on the same team, and have the same friends.

I observe Nathan timidly mumble something under his breath. Marcus approaches him and kind of leans in as he says something to him. It is much more cordial. Jessica leaves Tank's side and cozies up to Nathan as well, and the three of them talk. I realize I'm staring, hence why I go over to the keg and grab a beer. I can see Melissa, Abigail, Logan, and Webber sitting at the same table as before. I don't want to get stuck over there, so I take my beer back to the beer pong tables. When I do, I notice Jessica write something on Nathan's hand. I should have grabbed the opportunity to talk to Nathan when I had it while Jessica was by his side. But then Tank calls her over, and she goes running back to him. I'm about to get the courage to go over to Nathan when he turns and heads toward the keg.

"Hey. Bree, right?"

I turn and see a heavy-set guy with dark hair, wearing a T-shirt with a cartoon character holding a beer can on the front. *Classy.*

"Yeah," I say.

"Oh, cool. Thought so. I'm in your marketing class with Professor Gilford and Assistant Professor Cooper."

"Oh, yes."

"Sorry, I know your name because you got the internship this year. Congrats, by the way. That's huge."

"Thanks. So far, it's fine."

"I'm Aaron."

"Oh, sorry. Nice to meet you, Aaron. You play football?"

"No, Troy, my old roommate, does. He lives in this house now."

"Ah, I see."

"The application process for the internship, it was hard, right?"

"What do you mean?"

"I mean, it was difficult. Essays to complete and then an interview. I only got to the second round. But I know for a fact that there can be several rounds before they even decide on the finalists."

I'm speechless. I had no idea.

"Last time I applied, Cooper said my essay bordered on that of a high school student, and I had a four-point-oh average. Whatever you wrote must have been pretty spectacular."

Maybe it's the beer that is making my brain unable to fire on all cylinders, but there is no way he is talking about the same internship.

"Yeah, you know, mine was about marketing solutions on campus—how to market to the masses, but attract the best talent," I lie.

"Interesting. I can see how that might grab his attention."

"Yeah, well, I guess it did." I laugh.

"My friend had the internship last year, and he said working with Cooper was awesome. He is brilliant. That's why everyone wants it so badly. He's like the second coming of professors at this school. Rumor has it, he turned down Duke, Vanderbilt, and Columbia, all to come here for this program. Gilford made such a big deal about him when he came here. Rolled out the red carpet for the guy."

Strange, Assistant Professor Cooper doesn't seem like the second coming. After all, to advertise for the internship, his best idea was to leave a flier. I must be missing something.

"Well, I'll be sure to let you know how the year goes."

"Yeah, please do. More than anything, I'm curious to see if he makes the internship different from year to year or what."

"About how many students apply each year?"

"The year I did, I think there were forty of us."

I almost choke on my beer I was taking a sip of. *Forty?*

"Wow, I didn't know."

"Yeah, but I heard, this year, the process was much faster. He must have it down pat and know what he is searching for."

Either that, or he wants to torture me and make my life hell for the next year, I think.

"Hey, Bree."

I turn toward the beer pong tables.

"Hey, Melissa, Logan. This is Aaron. We are in the same marketing class."

"Hey, you guys ever been to this party before?"

"Nope, first time," Melissa responds.

"Cool," he says.

"Where is everybody else?" I ask as I peer past them.

"They left. Nathan had to take his roommate home."

"They?" I ask.

"Yeah, well, just Abigail and Nathan. They needed to take Webber home. He had a few too many and too quickly."

"Lightweight," Aaron says with a chuckle.

I am more interested than anything about how Abigail managed to leave with Nathan after only meeting him only a few hours ago.

"Huh. Well, that was nice of her," I say, trying not to imply that I might be a little jealous.

"You want to go listen to the band?" Aaron asks me.

"Sure. Why not?" Before I head over to the band with him, I whisper in Melissa's ear, "Don't leave without me, okay? Seriously." I give her a glare, and I think she understands I mean it.

"Oh, yeah. Of course not."

Aaron and I watch the band for about an hour. I have two more beers, and I know I'm at my limit. He tried at one point to put his arm around me, but I'm positive he got the picture when I shot daggers at him with my eyes.

Not interested, Aaron.

I can see Melissa and Logan working their way through the crowd toward me. I wave them back and turn to Aaron. "Hey, see you in class!" I yell over the music.

I make my way back through the crowd to Melissa and Logan.

"Ready to go?" Logan asks.

"Yeah, definitely," I say as I head toward the back gate.

It's time for me to call it a night. This time, I'm trusting my instincts.

Nine

I'LL WALK YOU HOME

Three grueling weeks are gone, just like that. I can hardly remember what
I've done because the days have blended together.

I met a guy at a party last week. He seemed cool enough, but once we
started making out, I panicked.

"Dude, slow down, will you?" I barked.

"What's the problem, babe?" he said, barely paying any attention to me,
despite his lips being all over me.

He started to pull up my shirt, and I was instantly taken back to
Dashiell's party and my first night of college. *What was it with guys thinking we
were going to get down to it immediately? Didn't anyone freaking give a shit anymore?*

"I thought you were cool," he said, like me not screwing him somehow
equated to me not being freaking cool.

"What?" I said, obviously irritated.

"Don't get pissy, sweetheart."

"I'm not." *The hell I'm not*, I thought.

"Good." He tried to kiss me again.

"Can you hang on for a minute while I use the bathroom?"

He smiled at me. "Of course, Bryce."

I didn't bother to correct him.

I smiled faintly in return, but then I left the room and hurried through
the crowd until I found Casey.

"Can we please get the hell out of here?"

Her eyes wide, she said, "Sure, Bree. You okay?"

"I will be if we can leave...now."

Quickly, she grabbed my hand and led me through the crowd and up
the stairs of the old basement. Within seconds, we were out and in the cool

fall night. I welcomed the brisk air and took a deep breath in. I was free again. I noticed she didn't let my hand go as we began hiking down the street and back to our dorm. I glanced at her, and she smiled back. I nodded, and we continued our way home in welcomed silence, hand in hand.

I find myself back to the grind. It's Monday afternoon, and I'm sitting with Ashley, Mallory, and Mila, discussing our project. I glance at my watch, trying not to be obvious that I'm watching the time. I'm used to busy days, but college life has definitely presented some challenges to me in more ways than one. Trying to excel in everything can be pretty darn exhausting.

"Do you have somewhere you need to be?" Ashley says in a bitter tone.

I peek up and notice her glaring at me. Her piercing eyes tell me she has a story, one I'm not sure I want to be a part of.

"Well, yes, in fact, I have to be at my internship at six," I say defensively. I glance at the other girls to gauge their reactions.

"We should be done by then," Mallory adds kindly.

"And if we aren't?" Ashley says rather provokingly.

Mila snaps her head up and stares at her. "Ashley," she whispers.

"Well, it's due in two weeks, and we hardly get time to meet, so if she can't do her part—"

"I never said I wasn't going to do my part." I don't know where this is coming from, but she seems upset at me.

"That's not what she meant," Mallory chimes in.

"Yes, it is." She folds her arms across her chest.

I glare at her and say, "We have twenty more minutes until I have to leave. Let's not waste it discussing a nonissue, okay?"

She starts to open her mouth to respond when I see Mila put her hand on her arm.

"Yes, okay? We all agree," Mila says. "Right?"

"Fine," Ashley barks. "Let's continue."

And we do.

It's awkward when I have to leave, but thankfully, Mallory leaves with me.

"Hey, sorry about that back there," she says as we vacate together.

"I have no intension of not doing my part, just so you know," I say firmly.

"Never had a doubt, Bree." She pauses, and for some reason, she looks concerned, as though something is on her mind. Then, slowly, she adds,

"You know…Ashley can be a little unpredictable at times. Hard to put into words. It's just something about her."

"Really? Like what?"

"Well, I'm friends with her roommate, and she said—" She is about to say something that I can tell is weighing on her mind when, unexpectedly, Mila and Ashley can be heard exiting the library doors.

"Well, anyway, I gotta run. See you later."

"Bye, Mallory," I say. Before I get caught in a crossfire with Ashley, I quickly scamper toward the Draper building.

Since, at this point, I know I'm already late and I have been working nonstop for several hours, I decide to grab a latte before I start reading the essays. On my way to Draper is a little café on campus that sells coffee and quick snacks for on-the-go students in between classes. Thankfully, I get inside right before it closes.

"Can I have a latte with skim milk, please?" I find myself dozing from time to time, particularly during those poorly written essays.

"Anything else?"

"Sorry, can you make two of those?" *Why not try to make friends with the great professor who doesn't seem to like me?*

"Sure."

It's time to butter up Cooper a little. He has hardly spoken a word to me these past weeks, and honestly, if all he wanted was an essay reader, well, I'm sure he could have picked anyone off the street to do what I've been doing.

I take the lattes and hurry to the Draper building. As I pass my office, I can see his door open, and the light is on. I take a deep breath before I enter.

"A few minutes late," he says, not glancing up from his paper.

I notice the clock on his wall, and it reads eight minutes past six. *He has got to be kidding me.*

"It's a latte with skim milk," I say as I put the cup on his desk.

I walk over to the shelf where I grab all my papers and my notebook. Then, I turn and leave.

So much for making a friendly gesture.

I plop down in the desk chair and open my notebook to where I left off.

Two hours fly by, and I'm wide awake, thanks to my latte. I finish reading the last essay in that pile and finalize my notes before I stand up, put on my jacket, and head down to Cooper's office to return my items.

I'm not surprised to see him sweaty and in his gym clothes. He peers up and smiles at me. I think he only smiled at me because he didn't know it was me. He must be expecting someone else.

"Ms. Van Tousen." He nods at me as I place my items on his shelf.

I notice the latte is untouched.

"Good night."

"I'll walk you. I'm just leaving myself."

"Thank you, but you don't have to go to any trouble for me."

"I understand. Thought we might catch up."

My cheeks are rosy. All of a sudden, he is friendlier toward me. I'm skeptical, to say the very least. He now has my full attention, and I can't wait to see what this is all about. He has to have a motive for wanting to escort me home.

"Okay," I respond slowly. I step out of his office and don't look to see if he is following me.

"Mind if we go out this way?" he asks. "My bike is back here."

"Sure," I say as I turn and follow him.

I have a funny sensation I can't seem to shake. I'm nervous, and I don't know why.

We exit out the side door, and sure enough, his mountain bike is locked to the bike rack. He unlocks it and starts to mosey toward campus.

"You know, if you just want to ride your bike home, we can catch up on Wednesday."

"Ms. Van—"

"Please. Can I ask that you please call me Bree?" This time, I'm pleading. I hate being called Ms. anything.

He stops and gives me a pained expression. "Okay, I can do that."

My God, he seems terribly uncomfortable at the thought of calling me by my name. So weird.

"Thank you."

He continues to walk. "I assume you live across campus?"

Most of the freshman and sophomore dorms are on the opposite side of campus.

"Yes, I do. Willis Hall."

"Wonderful."

"You?"

"Um, I can tell you that I do not live on campus." He is formal when he speaks.

I realize that, despite his age, he is still an authority at the university, and I should not have asked him that.

"I'm sorry. I'm so used to asking people on campus that I forgot, you know, that I should not have asked that. I apologize."

His face softens. "No need to."

I'm not sure if he is walking with me to talk about school or more get-to-know-you type talk, so I wait for him to ask me a question.

We continue on in silence for a few minutes, and we cross the main road. I'm dying inside.

Finally, he speaks, "You enjoying the internship?"

Crap. "Yes, totally," I lie.

He hesitates and then smiles. "What have you enjoyed the most thus far?"

Ugh. "Well, you know, reading the essays." Because it's the only damn thing I've done for over a month.

"One could say, that's all that I have assigned to you." His tone is slightly sarcastic.

I am annoyed. Thankfully, I can see Willis Hall up ahead.

"Coop—"

His eyes get wide.

"Assistant Professor Cooper," I say in a huff, "since that is all you have allocated to me, then why ask me to tell you what I have done and what I like? Am I not performing to your standards? If that is the case, then I would like you to tell me, so I can try to improve."

He stops and turns toward me, resting his hand on his handlebars. I am quickly regretting my words and, more importantly, my tone.

"I was simply asking for specifics."

Unwilling to apologize, I say, "I would specifically like to do more than read essays. I have enjoyed reading a few, but some of them are just crap and hard to even get through, to be honest."

"You seem like the type of person who is," he says with an edge. He continues forward.

"The type of person who is what exactly?"

"Straightforward."

I hurry to catch up with him. "I never said straightforward."

"Well, brutally honest might be too strong."

I either want to burst into tears or claw his eyes out. I'm torn. He seems to speak in riddles, and I can't figure out the meaning behind any of his words. I continue on and try not to let him get the best of me. I stare up at the night sky and observe the stars above as I think of happier thoughts—Claudia and Eva, swimming in the ocean, strolling along the beach. My shoulders begin to relax.

"Bree—"

"Well," I quickly interrupt, "thank you for the escort home." I don't wait for him to respond and briskly approach the front of my dorm. I don't turn around.

I enter the building and straight to the elevators. Once inside my room, I go over to my windows to draw my shade when I see him with his back to my dorm. He gets on his bike and rides back in the direction we just came.

"Well, that sucked," I whisper.

I get ready for bed. I climb in, switch on my TV, and watch Eva's movie for about the fifteenth time. I'm frustrated and confused more than ever. I try really hard at school. I always have. However, his morose tone is making me guess what I've been putting into it.

Knowing that I will not be able to figure this out tonight, I reach over to my nightstand, grab one of my sleep aids, and wash it down with water. At some point, before Eva discovers she cannot have the man she wants, I fall asleep.

I am unequivocally dreading going to my internship. There is nothing worse than working for someone who doesn't seem to give a shit about you. I peel myself out of the chair in the cafeteria and wave halfheartedly to Casey and Jen before exiting out the side door. I meander over to the Draper building. The campus is changing, the leaves have turned, and the smell of the air is crisper than before. I notice it is much cooler tonight than it was the past few evenings.

I am pleased to find that Cooper is *not* in his office although I know he is close by because his coat is on the back of his chair. The light on his desk is on, and it's shining directly on the latest copy of the student paper, *The Weekly Blue*.

I quickly grab my notebook and folder and hurry down toward my office, praying that I will not see him.

I put all my thoughts aside, so I can concentrate on the essays. I read the last seven essays and make all the appropriate corresponding notes in my book. I glance at my watch. It is already ten minutes until eight. I am relieved that I have not seen Cooper pass by once. I get up, gather all my items, and make my way back down the hall, hopeful that he is gone.

Instead, I find his door closed. The light is on, and two male voices are talking inside. I take a deep breath and sit on the chair outside his office. It scratches on the concrete floor and makes another loud noise. I don't care because I want to return these papers and leave.

I wait a minute, and then the door swings open. I glance up and am stunned to see Officer Murphy, in full uniform, exiting his office.

"Hello, Bree," he says a bit too loudly.

"Officer," I say under my breath.

I'm afraid that the officer shared his suspicions about what happened to me. *What if Cooper now knows my deepest and worst secret? The reason for my pain. The reason I am so bitchy and horrible every day.*

Officer Murphy continues on down the hall, not glancing back at me, so I hesitate only for a moment before entering Cooper's office. The door is open, and he must know it is near the time for me to leave.

I enter the room to find him standing, putting on his coat. He looks handsome, dressed like he is going somewhere. I'm presuming a date or something.

I hate that I know my cheeks are blushing.

"Hello," he says.

I try to figure out his tone, but quickly realize I have absolutely no clue when it comes to reading him or analyzing his tenor. I am at a loss.

"Hello. Just need to return these." I place my stuff on the shelf.

"You're finished?"

"Yes, all completed."

"Okay then. Well, I'm heading out, too. Let me walk you back."

Shit.

A part of me is kind of glad he is still willing to walk with me, considering our exchange on Monday; however, a stronger part of me wishes I could just enjoy the walk home alone regardless of how afraid it might make me.

I turn and head toward the side door.

"I don't have my bike tonight," he says.

I spin back around and follow him out the main door. I zipper up my leather coat and put on my beret. He gives me an interesting smile as I straighten my hat. I want to ask him what he is smiling at, but I can't.

In fact, we don't speak until we cross the street.

"How do you know Officer Murphy?" he asks.

I have to think fast. "He came into our dorm, and I met him." I am vague, and it is on purpose. Quickly, I add, "How do you know him?"

"He keeps a good eye on the students and informs me of anything going on."

I swallow hard. "I see."

"See what?"

"The connection."

"Connection?"

"Yes, between you and him. I understand why he was in your office." I can smell his cologne as the wind picks up. I like it. It's unusual, but it's pleasant. It's similar to Old Spice or something woodsy.

Before he can add anything, I say, "I'm curious about what I'll be doing next. What other projects do you need help with?"

He smiles, and I find myself starting to smile as well until he says with a laugh, "I don't need help. It is more about your experience and learning from all of this."

I decide yet again not to get sucked into his remarks because he's baiting me for some reason. And I am not willing to take the bait…yet.

"Well, I'll think about it and get back to you," I say, knowing I haven't addressed my experience with the internship, nor have I acknowledged his remark. Again, before he can respond, I say, "Thanks again for chaperoning me. I'm going to the Union. I'll see you tomorrow."

"Wait," he says, "you're not going home?"

Surprised by his remark, I respond, "No, I'm going to the Union. You know, like most of the students on campus do." I smile at him, hoping he'll lighten up.

He glances at his watch and doesn't say anything.

"Good night," I say.

He hesitates and then seems not to know what to do next. "Um, okay. Yes, good night, Bree, and I'll see you tomorrow. Six. Um, six sharp."

His words came out so awkwardly that I almost whirl back around so I can ask him what his problem is. But, instead, I keep making my way toward the Union.

Once inside, I stroll down the hallway in front of all the stores. This hallway is conveniently encased in all windows on the side facing campus. I can see Cooper out of the corner of my eye, and he is walking back toward the Draper building, not toward the dorms. Part of me wants to call him out on this, but knowing how painful it can be to have even a simple conversation with him, I decide I'll leave it be. He is a confusing puzzle that is missing some pieces, and I can't seem to find them to put it all together. Then again, maybe this is how he always is. Sometimes, brilliant people are just plain odd. But I get the sense, from the way he carries himself, that he is not, in fact, odd but maybe overly confident. I'm perplexed.

I arrive down by the mailboxes and search for number 4817. I open it and am delighted to find mail inside. I scan through the pile as I close the small mail door and lock it. I walk out into the main lounge area and grab a seat on one of the couches. I remove my hat and open my jacket. I notice a letter from Nelly and cautiously open it.

Longing to Be

October 19, 1995

Dear Bree,

How are you? How is school? By now, I'm guessing you are settled in and hopefully having a blast. I am loving NYU, and I am so glad I decided to come here. Classes are good so far. Nothing earth-shattering to report here.

I heard through the grapevine that Joss broke up with Asher the day she left for school. Not surprised. Never got that attraction anyway. I am still sort of seeing Dashiell, but it's nothing serious. Joss and I are not talking, but it's probably for the best, considering what a bitch she always was to me. In many ways, I guess I like Dashiell to spite her. You know I'm not like that, but I couldn't help myself. I don't regret getting the last laugh, and for some reason, I'm guessing you probably agree with me.

I pause reading the letter and start to reflect on my friends from home. I like some parts of where and how I grew up with my family, but I wish I'd had better friends than Joss and Asher. I wish I had better friends here, too, but I'll get there. I gaze around the Union, wondering if maybe my actual best friend is somewhere here at school. I desire to find that one person I can tell everything to. Again, I think of Nelly and Joss and how I'd never tell them what happened to me. Ever. Period. They'd probably tell everyone, like it was hot gossip, never paying any mind to my feelings about it.

My spirits start to grow dark. I contemplate not even finishing reading her letter. But I can't help myself.

Anyway, how is that hot brother of yours? Still in California? I hope he comes home for Thanksgiving. I'd love to see him. Hope to see you, too.

I know the summer kind of ran away from us, and I was all into Dashiell and Joss and Asher drama. But I'm past that now. You know, at least until we all return to the Hamptons.

Write me back and fill me in on what you are up to!

Love and kisses,

Nelly

"Hey, Bree."

I'm startled to hear my name. I glance up from the letter in my hand. "Oh, hello."

Jason is standing in front of me, holding a cup of coffee. "Mind if I join you?" he asks.

"No. Sure, of course not."

"I heard through a friend who is in your marketing class that you got the internship this year."

"Yes, I did."

"Congratulations." He smiles so sincerely at me that he almost makes me feel instantly comfortable with him, despite my limited interaction with him.

"Can I ask you something?" I say.

"Shoot."

"Is it that big of a deal? This internship?"

"Totally."

"Really?"

"Yeah. Why? Isn't that why you applied for it?"

"I mean, yes. I didn't understand the scope of it. Everyone has been congratulating me, and it seems excessive."

"Hey, take the credit when it's due," he says with a goofy grin.

I smile back and say, "I suppose you're right."

"Hey, Nathan!" he yells across the Union.

I turn slightly and see Nathan Ryan making his way toward us. I have to will myself not to let my jaw drop open. My God is he hot. His tall, lean, and muscular body moves so fluidly across the hall. He doesn't have a strut or cocky approach about him at all, which makes him even more likeable. He's gorgeous, in perfect shape, and a Division One athlete—the starting quarterback to boot—and he seems sweet and unaffected. He is definitely too good to be true.

"Hey, Jay," he says with an enormous smile as he approaches.

I know I'm staring, but I literally cannot help myself.

He eyes me and smiles. I want to melt.

"I'm sorry. I know we've met?"

"Yes, um, at the football party about a month ago. I'm Bree." My words sound incredibly lame because I remember exactly when I met him.

"You are friends with my roommate, right?"

"Well, he got us in because I'm floor mates with Abigail, and she…" I pause as I see his face change at the mere mention of Abigail's name. He seems to light up, and I can't help but feel a bit jealous. "She is friends with Webber. Good friends, from what I'm told," I stress.

"Well, I hope so. They are lab partners," he says with a wink.

"Yeah, I was chatting with Bree here because she got the marketing internship this year."

"What is that?"

"Well, it's a big deal in the marketing department," I say with a straight face.

"Well then, I suppose congratulations are due."

"Thank you, Nathan."

"Welcome. Well, I gotta run. Jay, see you tomorrow."

"Bye," I say as sweetly as possible.

I watch him as he walks away. In fact, I find it almost impossible to take my eyes off his backside.

"Anyway," Jason adds, "I should be going, too. We have a big game this weekend."

"But you play? I'm confused. Aren't you the backup?"

"Um, yeah, Bree, I do. I mean, I practice each and every day and—"

"You know what I mean," I quip.

"Yeah, I do. But, hey, good to see you, and I'm sure I'll see you around."

"Hey, is the football team going to the Sigma Halloween Party?"

"Nah, we have our own party each year. It's a blast. You should come."

"I can't. We got tickets for the Sigma one. Maybe next year."

"Yeah, next year. Sure." He stands up. "Bye, Bree."

"Bye, Jason."

I decide to leave myself.

As I exit out of the Union, I glance over my shoulder to make sure no one is following me. My heart picks up speed as I see a man approaching the double doors as I pull one open. I avoid making eye contact with him. Once on the brick pathway in between buildings, I start to pick up my pace and jog slightly back toward my dorm. I can see the lights ahead, and the front door is only a short distance from where I am.

Then, someone yells, "Hey!"

I glance over my shoulder again and am relieved to see two people, shaking hands and meeting by the Union. I sigh deeply. I fumble for my keys in my bag as I approach the door. The emergency button post is only inches from my hand, which gives me a static sense of peace for the moment, as I put the key in the door.

I pull it open. "Deep breaths, Bree. Deep breaths," I whisper to myself as I enter my dorm. "You're safe."

Once inside my room, I lock the door, sit at my desk, and browse through the rest of my mail. There's nothing of significance, and I end up throwing most of it away.

I start studying for my marketing midterm, but all I can think about is Nathan. I have to find a way to get to know him better. I'll have to butter up to Abigail and Webber or maybe even Jason, so I can get closer to Nathan. I need to form a plan.

Unfortunately for me, I spend most of the night not studying for my midterm. I can't concentrate. I'm not necessarily worried that I won't pass. But I have to get a hundred, or I will feel like I failed. Being a perfectionist has its ups and downs. I refuse to settle for anything but gold. I'm exactly like my father that way.

I walk out of my afternoon class and spot Laura heading toward the cafeteria.

"Laura!"

She turns and sees me. "Hey, Bree!"

I hurry to catch up to her. "Going to lunch?"

"Yep, later than usual, but I had to get my laundry done while the machines were not being used."

"Next time, give your laundry to me. I send mine out to get laundered."

"Oh, wow, I didn't know we could do that."

"We can't. But I do," I say with a grin. "I send them to get dry-cleaned at a place down the street."

"I see." She laughs slightly at me, and I kind of like that she lets some of my remarks roll off her.

As we enter the cafeteria, I notice that it is almost empty.

"I'm going to grab a salad, and I'll meet you at our table."

"Sure, I'm just getting a sandwich," she says as she enters the deli line.

Laura and I sit and eat, chatting mostly about our classes.

I try to change the subject to something I'm more interested in. "So, next weekend, are you excited for the Halloween party?"

"Yeah, of course. Should be dope."

"Dope?"

"Yeah, you know, cool."

"I don't think we should say dope. It sounds…" I hesitate as I observe Laura's cheeks pink but decide I need to just be direct with her. "Adolescent."

"All right then," she whispers.

"Anyway, don't worry about it. You didn't know."

I watch as she picks at the crust on her sandwich. She appears wounded, and it surprisingly bothers me. My friends at home could take a verbal lashing, and they would bounce right back. We all did. It was how we survived. I can tell my attitude offended her, but it's how I am. But I must try to make it right.

"Hey, I have an idea. How about, tomorrow night, we bust out of this town and go somewhere nice for dinner? My treat!"

I watch as she quickly perks up.

"Really? Where?"

"My father told me of a place, about fifteen minutes from here, with exceptional steaks. You like steak?"

"Yeah, I do."

"Good, it's settled. It will be awesome to get out of here for a night."

"Agree. Should I ask Abigail to join?"

I have to think fast, which I'm good at, but in this case, I need to choose my words with care. If she comes, then I'll be forced to spend time with her, but then maybe I can pick her brain about Nathan and see what she knows. I've had so few good friends in the past, I think I can only win them over one at a time—hopefully.

"Totally up to you."

She contemplates for a moment then she responds, "No, we can go, just us. Sounds like fun."

"Perfect. We'll leave at eight. The thought of good food is making this salad seem so disgusting to me. I'm throwing it away. Yuck."

"Me, too. I'm done with the cafeteria for now," Laura says. She sounds like me, which I find amusing.

We both get up, put our trays on the belt, and head back to our dorm.

I can't think of anything less inviting right now than studying, but I've left myself with no choice in the matter. "Hey, you want to study in the common room?"

Laura pauses before my door and smiles. "Sure, I could get some studying done. I'm working on a paper for a class."

"Okay, I'll grab my bag and meet you down there."

"Sounds good."

After I retrieve my messenger bag, I take the stairs down to the first floor and into the common area off the center lobby. The common area— or commons, as everyone around here calls it—is directly across from the recreation room, so it can get noisy for studying, but I find the distraction comforting.

With only three other people studying in here, it's easy to find a table near the windows, so I can peer out across campus.

I glance up as I see Laura enter. As I'm about to draw my eyes back to my notes, I notice Abigail is right behind her. She's like a blonde vision, despite the fact that she is only wearing jeans and a T-shirt. I'm starting not to like her even more. I think the real reason is that everyone says she is nice, and I know most people think I'm mean.

"Hey, guys," I say with a painfully cheery tone. I wish it felt more natural, but Dr. Leo said, in time, I might start to feel happier in general. God, I hope she is right.

"Hey, Bree, how are you?" Abigail asks me.

"Fine, considering I'm sitting here, studying."

Laura plops her bag down on the table, and I jump.

"You are not going to believe what I heard. Sigma's Halloween contest this year...first prize is one hundred bucks! Imagine that, a hundred dollars."

Really? A hundred dollars? Is that a big deal? I think. *Well, maybe for her, it is.*

"Super cool," I say. "At our next floor meeting, let's come up with ideas then. Sound good? We only have a week to get our costumes."

"Sure," Abigail chimes in.

"Sounds good," Laura says.

After studying with Laura and Abigail, I find myself excited about my internship this evening. The air is crisp and cool as I make my way over to the Draper building. I enter the building a few minutes before six and make sure I'm standing in front of Assistant Professor Cooper's door promptly at six.

"Hello," he says.

I notice again that he is dressed in gym clothes, a bit unorthodox for a professor, but I know I tend to judge.

"Working out?" I ask with an edge in my voice. I, in contrast, opted to dress the part. I'm wearing pressed black pants and a dark green silk blouse, and I pulled my hair back in a ponytail.

"Yes, and you? Going somewhere?"

He eyes me up and down, and when he does so, the blood rises to the surface of my skin. I feel warm inside.

"Yes, to work. What do you have planned for me this evening?" I enter his office.

He gives me a wicked smile. I like that I'm able to strike a chord with him, considering he has hit a few of my nerves.

"Glad you asked. I'd like you to help me create a new curriculum for next year. I thought about what you said about the essays..."

My mind starts to drift. *He actually thought about what I'd said.* I snap back to reality once I realize he is still talking.

"There seems to be a disconnect in the quality of work handed in by my students, and I'd like to understand why. Then, we can fix the issue better, therefore creating a much more robust and thoughtful agenda for next year. But it needs to be more challenging. Therefore, I'm open to your ideas."

I notice that I'm still standing in the middle of his office. I'm almost too stunned to move.

"Please, sit."

I walk over and retrieve the notebook from the shelf. I sit in the chair across from him, crossing my legs. I notice his eyes light up a bit. I smile inside.

"Well, Assistant Professor Cooper, I think…" Then, I stop talking and peer up at him. I blurt out, "Do I have to call you that, or can I call you Cooper, like everyone else does behind your back?"

He smiles wide. I can't help but notice what an attractive smile he has.

"They do, do they?"

"Yes, like, everyone calls you that."

"Well, my real name is Adam, but please call me Cooper if that is easier."

Adam Cooper. I like it.

"Okay. Do you have a copy of next year's curriculum? Maybe, if we can decipher what not to do, we'll discover what we should be doing."

He smiles slightly and picks up a folder in front of him, handing it to me. "Last year, the intern tried to make improvements with Professor Gilford, but he wasn't pleased with the changes and decided at the last minute not to implement them. I think that might have been a mistake. But, for now, these are your copies. Same rules apply. If you could keep them here in my office, I'd appreciate it."

"Of course," I say as I lean forward to grab the folder. My fingers slightly touch his, and I sense something unusual happen. I lock eyes with him, then bashfully mumble, "Mind if I take a minute to read through these?"

"Of course. You can stay in here, no need to leave. In case you have questions, that is. I'll be back in twenty minutes."

"Okay."

I open the folder and am truly surprised to see such a lackluster agenda staring back at me. There is no discussion on pharmaceutical marketing research or product innovation, but what I'm even more disappointed in is the lack of retail and sales management, which is obviously dear to me. But the very worst of it all is there is zero mention of marketing high-technology products and services. I mean, come on. I got my first email address last year, and computers are going to be our future whether we like it or not. But the fact that I can get a note to someone around the United States in seconds is pretty powerful stuff. We should—no, we must, try to understand how technology can be profitable for those who understand how to market. *Ugh, Cooper and I need to start from scratch.*

I begin feverishly making notes in my book. I don't notice him come back in, but I can smell his cologne. It's strong, but I like it. I quickly peek up to see him leaning over my notes. His hair is wet and pushed back, and he is now in a pair of brown pants and a navy sweater.

"Sorry, didn't mean to startle you. You seemed like you were in a zone," he says.

"Yes, the ideas are coming."

"Good, good." He sits down in his seat and eyes me. "Let me start by asking, what was your initial reaction to the curriculum?"

Shit, Bree, think. Think!

"And be honest."

"Like, how honest?"

He smiles and runs his hand through his hair. "Bree, honest. I think you know how to say exactly what you mean."

I can't help but smile and think that, for once in our screwy relationship, he actually gets me.

"It's awful, and I'm not surprised that it is falling flat. It's not current, and it does not address major divisions, like technology or pharmaceuticals or even retail, which, as I'm sure you can tell, is near and dear to me."

He returns a smile.

I continue, "I'd use the word *uninspiring*, if I'm being honest."

He leans back in his chair and peers up at the ceiling. Of course, now, I'm afraid that I've been too honest.

"Interesting," he finally says. "What do you propose?"

"Well, have you ever attended another university's marketing class? Have you done any digging into what makes other courses successful? Since you and Professor Gilford work so closely and run this department, is there a way we can find out what the current class trends are outside of OSU?"

"I see. Not where I thought you'd go, but continue."

"Well, that's one avenue. It wouldn't be the only one."

"Okay."

"Guest speakers. Bring in business people from around the area, ones who would volunteer their time for a lecture series. From there, maybe create teams to complete marketing campaigns and projects. Working and collaborating with those who might not necessarily have the same views as you is what marketing is all about. Reaching the masses when the masses have conflicting ideas and needs to fulfill. Make your students collaborate more, and, in turn, you'll give them more real-life experiences versus essays and textbooks."

He shows me little reaction. "Okay, what else?"

I talk almost nonstop for the next hour. I'm mentally drained.

I glance at my watch. It is half past eight. "Oh, wow, I'm sorry. I didn't realize the time."

He laughs. "Yeah, I've probably made you late for a party."

"Kind of. I'm supposed to go to this frat party with my floor mates, but—" I realize I'm telling him way too much.

"Funny, you don't strike me as the frat-party type."

"I'm not sure how to take that." Because I'm not. I'm definitely not. I can't seem to find my niche at school yet.

He starts to stand. "I'll tell you why I think that on the walk back."

Again with the escorting me home. I do like that it's safer, and I should try to appreciate it more. Particularly on a Thursday night. The natives do start to get restless and drunk.

"Okay."

Once we are out the front door, he says, "What I meant is, my experience with frat-parties is that they get a little rowdy."

I glance up at him and smile. "I suppose."

"Come on, you know exactly what I mean."

I start to laugh, and he does as well. I almost can't believe he is loosening up so much and talking like this.

"Crazy?"

"No, more like, sweaty and filled with testosterone."

"Sweaty, huh? I was not expecting you to describe a party that way, but yeah, that could be true."

We are close to my dorm now.

"Well, next week, I'll let you know how the sweaty party was."

"I look forward to it," he says with such a sincere smile that it makes me start to wonder what happened to the former Assistant Professor Cooper.

"Have a fabulous weekend."

"You, too."

As I enter the dorm, I am happy for the first time in…I don't know when. This surprises me.

Why the burst in happiness? I wonder. *Could it be the new project I'm taking on in the internship? Or, could it be that I finally think Cooper and I are getting along? Or, is it that I'm starting to make friends and not feel so damn bitchy all the time?*

I suppose it shouldn't matter as long as it's happening.

Ten

I'LL DRIVE YOU HOME

I stroll down the hallway toward my room. I am thrilled to hear the sound of blow-dryers and music wafting in the air. I knock on Jen and Casey's door.

"Come in!" Jen yells.

I open the door and find the two of them nearly dressed.

"Jesus, Casey, what the hell are you doing?" I grab the eyeliner from her hand. "Goth is not a good look, no matter who tells you it is."

"I got a little, you know…"

I regard her and realize it is not a lack of skill that is preventing her from doing it right. It's her wavering and unsteady body.

"Ah, I see. We got into the liquor a bit early."

Jen rolls her eyes at me. "Want some?"

"What is it?"

"Vodka and Hawaiian Punch."

"Seriously?"

"Yeah, taste it. It's delicious." Jen pours some into a Solo cup for me.

I notice it is blue, and I turn my nose up to it. I am a bit curious as to how this blue liquid I now have in my hand tastes. I take a big sip. It tastes good. It's sweet, and it burns a little as the alcohol hits my throat.

"Wow, how much vodka did you put in this?"

"All of the vodka," Casey slurs.

"Well, ladies, I'm taking it to go and letting you finish getting ready."

"Maddie mentioned another party across campus. We are thinking of going to that one," Jen says.

"Which one is that?"

"Phi Beta Kappa. They have the hottest guys."

"Well then, we should go to that one," Casey says, albeit awkwardly. "Plus, I hear that is where the athletes go when they don't have parties."

My ears perk up, but I play it cool. "Sounds good. I'm going to change, and then I'll be ready. Come by when you are all set."

I enter my room, and when I take one glimpse in the mirror, I know there is very little for me to do to get ready. I change quickly, slip into a pair of designer jeans I got from a photo shoot last year, and decide to keep my green silk shirt on and wear my leather jacket. I touch up my makeup, and now, I have to wait. I sit at my desk and gaze out the window across campus.

I can't help but feel slightly alone at this big university. I hoped, by now, I'd have felt much different about being away at school. A sense of freedom from home I'd never had, but all I have is a sense of desire to be back home, safe under my father's roof.

I take a few sips of the concoction Casey gave me and decide I'll call Claudia and see if she's around. It's nearly nine, so I'm hoping I can catch her resting or watching her favorite show on TV.

"Hello?"

"Claudia, it's me, Bree."

"Senorita! Wonderful to hear from you. *¿Cómo estás?*"

"I'm doing well. And how are you?"

"Very well. It's quiet around here without you."

"I know, but I'll be home in less than a month for Thanksgiving break, and then a few short weeks after that for winter break."

"Do you have any jobs lined up for over winter break yet?"

"No, not yet. I don't think I've told you, but I am working at school. It's volunteer—well, an internship. Pretty prestigious from what I've been told."

"I'm sure it is, dear. How great for you."

"Yes, it's in marketing, so I'm excited to see where this takes me."

"Wonderful, Bree."

"Thank you."

"This should be a good one," she says.

"What is a good one?"

"Oh, sorry, dear. *Dateline* is on next."

"Ah, yes, of course."

"Looks like a good one."

"Don't they all?" I say with a laugh.

She loves *Dateline*. I have come to love it, too. I have spent many nights sitting at her feet, watching the show with her. Sometimes, when I can't sleep, I go down to the lounge and watch *Dateline* to feel closer to home.

"Knock, knock," Jen says as she pushes open my door.

"I have to go," I say to Claudia as I wave Jen inside.

"Of course, dear. Good to hear from you. Please be safe."

"Good-bye," I say.

"Good night." Claudia hangs up the phone.

I try to reason with myself as terrible excuses pop into my head as to my limited conversations with her. I don't call her as much as I would like. I fear she'll hear the pain in my voice. Hence, I have been avoiding her, and I feel awful about that.

I hang up and turn to see Casey, Jen, Maddie, and Melissa standing in my room. Casey is swaying, and I question whether or not she should even be going out. I do not want to babysit tonight, not one bit.

I take a deep breath before I stand up. I turn to them. "You ladies ready?"

Maddie gently rolls her eyes at me and motions toward Casey. "I think we all are."

"Oh, please," she slurs. "I can handle my liquor."

I glance at her as she steadies herself on my dresser.

"Okay then," I say as I motion for them to exit. I close my door behind me and follow them to the elevator.

"Where is Phi Beta Kappa?" I ask.

"Close. It's on the back side of campus," Maddie answers.

The back side of campus is more prestigious than where all the dorms are because that area is where the upperclassmen can opt to live. Parkers Village is an area of newer apartment buildings that resemble townhouses you might find in Boston. Each townhouse has three separate entries. Each building is rather large and can house between twelve to fourteen people. With the limited number of spots, there is a mad dash at the end of each year to get into the lottery for one of the residences.

We walk through the Village and can hear the beat of the music as we approach Phi Beta Kappa. At this time of night, there is hardly a line out front anymore, which I'm obviously thrilled to see.

I approach first.

"It's five apiece," the tall kid with the Soundgarden T-shirt says.

"I'm paying for all of them," I say.

"Cool," he says back as he winks at me.

I hand him the money and wait for the rest of the girls to go ahead of me.

"Thanks, Bree," Melissa chimes in.

"You didn't have to do that," Jen adds.

"You're welcome," I respond back. I'd hate to think that the only way I know how to be kind is by paying for things, but it's a start for me. I have to start somewhere.

He then opens the door, and we enter. I stop dead in my tracks. There, standing in front of me, is none other than Nathan Ryan.

I wake up the next afternoon with a pounding headache. I have no idea what came over me. I drink the rest of the water that I thankfully left next to my bed last night. Although I don't remember doing it. I glimpse down at my body and am grateful I'm half-clothed. I have a vague recollection of last night and am almost too afraid to put together the pieces. Something horrible could have happened to me, but I made sure that, no matter what, we all stuck together. Dr. Leo has repeatedly told me that I can't go into every situation fearing the worst, or I'll never leave the four walls of my room. I have to start living my life. I might have taken that a bit too far last night, however.

I finally stand. My head starts to spin something awful, and I have to hold on to my dresser. Once I can steady myself, I grab my shower basket, and with my head down, I hurry toward the showers.

I'm in and out in no time, and my hangover is dissipating although I think today calls for delivery service. Once I dress, I call my favorite pizza place and order a basket of French fries and a house salad. I tell the guy I'll pay him an extra ten dollars if he'll bring it up to my door on the sixth floor. He quickly agrees, and I lie back down on my bed as I wait for him to knock.

I'm drifting off to sleep when he thumps on my door. I barely crack it open. I hand him the money and take my food. I eat all of it. I mean, all of it. I wish I had ordered more. At least I'm going out to eat at a high-end restaurant tonight and will indulge on much finer foods.

My phone rings, and reluctantly, I pick it up. "Hello?"

"Bree, it's me, Laura."

Oh, sweet Laura. The one who stuck to me all night, never leaving my side. She is a good friend, more than she knows.

"Hey, Laura."

"I wanted to check in with you. Everything okay?"

"Yeah, why?"

"Oh, well, no reason."

"Okay, you sure?"

She sounds like she wants to ask me something important, but can't spit it out.

"Yeah, are we still on for dinner later?"

"Yes, I made a reservation for eight. So, come here at seven."

Maybe she is reluctant to go to dinner?

"Okay, great. I'll talk to you later then."

She sounds strange, but I don't want to talk on the phone anymore.

"Sounds good. Bye."

"Bye."

I switch on my stereo and close my eyes. I drift back to sleep. And I sleep deeply until six.

I finally get up and crack open an energy drink. I keep them for just these sorts of occasions. I used to drink them a lot when I was modeling nonstop during the summers because coffee was just too harsh on my stomach.

I pick out a navy-blue dress and nude heels for dinner. I opt for my burgundy trench coat and matching clutch. As soon as I finish my makeup and hair, there is a knock on my door.

"Come in!"

"Hey," Laura says as she comes in the door.

She is wearing a pair of black pants, black heels, and a bright blue turtleneck, which is perfect with her short bob tucked behind her ears. "Wow, Bree, you look great!"

"Thank you. So do you."

"Well, thanks. Coming from you, that's a real compliment."

I smile sweetly. "Ready to go?"

"Sure am. I'm excited for dinner. You know, you're the first date I've had in college."

I can't help but burst into laughter. "Oh my God, you're my first date, too."

She laughs and adds, "Could be a lot worse."

"True," I reply. *If only she knew.*

We drive the twenty minutes or so to the steak house, singing almost the whole way there to whatever comes on the college radio station, WOUR97. It was hip-hop night. Laura knew more of the songs than I did.

I park in the lot of Prime Bistro.

"Follow my lead," I say with a wink as I pull open the solid mahogany door.

The hostess promptly greets us, "Good evening, ladies."

"Good evening. I have a reservation under Van Tousen. We are a bit early, so we don't mind waiting at the bar."

"Of course, Ms. Van Tousen. And, yes, your table should be ready within the half hour."

"Thank you."

Laura follows me into the bar area. I take a seat in one of the high chairs. I sense Laura hesitate, but finally, she takes the seat next to me.

The bartender comes over, and I order for the two of us. "Two glasses of the California noir. Thank you."

"Yes, of course," the bartender says.

I make note of his name on his shirt.

He returns with two glasses.

"Thank you, Michael."

"Yes, thank you," Laura whispers.

"You're welcome, ladies. Enjoy."

I pick up my glass and again wink at Laura. She picks up hers, and we quietly clink our glasses.

"To a lovely meal," I say.

"Yes, to a better meal than we would be having," Laura adds.

I watch her take a sip, hoping she likes it. "Delicious, right?"

"Yes, very."

"Glad you like it. There is this restaurant in the city that I love and typically go to with my father. This wine is our favorite."

"I can taste why," she says with a goofy grin. She takes another sip. "Are you working at all? I mean, modeling this semester?"

"Well, it is work, silly," I say playfully. "But, no, I finished up a job in September, but haven't had time to focus on trying to land other gigs. Besides, I promised my father I'd give it my all here, and I need to. I mean, I owe him that at least."

"Makes sense. I, alternatively, need to find something to do. A club, job, something. I'm uninspired, and I need something to keep my interest. I can't go to classes and have nothing after to do but study."

"Well, what do you like?"

"Well, I love music."

"What about a job at the station?"

"I never thought of that, but that could be totally cool."

"You have got to check out that board next to it. Even better, I'll go in with you. I'll sell them on you in a second. You know, being the marketing whiz that I am."

"Ha, funny. But, seriously, you'd do that for me?"

"Of course I would. We're friends."

I see her eyes light up a bit, and it makes me happier than I've been in a while. She takes another sip of her wine, as do I.

We chat for another fifteen minutes and each have another glass of wine. I am enjoying the conversation so much that I don't notice the time. It's now quarter past eight.

Michael hands me the bill, and I settle up as I hear, "Ms. Van Tousen, your table is ready."

"Thank you."

After two glasses of wine, I could use some food. I stand and have to steady myself a bit. I notice Laura giggle, and I grab her hand as we follow the hostess to our table.

Once the hostess hand us the menus, Laura leans in and attempts to whisper, "I can't believe they let us drink wine here."

My eyes flicker as I say, "That's because my father is part owner."

"Holy shit. Of this place?"

"Shh. Yes, silly. Now, keep it down, will you?" I smile as she starts to laugh.

The waitress approaches. "Ms. Van Tousen, we have a few specials I'd love to tell you about."

I glance at Laura and smile. "Yes, continue."

"Tonight, we have a ten-ounce porterhouse steak. A six-ounce filet and a ten-ounce bone-in pork chop. For our sides this evening, we have truffle fries, brussels sprouts with pancetta in a Dijon mustard sauce, and lastly, a goat cheese house salad dressed in a light raspberry vinaigrette."

I see Laura's eyes get wide.

"Can I get you ladies another glass of pinot?" the waitress asks.

"Yes, please, and a bottle of sparkling water, too," I say.

"Great. I'll be back with your drinks," The waitress responds as she turns to walk away.

"Thank you. Laura, what are you thinking about ordering?" I ask her.

"Oh, boy, it all sounds so wonderful, and I'm starving!"

"I recommend the filet. Very delicious," I say.

"Okay, and I'm going to get the truffle fries and the salad," Laura decides.

"Perfect. I'll do the same."

The waitress brings back our drinks, and I order for the both Laura and me. We chat mostly about music, and I notice how much she lights up. I'm even more determined now than ever to get her a job at the station. We devise a plan for when we get back to campus.

"This is going to be so exciting, our very own DJ in our little clique. Super cool," I say, smiling ear-to-ear.

Her cheeks burn pink. "Enough about me," she says. "I hear you had quite the good time last night." She laughs slightly, only I have no recollection as to what she is talking about.

"What is that supposed to mean?"

"You know, you, last night, and the guy you hooked up with! All the girls were talking about it today."

I stare blankly at her. I don't like being embarrassed or afraid for that matter, and I'm starting to feel both ways.

"What are they saying?" My response is cold.

She stammers, "Oh, you know, that you hooked up with the quarterback!"

Oh my God! Did I hook up with Nathan Ryan and not remember it? No, that would never happen.

My heart starts to beat fast, and I'm beginning to panic.

"Shut up. Nath—"

"Jason, the backup quarterback. Don't you remember? You were all over him."

My eyes must be the size of dinner plates. I have no memory of hooking up with Jason. In fact, all I can remember is entering the party and seeing Nathan Ryan, that handsome specimen of a man, standing there. I remember flirting with him, not Jason.

I ponder my encounter with Jason. *What came over me?* In many ways, I'm glad I can't remember the party last night. I mean, I know I got home safe and all that, but the embarrassing part is when you can't remember the real details.

"Yeah, that. No big deal. So, I made out with him a little. Not my first time and won't be my last."

I'm so pissed at myself. I now have some serious ground to gain if I'm going to have any chance with Nathan. I mean, I do remember talking with him, and he was polite and smiled a lot. But hooking up with one of his teammates is about the best way possible to make sure I never have a chance with Nathan. Nathan is like filet mignon in a fine restaurant, such as this. Jason is like coming here and ordering the only chicken dish on the menu. Sure, it will be delicious, but you'll wish you'd ordered the filet.

"I'm surprised the girls are even talking about it," I continue. "I mean, talk about immature." Deflect, deflect, deflect, and you'll always have the upper hand.

I can hear Joss telling me, *"Deflecting is Bitch one-oh-one."*

I try to shake her from my mind.

"Sorry. Thought you'd want to know." She lowers her eyes.

My heart softens. She's right. I'd rather know what they were saying.

"You're right, and I'm sorry. I do appreciate you telling me. And, to be honest, I had no recollection of last night, which scares me."

"Yes, I know. We were all a little drunk, if that makes you feel better."

"Maybe a little."

I'm in serious need of a distraction. When the food arrives, we hardly speak as we devour our delicious meals in record time. I try to keep my manners per usual, but I'm past the point of starving.

"Oh my God, your father knows what he is doing. This is fantastic. We don't have steak houses like this in Stockbridge."

"Glad you like it."

"Like it? I love it."

Now, normally, I would have scolded her for talking with food in her mouth, but I'm too hungry and somewhat drunk to protest.

I put the meal on my father's charge account at the restaurant but make sure to leave a cash tip for the waitress. Laura and I start to stand when, out of the corner of my eye, I catch someone approaching me. For some reason, it startles me.

Laura whispers, "Holy shit, he's hot."

I glance at her and then at the man approaching. My cheeks burn redder than the pinot I've been drinking as I see Cooper near my table.

Where the hell did he come from? I think.

"Hello, Bree."

I struggle to find my voice. Maybe it's all the wine, but he does look hot and more relaxed or something. I can't quite put my finger on it.

"Cooper, hello. Didn't see you here," I stammer.

"Who's this?" Laura asks.

"Oh, sorry. Um, this is Coop—er, Assistant Professor Cooper. This is Laura."

Laura stumbles a bit forward and reaches out her hand.

He reluctantly takes it, but smiles politely. "Nice to meet you, Laura."

I notice a woman standing slightly off to the side of him. She hasn't spoken, but I'm presuming she is with him. She appears older—maybe late thirties—but it's hard to tell. She doesn't strike me as his type at all. She is dressed in a conservative white oxford and tan pants. She is wearing no makeup and has let what little gray hair that she has shown in her mousy brown hair.

"I'll meet you outside," she says quietly.

"Thank you, Anna."

"We were leaving, too," I say as I put on my jacket. I rummage in my bag for my keys.

"After you," he says.

Laura walks toward the door first. I wave slightly to Michael behind the bar and then say good-bye to the hostess.

Once outside, I notice Anna is not there.

Cooper gently grabs my arm. "I'm driving you girls home. And please don't try to argue with me, okay?"

Laura is up ahead.

I stop and turn toward him. "Were you watching us?"

He lowers his eyes, but then quickly meets mine. "Yes."

My heart skips a beat, and I'm confused.

"Where is Anna?" I ask, trying to change the subject.

"She is driving her car."

"What about yours? Or do you—"

"I'll get it tomorrow."

"Don't be silly. Take your car, and I'll see you on Monday, six sharp," I say mockingly as I wave my finger.

"Bree, please give me your keys."

"Coop, you know you don't have to be so serious."

"You think, if I see one of my students drinking, that I should turn a blind eye and let them drive?"

"Just one of your students, huh? Okay then. Have it your way."

It's not like we work together, I think sarcastically. *God, just when we've lowered the wall a bit, he goes and builds it back up.*

I hand him my keys and turn to walk toward my car. Laura is leaning on the back of my car, her eyes heavy. I know he is following because I can hear his steps behind me.

"You have to ride in the back. We have a special guest," I say with a snicker.

She picks up her head, and I can see her face light up as she moves to the back door.

"You'll have to unlock it!" I yell as I go around to the front passenger door.

He unlocks the door and gets in. "Let me guess, your graduation present." He starts the car and puts on his seat belt.

"Correct," I say with an edge. "I really did a great job in high school."

"You must have," he returns with an equally sarcastic tone.

"Straight As," I mumble.

"You all buckled in?" he says as he glances in the rearview mirror.

"Yes," we both say.

He starts to back up out of the space.

"Professor, what do you teach?" Laura slurs.

"Marketing."

"Ah, and Bree is in your class?"

"Yes, she is also doing the internship for the department this year."

"Oh, right. Super cool." Laura hiccups.

He quickly glances at me. His stare sends a shiver down my spine.

"Yeah, and Laura is going to be trying for a job at the radio station."

"Are you a communications major?"

"No, I just love music."

"Ah, well, I know some people who are heavily involved in the station, so please let me know if I can put in a word for you."

"Don't think she can get it on her own?" I am purposely being snarky, and I know this, but God, he can rub me the wrong way sometimes. He gets under my skin.

"Bree," Laura says.

"What?"

"I would appreciate that, if you can. My last name is Chase."

"Sure thing. I hope you know that I wasn't insinuating that you'd be unable to get anything on your own. With half of the semester behind us, it can't hurt to push a little hard to see if the station can squeeze you in."

I stare out the window so my big mouth doesn't get me into trouble before Monday. The rest of the ride, we are all silent until we pull into campus.

130

Laura says, "Oh, boy, I'm awfully dizzy."

"You'd better not puke in here," I bark. I see him glare at me. He seems perplexed, and I know my tone could have been a little softer. "I mean, you okay? Let me roll down the window."

"I'll drop you off at the front." He glimpses at me as he pulls up. "Go ahead, and I'll park your car."

"How will I get my keys?"

I notice his hands tighten around the wheel. "Take care of your friend, and I'll get you your keys on Monday, okay?" He sounds like he is scolding me.

I get out of the car and open the door for Laura. She stumbles out and lands on her knees on the pavement.

"Come on, let's go," I say through gritted teeth. As I stand her up, I notice Cooper is next to me.

"You guys need some help? Here, let me at least get the door."

I hand him my dorm key.

He walks up to the door. He puts the key in, and pulls it open. He holds open the door, allowing us to enter the building.

I turn slightly toward him. "Take care of my car."

"Just take care of your friend," he replies. "Please." He turns quickly on his heel and heads back to my car.

I get a funny sensation in the pit of my stomach as I watch my brand-new car drive away with Assistant Professor Cooper behind the wheel.

Eleven

TOE THE LINE

"I'll go make copies," Mallory says as she gets up from the table. She takes our final outline and goes over to the copier to make a few copies for each of us.

"I don't know, guys. I think something is missing in our presentation," Mila says once Mallory gets back and hands us each the copies.

"Me, too. Something is missing—" I say.

"Bree, why don't you take this to Professor Cooper and ask him for some advice?" Ashley says brazenly.

I glance up from the papers in my hand and narrow my eyes at her. "Why would I do that?"

"You know..." she says with a cruel grin.

"No, actually, I *don't* know," I quip back.

I'm getting real tired of working in this group. The headache is not worth the grade on this presentation. That, I am sure of.

"What I think Ashley is trying to say," Mallory cuts in, "is that we all think something is missing. But we should try to figure that out before we ask for assistance. Wouldn't you all agree?"

Breathe in for ten seconds, Bree, just like Dr. Leo told you this week. Breathe in, and focus on your breath to avoid saying things you might regret later.

"Yes, I agree," I say calmly. "Why don't we try moving this," I point to one line item, "then move this here, and lead with this? This is our strongest point by far, and I think if we lead with that—"

"I like it, Bree. Great idea," Mila says.

"Me, too, Bree. I completely think that is the way to go," Mallory adds.

I notice Ashley cross her arms over her chest and sit back in her seat. We all stare at her.

"Ashley, what do you think?" I ask as politely as possible.

"It's fine with me. If the team agrees…then I'm fine with it." It is obvious by her tone that she is *not* fine with it.

"Good. I'll make the changes, and we can reconvene on Wednesday to finalize it," Mila chimes in.

"Great, thanks," I say, glancing at my watch. "Shit, I have to go. Sorry, guys, really, but I must leave." I stand and pull on my jacket.

"To your internship, we know. We get it," Ashley says under her breath with a slight roll of her eyes.

I am about to ask her what her problem is, but then I remember the first day I met her—how she wanted to know how I'd gotten the internship and said how she had tried herself to get it. So, that must be it. She is jealous and hurt that I got it, and she didn't. My shoulders relax a bit as I zip up my coat. I think we've all had similar emotions about something or someone at one time or another.

I give them all a faint smile. "Very sorry. I'll see you guys later."

I hang my head low as I make my way across campus toward Cooper's office. I'm trying to seem casual, but I just can't. I know my car is safe because it's been in the parking lot for the past day, and I've been too embarrassed to seek my keys out until now. I'm hoping he won't make me ask for them.

I approach his door and take a deep breath before I enter.

"Hello, Bree."

"Hello."

"How are you?"

"Fine. And you?" The small talk is weird and makes me more uncomfortable.

"Good. We have a lot to get to tonight. Please have a seat," he says as he points to the chair across from him.

I gently lower myself into the chair, trying not to make any sudden movements. I don't want to give him any reason to browbeat me for the other night.

"I think we need to think of this curriculum from a higher level."

"Higher level? Okay."

"Yes, what am I trying to say?" He glances up toward the ceiling.

I notice the glimmer in his pretty eyes from behind his glasses.

My God is he handsome, I think. *But so untouchable. Concentrate, Bree. Focus.*

"Start from where we want to end up. Is that what you mean?"

He peeks at me, and a slight smile draws across his lips. "We need to start where we want the students to end. Exactly what I was thinking."

"Great. I completely agree. Starting from marketing one-oh-one doesn't tell us at all where we should end up. So, what is the end then?" I ask.

"Good question. Let's think about what makes the most sense." He stands up and goes over to the chalkboard in his office where he begins jotting down his ideas and then mine.

For the next two hours, we brainstorm constantly to the point where my voice is harsh, and I'm in desperate need for a drink.

"Well, I think I need to grab a drink. Okay with you?"

"Bree, I can't drink with my students." His response catches me off guard, and I can feel my face burn.

"No, sorry, I meant, I need some water or a tea or something." Now, it's his turn for his face to turn red.

He tries to recover by saying, "I was only kidding."

But I can tell he is totally embarrassed, and I have to give him a slight smile to let him know I've noticed.

"Well, I'll see you on Wednesday."

"I'll walk you," he says.

"Can you be seen walking with your students?"

"Funny, and yes, as a matter of fact, I can."

"Well, all right then."

As I meander alongside him, I observe him out of the corner of my eye. I wouldn't say he seems at ease as he walks with me. He's leaning around a lot and almost shielding me as we make our way across the campus. I want to ask him where he lives and why he insists on accompanying me home every evening. Boldly, I'd love to ask if he has walked all the intern's home or if it's just me.

Next thing I know, we are close to my dorm, and there is one question I have to ask, "Can I please have my car keys?"

Thankfully, due to the darkness, I can't see his face perfectly, but I notice him scowl.

"Yes."

He reaches into his pocket and pulls them out. He goes to hand them to me, and as he does, our fingers touch. I instantly have this sensation wash over me that I have never experienced before. I tingle and have to draw my hand away from his. He watches me for a moment. I divert my eyes.

"Bree, I hope I don't have to drive your car for you again. In fact, I hope no one does. You should be more careful."

There are two ways I can handle this. I can be a total bitch and tell him to mind his own business, or I can say that I'm sorry he had to do that and that I screwed up his date.

I have to react swiftly, and without warning, I say, "Well, sorry I screwed up your date, and you don't have to worry about me doing that again, okay? Happy?" I realize, as I'm speaking, that I'm half-bitch and half-nice, but I should have been all nice.

"Yes, that does make me happy. I'll see you on Wednesday." He turns and starts heading back in the direction from where we came.

"Where are you going?" The words fly out of my mouth.

"Good night, Bree," he says with his back still toward me as he gives a slight wave.

In my marketing class, I'm anxious to see Cooper and tell him about this brilliant idea I have for the new curriculum. I spent most of Tuesday at the library researching a marketing concept I'd worked on for my final project in high school. But, now, with access to a university library and a wealth of knowledge at my fingertips, I am reinspired. I think it might be what Cooper needs to advance the curriculum into something spectacular. I trust, if he can help develop a way to integrate the use of technology in marketing, we might be on to something.

For example, in advertising, we are beginning to understand the Internet. *How is this helping people become more connected across the globe? What impact will this have on how products and services are sold? What role will it play?*

I am excited to see where this theory can go.

About fifteen minutes into class, I realize Cooper is nowhere to be seen. Sometimes, he lurks in the back and observes his students to see who is truly engaged. I know this because I asked him once why he seems to gaze around more than teach. He assured me, he learns how to be a better professor by knowing his audience. It makes sense, I suppose.

I rise at the end of class and hear Professor Gilford call my name.

"Yes, Professor Gilford?"

"Bree, I need you to take these papers to Professor Cooper's house, please."

"Um, Professor, are you sure that is okay? I have no idea where he lives. Are you sure he wants one of his students stopping by, unannounced?"

"Relax, Ms. Van Tousen. He is expecting you for your internship this evening. He mentioned you'd made great strides in such a short period of time, and he'd like to keep the momentum moving forward."

"I see. And is there a reason—"

"They are shutting down the building tonight. Maintenance on the pipes, and they have to shut off the water."

"Okay."

"His address is on the top paper there. He is expecting you at the usual time."

"Thank you, Professor. I'll be sure to get him the papers."

As I step out of the building, I see a large van with *OSU Plumbing and Heating* scrawled on the side. Two large men in dark blue jumpsuits get out and open the back, taking out an assortment of tools.

I head directly back to my dorm room and start to better organize my notes from my research in the library. I recognize the street name and know it is on the other side of campus, back in the direction of the marketing building. I've driven the road a few times while trying to escape from my thoughts. Unexpectedly, I have the strangest feeling in my gut, an uneasiness I can't place.

I'm busy studying my notes when I abruptly realize it's quarter until six, and I haven't eaten dinner or anything. But there is no time. I gather my papers and glance at my reflection in the mirror. I grab my brush and run it through my hair. I dab on some lip gloss, and I spray a bit of perfume on my neck. I snatch my car keys from my dresser, sling my bag and coat over my arm, and quickly leave my room.

I get into my car, and some sad, depressing song is playing, so I quickly change it to the college radio station, WOUR97.

Laura secured a spot as a DJ on the station twice a week. She interviewed with the station manager, and because of her vast knowledge of music, she was an easy contender to slide into their open spot on the airwaves. She was thrilled when she got the job, so at least something great came out of the night Cooper drove us home. She's quite good, and she seems very natural.

I listen to her announce the next song, which I happen to appreciate.

"This one is for all you girls out there tonight. We should all aspire to be fierce, vulnerable, and unapologetic, much like her. Here's 'You Oughta Know' by Alanis Morissette."

What female in college doesn't like a little Alanis Morissette? I think.

It's a short drive to his house, and I park my car in the front. I'm having untold emotions as I open my car door and step out, taking my bag with me.

I advance soundlessly toward the front door, as if I don't want to alert him of my presence, which makes zero sense. Maybe it's the neighbors I don't want to alert. Being here seems wrong on so many levels, and I'm nervous because of it. Partly because I am a student, and he is a professor, and the other part is because he is wildly attractive, which I suppose could confuse anyone at my age.

I walk up the steps to the beautiful front porch. There is a double-seated swing on one end and three Adirondack chairs on the opposite end of the porch with a small table in between. The porch is surrounded by high rhododendrons gently touching the railing, giving the porch a nicely shaded view of the street.

As I'm about to knock, I take a deep breath and hold it. I knock twice on the screen door. Within seconds, the front porch light comes on, and the door is opening. I exhale.

"Hello, Bree," he says coolly as he opens the door.

He seems different. Maybe it's because he is wearing jeans and a T-shirt, but he seems more comfortable, which makes me a bit calmer, despite his formal tone.

"Hello, Cooper," I say. I see him roll his eyes at me. "What?"

"How about, in class, you can call me Professor Cooper, but in my house you can call me Adam?"

"Okay, but behind your back, I'll still call you Cooper." I smile.

"Deal. Now, please come in, so I can close the door."

I enter the expansive old Victorian house. It is quite unlike the home I grew up in. Much more charm and detail than the monstrosity of a home my father had built.

"Wow, this is lovely. How long have you lived here?"

"Two years. It wasn't easy, finding a house close enough to campus to rent, but secluded as well."

"Yes, I've driven down this road many times."

He gives me a quizzical glance.

"You know, just out driving, enjoying a little time away from campus."

"Understandable. I'm sorry you had to come here. I assure you, I don't make it a habit of having any students in my house."

"Well, I didn't think you did," I say under my breath.

"Right," he says with a laugh. "But come in. We can sit in the kitchen."

"Okay."

As I follow him to the kitchen, I have to will myself not to stare at his backside. Maybe it's the jeans he has on, but my, he sure is amazing. I start to imagine what he must look like without his jeans on, and I stop.

Cut it out, Bree. He's your professor and kind of a jerk. Shake it off. Nathan Ryan is what you need, someone who can keep you safe on campus, I think as I enter his kitchen.

The kitchen is a bit outdated, but has a lot of appeal. There is a large farm table off to the side, and he motions for me to sit as he opens the refrigerator.

"Can I get you something to drink?"

"Yeah, wine. You know how I *love* my red wine." I am attempting to make a joke, but he quickly whips around and stares at me. I nervously tuck a strand of hair behind my ear.

"Maybe some other time," he says, which almost knocks me out of the chair I am sitting in. "How about water?"

"Sure, water is fine."

He pours me a glass, but grabs a beer for himself.

I narrow my eyes at him. "Hey, I'm of age, remember?" he remarks as he takes a sip of his beer.

"Hard to forget when you keep puffing your authoritative feathers around me."

He takes another drink of his beer, and I can see his cheeks turn red.

Then, he says as his eyes lock with mine, "You know, I question whether I made a mistake in choosing you for the internship."

I'm glad I wasn't drinking any water or I would have spit it right out. "Wow. Okay, well, I can just—"

He interjects, "You don't get a lot of rejections, do you?"

"I don't think, in the short amount of interactions we've had, that you know me even *marginally* well enough to make such an assumption."

"Tell me then, who is Aubrey Van Tousen?" he asks as he takes the seat across from me.

Who am I? What the hell kind of typical stupid-ass question is that? I think.

"Well, for one, I go by Bree, and two, I'm the type of intern who spent the past two days researching in the library," I begin as I lean over and retrieve all my papers from my bag. "I think an idea I had for my senior year project could, with your elderly wisdom, be turned into something great. This," I say as I push the papers in front of him, "could be the end of the curriculum we spoke about the other day. If we end here, I think we'll be able to construct and pull together some new and exciting projects for students."

He starts to scan the top page of my notes, and I can see his eyes get wide. I wait while he reads one page and then another and another, never peeking up at me or saying a word. The silence is killing me.

As he flips to another page, I have to break the quietness. "And, yes, Professor Cooper, to answer your question, I have gotten and continue to get rejected in all aspects of my life. Modeling, school, friends. Hell, even boyfriends. No one gets away scot-free. It's not possible."

A sly smile crosses his face. He sits back and takes a sip of his beer. I eye him, wishing I had a cold beer myself.

"You say you did this in high school?"

"Yes, my senior year. Here, I kept my notes from high school. With access to the library we have here, I was able to research and tweak some ideas I couldn't get past. I mean, there is a lot more to do, but I think it's a good start."

I hand him my notebook from high school. He takes it and quickly flips through it.

"Well, Bree, we have a good base here, honestly. I think we can take this somewhere."

"Have I earned myself a cold beer perhaps?"

His eyes sparkle a bit as he peeks up at me. I hold my eyes steady on his.

"If I say yes, can I trust you not to tell anyone? I could get in trouble. Big trouble."

"Promise, Adam, your secret's safe."

"Help yourself then."

I get up and open the refrigerator door. You can learn a lot about someone by what is in their refrigerator. I'm not surprised when I see tons of fruits, vegetables, and healthy items on the shelves. His refrigerator is well stocked. He seems like he cares about what he eats.

"So," he says with a laugh, "what does my fridge say about me?"

"Funny, you know about that theory?"

"Of course. You know the saying, *You are what you eat.*"

"Let me ask you then, knowing I was stopping by, is this what you usually have in your fridge?" I ask as I sit back down in my chair.

"Would you believe me if I said yes?"

"You haven't given me a reason *not* to believe you."

"I bought groceries right before you arrived. I was running late from classes, so I'm a bit behind today."

"Me, too. I couldn't believe the time—"

"You haven't eaten dinner?"

"No, but I'll—"

"Let me throw on some turkey burgers and make a quick salad, okay?"

"No, you don't need to do that."

"Well, technically, I still have you for another hour and a half."

"I suppose that is accurate."

"All right then, it's a working dinner. I'll start cooking while you walk me through your ideas."

Several hours later, I'm sated, and I think I've actually accomplished something at school for the first time since moving on to campus nearly three months ago.

"Oh, boy. I'm sorry, but it's nearly nine." I glance at his clock on the wall.

"Wow. Okay, sorry I kept you, but we made some real progress," he says.

"I didn't mind, obviously. But, before I go, can I ask you something?"

"Sure."

"Still regretting your decision to give me the internship?"

"No, Bree, and I'm sorry I said that."

"But why did you? I mean, I've done everything you asked of me."

He starts to stand up, and I can see the expression on his face grow somber. He places a few dishes in the sink and peers out the window. "See, it's hard, you know. I realize that I'm only a few years older than the students here, than you." He turns to gaze at me, and when he does, his cheeks pink. "And I have to toe the line. I have to find the balance, but it's difficult at times. I question all my decisions, Bree. It's who I am. If I don't, then I can get careless, and I love what I do. It means everything to me. Teaching—it's all I've ever wanted to do."

"Well then, don't question your decisions. Because it sounds like you've made a lot of good ones to get to where you are today." I smile wide and pick up my bag. "And that includes picking me for the internship."

He laughs slightly.

Maybe it is the one beer I've had or just that, for the first time in months, I'm relaxed around someone, but as I start to make my way down the hallway to the front door, I turn slightly before placing my hand on the door as I say, "Does this mean you won't be a dick to me sometimes?"

"I'm a dick sometimes?" He genuinely appears shocked.

"Yeah. I thought you knew."

He laughs and shakes his head, but doesn't respond.

"Here is the deal. I'll know you need to toe the line, and we'll work even better together. I won't tell anyone that I was here and that I had a beer. Promise. I know how to act accordingly. I've had to my whole life."

I grasp for the doorknob.

He reaches from behind me and pulls the door ajar. "Thanks, Bree. Great work tonight."

"You're welcome. I'm enjoying it."

"Good. See you soon. Get home safe."

I want to ask him why he is so concerned about me—or anyone, for that matter—getting home safe. He obviously supervises my safe arrival to my dorm, but I think I'll save that discussion for another time. It's a bit too close to home for me anyway. I'm not prepared to talk about campus safety or lack thereof.

"Good night."

When I'm finally in my car, I let out the biggest sigh I have ever had inside me. It's as though I was holding my breath the entire time.

"Holy shit. That went a hell of a lot better than I'd thought it would. Thank God," I whisper to myself.

I start my car and start my quick drive back to campus, but before I do, I need to stop at the drugstore on the corner. I pull in and go in to grab some toothpaste. As I enter the drugstore, I go over to the oral care aisle.

Why they call it that, I don't know, but it sounds dirty, and it makes me giggle.

I'm searching for my specific brand when a deep voice says, "Excuse me, please. Just need to reach—"

I glance up to find Nathan Ryan standing over me, reaching his long, firm arm over my head. My cheeks redden and burn as we lock eyes.

"Hello," I say sweetly.

He's caught me in a very good mood.

"Hi," he responds. "I'm sorry. I know we've met."

"Yes, I'm Bree." My heart sinks. *He doesn't remember me? Ugh.*

"Gosh, right, of course. How are you?"

"Good. And you?"

"Good. Just jogged down here. Killing two birds with one stone, so to speak."

"How so?"

"Um, well, exercising and getting my toothpaste."

"Oh, right, right." I notice the sweat on his brow, and a tingle comes over my body.

"No big party plans tonight?"

"Nope, not tonight. Saving it for this weekend. What about you? Any big plans this weekend?"

"Yeah, have a game on Saturday and then maybe the big Halloween party at The Ridge."

"Ah, but you do know the one at Sigma is much better."

"How so?"

"They have a contest and all that. We're in it. You should check it out."

"A group contest?"

"Yes, all the girls from my floor. Our costumes are killer. We are totally going to win."

"Well, you sound so confident. I suppose you must know then." He smiles wide at me.

"Of course," I say, giving him my winning smile.

"Well, I think I have all I came for." He shows me his toothpaste, and it's the same as mine.

"Good choice." I show him mine, and he then gestures for me to go ahead of him to the checkout counter.

I approach the heavy-set woman behind the register, and as I do, I whisper, "I'd like you to charge me for two of these, please."

She gives me a quizzical stare until I motion behind me, and she glances past me.

"Okay, sure." She gives me a sly smile. She rings me up, and I pay. "You're all set, hon."

As I start to walk out the door, she says to Nathan, "This young lady paid for your toothpaste."

"Wait, what? Bree, no. Please, you—" he says as he follows me outside.

"Need a ride?" I ask as I approach my car. I see his eyes light up when he sees the shiny, gorgeous Mercedes in the parking lot.

"Wow, this is your car?"

"Oh, this? Yeah. You know, my dad wanted me to have a safe car at school."

"A safe car at school." He laughs as he approaches me. He peers inside. "I mean, Bree, this is gorgeous."

As the words flow out of his mouth, I want to dive across the hood of my car and kiss him deeply. But I must play this right. He might know about Jason, so I need to be cool, and this money thing can sometimes be too intimidating for people. And, considering I know so little about him, the money can either be a total turn-on, or it might make him go running in the other direction.

"Want to drive it?"

"No. Oh God, no, I couldn't do that."

"You don't have a license?"

"No. I mean, yes, of course I do."

"Why can't you drive it?"

"I mean, I can. It's just—"

"Come on. You'll love it."

"Ah, I see. You want to get me into your car."

"Ha! No. I'd like to think it wouldn't be so hard to get someone—I mean, you to drive a car like this."

I watch him as he runs his fingers over the side of the door. My mind starts to race, and I can't help but imagine him next to me in the car, running his fingers over my legs, while I kiss his neck as he drives faster and faster down the street.

Doesn't he know, we could be the king and queen of this campus? Rule the freshman class from now to all the way until graduation. We'd be the definition of a powerhouse couple. I'd finally be untouchable—literally. No one would dare mess with me again, or they'd have Nathan Ryan, one of the most popular and well-known student athletes on campus, along with a rather large team of players to deal with. I'd never be in fear again.

"My heart rate has cooled down, so I could skip the rest of my run."

"Your heart rate is down? Huh, well, let's see what we can do to get that back up," I say as I climb into the passenger seat.

Dr. Leo suggested that I not hold back from pursuing an intimate relationship. She mentioned that, in her thirty-plus years of practice, she believed in encouraging women not to blame themselves for what had happened or to allow one person—she actually used the word *asshole*, which made me laugh—to pave the path for future relationships. Rather, we must learn and grow from each situation and turn them into opportunities to make and develop better and more meaningful relationships.

I have her advice swirling in my head as I note Nathan's lean, long body get in the driver's seat. He moves the seat all the way back to accommodate his height. I don't know about him, but I can sure feel my heart rate increase as he places his hands on the steering wheel. He has great hands, I notice. They are big with long fingers, not calloused or anything like that. His clutch on the steering wheel is tight, and I swallow hard as I think of him gripping those large hands of his all over my body.

He starts to back up out of the parking spot.

"Nathan, how's school been for you?"

"Fine, I suppose. Football and studying keep me real busy, so there's not much time for anything else."

"What kind of life is that?"

He peers over at me and gives me a strange expression. I think I've struck a chord with him.

"You know what I mean. You've got to have fun, too."

"I know. It's hard. That's all. I really need to make my mark on the team and in school, so it doesn't typically leave time for anything else."

He is so dedicated to his team, I think. I commend him for that. It must be hard to balance it all.

"Well, you never know when an opportunity to have some fun might sneak up on you in a drugstore." I can see him smile out of the corner of my eye. *Good, he's not all business*, I think.

"Ha. I suppose you're right. Didn't think I'd be driving *this* car tonight. By the way, this is a beautiful car. You're sure lucky to have this."

The car wasn't exactly what I had in mind when I was referring to fun.

"Thanks. I have a Jeep, too."

"Wow, two cars?"

"Yeah, two cars."

I notice him turn the corner and head toward his dormitory. My heart sinks, and I can't think quickly enough to come up with another plan to keep him in my car longer.

"Well, Bree, thanks for the fun. Glad it snuck up on me," he says as he puts the car in park.

He smiles so sincerely that I literally catch my breath. He seems so unaffected. Deep down, I suppose I didn't really expect that from a Division One star quarterback, but there does not seem to be a conceited bone in his body. He's unlike the other athletes I've come to know.

He opens the door and climbs out.

I open my door and get out as well. "You are most welcome."

"And thanks for the toothpaste."

I'm hoping to meet him in front of my car, but he moves around the back and toward the walkway to his dorm.

"Bye, Nathan."

"Good night."

I climb back in the driver's seat and watch him as he enters his dorm, never turning back to wave at me. My hearts sinks, but I'm even more determined than ever to make him mine.

Twelve

POIGNANT RELATIONSHIPS

The Halloween party was a total bust. We won the contest, but it got me little attention from Nathan, despite the barely there outfit I was wearing. In fact, I had to watch him flirt with Abigail for an hour. Then, what was worse, after she abruptly left, this other girl dressed as a sexy nurse was hanging all over him for the rest of the night. I couldn't even get near him.

I haven't seen Nathan for weeks. However, I just watched him, laughing and giggling with Abigail as they went into her room. I know Laura is gone, so they are now all alone, and my blood is boiling with jealousy.

I'm glad to be going home for Thanksgiving. I need to develop a better game plan to grab his attention, and there is no one better to ask than my friends from home. They know how to give me straight-forward advice. They don't sugarcoat anything, no matter how much it might sting. Although I'm not pleased with all the shit that went down between Asher, Nelly, Dashiell, and Joss, I have to admit that Nelly knows how to get attention from a man. *Could she be the one who holds the secret as to how to get someone to notice you?* She stole Dashiell from Joss, and I'd thought that was all but impossible, yet she managed to do it under the cover of darkness.

There is, of course, a goodness in me that also wants to make sure Joss is okay. We were, despite our loathing for each other at times, friends. Maybe not the picture-perfect friends you read about in fairy-tale stories, but we were all we had in an environment that thrived on bitchy and backstabbing behavior.

Notwithstanding all that, what the four of them did to each other was inexcusable. They royally screwed up.

My father calls me from his cell phone in the car.

"I'll be right down, Dad."

"Okay, sweetheart."

Since I have all my clothes laundered and an entire wardrobe back at home, I have little to carry down. All I have to carry is my messenger bag and my Louis Vuitton suitcase.

I lock my door and pop my head into Jen and Casey's room.

"Happy Thanksgiving. See you guys soon."

"You, too, Bree," Jen says.

"See you in a week. Have a good one," Casey adds.

"I will, and you, too."

I walk down the stairs and out the front door. I take a deep breath. The cool air fills my lunges. I am nervous that my father will be able to see right through me. He was a lawyer, and he knows when people are lying. I try to get my emotions in check.

When something is wrong, I tend to burst into tears when I see my dad. Like the time I let Joss drive my Jeep. She flipped it on the beach, and I had to have it towed to a garage. I thought of a thousand things to tell him, but as soon as I saw his face, I burst out crying and spilled my guts to him. He knows how to solve my problems, and I want to tell him everything. He'll know how to make me feel better. But I know I can't or I shouldn't or I'm just too afraid to.

I took a muscle relaxer about an hour ago to help calm me. I haven't seen anyone in my family since I started school four months ago, and I know my father will be asking me a lot of questions about how I'm doing and so on. I hate lying to him; therefore, I need to put on a good show. I don't want to ruin the holiday by telling my father I was sexually assaulted on my first night at school. My parents might not let me return, and that would be awful.

My father is sitting in his Range Rover. I toss my bags in the back as my father climbs out to give me a hug. He might not always pay the most attention to me, but I know he loves me, and he does take every opportunity to show me. Both monetarily and non-monetarily, I take what I can get.

"Daddy!" Oh, the mere sight of him is enough to bring mist into my eyes. It feels like forever since I saw him.

"Bree, sweetheart, you are beautiful." He squeezes me so tightly that I groan.

"Thank you, Dad. You look as handsome as ever. New suit?"

"Yes. You like it?"

"Yes. Burberry?"

"Of course."

"It's divine." I smile widely at him. I can't help it. I've missed him dearly.

"Come, let's get going."

I open the car door and climb in. My father and I talk almost the entire way home. We listen to the oldies station, and he tells me about how each song reminds him of a special time of dating my mom or his high school days. I get to know my father better and better each time we listen to The Four Seasons with Frankie Valli or Fred Parris and The Five Satins, and this time is no exception. I need this distraction, so I don't have to talk. I make him tell me stories he's told me a hundred times, and eventually, I fall asleep. I sleep for the last two hours of the ride.

When we finally arrive at home, I am delighted to see Claudia waiting for me. She opens the garage door.

Once my father walks in, I eagerly hug Claudia.

"Bree, senorita, oh, how we have missed you around here."

I can assure you, Claudia, I have missed you more.

"Claudia, I've missed you, too." I have to will my tears back as the sight of her makes me want to curl up on her lap, like I did as a little girl, and tell her of all my worries, so she can make my pain go away.

She hugs me, and I squeeze her back.

Then, my mother calls from the other room.

"Bree, darling, are you home?"

My shoulders tense at the sound of her voice.

"Yes, Mother, I'm home." I notice she doesn't come and greet me, so I stroll through the kitchen, the front room, and into the large sunken living room that pokes out over the ocean.

My mother is lounging on the couch, dressed perfectly in a navy suit and white silk blouse, her hair pinned back. She mimics a million bucks, but she usually does. She quickly rises and hugs me, so she can draw back and inspect me, turning my face from side to side. I can't make eye contact with her. I never could. I can't wait for this moment to be over. It's too painful for me to be so scrutinized.

"Is that a scar on your lip, dear?"

Shit, she noticed, I think. I forgot to put on my dark lipstick to cover it. I curse myself.

"Ah, I got hit by a door swinging open. I didn't see it, and I bumped into it on my way to class."

"Does the school know?"

"What? The school? No. I bumped it. You can't see it when I have lipstick on. It's fine. It's still healing."

"I'll have Claudia get you some vitamin E."

"Thank you, Mother. So," I say, eager to change the subject, "are you excited for the holiday? Are the Jameson's stopping by?"

Mr. Jameson is my father's business partner in the city and comes by every year for Thanksgiving. Their whole family does, which livens it up around here. Otherwise, it would just be us. My brother doesn't usually come home for Thanksgiving. He saves his holiday trip for Christmas, mainly so that he can go skiing. One of the Jameson's' sons is around my age, a bit older if I remember, and goes to Harvard. So, at least I have someone to talk to besides my parents and his.

"Yes, of course. They will be here by noon on Thursday. You should ask John about Harvard. I hear he's doing very well."

"I'm sure he is, Mother."

I notice she has yet to ask me how I'm doing in school.

"Darling, why don't you get settled? Then, tomorrow, we'll go get our nails done. Sound good?"

"Sure, Mother, sounds great."

I walk up the stairs and to my room. It's been nearly four months since I last stepped foot in my room, and as soon as I open the door, I realize how much I've missed the luxury that is my bedroom. I drop my bag on the floor next to my bed and approach the window. I watch for a few minutes as the winter waves crash onto the shore. I spent the better part of my youth gazing out this window, experiencing a myriad of moods as I viewed the ocean. I've been amazed by how something so terrifyingly beautiful can make you feel so small and alone, like a speck of sand on a beach. I love the ocean, but during times of sadness, it pains me to be close to it.

This is one of those times. I don't have the distraction of friends at school or my internship to keep my mind active. I close my drapes, walk over to my bed, and fall back on it. The comfort is almost more than I can bear, and I find my body sinking deeper and deeper into the mattress, as though it is swallowing me up. I close my eyes and try desperately not to think about my first night at school.

Without warning, he stands up. His eyes are dark and hollow. He grants me a mean and disturbing smile. My body shivers, but I lie still, lip bleeding, and my cheeks burn from his tirade of slaps to my face. My mind is racing, but I try not to think about what is coming next. I squeeze my eyes shut and then slowly try to open them. When I do, I find him leering over me, chest heaving, as he draws in another breath.

"You're too stiff to screw," he barks.

Then, as though it happens in slow motion, he spits on me. I start to scream.

"Bree, Bree, wake up! You are having a bad dream."

My body catapults forward as I sit up in my bed. For a brief moment, I have no idea where I am or who is touching me. I go to push them away.

"Bree, it's Claudia. Bree—"

"Oh God, I'm so sorry. I was, er…dreaming or…"

"What were you dreaming about?"

"I don't remember…thankfully."

"Well, you're drenched. Come, let me get you ready for the day." She turns on the shower and hangs an outfit for me behind the door. "I'll grab you some water and a coffee. Your mother is waiting for you to go out and get your nails done. I've made an appointment for eleven."

"Oh, thank you. What time is it?"

"It's ten. You've been sleeping for a long time."

Yes, I have, I think.

I shower and dress quickly. I don't want to keep my mother waiting. I put on my jeans, a navy silk shirt, and a tan scarf. I spend most of my time blow-drying my hair and applying my makeup. My mother will have some comment about my appearance if I don't.

I pull on my knee-high brown leather boots and grab a matching bag. I hurry down the stairs to my mother waiting in the grand foyer.

"Good morning, Mother."

"Bree, darling, did you sleep well?"

"Yes, of course."

"Good. Now, let's be on our way."

My day has been relatively painless. I spent it getting my nails done and lunching at Dexter's restaurant, which is one of my favorites, while chatting about my friends at school. I might have alluded I am closer to them than I am. See, I know my friends at school are so unlike my friends here, and I want my mother to think that I'm making good friends. As a result, I might have embellished my relationships a little. I spoke mostly about Laura and Melissa, which was easy to do since I know them the best. I mentioned my internship and briefly told her about my curriculum project. She seemed somewhat interested in this, but she could not get past the fact that I was working for free. I kept telling her it is not work per se but an internship, and I thought the difference was clear. She disagreed.

I get back to the house and decide I should call Nelly. I'm not surprised when I speak to her father to find out that she is over at Dashiell's house.

"Can you tell her to call me? I'm home."

"Of course, Bree. And tell your family happy Thanksgiving."

"I will. The same to you."

I hang up and decide at least I can put my time to good use, so I go down to my father's office and work alongside him on my project. I know he'll have some good ideas, and I'm eager to show him what I'm working on.

"Daddy?"

"Come in, Bree. Hello, honey. How was your day with your mother?"

"Fine. Mind if I work with you?"

"Work?"

"Yes, I wanted to show you what I've been working on for my internship and see if maybe you could toss me some of your good ideas."

He takes off his reading glasses and glances at me. My father is a very handsome man. As strange as it might seem, he has gotten better-looking as he has aged.

"Of course. And close the door, please."

My father never closes his door. I slowly push it shut.

"Before all that, let's sit for a minute."

"Okay."

"How is school? Are you liking it?"

"Yes, very much, Dad."

"Think you chose the right place for you?"

"Yes, Dad, I do."

He gives me a quizzical stare, and I lower my eyes, as I'm unable to meet his.

"I'm glad."

"What is it?" I ask, knowing full well my father has something to say to me.

"Miguel came by my office last month. I kindly requested that, while you're in school, the two of you put any and all photo shoots on hiatus, while you are getting acclimated to university life. He didn't seem to know what I was talking about and mentioned he had not seen you since July."

Busted.

"Something you want to tell me, Bree?"

I have to think quickly, and I'm struggling to find the words. "No. I wasn't so sure after my first day that college was for me." At least I'm not lying. After my first night, I definitely had good reason to think college was not for me. I wasn't going to survive. "I wanted to get away, be alone, and think about what I really wanted."

"And what did you discover?"

"That I did—I mean, I do want to be at school. See, I thought I had no purpose really, and before I wasted one dime of yours, I wanted to be sure that OSU was right for me."

"Okay, I can appreciate that. But I'm not happy you lied."

"Did you tell Mom?"

He gives me that smile, the one he's been giving me since we made our first pact as father and daughter nearly sixteen years ago. It was when I first realized that, no matter what, my father would always have my back.

"Thanks, Dad, and sorry I had to lie. I apologize." *I'm sorry I'm lying right now, but I can't tell you, Dad, about what happened to me. I just can't. I have to put it behind me.*

"It's all right, Bree. Now, tell me more about this project."

For the next two hours, my father and I pour over my ideas, and he helps me craft a proposal that I'm almost positive will knock Cooper out of his chair. It's even better than what we accomplished at his house a week ago.

"Bree, you in there?" Claudia says as she quietly knocks on my father's door. "Nelly is on the phone."

"Thank you, Claudia. I'll get it in here." I go over to my father's desk and pick up the receiver. I can hear a ton of background noise. "Hello?"

"Bree, get your ass down here!" she yells.

"Where?"

"Cuffy's! It's the night before Thanksgiving, greatest drinking day for all college students. Come on, join us!"

I peer over at my father, who is grinning from ear-to-ear.

"Tell her I can hear her all the way over here." He snickers.

"All right. I'll come down. Joss with you?"

"Yes, bitch, we are all here." I'm not all that surprised to hear this, considering Joss's philosophy has typically been to keep her enemies close—so close, in fact, that they become her best friends. So, no doubt, she wants a front-row seat to the Nelly and Dashiell show.

"Okay, I'll be there in thirty."

"No," she says in a deeper and darker tone, "you'll be here in twenty."

Then, the line goes dead.

Jesus, bite the head off of one queen in the Hamptons, and another rears her ugly head, I think as I place down the receiver.

"Please be safe, okay?"

"I will, Dad, promise."

I start to exit his office, but I stop. I turn and head right back toward him. He stands and gives me a big hug.

"I love you, Dad."

"I love you, too, Bree. Always. Now, go see your friends."

I have this unwavering knot in the pit of my stomach as I pull open the door to Cuffy's. The music is blaring, and it is incredibly crowded. I immediately spot Nelly, and she locks eyes with me. She screams in this high-pitched valley-girl yelp that literally makes me want to turn around and immediately get back in my car.

But, instead, I hear closely in my ear, "Better go see her, girl. She's been waiting all night for you."

I spin around. "Dashiell, hi. How are you? Long time."

"What's up, Bree? You are as hot as ever, babe."

"Thanks, Dashiell. You, too."

"Bree!"

I spin back around and am nearly battered by Nelly as she throws her arms around me and gives me an overwhelming back-and-forth hug.

"Nelly, good to see you."

"I know, isn't it? You get my letters and such? You never wrote back, you snob." Of course, the entire time she's speaking this way, she is grinning from ear-to-ear, so in her mind, she truly thinks she is being kind to me.

"I know. Sorry. I'm working, and I have been so—"

"Gross. You are working at college? Why? Why not just take a break, girl?"

"Well, it's an intern—"

"Like, as in, for free? Wow, Bree, I guess college really does change people now, doesn't it? But, seriously, that is cool. I mean, if you're happy?"

"I am."

"Good. Now, let's grab a drink, and you can tell me all about this so-called charity work."

I shake my head and don't bother correcting her. She grabs my hand and pulls me toward the side of the bar where I see a lot of my classmates.

"Wait until you see Joss. Oh my God, she's gained, like, ten pounds. She looks terrible."

"Joss, heavy?"

She completely ignores my question. "What do you want to drink?"

"Vodka soda."

There is a slight tug on my shoulder, and I quickly spin around. "Joss, hi!"

"Bree, good to see you."

"You, too. You look great."

She's maybe put on five pounds, tops, but it suits her.

"Oh, thanks. Packing on some pounds."

"Didn't notice," I lie.

But I do notice she seems different—quieter and not as obnoxious. It seems like Nelly drank all the obnoxious juice.

Nelly comes bounding over with my drink. "Here. Ugh, where is Dashiell off to now? I know when he's not around because he usually has his hands all over me." She glowers through the crowd and pretends to search for him. I watch Joss playfully ignore her. "Ah, I see him over there. I'll be back. We have so much to catch up on, I'm sure." Nelly yells for Dashiell as she crosses the crowded floor.

"It doesn't bother you? I mean, the two of them?" I ask Joss.

A wicked grin grows across her perfectly painted pink lips. "Oh God, no. I mean, why would it?"

"Well, it's just—"

"Please, don't you know me by now? Dashiell and I still hook up. Nelly has no clue." She tosses her hair to the side, and within moments, the old Joss is back.

I can't help but shake my head and laugh slightly. I should have known that Joss would win in the end. Nelly is no match for her. She never was.

"Well, since you are such a man-eater, what's the secret to getting the man you want? I mean, in your opinion." I planned to ask Nelly how I could score Nathan Ryan, but seeing that Joss had always been in control of the situation, I figured I'd ask her.

"It's not about getting the man you want. Sometimes, it's about getting the man someone else wants."

"Really?"

"Yeah, I mean, it's all about how you play it. Make them come to you, Bree. For Christ's sake, one, you're a freaking model, two, filthy rich, and three, smart as hell. Whoever doesn't want you is a total idiot. And I apply the same logic to me. It's not that I even like Dashiell anymore, but just knowing he'll come back to me at a moment's notice is satisfying enough for me."

"Oh, Joss, how I've missed you."

"You mean, you've missed my honesty. I bet you, no one at OSU is as honest as I am."

Honest or as abruptly cruel, I think. "You got that right!"

"Good. Let's have another drink then, shall we?"

"Sounds good."

We snuggle up to the bar and order two more drinks. At some point, I notice Asher come in. He appears disheveled and out of shape, which makes me secretly happy.

"Whatever happened to you and Asher?" I ask quickly before he approaches.

"Nothing really. He got all weird on me, and we just weren't a match, like, at all. So, I told him bye-bye."

"Yeah, here he comes."

Joss turns with conviction toward Asher, and I can tell, by how his eyes dance back and forth between us, that he is terribly uncomfortable. I know I don't plan to make this easy on him, and if I know Joss as well as I think I do, she'll make him want to crawl in a hole and die.

"Asher, you're looking…well, not up to standards. How's school?" Joss quips.

He lowers his head and peeks up at her. "Fine." Then, he looks at me. "Hello, Bree."

"Asher."

"You guys seem well."

"We know," Joss says as she bats her eyes at him.

"Thanks, Asher." I'm trying not to let my blood boil as I play it cool since Joss has no idea what happened between us at Dashiell's graduation party. Or at least I don't think she knows.

"Buy us a drink at least. Jesus, where are your manners?" Joss barks.

He raises his hand to the bartender and yells over the music, "Can you make the ladies two more and I'll have a Heineken."

The bartender pops the cap off and hands it to him.

"You can leave my tab open for these two tonight."

I just want him to leave. I don't want to be reminded of the night with him.

"Thanks, Asher, but if you don't mind, Bree and I were way deep in a convo, so if you could give us a sec."

"Sure, I'll check back with you guys later."

"Dashiell is over there," Joss says with a flick of her wrist.

"See you."

"Excuse me one sec," I say to Joss.

Before he can walk away, I quickly grab his arm. "Asher, listen to me."

He bends down closer to me.

My heart beats uncontrollably, but I will myself to speak my piece. "We were friends, and you took advantage of that. On graduation, you treated me like shit, and you never said you were sorry."

He goes to speak, but I quickly continue since this moment has been eating away at me for months. It's finally my turn to face a friend who hurt me.

"I don't want your apology. 'Cause, deep down, it's you who has a fucking problem, Asher. So, get some help, and for God's sake, don't treat women like objects…or worse. I was your friend, but please know, I am not anymore. No amount of drinks at a bar will ever change that."

"Bree, I…I can explain."

"Save it, Asher. And stay away from Nelly and Joss. If I overhear that you even attempted to put your paws on either of them, believe me, it will be the last thing you do. Now, please, just leave me alone."

I turn quickly and head back toward Joss. Out of the corner of my eye, I can see that he has left. I'm relieved that he is gone.

"What was that all about?" Joss asks.

"I just wanted to say my piece about this summer. You know, the mess that we all found ourselves in."

"Good for you," she says.

"I suppose."

She observes me. I know her mind is spinning, but I pick up my drink and take a sip. I play it off.

"By the way, drinks are on me tonight. I don't need Asher's freaking tab." I smile wide.

"Amen to that, bitch. So, back to us."

"Yeah, back to us," I add.

"I gather you have got your eye on someone?"

"Yeah, I do actually."

"What's his name?"

I panic for some reason because I wasn't expecting to get into details.

"Cooper." I can't believe his name just flew out of my mouth, but now, I have to go with it. Although, deep down, the idea of being with him is quite intriguing. He is smart, established, serious, kind, and seems to be surer of himself but not in a bad way. His confidence is earned, and that is very sexy.

"Cooper? That's cool, I suppose."

"Yeah, so, like, how do I land this guy? He's kind of a big deal on campus, you know. Like, well-known."

"Yeah, and soon, you will be, too."

"I know, but this is different." In this moment, I'm confused as to whom I'm referring to—Nathan or Cooper.

"You go up to him and ask him to call you, plain and simple. He'll say yes."

"Really? That simple?"

"Or do what I did, and tell the guy you want that the girl he wants is interested in someone else. Plant the seed of doubt and then swoop in and be there for him when he's searching for a girl who actually is interested in him. If he's that big of a deal, trust me, he chases no one."

She is a master of her craft, no doubt about it. She knows exactly how to manipulate men. I can't believe I thought for one second that she'd crumble to Nelly. I should have known better. I wasn't all that thrilled to come home and see my old friends, but now, I'm glad I did. I have a renewed sense of confidence, which is usually not a problem for me, but I've been knocked down, and now, I'm about to get back up.

Thirteen

PLANS UNCOIL

Thanksgiving was fine. The Jamesons came as planned, and I spent most of my day and evening talking with John about his life in Cambridge, Massachusetts, his classes, and—unbeknownst to his parents—his boyfriend of nearly a year, Drew. It became sort of an inside joke to us every time one of our parents would meander by us, all cozied up on the couch, sipping a glass of wine. They'd have stars in their eyes and ask us how we were getting along. We knew they were envisioning the two of us married with babies and brilliant careers. Unfortunately for John's parents, I am the furthest thing from John's mind.

What did I get out of it, however? A great, real new friend. I actually believe that, by taking any sort of sexual tension out of the equation, it made for tremendous conversations and a relaxed evening, so much so that I plan to visit him at Harvard over the summer. I love Boston and can't wait to spend some time there with him and Drew.

As my father waits for me in the car to drive me back to school, Claudia comes into my room. I almost can't say good-bye again. She seems sadder than I anticipated, but I'm assuming, by the way she holds me tight that it's pretty quiet in this big house without me. If only she knew that OSU was quite big and intimidating without her there to brighten my days.

I hesitate as I exit my room. The solace the last few days has brought me is now leaving my body as anxiety begins to swiftly creep in. I make my way down the stairs and enter the living room where my mother sits, reading a book.

"Good-bye, Mother," I say as I lean in to give her a hug.

"Good-bye, darling, and good luck on your finals and in your internship. I'm proud of you."

I almost can't believe my mother has said that. Deep down, I know she is proud of me, but she rarely expresses it.

"Thank you Mother. I'll talk to you soon. I love you."

"I love you, Aubrey."

I start toward the garage when she yells, "Oh, there was a huge article in the paper about a boy, a quarterback at your school? Some freshman phenom? Maybe you know him?"

My skin prickles at the thought of him. "Yes, I do know him. Nathan Ryan."

"Yes, right. Nathan."

"We're good friends actually."

My mother's eyes flicker.

"How wonderful. Please extend our congratulations. You must know his girlfriend, too."

What girlfriend? I think quickly. "He's pretty casual—you know, dating and all as a freshman. No biggie."

"Good. You kids should date. Don't get tied down. You have your whole life for that."

"I'll take the article with me. I'm sure he'd love an extra copy."

"Great idea. Here."

She hands me the article, and I tuck it under my arm even though I'm absolutely dying to see who the hell this girl is.

"Your father is waiting. Safe trip back."

"Bye," I reply.

I knew it. It had to be *her*, right? Little Miss Too Good to Be True—that's who. The picture of Nathan and Abigail holding hands has steam coming out of my ears, and what's worse is, they look awesome together. You'd think this might push me down, but no, I'm even more determined now. Laura mentioned in passing she has a high school boyfriend, and I bet poor Mr. Nice High School Guy has no freaking clue. Damn, Joss was spot-on. I'll make sure Nathan knows she's interested in someone else, and voilà, he'll be mine.

After my father drops me off, I head up to my floor. No sooner do I open my door than I have Laura on my heels.

"Hey, drop your stuff and let's go to the cafeteria. I'll explain when we get there."

"Okay, okay. What's the rush? And how are you by the way?"

"Sorry. Hi. How are you? Have a great Thanksgiving, I assume?" she says hastily.

"Yeah, I did—"

"Great. We can catch up over dinner."

She grabs my hand, and I reach for my ID badge before she pulls me out of my room. We wait impatiently for the elevator.

"It's going to be long because everyone is back with all their laundry," I remark as I watch her hit the down button a few more times. "We can take the stairs, you know."

"No, it will come."

"Suit yourself."

The elevator door beeps and begins to open. We step in and turn to face the hallway. I glance up and see Nathan coming through the door from the stairwell. He is nervous or something. I can't quite place it.

"Hi, Nath—" I say but the doors shut.

I hear Laura exhale deeply.

"Okay, what gives?"

"What? What do you mean?"

"What do you mean, what do *I* mean?"

"Nothing gives."

"You're way too transparent, Laura, so give it up."

We step out of the elevator and walk toward the glass doors. I have no intention of letting this go.

"You rushing us out the door to the cafeteria have anything to do with Nathan arriving on our floor?"

We enter the cafeteria and hand the lady our badges.

"Yes. I mean, no. I'll explain. Meet me at our usual table."

Laura scurries off to the deli line to get a sandwich. I get a salad and go over to our table and wait for her.

"So, what's up?" I ask as she puts her tray down.

"I wanted to give Abigail some space, and I was hoping not to cause a scene with everyone on the floor, you know."

"Cause a scene?"

"Yeah, she's pretty upset, and he's coming over to talk with her."

"So, what happened?"

"You saw the article, right?"

"What article?" I respond, playing dumb, of course.

"Oh, boy. Um, okay. So, every year, the *Sunday College Spotlight* does this big article about an athlete, and…well, this year, they picked Nathan Ryan. It's a super-big deal, and it's a lot of recognition for the school."

"And? I don't see the problem."

"Abigail was in one of the pictures, holding hands with Nathan."

"What? Oh, how scandalous," I respond, rolling my eyes.

"Well, you say that, but it kind of is. See, it's clear from the picture's caption that this was taken back in late September after his record-breaking game, and...well, Abigail had a boyfriend."

"*Had* a boyfriend?" I am super focused on the fact that she is using the past tense.

"Yeah, he wasn't too happy with her."

"Oh, young love. They'll get over it."

"I'm not so sure."

"Why's that?"

"He broke up with her."

"Who?"

"James, her boyfriend. Duh."

Boom. It's like she punched me in the gut.

"Oh, for what? Holding hands with some random guy? Give me a break. I'll help her win him back. You just watch." I couldn't care less about the Abigail-James saga unfolding in front of me, but as long as Nathan remains an option for her, I have to fight. So, I have found my new calling—keeping antiquated love together.

"I'm not so sure that's a good idea."

"Why not?"

"You know, I've gotten the impression from her that maybe James isn't the right one for her."

"Really? And you know this how?"

"It's more of a hunch than a fact. And, you know, obviously, Bree, I'm her friend. I get it."

"Okay, but what if you're wrong?"

"But what if I'm right? And what if that article is the reason that Abigail gets a new chance at something great?" she says with a dreamy smile on her face.

Shit, Laura is totally on her side.

I have to try to stop this.

Operation Destroy Abigail's Chance at Something Great, commencing 3. 2. 1.

It's been about four days since I saw Nathan come up the stairs in our dorm. I've been hoping to run into him and plant my seed of doubt. Thankfully, as I'm coming out of class, I see him.

"Nathan!" I yell from across the courtyard out front of the Student Union.

He jogs over to me. For some reason, he echoes sadness. "Hey, Bree. What's up?"

"Nothing. How are you?"

"Oh, fine, I guess."

"So, can you believe that about Abigail and James?" I watch his eyes widen.

"What about?"

"Not sure, but Laura mentioned they might be getting back together."

"Really? Is that so?" he replies sadly.

"Yeah, that's the rumor."

"But it's only a rumor?" He perks up a bit.

"Maybe. Who knows? You know how high school sweethearts can be so fickle and dramatic."

"Sure, I suppose you're right."

I recognize Abigail across the way, shoulders hunched as she ducks behind the English building. "So, anyway, you should call me sometime. Here," I say as I take out a pen from my bag, "give me your hand. I'll write my number."

"Okay," he says.

Then, I watch her head right for our dorm. A perfect opportunity for me to drop a bomb on her.

"Great. I anticipate hearing from you soon. Bye, Nathan," I say as sweetly as I possibly can.

I rush over to our dorm and take the stairs all the way up, two at a time. I bound down the hallway to Laura and Abigail's room. The door is slightly ajar.

"Laura, oh my God, you're never going to believe this! Nathan just asked me out. He's so hot, right?"

She pushes me out of the door. "Come on, let's go grab a drink."

I can tell by the expression on her face that Abigail is in the room. So, I know she heard my news, and maybe that will push her right back into James's arms.

One point for me.

Unfortunately for me, my second and third points never come. Nathan never calls either. Not only does he not call, but also, the most embarrassing thing possible happens to me.

One night, when we are all studying in the library, he stands up in front of all of us—Webber, Laura, Abigail, and me—and he basically professes his love for Abigail, insisting that she leave with him. Regrettably for me, she does.

"Abigail, I've had a terrible few weeks," he begins. "I'd like you to come with me, so I can try to explain to you— no, actually, I *need* you to come with me, please."

I swallow hard as, just moments before, I attempted to push him to make a decision.

"I don't wait for anybody, Nathan," I said as we approached the library. "Abigail is still in love with James by the way. So, maybe you are barking up the wrong tree."

"Really? Is that so?" His eyes seemed sad.

There was a part of me that hated what I was doing. I was lying, and I knew this. Deep down, I was better than this.

But, despite my efforts, he's still choosing her, and not only has he chosen her, but he's also doing it right in front of me.

We watch as the two of them leave the library together. I am embarrassed that Laura has witnessed all of this because she knows I told her he asked me out. This is now an obvious lie. But, as Laura smiles while the two of them leave, I know what I've known all along. It was never meant to be.

I leave the library with Webber and Laura and head straight to my car.

Notwithstanding my realization, I can't help but feel devastatingly rejected as I drive over to my internship. I decide to drive because of the heavy snow falling, and I don't want to trek across campus in this weather.

I'm already in a mood when I climb out of my car and enter the building, only to find the entire hallway empty and dark.

"Seriously? You'd think, in this snowy weather, Adam would have told me he was going to cancel," I mumble as I turn on my heel and head back to my car. Pissed off, excluded yet again, and slightly concerned that I have not heard from Adam, I decide to drive over to his house.

The roads are slick as I turn down the street toward his house. There is a car parked in his driveway, right behind his car. I pull past his house and park. I look toward the door and watch as Ashley steps out onto his porch while Adam waves slightly to her. She zippers up her coat and hurries down the stairs. They both don't notice my car, thankfully. I watch her as she gets into her car and slowly backs out of the driveway. He closes the door, and I wait a moment before opening my door and climbing out.

I'm fuming. *He didn't bother to cancel on me because he was entertaining Miss Ashley instead?*

I knock on his door. I can hear him unlocking it, and he pulls it open.

"Oh, Bree. I wasn't—"

"Expecting me?" *Well, you didn't cancel, and you weren't at the building, so did you assume I'd simply disappear? Don't you expect me to always be on time, no matter what?*

"Well, yes. Are you all right, Bree?"

"No, actually, I'm not." *I'm pissed off!*

"Come in. Here, let me take your coat."

I shake off my coat, my anger rising at his kindness.

I walk down the hallway toward the kitchen. The glass on the counter has lipstick on the rim, and my blood begins to simmer again. I boldly go over to his wine cabinet and pour myself a glass from the bottle of red that is already opened. He watches me, but he says nothing. I take a big sip of the wine, finishing half of it, and then I pour more in my glass.

"Hey, go easy, will you?" he says delicately but firmly.

"Why should I?" I say as I turn to him. It's then I notice he is wearing well-fitted dark jeans and a white T-shirt that perfectly hugs his chest and shoulders.

"Why? Because the roads can't be good, I'm sure, and—"

"If you're so worried about me, why didn't you cancel tonight?"

"I did cancel."

"When?" I bark.

"I left a message on your voice mail."

"Really? Never got it." *Because I was at the stupid library, realizing what an idiot I had been, chasing someone in my head that never even once considered me as a possibility.*

"I can see that."

I take another sip of my wine. I'm having a hard time meeting his eyes.

"Bree, what's going on? You okay?" he asks compassionately.

I take another drink.

He goes over to his refrigerator and takes out a beer before sitting at his table. "What's up?" he asks.

I reluctantly sit in the chair next to him. The alcohol starts to take effect, and as I finally meet his eyes, the words fly out of my mouth. "I saw her leave, Adam."

His eyes drop. "And?" he says with a coolness in his voice that seems very unlike him.

"And is that what you meant by toeing the line? Is that why you canceled our meeting? Because, if that is why, it's kind of a bullshit move."

"Bullshit move, huh?" He chuckles.

"Yeah, I don't like to be kept waiting." I don't even know what I'm mad about anymore. I'm just angry.

"Bree, please don't. My personal life—"

"Personal life? Are you kidding me?"

"Listen, Ashley and I...well—"

"Oh my God, are you *dating* her? Your student?" I can't believe it. Now, I know why she was so pissed she didn't get the internship.

"Bree, please, it's not like that. You have to understand—"

"Understand what?"

"Ashley and I dated briefly. Nothing serious."

"Nothing serious?" *And that is why she has such a major issue with me.*

"Yes, at the time, she wasn't in my class. I didn't even know she was a student at OSU, and... now, she is having a hard time and wanted to make certain Professor Gilford didn't know of our relationship."

"Relationship?"

"Yes, I use the word loosely. We went on a few dates, if you will."

Jealousy swirls in my blood. I hate being jealous. I fantasize about the two of them out on a date.

I wonder, *What makes her so desirable to him? What makes Abigail so desirable to Nathan? Am I not desirable to anyone but predators?*

I finish the rest of my wine and stand. He pushes back his chair and stands in front of me. I can smell his cologne. I briefly close my eyes. He touches my hand, and a warm response carries over my body. It's something I have never experienced before. I open my eyes to him standing closer to me.

"Bree, are you sure you're all right?" His eyes show real concern.

"I'm fine." I keep my eyes toward the ground.

"Listen, I know how it seems...dating my students, but in reality, I'm merely a person, at a job, around lots of people close to my age. If you think about it, it's only natural that I date someone my age, right?"

"I suppose."

"Look at me, please. I'm still the same person. I just happen to be surrounded by some beautiful, highly intelligent women." He touches my arm.

I glance up at him and watch a slight smile grow across his gorgeous lips. I can't explain the sensation that comes over me, but before I know it, I'm leaning forward, up on my tippy-toes, and kissing him. His lips are soft and full, and I can feel an energy pass between us. It's one of the best kisses I've ever had. He starts to kiss me back, but suddenly, he grabs my arms and pulls away.

He gently wipes his lips with his hand. "Bree, I can't...please understand..."

My cheeks burn with embarrassment as he rejects my advance. I push past him, and I hurry down the hallway. "I'm sorry I came over. It won't happen again."

"Bree, please wait, will you?"

I start to turn. "I'm terribly sorry I did that, and it—"

"I'm not," he responds loudly.

It catches my attention.

"I'm glad you did. Err, I was hoping you would."

"What?" I can't believe he said that.

He reaches for my hand. "You remember the other night when I said I had to toe the line?"

I swallow hard. "Yes?"

"I meant with you."

"Me?" My legs are weakening, and my heart is beating wildly.

"Of course you."

My pulse quickens more as the fear or excitement—I can't quite decide—of being alone with him hits me. "I'm sorry." I rush toward the door, open it, and hurry down the stairs.

The snow is falling hard. I run to my car and climb in. As I put my hands on the wheel and breathe in deep, I can't help but laugh slightly to myself as I realize I don't have my jacket and, more importantly, my car keys.

I sit, contemplating the advice Dr. Leo has bestowed upon me after I expressed my confusing relationship with Adam over the past few months. I consider the man inside the house, only feet away from me, and I can't help but wonder what he is thinking right now. Kissing him was wonderful, and I'd love to do it again. I want to experience it again.

"I am not broken," I whisper. "I must live in the moment."

I peer over at his house and notice his silhouette in the window. My heart quickens, and I sense this incredible tug back toward him. Before I can truly comprehend what I'm doing, I am opening my door, climbing out, and wandering back toward the house. The snow falls on my shoulders. I glance up and marvel at the beautiful scenery.

"Live in the moment," I whisper again. "I am not broken."

As I march up his steps, my face and hair soaked from the snow, I approach the door and knock on the wood frame. I breathe out deeply as I hear him turning the door handle.

As he opens the door, I note that his expression is forgiving and warm. He reaches forward and takes my hand. I swallow as I step closer to him.

"Bree, I don't want you to leave."

My head is spinning as he begins to lean in closer to me. His breath is now on my face, and his lips touch mine. He gently puts his hands on my hips and pulls me into the house. He closes the door. Our bodies are now touching, and I almost can't believe that I am here with him.

He kisses me again. He is so gentle and deliberate as he runs his hand up my body, resting it on my cheek. I'm free and at ease. This is my choice. I want to be here. I am safe and unafraid of him. His kisses let me know that, in this moment, I don't want to leave either. I want to stay here, with him, as two consenting adults, and enjoy whatever this is…together.

I draw back from him. My heart is beating soundly within my chest.

He gazes at me and smiles. "Tell me you'll stay."

"It's hard to say no to you."

"Oh, is it?" he says with a devilish grin.

I can't help but return his smile.

"Good." He takes my hand again and leads me up the stairs.

My thoughts swirl as I climb the stairs, watching his beautiful backside move up each stair in front of me.

We get to the top, and he turns suddenly to me and wraps his long, lean arms around my waist. He kisses me again, only with more passion than before. He starts guiding me backward. I assume we're going toward his room. My head is whirling with an incredible array of emotions. I'm nervous and excited, only I'm not certain which one is holding more power over me in the moment.

He pushes open a door to a dark room, and suddenly, a wave of anxiety washes over me.

"Adam," I whisper, barely able to find my voice.

"Yes, Bree?" he whispers back.

He starts to pull my shirt up over my head, and I attempt to resist, only I do nothing. He tosses my shirt on the floor.

"I'm—" I begin to speak, but he kisses me again.

I don't want him to stop, but I'm not sure I can go further. I'm panicking. He moves me back into the room as he runs his fingertips over my skin. I hear him moan as he touches me.

Then, I sense the backs of my legs touch the bed, and I freak. He pushes me backward, and I land on the bed. It's dark, and I can't make out his expression. I'm immediately brought back to my first night of college when *he* pushed me on the ground. I freeze.

He starts to climb on top of me as he reaches his hand up my leg before landing on the button on my pants.

I suddenly sit up. "Adam, I can't."

I slip out from under him and cross the room toward the only light peeking out from the window shade. My heart is pounding with might. I attempt to do the breathing exercises Dr. Leo told me about. For fear of hyperventilating, I put my head down and close my eyes.

I chant over and over in my head, *Breathe, breathe, breathe.*

Within moments, he is behind me. He carefully wraps his arms around my waist. I jump slightly, and he releases his touch.

"Bree, we can take this slow. It's okay, I promise." His voice is so kind that I have to turn to him.

I rest my head on his chest and breathe in deep. I contemplate telling him, but I can't get the words to come out. I'm too embarrassed for him to know, but I feel so broken and unable to connect deeply with anyone, with him, no matter how badly I want it to happen.

He starts to stroke my hair, and my body begins to relax.

"I'd still like you to stay."

"Really?" I ask. "Why?"

"Why wouldn't I?" He pulls back and lifts my face upward. He leans down and brushes his lips on mine.

He then steps back and crosses the room. He switches on a light. It takes my eyes a moment to focus, and once they do, I notice him standing before me, his eyes wide.

"Bree, you are beautiful."

I gaze down at my body and feel the heat in my cheeks. "Thank you," I whisper.

He picks my shirt up off the floor and brings it to me. He lifts it up to my head and slips it over me. "I was kind of hoping I'd be undressing you," he says with a slight laugh.

I lower my head, as I'm too humiliated.

He goes over to his bed and sits on the edge. "Come here," he says as he pats the empty spot next to him.

I shyly step toward him and sit down on his bed.

His room is pleasant and actually decorated rather nicely. He has two dressers, one with a mirror on top. A wingback chair is in the far corner, cozied next to a small table with a lamp, newspapers, and books on it. There is a door, and it is slightly ajar, revealing the master bathroom.

"So, this is my room," he says with a slight chuckle. He places his arm around my shoulders and gently squeezes.

"I'm sorry, Adam."

"Please don't be."

"I can go."

"Stay and have dinner with me," he says.

I peek up at him, and his face tells me all I need to know.

"That all depends on what you're making." I give him a wink.

"And there's the girl I know." He laughs and starts to stand. "Come," he says as he reaches his hand out for me to take.

I gladly put my hand in his, and he pulls me up to him.

"Let me pour you a glass of wine this time, and let's relax for a little while."

"That sounds wonderful."

I follow him down the stairs and into the kitchen. I think he can sense that I'd rather be moving than sitting still.

"Would you mind helping me?" he asks as he opens the door to the fridge.

He takes out a few tomatoes and hands them to me.

"Of course not. What are we having?"

"Does a caprese salad with grilled garlic bread sound good?"

"Um, that sounds wonderful. So, slice the tomatoes?" I ask as I go over to the sink to wash the vegetables.

"Yes. But first things first," he says as he pours me a glass of wine and hands it to me.

"Thank you."

We work side by side, making dinner, mostly in silence. The snow is coming down harder as I watch out his window.

I can't believe the last hour of my life—how quickly I went from agony to being pissed off to lust, then to being frightened, and now being content. My mind is spinning with so many emotions, it's hard to tell which end is up.

Adam draws me away from my thoughts. "Quite a storm, huh?"

"Yes, I didn't know it was supposed to come down so hard," I say.

"I'll be right back," he says.

While he's gone, I serve us each the salad and slice the fresh garlic bread that smells so delicious, I am eager to taste it. He comes back a few minutes later.

"Let's eat in the living room," he pronounces.

He hands me one of the plates as he takes the other. He gestures for me to follow him down the hallway and toward the front of the house. As I do, I can hear the crackle of wood.

"Oh, how perfect," I whisper as I enter the room and find it warmly lit by the glow of the fire.

"You don't mind sitting on the floor, do you?" he asks. He's lined the front side of the couch with pillows, and there are two lap trays placed in front of them.

"No, this is great."

I take a seat on the floor, and put my plate on the tray. This is a much more rustic way of eating than I'm used to, but I like the unpretentious, non-stuffy sentiment this gives me. I slide the tray up over my legs as I stretch them out along the floor. He sits next to me.

"Enjoy," he says.

"Thank you. This is wonderful." I bite into the amazing grilled garlic bread and can't believe how amazing it tastes.

After we eat, he takes both trays and places them to the side. "I'll pick clean up later."

"That was wonderful. Thank you again."

"You are welcome. I'm glad you stayed."

"Me, too," I reply nervously.

There is something about the way he studies me. I can't describe it, but he almost regards me as a real person, not as the wealthy model girl from the Hamptons. He speaks to me as though I'm something much more.

"Bree, there is one thing I want to say." He takes my hand and turns toward me. "I need to know that I can trust you."

My eyes get wide. If only he knew that I am the one who needs to know I can trust him. Trust him to treat me right.

"Yes, you can," I say with conviction. "I would never tell anyone about this," I add.

"Good. It's important we stay on the same page; otherwise, people can get hurt."

"I understand. And I want to be able to trust you in return. Take it slow and know that you won't treat me differently."

"Of course. You have my word."

"Good." *Thank God,* I think.

"We need to be careful; it's important."

"Agreed."

"So, let me get rid of the dishes while you finish your wine."

"No, please, let me."

"No, I insist." He smiles warmly and starts to stand up.

"Okay. I appreciate it."

He takes the plates and enters into the kitchen.

He comes back a little while later. "Bree, I prefer you don't drive home, okay?"

The alcohol has made me sleepy, and the fire has made me relaxed, so much so that the mere thought of the drive home is not a welcome one. But I can't help but be nervous about being here, about sleeping at his house. That seems absurd.

"I don't know, Adam. It doesn't quite—"

"Listen, the roads are bad, and I served you more wine than I'd like...partly because you helped yourself."

He laughs a little, and this puts me at ease.

He's right.

"Okay," I reply sheepishly. "I could fall asleep right here, in fact."

"How about a comfortable bed instead?"

My heart picks up speed again as he eyes me.

"Sounds good." I climb to my feet and have to steady myself.

He takes my hand, and I follow him up the stairs.

"If you are more comfortable, you can sleep in here," he says as he opens a door to an extra bedroom.

The room is respectfully adorned.

"Thank you, Adam," I say as I enter the room.

"I'm going to take a quick shower, and then I'll come back and check on you, okay? There are some extra T-shirts in the dresser over there that you can sleep in if you want."

He leaves the room, and I undress and toss my clothes on the chair. I open the dresser and take a shirt out. I slip it on and go to pull the sheets down when I pause and have this burning awareness in my stomach. The next thing I know, my feet are carrying me toward the door. I open it and head toward his room.

I can hear the shower running in his bathroom as I push open the door. I locate a picture on his dresser, and I lean forward to get a closer peek. It appears to be a photo of his parents, if I had to make an educated guess. I can see where he got his good genes from. His mother is striking, and his father is equally attractive.

"Those are my parents," he says quietly, which startles me.

I whip around. He is standing in front of me, dripping wet, with a towel wrapped around his waist, hair perfectly pushed back. I find my mouth drops open slightly at the sight of him.

I stumble for something to say. "Oh, sorry. I hope you don't mind me looking…"

"At what? Me or the picture?"

"Cute." I give him a crooked smirk.

"I wasn't going for cute," he responds playfully.

I can't believe I'm actually in the same room with him, let alone with both of us being half-naked.

"I, um, meant…"

"You look good in my shirt," he adds as he crosses the room.

His body is amazing, and I am mesmerized by him.

"You need anything?"

"No, I thought I'd come in and say good night."

"It has been, hasn't it?"

I can't help but smile at him. "Yes, and thank you for letting me stay."

"Of course," he adds. He strides toward me.

I swallow hard as he approaches.

"Did I mention, you look great in my T-shirt?"

My cheeks burn with heat. "Yes, you did say that a minute ago, and…" I whisper.

He comes even closer, "And?"

"And…did I mention how great you look in that towel?" My eyes shift down toward his waist.

"No. As a matter of fact, you didn't mention that."

"I'd be willing to bet you'd look even better without it." *Where is this boldness coming from?*

It's him. He makes it so easy to feel this way.

The sexy smile that spreads across his face is so incredible that I know, if I don't walk out the door right now, I never will.

He stands directly before me now, chest still misty from the shower. "I wager you'd look better without that shirt on, too."

"Really? Is that so?" My breath is barely able to push out the words.

He reaches forward and tucks a strand of my hair behind my ear. I gently close my eyes as his fingertips caress my cheek.

"Yes, and I'm also confident in saying that you'd have a much better night's sleep in here with me than anyplace else."

My eyes flash open. "You're positive of that?" I inhale his scent.

He puts his arms around my waist. "Uh-huh," he whispers.

His lips gently trace over my cheek and down my neck. A tingling responsiveness runs down my body as his kisses become longer and more profound. Finally, his lips meet mine, and I'm overwhelmed by the powerful sense of longing that is pulling me toward him. I wrap my arms around his waist, noticing the smoothness of his skin, and I draw in the smell of his body wash as my breathing deepens.

He starts to back me up again toward the bed, so I begin to turn my body slightly to the side. He steps back and gazes intently into my eyes. I know he can sense my hesitation because it is impossible for me to hide.

"Anytime you want to stop, please tell me, okay?" he whispers.

A small sense of relief comes over me. "Okay…can we, um…"

"Let's take this slow, okay?" he adds in.

I can tell he knows what I was trying to say.

He takes my hand and leads me over to the side of the bed. My heart is racing in double time. He switches off the light near his bed. Then, he kisses me.

"I've wanted to know what it would feel like to hold you, Bree."

I'm glad it's dark in here because I don't want him to take notice of the anguish on my face. I long to be held by someone, a man and lover, someone to connect with me.

Could I be lucky enough tonight to have that? An intelligent man who knows how to treat a woman right?

I turn and rest my head on his chest. The beat of his heart is slow and calming.

"That is exactly what I need," I whisper as he reaches his hand up and strokes my hair.

"Then, that is what you will get."

Fourteen

WEEKEND AWAY

It's been three weeks since Adam and I spent our first night together at his house. He has been wonderful, taking it slow, and it has made me more comfortable with this newfound and quite secretive affiliation.

I expressed my feelings about my relationship with Dr. Leo; although I have to admit I did not tell her he was my professor. One step at a time. The heart cannot help whom one falls for, and since I have overcome some intimacy issues as my relationship with Adam has progressed, I don't feel badly for lying to her. I know, eventually, I will tell her.

Adam's fingers trace the curve of my back as he tries to wake me. I moan slightly and turn my head to face him.

"Good morning," he says.

"Morning."

"I made you some coffee."

"Mmm, thank you. It smells wonderful." I stretch and sit up against his headboard, pulling the comforter up, before I take the coffee from him.

"When is your first class?"

"Eleven thirty." I yawn.

"And when is your last?"

"Ends at three."

"Good. How about I take you away this weekend?"

We have done little in the way of actual dating. It is quite difficult to be out in public and not be seen. We ventured out last weekend for dinner, but we had to drive an hour away. So, mostly, we prefer to stay in—eating dinner, sitting by the fire, and talking about his love of biking and my life back home as a model in the city. Trying through conversation to get to know each other on a different level. We have, for now, steered clear of any talk of past relationships, which is fine with me.

"What do you have in mind?"

"I want to surprise you, if that's okay?"

I take a sip of my coffee and eye him. Then, I smile. "Surprise me, huh?"

"Yes," he says playfully as he kisses my arm.

"All right then. Can I ask what I should pack or bring?"

"Dress for warmth, but you won't need much," he says with a sly grin. "I'll take care of all the rest."

I feel the heat rush to my face. "You have definitely piqued my interest."

"Good. So, if you want, drive here after your class. We can leave from here."

"What? You don't want to pick me up in front of my dorm?" I say with a grin.

"I know, I know. We both wish it were different. But I hope it will be worth the trouble of sneaking around for a while."

I fantasize about the nights I've spent with him, and I can unequivocally say that he is worth the trouble.

My car is packed. All I can think about is leaving for the weekend. But I'm stuck in my psychology class, tracing with my eyes the curls on Jessica's head as she sits in front of me.

She turns slightly. "Got plans this weekend?" she asks.

"No," I lie. "You?"

"Not sure. I might hang with Tank on Saturday."

"You guys back on again?"

Jessica and Tank have been on again, off again for practically the entire semester.

"Sort of. Who knows?"

I'm not surprised by this in the least. The rumors are swirling about the two of them and their tumultuous relationship. From what Jessica has told me, they are on some level bordering between sexy and sad. He is moody, but appears to be into her.

"That's cool."

I'm not sure if I should encourage her to keep trying with him or to go running for the hills. He seems, from what little I know, to have a hard time with commitment. He parties hard and doesn't always handle himself well.

Our professor clears his throat and stares directly at us. Jessica turns back around to face him.

"As I was saying, the final will be next Friday, so please take this week to study chapters eighteen through thirty, concentrating on chapter twenty-eight for your final essay. Any questions?" He pauses and glances around the classroom. When no one answers, he says, "Okay then, you are free to go. Please have a safe weekend."

Not wanting to get into a long discussion with Jessica, like we usually do, I say, "Oh, shoot, I forgot to ask Professor Walsh something. I don't want to make you wait. So, I'll see you this weekend maybe?"

"Cool, yeah. He can go on and on..." she says with a roll of her pretty eyes.

I laugh. "Right, so I'll see you." I take my time putting my book and notebook back into my bag. I even pretend to be searching for something. Once Jessica is gone, I head toward the door. "Have a nice weekend," I say sweetly to Professor Walsh.

"You, too, Bree."

I hurry toward my car and pray I run into no one I know. I am excited at the idea of going away with Adam for the weekend. I climb in my car and head straight for his house. When I turn down his block, his black Toyota 4Runner is parked out front of his house. I turn into his driveway and see his garage open. He steps out onto the porch. He looks awesome in his jeans and red sweater with his hair perfectly pushed back and his glasses on. He's breathtaking.

I roll down my window.

"Park in the garage," he says. He smiles wide.

I pull forward and park in his garage. As I climb out, he approaches my car.

"Hi," he says.

"Trying to hide me?" I laugh.

"Something like that." He leans down and softly kisses me on the lips.

My God, is he a wonderful kisser.

"You'll also thank me when your car isn't buried under snow when we get back."

"Ah, so thoughtful of you."

"Come on," he says as he opens my back door and takes out my bag. "Got everything you need?"

"Yes, I have everything I need." I smile and follow him to his idling car. It's warm inside as I get in and close the door.

"How was class?" he asks as he buckles his seat belt.

"Oh, fine. Finals next week."

"I know." He laughs.

"Right. Of course."

Not wanting to talk about school, I ask, "So, where are we going?"

"You'll see. We have about an hour drive."

"You definitely have my attention."

"I hope so."

A sly smile cultivates across his face.

He drives about forty-five minutes north of campus, and the further we get, the more we seem to be out of contact with civilization. He gets off an exit. There is one lonely gas station right off the exit, and as we pass that, I realize that is probably all there is in this town.

We turn down a poorly paved road about five miles from the gas station. It's dusk now and hard to decipher what exactly is up ahead. As we bounce down the road, I notice a mailbox with the number eighty-six on it. At this point, I'm surmising we are going to a hotel of some kind.

He drives around the corner, and there is a slight clearing. Then, this small but spectacular wood home pushed back on the property appears. There are stairs in the center and a wraparound porch on the front. A big wood door with glass around it makes the front seem modern but rustic.

"What do you think?"

"Wow. What is this place?"

"I'll show you. Let's go inside, and I'll get the bags in a minute."

We stroll up the porch, and he takes a key out of his pocket and unlocks the front door. The door creaks as he pushes it open. He flips on a light and illuminates the kitchen that is set to the right of the door. It has an island in the middle and relatively modern appliances. The rustic cabinets are made of all wood, and the simplistic feel of the large farm table beyond the island makes the kitchen so welcoming. But what I notice even more is the grand fireplace in the center of the room. It is made of large stones and goes all the way up to the second floor loft. To the left of the front door is a quaint living room with two leather couches and a coffee table. He goes in there and switches on a table lamp next to one of the couches.

"Adam, this is beautiful."

"You like it?"

"Yes, very much. How did you find this?"

He comes up behind me and puts his arms around my waist. I turn toward him. He takes his hands and places them on my face, drawing me toward him and passionately kissing me.

"I've been wanting to do that since you left this morning," he breathes.

I kiss him back and whisper, "Me, too."

He starts to pull off my jacket, and it drops to the floor. I begin to tug on his sweater, and he stops me.

"You're going to have to wait," he says as he releases me and approaches the main door.

The little temper I have starts to surface. He exits out the door, and I know he's going to get our bags.

I wander over to the other side of the double-sided fireplace and gaze upon the large master bedroom with a huge four-poster bed made out of birch trees. It's absolutely beautiful. The bed is dressed with tan and white sheets and a matching comforter. There is a plush white faux fur spread on the bed as well. I run my hands over it and smile to myself. It is so soft and welcoming. There are also minimal pillows, but it suits the vibe of this place very nicely.

He opens and closes the door a few times, and then I assume he is in the kitchen putting away groceries.

"Bree, I'm starting a fire. You okay?" he yells to me as he wrestles with some wood logs and then strikes a match.

I don't answer him on purpose. A few minutes go by.

"Bree?" he says again as his voice gets closer to me. He comes around the corner and into the room, the glow of the fire lighting the room.

"Oh, wow," he whispers. He sees me partially naked, in only my bra and panties, lying belly down, on the faux fur comforter on the bed.

"I don't like to wait," I reply.

"I can see that," he says as he starts to kick off his shoes.

He comes closer to me, and as he does, he pulls his sweater and T-shirt off at the same time. Without a care, he drops them on the floor. I bite my lip as I watch him draw nearer. He runs the tips of his fingers up my legs, over my backside, and up to my shoulders. Gently, he turns me on my back and leans down. He kisses me deeply.

"Do you always get what you want?" he asks in a husky voice.

"Yes," I answer.

He starts to kiss me harder, down my neck and across my shoulders and to my breasts. He softly touches me at first and then massages my body to where I might explode. Then, suddenly, he stops.

"But you are going to have to wait," he says.

As I open my eyes, a devious smirk grows on his face.

I'm about to protest and say no one has ever kept Bree Van Tousen waiting when he quickly adds, "And no pouting."

I'm floored, furious, and feeling terribly rejected, but I can't respond. He has not only left me speechless, but he's also left the room. I hurry off the bed with a huff. I slip back on my jeans and T-shirt. I pile my hair on my head and make my way back into the front room.

I hear the pop of a cork out of a wine bottle as I saunter into the kitchen. He turns with a glass and pours me one with a smile.

"You can lose the smile," I say as I take the wine.

"How can I possibly with you in the room?"

Ugh, he's maddening.

"What a witty response."

"It's true."

I can tell he has something more pressing on his mind by the way he runs his hand through his hair. "What is it?" I ask.

"I know we talked about this before, but did you take your pill?"

I'm caught off guard that he asked me that since we haven't actually had sex yet.

I swallow nervously. "Yes, I have every day for a year." *Ah, the burden of being a woman sometimes.*

"Good. Just want to be safe."

"Me, too, Adam. It's my top priority. Trust me, I do not need to be reminded to take it."

I give him a slight grin and feel my cheeks scorch as the anticipation of sleeping with him builds even more. I lower my eyes. Sensing my apprehension, he comes around the island and stands behind me, placing his arms around me.

"I'm glad we've waited, Bree, because I know you're worth it."

"Thanks," I whisper.

He squeezes me tightly and then releases me.

"So, what do you want to do now?" I ask as I take a seat at the farm table.

"I'd like to make you dinner."

"Are you some kind of chef in training? What? Being a professor at your age isn't enough?"

He laughs. "I do love to cook. I had to find a hobby I could do that didn't require a weather report."

"That's a good way of thinking about it."

"I love to bike, and unfortunately, in this part of the world, that's only weather-permitting."

"True."

"So, how about chicken marsala?"

"Sounds wonderful. Thank you, Adam," I say sincerely.

He's been so wonderful and kind these past few weeks, and I find myself getting lost in being with him.

"Good, it's settled. You sit there—"

"And I'll watch you cook, shirtless."

"I don't typically cook this way," he says shyly.

"Oh no? This isn't how you draw all the women in?"

"Very funny, but no."

He starts to get the pans out, and it dawns on me, as he is making his way around the kitchen, that he is familiar with being here.

"So, I'm deducing by how familiar you are in here that you or your family came across this place?"

"Oh, right. My parents purchased this land when I was little, and then they built this property about ten, maybe fifteen, years ago. I was going to live here when I got the job at OSU, so we put some money in updating it. Then, I realized that, with my schedule and all that I wanted to accomplish at the university, it was too far for me to commute every day. So, I got the place closer to OSU, and I come here a lot on weekends to get away from the parties and craziness near campus."

"Craziness on campus?"

He smiles. "Don't get me wrong; it's a rite of passage, no doubt, but I can't get drawn into that, as much as I'd like to."

"Really? You?"

"Yeah, of course. I finished grad school, and here I am, back on a huge campus. It's easy to know what you are missing."

"Makes sense."

"But, back to dinner, you like mushrooms?"

"Whatever you are making, I'll eat."

"Really? Glad to hear it."

"You know, I've sort of tried it all."

"Of course you have," he adds with a laugh.

"It's true. When you grow up with a chef living in your home, you tend to eat many different things."

"Oh, boohoo."

"Adam." I scowl. "You know what I mean."

"Do I?"

"Are you making fun of me?" Now, I'm pouting.

"No, I'm not, Bree. I'm sorry if that is what it sounded like."

"I'm..." I hesitate, putting my head down.

He comes over toward me and pours me another glass of wine.

"Don't worry about my joking around, please. We are simply two people in a cabin in the woods."

I gaze up at this beautiful, bare-chested man smiling at me, and my shoulders begin to relax. "Do you always know the right thing to say?"

"No, I rarely do, in fact. But, when I do, if you could point that out, it would certainly help me in the future. Not to screw up, that is."

"Okay, I'll do my best." I get up. "Want me to put another piece of wood on the fire?"

"Yes, and thank you."

I gradually place the wood on the top, making certain not to burn my hand as I do. I sit in front of it and warm my body as I watch him chop, sauté, and effortlessly move around the kitchen.

"This fireplace is truly beautiful. I mean, with where it's placed and all."

"Yeah, we wanted it to sort of become the wall between the front living space here and the master bedroom."

"It is a lovely place," I add.

The wine begins to relax me even more, and I'm feeling happier than I have in a long time. I want to tell him that, but again, it might be too fast.

Will he think I'm some silly, young, soon-to-be nineteen-year-old college student, falling hard for her professor?

In many ways, I wish I had asked him more about his relationship with Ashley.

Why did it only last a few dates? Does he consider these nights I spend with him as dates? Is he a serial dater, only staying with a person for a little while and then carelessly moving on to the next? As quick as, say, the time it took to walk Ashley out of his door and me in?

"Dinner is ready." He takes me out of my thoughts and to the wafting aroma of the chicken marsala.

It smells fantastic, and my mouth is watering.

"Smells wonderful."

I sit at the table, and he sits next to me.

"I'm glad you are here," he says as he raises his wine glass to me.

"Me, too."

Adam insists on cleaning up while I put another log on the fire. I go into the living area and curl up on one of the leather couches that faces the fire. I watch Adam as he pours himself another glass of wine and works in the kitchen.

My mind is more relaxed than it has ever been as I twirl my glass of wine in my hand and watch the reflection it makes with the roaring fire behind it.

He finally comes in the room and sits on the floor near me, leaning back on the couch. From where I now lay, I am able to watch him watch the fire, and a slight smile grows across his face. I reach forward and run my fingers through his beautiful thick, wavy hair. His eyes slowly lower with each stroke of my hand in his curls.

"It's nice that you're so relaxed, Professor."

He chuckles deeply and takes another sip of his wine. He turns, and his expression darkens. "I'm not a professor now, Bree."

"So, what are you? Now, that is."

"I'm here with a friend, enjoying this magnificent fire."

"I want to know more about you. How did you get into teaching? I should say, how did you get to where you are today?"

"I'd love to tell you, but right now, I'd like to *not* talk about my job. I'd simply love to enjoy my time…with you."

I slink down lower on the couch. "I understand."

I watch his chest rise and fall as the glow of the light touches his upper body. I'm almost obligated to get to know him better, but I completely understand the idea of anonymity.

"I hope so. I mean, I rarely get a chance to spend time with such a beautiful woman that, right now, it's all I want to do."

"Thank you. I appreciate the compliment."

He turns his head toward me and smiles. "You must know that. Aren't models, by definition, beautiful?"

I start to think about the episode in the library with Nathan and Abigail. "I'm not everyone's definition of beautiful."

He smiles at me and says, "Well then, they're the fool, Bree."

He reaches his hand up and caresses my face. I swallow hard as his eyes meet mine. He smiles as he puts down his wine on the table. He leans up on his knees to face me. He takes off his glasses and puts them on the table as well. His eyes are so remarkable. Then, he takes the wine from my hand and puts my glass next to his.

He reaches up to my hair and with ease loosens the rubber band from it. I feel hypnotized by his attention. Then, he releases the bun, allowing my hair to fall past my shoulders. He runs his fingers through my hair, pushing it back from my face. I can feel my pulse quicken. He lowers his hands toward my waist and slowly pulls my T-shirt up over my head before tossing it on the floor. He reaches under my back and unhooks and removes my bra. The coolness from the leather as it touches my skin sends a tingle down my vertebrae.

I want him to speak, to say something, but he gently runs his fingers down my skin while keeping his eyes locked on mine. My heart is beating wildly. I'm positive he can hear it.

He leans in. My lips part, and he kisses me deeply. My mind is racing as I run my hands through his hair and down his broad shoulders before resting my hands on his arms. He puts his arms around me and pulls me to him. Our bare chests are now against each other, and he feels so wonderful that I find myself wanting him more than ever.

He reaches down with one hand and starts to unzip my jeans. He slides them down with my help. I'm naked on his couch. He stands, his eyes still on mine, and deliberately unzips his jeans. The glow of the fire behind him is unreal. It shows the outline of his perfect body.

I almost can't believe this is happening.

He gently climbs on top of me. I love the weight of his body. He kisses me across my belly as he kneads my breasts. I moan, as his touch is so welcoming and wonderful that I relish in each second. He takes his time, continuing to make me wait. But, this time, I want to remember each moment like a still frame.

"Bree, you are stunning."

I pull my hands through his hair again, trying to bring him closer to me. "Adam, please kiss me."

"Be patient," he says as he peers up at me.

I am.

I protest silently in my mind, but am so glad that he and I have waited. I wasn't ready before. But, now, I feel so safe in his arms, and I need to be in order to be here. His kisses and touch are too good for me. I can't resist the temptation that he represents. I think he knows this and takes pleasure in watching me.

He runs his hands in between my legs. I gasp. He looks up again at me and smiles. I tip my head back, my eyes lowering half-way as I enjoy the sensation. He touches my belly and traces the tips of his fingers across my hip, down my backside, and back underneath my thigh. He draws my leg up, wrapping it around his back. He slides his body up mine and hovers over me, his arms on the sides of my shoulders.

He watches my eyes and starts to slowly move on top of me. He feels so fantastic, but I have to keep from getting ahead of myself. I lean up and wrap my arms around his neck. I bring my face close to his and nibble slightly on his ear.

Then, I whisper, "I'm so glad this is with you."

I can hear him moan as goose bumps form on his skin.

I keep going until he finally gives in and kisses me. This time, his passion is unmistakable, and I return his kiss with equal intensity. Suddenly, he is inside me, and as he moves with fever and passion, I groan with pleasure, letting him know I have needed him badly. He needs to satisfy something in me that I cannot explain.

At some point, I'm not sure when, I sense Adam scoop me up off the couch. I must have fallen asleep and quite soundly. The fire is fading as he carries me past the stone fireplace to the bed. He lays me down, and I curl up into a ball. He goes around to the other side of the bed and climbs in. I note the warmth of his body next to mine as he cuddles up next to me.

"Sleep well, Bree," he whispers in my ear.

I mumble, "Good night."

I'm awaken by the smell of coffee. I spread out my hand next to me and am not surprised to find Adam gone.

I climb out of bed and put on a T-shirt and workout tights. Then, I make my way into the kitchen. I am pleased that he is standing before me, in nothing but his boxer briefs. He turns, messy hair and all, with his glasses on, and I want to run and jump into his arms. I restrain myself, but damn, he looks perfect.

"Good morning," I say.

He smiles. "You're gorgeous this morning. Coffee?"

"Um, I'd love some. It's actually what got me out of bed."

"I had to try something."

"What time is it?" I ask.

"Almost nine."

"I can say I'm usually not afforded an opportunity to sleep in until nine—at least, not during the week."

"And on weekends?"

"Occasionally, I'll sleep in."

"I'm usually up, either working or taking a bike ride or something. But I rarely sleep in either."

He pours me a cup of coffee while I sit at the table.

"So, what do you have planned for the day?" I ask.

"I thought I could show you around the property, go for a walk."

"Sounds good."

After a breakfast of poached eggs and toast, we both forgo a shower and throw on our warmest clothes, ski jackets, and boots. Then, we head out the front door. He takes my hand as we walk to the side of the house and into the back. The most amazing view is revealed as the rolling hills and snow-covered trees are spread out before us.

"This is beautiful, Adam."

"Isn't it? In fact, if we stroll through these woods here, for about a mile, we'll actually come out to a main road."

"That's convenient."

"Yes. So, once I'm here, I usually walk to the store."

As our feet crunch through the semi-frozen path, I can't help but feel oddly comfortable with him. There is a calming factor about him that I didn't expect before. Part of me understands the facade he has to keep in order not to lose his position at the university, but I'm even more surprised by his sensitivity and, in some ways, his control over each and every situation.

"So, you asked me before why I became a teacher or how I got to where I am today."

"Yes," I say.

"Well, to be honest, I wasn't certain what I wanted to do after grad school until Professor Gilford read a research paper of mine and asked me to come and essentially be his apprentice, but please don't repeat that. No one is supposed to know he will probably be retiring in the next few years, earlier than planned."

"That actually makes sense. And I think you'll do wonderful, following in his place."

"What makes sense?"

"It makes sense why he has given you carte blanche to create a new curriculum. He wants you to make your mark at the school. That way, it will be easier for him to justify when he announces he's going to retire."

He gives me a quizzical stare and then smiles. "Nothing gets past you, does it?"

"I've had to be savvy and resourceful. I started working when I was twelve, and I had to catch on to the ways of the world a bit sooner than others my age."

"I didn't know you started working so young."

"Yes, my mother had me in modeling early on. In hindsight, probably too early."

"I'm guessing you didn't need the money." He chuckles.

"True. But it almost made my family question everyone's intention. Did the agents want me or my parents to invest our money in whatever fame they were trying to sell us? Simply because my parents had money doesn't mean I couldn't be taken advantage of."

"I suppose that is true."

"In fact, money can do the opposite. You'd expect to have a sense of freedom by having money, but in many ways, I watched my father constantly second-guess his friends, business partners, and people coming in and out of his life. He kept his guard up a lot, and it taught me to do the same."

"I can already see a difference in you in such a short time. You seem more relaxed than when I first met you."

"Really? How so?"

"You're much more content than I expected you to be. You don't seem like you are missing out on modeling, parties, the face-paced life you've describe to me."

Oh, Adam, you have no idea what I've gone through. The only reason I'm comfortable is because I am hidden in plain sight. Despite only knowing you for a few months, you make me feel safe and secluded. You have been the perfect distraction away from the fast-paced freshman life I now fear.

"And I must say it's easier being with you than I thought it would be."

He laughs and squeezes my hand. "Like I said, once I can be myself and away from school, it's much easier."

We come out to a small path and follow it along for about three minutes. Then, we hit the main road he spoke about before. Almost directly across from the road is a small store. On the front, the sign reads Ashton's Country Store.

We cross the street and enter the quaint, simple store. The man behind the counter greets us with a crooked smile.

"Pleasant day for a walk," he says.

I smile and nod.

"Sure is, Ashton," Adam replies.

"Perusing for anything in particular?" he asks.

"I need some tomatoes and an onion."

"Mmm, what are you creating tonight?" I ask.

"I thought I'd make chicken tacos."

"Oh, that sounds great."

"Good."

He grabs the vegetables he needs and another bottle of wine and pays for them as I flip through one of the *People* magazines near the front of the store.

"Ready?" he asks as he approaches.

"Yes I am." I place the magazine back on the rack.

We trek back through the woods and toward the house, which appears equally inviting as we approach the back of it.

"You mind bringing this in while I grab some more wood?" He hands me the bag, and then he bends over and pulls back a large wood top. He pulls out a few pieces of wood and stacks them in his arms.

We go inside and kick off our boots. We take off our jackets and hang them near the front door.

"You're welcome to take a shower while I start the fire," he says.

"That sounds great. I think I will."

"Everything you need is in there."

The bathroom is beautiful. No question this place was professionally designed. The large farm sink is actually made out of reclaimed wood that has been treated and sealed in order to be used as a sink. The floor is heated, which is a wonderful touch, considering most of the house is on the chilly side. The shower is double-sided with showerheads going all the way up and down each side. It's nicely tiled in a dark marble stone.

I step in and turn on the showerheads on one side. Then, as the water warms up, I turn on the others, allowing my body to be drenched equally on the front and back. I tuck my head under and relish the water running over me. I rub my face and start to turn to let it run down my hair.

"Aren't you glad there is room for two in here?"

I nearly jump. "You scared me."

"Who did you think it would be?"

"You know what I mean," I say with a smile as he steps into his side.

I watch the water run over his head, arms, and chest.

"Soap?" he says as he hands me a bottle of body wash.

I go to take it, but instead, he grabs a sponge off the shelf and pours the soap into it.

He squeezes the sponge, bringing the suds to life. "Turn around."

I do as I am told and turn. I can hear him slightly whistle, and I know he is eyeing me up and down. He starts to wash my shoulders, slowly at first, running the sponge back and forth. He draws my wet hair to the side and begins kissing me on the ear and neck, licking the water as it runs down my skin. As he gets closer to me, he moves the sponge down my back and over my buttocks.

He groans deep within his throat. "You have a spectacular ass."

I smile to myself.

He pushes forward and presses himself against me. I know that he wants me, and I want him equally as bad. He drops the sponge, and with his hands free, he runs them up and down my body, gently cupping my breasts.

"You're not going to make me wait this time, are you?"

"I don't think I can wait," he says as he steps one foot in between my legs, spreading them.

"Good," I whisper.

"What?" he says.

I know he heard me but wants me to say it again.

"Good," I say. "Don't make me wait."

And, before I can say anything else, we become one as he pushes inside me. He holds on tight to me, and I relish the sounds of his quick, heated moans. I tip my head back and let the water overcome me. I secretly thank him for making a shower that fits two.

After a memorable shower and a delicious meal, we play Scrabble by the fire while we drink a nice bottle of red he bought at the store.

"This has been an incredible weekend."

"Yes, it has. I'm glad you invited me." I smile warmly at him.

"I hope you'll come again."

"I'd like to."

"Good. But please understand that I…we need to keep the two parts of us separate. We can be completely different here than at the university."

"I know and understand."

"So, where will you tell all your friends you were this weekend?" he asks.

"At a job."

"Oh, what for?" he asks with a grin.

"A photographer wanted to use me as a model in his exhibit."

"What if they want to attend the exhibit?"

"They won't."

"Why not?"

"No one cares that I model. Most people assume it's a pretentious industry, which I suppose it has to be."

He shakes his head.

"What? You don't? Really?"

"Why would I?"

"I don't know. Most people—"

"I'm not most people. At least," he says as he comes over to me, "I'd like to think I'm not like most people."

I swallow hard as he leans down toward me. His face is only inches from mine. I want to speak, but his body so close to mine leaves me without words. He touches my face with his hand, and I get that familiar tingle all over my body.

"I wish this weekend wasn't coming to an end," I say breathlessly.

"It's not over yet." He takes my hand and pulls me up. "Let's spend what time we have left like this."

He leans in and softly kisses me. When he pulls back, I open my eyes to him giving me a suggestive and welcoming grin.

Oh my, if only a weekend were longer.

With a soft and full heart, I park my car in the student parking lot after leaving Adam's house. I'm floating on a cloud as I pull open the door to my dormitory with my bag slung over my shoulder. I glance to the right. The lounge is packed with students, which is unusual for a Sunday evening. Normally, I'd be on my way, but I recognize Jen and Casey and decide to go in and get an understanding of what is going on.

As I enter the room. All the dorm monitors from each floor are standing in the front of the room. The head monitor, Cameron, is addressing everyone. He appears serious.

"What's going on?" I whisper to Jen as I stand next to her and Casey.

I notice Laura, Abigail, Maddie, and Melissa are across the room. Laura waves slightly to me as we lock eyes.

"Where have you been? So much going on. Someone stole the master keys to a few of the floors," Jen whispers back with wide eyes.

Now, it's my turn for my eyes to grow wide. I turn to listen to Cameron.

"So, we are taking every precaution with security tonight."

Everyone starts to grumble.

"So, no one will be let in who is not a resident in this dormitory."

The guys in the room start to get rowdy.

One dude growls, "But my girlfriend is coming over tonight."

"Not tonight, guys. Sorry, we have to make sure the residents of this building are safe and secure."

"What the hell? Are we freaking prisoners?" another kid barks.

"Listen," Cameron says in a cool tone, "you are free to go to other dorms, but no guests here tonight. Understood?"

"When will the issue be resolved?" a girl asks.

"We will notify all of you once the locks are changed, and the situation is secure."

"What about the floors not affected?" a tall guy in the back asks.

Brittney, my floor dorm monitor, speaks up, "Everyone, we have to make certain that whoever took the keys does not have a chance to use them. We need to lock down the building, starting now, and make sure that nothing gets stolen or vandalized further."

"Vandalized further?" a girl asks, her voice shaking slightly.

"Yes, please understand that the only thing we are aware of currently is the lockbox with all the master keys. It was broken into, we presume, at some point on Saturday evening. We did not discover this until this morning, however."

"Now, please," Cameron adds, "know that the DMs will be on duty all night, and we have notified campus police. They will be doing perimeter checks all evening."

"What the hell, Jen?" I whisper.

"Seriously, what the heck is wrong with people? Are they that desperate to steal our stuff?" she whispers back.

"Makes me a little nervous," Casey says as she leans in toward us.

"Yeah, sucks for you guys," this dark-haired kid standing in front of us replies over his shoulder.

"How so?" Jen quips back with a bit of an edge.

"I heard from my DM that they only stole the keys for the women's floors."

Only the keys to the women's floors were taken?

My heart skips a beat and then begins pounding obnoxiously.

What if he stole the keys and plans to now terrorize the dormitories?

Oh, Jesus Christ. How am I going to sleep tonight, knowing that he possibly has a key to my room?

"Now, we are asking that you all head up to your floors and meet individually with your dorm monitors for a brief floor meeting. Again, we thank you all for your cooperation," Cameron says with authority. He leads the way out of the lounge area and to the floors.

Everyone is waiting for the elevator, so Jen, Casey, and I decide to take the stairs to our floor. Once we get to the sixth floor, we wait in the common area in front of the bathroom that divides the two wings. The elevator opens, and Maddie, Abigail, Laura, and Melissa step out with Brittney.

Laura gives me a concerned expression. I return a questioning face.

She tries to mouth something to me, but then Brittney starts to talk, "So girls, please let me know if you need anything from me. I have the later shift this evening, but I'll be in my room until then, should you need anything else. I'll be watching this floor. Trust me, okay? Any questions?"

"Thanks, Brittney," Abigail says sweetly.

"Yeah, thank you," we all chime in like lemmings.

But little do they all know that I have a hundred questions. *Do any of the DMs know the girlfriend of the guy terrorizing this campus who lives in our dorm? Or are any of them as afraid as I am? Anyone else wish they had a roommate right about now?*

"Okay then, ladies, you know where to find me if you need me." Brittney gives us all one last glance and then turns and enters her room.

Laura approaches me. "Hey, you okay?"

It's as though I'm translucent to her.

"Yeah, why?" I swallow hard. I have difficulty meeting her eyes.

"I knocked on your door Saturday night, and you never answered."

"I was away."

"Saturday night? You sure?" She gives me a concerned stare.

"Um, yes, positive. I was at a modeling job," I lie.

"Oh, huh. Maybe I am hallucinating, but we got home from a party, and I thought your light was on."

"Huh, no idea," I reply as we head down the hall toward our rooms.

I check my door handle, and it's locked. I put my key in, open my door, and switch on the light. As I peer in, nothing seems touched.

"I've had a long weekend. I'll talk to you guys in the morning."

"Okay. You know where to find us if you need us," Laura says with gloomy eyes before heading down the hallway.

I close the door and lock it.

After the fantastic weekend I had, I was not expecting to come home to all this dormitory chaos.

I drop my bag on my bed and then sit down. I press play on my answering machine. There is a call from my mother about a magazine that one of my ads was in. Another message is from Mallory about our project that is due soon; it's nothing bad, but she wants us all to meet on Tuesday in the library. Then, the final message plays. I lean in, trying to listen to the speech. I hear deep breathing into the phone.

Then, quickly, a voice whispers, "Bitch, stay away from him."

The voice and tenor make my skin crawl.

I reach over and hit the Delete All button on my answering machine. A chill runs up my spine. They must have had the wrong number; they had to. No one knows I'm even dating anyone. Adam and I are extremely careful; this, I am certain of.

Regardless of a call to the wrong number, I approach my window and draw the blinds, hoping that no one is watching. For effect, I drag my desk in front of my door.

It can't hurt, I presume.

I start to undress when it occurs to me that I might not be alone. So, hastily, I sweep through my room, despite the icy feel that has settled in my spine. I check under my bed and look into my closet. I stop and have to laugh to myself because I know there is no place to hide in here. It is virtually an open room with a shallow closet. Not exactly the place to sneak up on someone.

I grab the water bottle next to my bed and drink the remainder of the lukewarm water. It tastes funny, but it has been sitting there for a few days.

I start to dress, pulling my pajamas out from my drawer, when I abruptly freeze. Something does not feel right. Not right at all.

I turn and sense that perhaps a few items on my dresser have been disturbed, moved from their places. Normally, I'd say I wasn't an anal person, but Claudia taught me to be respectful to what I had and to make sure that I kept an orderly and neat room. With heavy hands, I reach over to my dresser and touch a few items that are not in their usual places.

My mind starts to question my emotions. *I've been gone for a few nights. Maybe I don't remember exactly where I put them?*

Not likely, I ponder as my fingers stroke my makeup brushes that are touching my powder makeup. I kept them in my drawer, only they are now sitting on my dresser. I know this because all the makeup I'm currently wearing is still in the bag I brought to Adam's house.

I turn to reach for the phone, but speedily, I realize that, if I report this, I'll have to tell the DMs and the police about what happened to me. They will want to know why, I believe, the guy that attacked me on my first night of college, has come back to terrorize me in my dorm. The attack will become public knowledge. I am not prepared to do that…tonight. I need a little more time.

I stop moving again. My breathing is rapid.

I assess my room and recognize that the picture I had pinned to the mirror's edge is gone. It was a photo of my grandmother on the beach, holding my mother as a child. I've always loved it for some reason.

Maybe it fell behind the dresser, I think.

It is heavy as I attempt to wedge myself in between the bed and dresser to get a better look. I try pushing it, but it is too substantial for me to move. I have to steady myself on the dresser. My mind feels woozy and foggy. I carry my body with heavy feet over to my bed. One step at a time, and I am slowly making my way. My pillow, albeit it's blurry, is only inches from me now as I draw near.

I want to reach for my phone to call Adam or Laura or someone to tell them that I am feeling funny right now about a lot of things, but more so, I feel incredibly tired.

I reach my bed and collapse down on the cushiony mattress. I tip my head back as the darkness washes over me.

For as long as I live, I will never forget this weekend. Or what I can remember about it…

I wake up, feeling groggy and confused. I can hear the girls in the hallway talking as I push my desk away from the door. I pull the door open.

"Survive the night?" I hear Melissa say as I look past the door.

All the girls are sitting on the floor, sipping their coffee, dressed and ready for a full day of classes.

"Yes, I suppose I did," I remark with a harsh tone. My mouth feels dry, and I taste metallic.

I glance over and notice Laura sitting there, eager to start the day.

She glances at her watch and then looks at me with a pained expression. Again, she asks me, "You okay?"

I glance over at the clock on the wall and note the time. It's a quarter till nine and late for me on a Monday.

"Yeah, fine. Needed to sleep in," I reply as I close my door. As I do, I stumble back toward my desk chair.

I steady myself as I sit down and quietly reminisce about the fabulous few days I had with Adam. Then, hurriedly, the last twelve hours of unnerving solitude come crashing around me.

Will I ever find true happiness in my life? I can't help but wonder this as I seek to pull together the puzzle of the weekend, one piece at a time.

I hear a faint knock on my door.

"Come in," I say with a scratchy voice.

Laura peeks her head around the edge of the door. "Got a second?"

"Yeah, come in. Close the door," I respond.

She comes in and sits in the other desk chair. "Thought I'd let you know that they have camera footage of the person who stole the keys."

My heart thumps loudly. "Really?" I'm barely able to choke out my words.

"Yeah, unfortunately, she had her hood pulled tight—"

"She?"

"Yeah, they said it was definitely a female. They could tell by her build. But they were unable to make out her face."

"Holy shit, a girl? But why?"

"Not sure. Probably wanted to steal clothes, bags—you know, items like that."

"Jesus, she a resident here?"

"They can't say for certain, but they figure, with the way she ran out of here, most likely not. She would be better off going back to her room and not running out and risking getting caught with any items. As an extra precaution, until all the locks are changed, they are keeping both front doors locked all day and night."

"That makes sense. So, what kinds of things was she seen leaving with?"

"Nothing that they could say. But I heard from one of the girls who dates one of the DMs that she stole a camera. Or at least they saw one in her hand."

"Camera? All this for a freaking camera?"

"Weird, right?"

I stare off across the room and think about how peculiar I felt last night.

"You okay, Bree? You seem off or something."

"Yeah, its that last night really freaked me out. You know, the mind starts playing tricks on you."

"Totally. When Abigail and I got back to the room, we started asking each other if we'd moved this or that. It was a total mind-screw, if you ask me."

"Right? Good, 'cause I did the same. I swear, my makeup was put away before I left, and I lost a picture somewhere. No clue where it's at." With my head in my hands, I add, "Then, I felt drowsy. You know, like, just exhausted," I say this almost as a question to myself.

"Really? You okay?"

"Yeah. You know, so much stress. I'm sure I was merely drained from the long weekend I had. Being in my own room and my own bed made me tired. I'm still not feeling one hundred percent."

"Yeah, I can tell. Well, I hope you're not getting sick before the holidays. That would totally suck."

"Yeah, right? I've probably been wearing myself down."

"I think we are all a little worn-out at this point, right? I can't wait for the semester to be over."

"Yeah, me, too. You working at the station over break?"

"Yeah, I'm coming back early to work. It will be quiet around here, but the radio station never truly gets a holiday." She smiles wide at me.

"Very true. Thanks for checking in on me. I'd better hurry and get dressed, so I'm not late for class."

"Lunch? Usual time."

"Sounds good. See you then."

She approaches my door and starts to open it.

"Hey, Laura?"

"Yeah?"

"Thanks for filling me in. I appreciate it."

"Of course. I'm guessing you're as relieved as we are that the weekend is over."

I smile at her as she walks out and think, *In some ways, I am. In other ways, I'd love to do it all over again.*

Fifteen

WINTER BREAK

I'm rereading the last line of a chapter in my textbook, only to realize that I have no idea what the chapter was about. I twirl a strand of my hair through my fingers and stare out across the campus.

Where is my mind? Back in the cabin last weekend.

My heartbeat deepens as my blood courses through my veins. I imagine Adam starting a fire. Then, he is standing before me, shirtless, as he reaches up and runs his fingers through my long hair. I welcome the warmth of the flames as they burn brighter.

"Bree, you okay?" Jen brings me out of my haze.

"What?"

"She asked if you are okay?" Casey interjects. "You've been staring out the window."

"Sorry. Yeah, totally fine. What do you say we get out of here? I'm not getting anything else done tonight."

"Me neither."

"Sounds good to me," Casey adds.

We leave the library and wander back to our dorm. I haven't seen Adam in what feels like forever, and I'm anxious to spend time with him before I leave for the holidays in four days.

I meander back with them and up to my room.

"Good night, guys. Talk to you tomorrow."

I enter my room and pick up my phone to call him.

"Hello?"

"Hey, it's me."

"Can I see you?" he asks.

I'm so thankful that he asked.

"Yes, I'll be over soon."

"I look forward to it."

I grab my bag and keys and quietly exit my room, hoping not to run into any of my floor mates. I make it out of the dorm without seeing anyone. I hurry to my car. I can't help when the fear of being alone on campus rushes back in. I wish it weren't like this, but for now, it is. I wonder to myself if and when I'll ever be safe here.

My heart flutters as I turn down his road and park in front of his house. He opens the door before I even have a chance to knock.

"Finally," he says with suggestive eyes.

"Oh, did I keep *you* waiting?" I say, returning an equally racy smile.

He closes the door. Then, he grabs me around the waist and pulls me in. "Yes, as a matter of fact, you did," he says.

He leans in and kisses me deeply. My knees get weaker as his tongue enters my mouth, and he starts to moan. I know, in this moment, that he has missed me as much as I have missed him. No words need to be spoken as he pulls apart from me and starts to guide up the stairs and to his room, gently pulling me along by my hand. I gladly follow him.

Once in his room, he turns to me and pushes my hair back. "Take off your jacket."

I take it off and drop it on the floor.

"Take off your shirt."

I do the same and toss it on the chair. Before he can ask me, I unbutton my jeans and slowly wiggle out of them. He is watching my every move, and I can tell, as he stands there, he is enjoying watching me. Lucky for him, I'm so used to being naked, in and out of clothes at photo shoot after photo shoot that I've actually learned to appreciate my body.

But, now, he's making me feel shy. He stands there, eyeing me. Then, he rubs his hand over his own face.

"Say something, please."

Only he doesn't. He traces his fingertips down my upper body, lightly touching my breast. I can hear his breath catch. I draw my head slightly back as merely his hand on my body, anywhere on my body, feels sensational. It seems so crazy, but he has this thing over me that I never thought I'd be able to have with anyone.

I aim to move my hand to his shirt to unbutton it, but he grabs my hand instead.

"I want to enjoy you for a moment."

I'm used to being the center of attention, but this is different. He is taking his time in appreciating me and treating me like I matter.

"Bree," he whispers as he strokes my shoulder with his lips.

His breath on me sends goose bumps up and down my skin.

"Uh-huh?"

"Will you stay with me?"

"I was planning to," I whisper back.

"No," he says as he kisses my neck, allowing his hand to drop down to my hip. "For the winter break."

I immediately step back and study him. His expression is serious.

"What do you mean?" I say as I bend down and pick up my shirt. I slip it on.

"Hey, what are you doing?" he asks playfully.

"What am I doing? What did you ask me?"

"To stay with me over the break."

I swallow hard. I can't believe he is asking me to stay with him. It seems so early in our relationship.

"But I can't live in the dorm then. It's too late to request—"

"I know. I want you to stay with me. At the cabin."

This is crazy. *How can I possibly stay with him? What will I tell my parents and my friends?* My head is spinning.

"You mean, while you stay here?"

He steps closer to me. "No, I'm planning on being there with you, silly."

"Don't make fun of me," I bark only because I'm nervous.

"Bree, I don't want you to go. It's a long time, and I'd like to keep what you and I have going. To get to know you even more."

"And, if I can't stay, then what?"

He avoids my question by saying, "I totally understand, considering the circumstances, if you think it's too sudden to tell your parents about us. I don't want to encourage you to lie to them. But maybe you could say you were staying to work for the school? And you'd be spending the time working on the curriculum project—which, by the way, we should be working on—so technically, it's not a fib."

To say my mind is racing with all kinds of thoughts would be a massive understatement. I'm having a plethora of emotions, however one is stronger than the others. Conflicting fear. Fear of being without him, fear of being with him, fear of falling way too fast for someone that I know, deep down inside, should be a forbidden lover. He could lose his job if the school ever found out about us.

Yet, here I stand, half-naked in his bedroom, and he is asking me, after only a month of being together, to stay with him in an out-of-the-way cabin in the woods, away from civilization, away from everyone.

And something inside me is saying, *Yes.*

I pack all my belongings in my suitcases and leave them by my door. Then, I wander down the hall.

"Knock, knock. It's me," I say as I push open Laura and Abigail's door. "Come in!"

"I wanted to say merry Christmas and happy New Year."

"You, too," Laura says as she gives me a warm hug.

"Yes, have a wonderful break," Abigail says in a cheery voice.

"I will. I'm excited to go home, get some rest, and get ready for next semester."

"When are you leaving?" Laura asks.

"I should be going now. It's a long ride, and I want to get on the road."

"Me, too. My parents should be here any minute." Laura adds.

"Abigail, you leaving today?"

"No, got a flight out of here tomorrow. Going to Florida to spend time with my grandmother."

"Sounds wonderful. Well, ladies, the Hamptons are calling me. Gotta run!"

I grab my bags from my room and lock it up. I say good-bye to Melissa, Jen, and Casey, who are all hanging out in Melissa's room.

"See you girls next year," I say with a wink as I drag my suitcase and bags to the elevator.

I struggle with them through the crowd of students waiting in the lobby for their parents to arrive. I maneuver through the snow and to my car, which, unfortunately for me, is buried by the recent snowfall.

I sit in it for a few minutes and let it warm as the blades scrape across the windshield while the heat blasts it, trying to melt the ice.

Suddenly, I hear a knock on my car window. It startles me. Then, I notice Jason peering in the window. I roll it down.

"Sweet ride. Fancy."

"Thanks, Jason."

"Got a car brush or scraper or anything?"

"Yeah, in the back."

"Were you waiting for me to come along?" he says with a smirk.

"Funny, but no. I was just warming up."

"Allow me then." He opens the back and gets out the scraper. Then, he works his way around my car.

It's not that I mind. It's nice actually and probably much safer than pulling out and driving with a car covered in snow and ice.

"Thanks, Jason," I say as he hands me the scraper.

"You're welcome, Bree," he says with a wink.

"Okay, great. Well, I've gotta run. Have a great Christmas."

He's not moving, and then it dawns on me that, the last time I saw him, we might have been seriously lip-locked, only I don't remember.

"Good to see you," he says with a slight laugh.

My cheeks blush. "You, too."

"Okay then, I'll definitely catch up with you when you get back."

"Okay," I respond, my eyes narrowing at him. I'm not one hundred percent certain what he's getting at, but regardless, it's time for me to leave. I start to roll up the window, and I watch as he jogs away.

I aim to shake off any thoughts of Jason when I have Adam to fantasize about. I remember every detail of our days and nights together, every single one, and that tells me something in itself.

I can't help but smile wide as I pull into his driveway and observe him standing on the front porch of the cabin. He returns an equally sly smile, and my heart skips a beat. He is wearing a red flannel shirt and dark jeans. His hair is perfectly messy, and he has his glasses on. I never, ever thought I'd be so attracted to a man in glasses, but they absolutely suit him. He doesn't need them to make him appear smarter because I know how intelligent he is, but my God, do they make him look sexy and distinguished.

He comes down the stairs to greet me. I climb out of my car, and before I can say a word, he wraps his arms around me and pulls me in for a long kiss. I fear the heat that is coming off my body might melt the snow I'm standing upon.

"Hi," he says, his voice husky and low.

"Hi back."

"Let me get your bags."

I open the back, and he grabs my suitcase and messenger bag. I enter into the house already warm thanks to the roaring fire.

"Make yourself comfortable," he says as he brings my bags into the bedroom.

I take off my jacket and boots and drop my purse at the door. I'm not eager to unpack; it makes me too nervous to be a live-in girl or whatever just yet. I still consider myself a guest and probably should keep it that way. Instead, I take a seat on the couch.

He comes back out from the bedroom and over to me. He sits next to me and wraps his arm around me.

"To winter break," he says with a devilish smile as he pulls me in and kisses me on the cheek.

"To getting our curriculum done, right?" I laugh. "Isn't that why I'm here?"

"To getting it done." He smiles in response.

"So, I believe I aced all my exams."

"Good for you. I'm sure you did. We'll get to work on our outline tomorrow. Supposed to get a storm tonight, so I thought tomorrow would be a good day to work."

"That sounds good. Besides, I was wondering, if we get it done sooner, maybe we could take off in a few weeks and go skiing?"

"How do you know if I can even ski?"

"Even if you can't, an athletic guy like yourself could at least try to keep up with me." I smirk.

"That's true," he says as he reaches over and gives me a squeeze.

Suddenly, the old phone on the wall rings loudly and startles us both. He crosses the room and takes the receiver off the phone.

"Hello?" There is a long pause, and then he says again, "Hello? Who is this?"

His tone is not friendly, and something about the way he stares makes me tense. I start to get up, but he gestures for me to stay seated. Then, he places the receiver back down.

"Who was—"

"There was no one there. Obviously, it was a wrong number."

"Oh, I see."

He comes back over and sits down next to me where he pulls me back in again. He sighs. A few moments pass between us.

I need to lighten the atmosphere, so I say, "So, what's for dinner tonight?" I peer toward the kitchen and smile.

"Oh, boy, have I spoiled you already?" He chuckles.

"No, not nearly enough."

"I bet. A girl like you is already spoiled rotten."

I smile wide. I can't hold my amusement inside. "Like my father always says, you don't have to like the money; you just have to understand it comes with the territory."

"Is that so?"

I love when my comments amuse him. It makes me laugh.

"Yes."

"He sounds like a smart man."

"He sure is." I beam.

"Must be. He's got you for a daughter," he says softly.

"Is that a compliment?" My cheeks pink slightly.

"Yes. Now, have I mentioned how glad I am that you decided to come?"

"No. How glad are you?" I raise my eyebrows at him.

He takes off his glasses and tosses them on the side table. He leans into me and says in a sultry tone, "Let me show you."

Oh my.

He asks me to follow him. He has a better route back than I remember. Then, he tells me to go in front of him. As I turn to look at him, I can hear him laugh. Then, without warning, he pushes me back onto the bed. I suddenly feel the urge to fight, to push him off of me, but I can't. He's holding down my arms. I try to scream, but nothing comes out. He tries to kiss me, but I move my head from side to side, violently trying to free myself. Then, suddenly, my arms are free. I can push and—

"Bree, Bree, wake up. You're having a bad dream…again," he whispers. Then, nothing.

"What? What?" I whisper back.

Adam is leaning over me, pulling slightly on my shoulders. "What's wrong? Are you okay, Bree?"

"Yes," I whisper as I turn on my side. "I had a bad dream."

I face the wall and begin breathing loudly, so he'll assume I've gone back to sleep, but really, I'm staring at the blank wall across from me, praying to God he won't realize that I'm wide awake and drenched in sweat.

Will these nightmares ever go away?

"How about I make you lunch today?"

He peeks up from the table, his hair unusually messy with at least a week's worth of scruff on his face. Yet, still, he is beautiful, as always.

"Sounds good."

We've been in the cabin for eight straight days now, and surprisingly, I am even more comfortable and at home than I was on day one. At least, for me, it seems to be getting easier than harder.

"Did I tell you that, if we can get this all passed by Gilford by the end of January, I might have an opportunity to meet with some professors from other universities at a conference in February?"

"How exciting!"

"Yes, it could be a great way to test the waters on this project," he says.

"Do you talk about what you're working on with your parents?" I ask. "Do they know what you're doing here at the university?"

"Absolutely. Yours?"

"Yes, they do."

I aspire to call home at least every other day. I plan to leave tomorrow to meet my parents in New York City for Christmas, but I told them I wanted to be back at school for New Year's Eve. They totally understood and think I'm coming back to some huge crowd of freshmen students, like me, to work away our winter break or get ready to let loose for the New Year. But, really, I want to come back to the cabin and ring in the New Year with Adam.

Adam, on the other hand, plans to leave tomorrow or the next day and go back to his house near campus for Christmas. His parents, aunt, and uncle plan to meet him there for the holiday. According to Adam, I'm not the only one who enjoys his cooking.

I make nothing special, a simple turkey sandwich. We are running out of food at the moment, but I plan to surprise him when I get back with groceries from this gourmet market place Claudia raves about in the city.

As I turn to put the sandwich down, I notice him yawn and stretch backward. He seems tired.

"Have you been sleeping okay?"

I know why he might not be sleeping all too soundly. It's because of me.

"Um, yeah. I mean, okay. You?"

"Me?" I attempt to play off his question.

"No, the other girl I'm lying next to each night," he says as he lowers his eyes. It's not what he says but how he can't meet my eyes that gives me pause.

Has this gotten to be too much for him? I wonder. *Is he regretting having me stay here?* I want to ask him, but I'm afraid of the answer.

"I've been sleeping fine."

He whips his head up. He seems like he wants to say something, but he doesn't. I can sense him watching me as I sit down across from him. I want to give him an opportunity to talk, to say what is on his mind.

Instead, he says, "Good sandwich."

"It's not an Adam sandwich, but I can actually make a few things for myself," I lie.

Who am I kidding? I've spent most of my nearly-nineteen years eating out at fine restaurants or having someone cook for me. It's a luxury that has left me with little culinary skills.

He simply smiles.

After several more hours of work on our outline, we are both exhausted and decide to call it quits. I rarely take the lead on this project even though we are constructing it off my ideas. At this point and after several days of conversation, Adam is much better versed in how we need to execute this in order to set him up for success to eventually take over for Professor Gilford.

"I'm going to take a shower," I announce.

"Sounds good. I'm going to start a fire."

During the day, we have decided to dress warmer and leave the curtains open to let the sun in and to conserve heat. I can honestly say, I've never conserved anything, let alone actual heat.

He stands as I gather our papers and books, and I put them away. Then, I stroll into the bedroom, undress quickly due to the coolness in the air, and get into the hot shower. I take my time, washing my hair and shaving my legs, feeling on top of the world. It's an emotion one might assume I've been afforded throughout my life, but I have not.

Once I'm done, I dress in a tight tank top, tights, and a sweater. When I enter back into the living room, he is finishing poking the fire and adding one last log.

"I poured you a glass of wine. I'm gonna grab a quick shower myself."

"Don't shave the scruff," I say with a wink.

For the first time since I've met him, he seems bashful as he rubs his face and says, "Really? You like it?"

"Of course I do."

"I'll be even quicker then."

I pick up my glass of wine and curl up on my spot on the couch. I love the fact that Adam seems to get me. I don't want to chug beer at fraternity parties all weekend. I want to enjoy a glass of wine, maybe two. But, still, it's much more sophisticated than guzzling some cheap Natty Light for four hours straight and then stumbling home.

Sure, I'm underage, but it's college, and it sort of goes with the territory.

The phone rings, interrupting my gentle thoughts. Since Adam is in the shower, I figure I should at least answer it, or it will ring and ring like it did the other night. Adam said they get a lot of wrong numbers at the cabin, and since they don't have an answering machine, it can be very disruptive to the otherwise welcome silence the cabin almost guarantees. I hurry over and pick it up.

I am going to hang up when I hear a female voice say, "Hello?"

"Yes, hello?" I answer.

Then, nothing. Just silence, and then the line goes dead.

"Huh. Weird," I say. I go back to the couch and curl back up in my spot.

Within five minutes, I catch him come out from behind the fireplace, wearing nothing but a pair of dark gray sweatpants. His chest is bare, but his face is still beautifully outlined by his beard. I want to lick my lips for effect, but fear it might be too forward.

"Hey," he says in a morose tone.

"What is it?"

"Nothing. Well, maybe I was just thinking about you being gone tomorrow."

"Really?"

"Yeah," he says as he pokes the fire.

"I plan to come back."

"I hope so."

"Of course," I say as I reach out my hand for him to come near me.

He does, and as he draws near, I can smell the soap on his skin. He leans in and kisses me. I slide my fingers through his thick hair and keep his lips on mine. I kiss him. I really kiss him, letting him know that I will, undeniably, be back.

He straightens back up and smiles as I reluctantly release my fingers from his curls.

"I thought I'd ask you to help me with dinner tonight."

"Oh God, of course. What can I make?"

"No, what I meant was I thought I'd ask you to *help* me."

"Oh, like your assistant?"

"Something like that. They usually call them a sous chef."

I uncurl myself off the couch. I follow him the few steps past the farm table and to the island in the kitchen.

"Come on this side," he instructs, pointing me to the same side he is on.

I do as I was told and come around to stand next to him.

"So, tonight, we are making pizza."

"Pizza?"

"What? You don't like pizza?"

"No, actually, I love pizza. Who doesn't, really?"

"Precisely. So, we are going to make thin pizza. They cook fast and are delicious."

He's thought of everything ahead of time, and somehow, he did it without me knowing it. The dough is ready to be rolled, the tomatoes crushed and seasoned, and the cheese is shredded.

"But how? When did you do all of this?" I ask as I pick up a piece of tomato and pop it into my mouth.

"Oh, you'd be surprised what I can get done when no one is watching."

I am too thrilled with making my own pizza to ask any more questions. I don't want to ruin the fun with inquiries.

"Are we cooking them in the oven? I should turn—"

His eyes light up. "No, on the fire."

"Seriously?"

He continues to surprise me.

"Absolutely."

"But how?" I ask, glancing over at the open flames as they crackle and pop.

He approaches the fire, grabs another log, and puts it on. He also takes what appears to be a grill grate, but with legs, and puts it directly over the fire. He comes back over, and takes both the pizzas we've made on the metal pan.

Then, he turns to me. "Ready?"

"For what, I'm not exactly sure, but yes." I follow him over to the fireplace.

He places the pan directly on the grate. "Grab that metal spatula and watch your pizza bake."

We both sit in front of the fire and watch as the thin dough rises and the cheese bubbles to perfection. He pulls them off in about eight to ten minutes, cuts them on the island, and then brings flawlessly cut pizza back to me on a plate.

We sit in front of the fire and eat every last piece of pizza with pure satisfaction.

"I'm not a bad sous chef, am I?" I ask.

"Ha. Actually, you are pretty good."

"I'm kidding. This one is all you." I laugh.

"You liked it?"

"Loved it."

For some reason, even though I'm only talking about the food, saying the word *love* in any form around him stops us both in our tracks.

He gazes into my eyes, so I swiftly add, "Awesome job, chef."

Unpredictably, he says, "Before we clean up, come here for a minute."

I lean into him in front of the fire, and he eagerly pulls me toward him. He holds me tightly with much more emphasis than he has before, like he truly doesn't want this moment to end, and neither do I. I can't find the words in my brain to tell him as such. I keep telling myself it's too soon to feel this way. I've been too fortunate my whole life for this to actually be true.

He pulls me out of my thoughts as he kisses me on top of the head. "In case I forget to tell you tomorrow, Bree, I hope you have a merry Christmas. More importantly, I hope you get everything you need."

I note he didn't say *want*. He said *need*.

He hopes I get everything I need.

What I need is to forget my pain. What I need is to believe it never happened. What I need is to continue to feel the way I'm feeling now and not the way I felt in September or October or November. What I need is for all of that to go away.

But what I *want* is him.

Sixteen

GLAD I CHOSE...

Like most holidays, Christmas flies by. The next thing I know, it's December 31, and I'm pulling back into Adam's driveway. I park the car and get out. My heart quickens as I approach the porch and open the door.

I don't bother to knock as I'm balancing grocery bags in my arms.

When I enter the cabin, I can't believe this is the same place. The living room is decorated with holiday garland and wreaths. White candles are lit throughout the house, and music is playing softly in the background.

"Hello?" I drop the bags on the island in the kitchen. "Adam?"

He comes from around the fireplace. "Finally," he says with a killer grin. "Like it?" He motions around to the house.

It reminds me of a set from a movie in which the house is so beautifully decorated that it had to take professionals days just to stage it. But, somehow, he pulled it off. Beautiful wreaths hang on all the interior doors with silver bows. The mantel above the fireplace has beautiful green garland wrapped around white pillar candles. Two large red floor pillows rest in front of the fire, and by the way, there is a book and white blanket tossed on one, I'd say he probably took a nap right there. The thought makes me smile.

Right when I thought he could not make this cabin more warm and welcoming, he has absolutely outdone himself.

I pick up a green candle off the table, and the smell of evergreen catches my nose. I inhale deeper. "It's beautiful. Did you do all of this for me?"

"For us."

"Thank you...from us."

The hum of Dean Martin singing "Blue Christmas" is a welcome sound coming through the speakers.

He comes near me, and I swallow hard as I take a good look at him. His beard is trimmed nicely, and his hair is sheared. The contrast is striking.

"You look wonderful."

"So do you," he says as he brings his hand up to my lips. He gently pulls down on my bottom lip with his thumb.

Oh my.

It's been a week since I've been in his arms. More importantly, it's been a week since I've been in his bed. The way his eyes are dancing all over my body tells me he's not in the mood for a recap of my Christmas. He leaves his hand on the side of my cheek, and without warning, he pulls my face to his and kisses me deeply and hard.

Before I can react at all, he's pulling my jacket off. It drops to the floor. Then, he's unbuttoning my new, expensive silk blouse and letting it fall to the floor. But I don't care.

He tosses his glasses on the island, and with one swift motion, he pulls his T-shirt up and over his back and head, balling it up and letting it fall where it does. He eagerly kisses me again. I longed for his warm lips on mine. Then, he softly draws his teeth over my bottom lip, and I get an excited tingle everywhere.

He starts guiding me backward while he continues to kiss me. He unbuttons my jeans, and I slide out of them as I move with him. He does the same, leaving a trail of clothing into the bedroom. He sits me down on the bed and gets one knee up next to me. He moves me back as he climbs on top of me. I love the weight of him on me, and I moan as I push my hips up toward him. I wrap my legs around his waist and my arms around his beautiful back.

He's breathing heavier now, but he leans up for a brief moment to glance at me. Up on his arms, he takes one hand and softly traces my face, pushing my hair back as he does. I can't help but smile at him.

"What?" he whispers.

"Nothing," I say.

He gazes intently into my eyes. He continues to deliberately move his hips, taking his time to make me wait. I know that he is ready for me.

I want him so badly that I want to scream, *Please, please, don't make me wait.*

But I don't.

Instead, I lean up and kiss him, making it all but impossible to resist me. And, once I reach my hand down his chest and between our legs I know most certainly that he will be unable to resist me. And, with deliberation, he doesn't.

Adam collapses down next to me. His chest is rising and falling fast as he tries to catch his breath. The soft glow of candles casts a silhouette of his body on the wall, and I simply have to sit up and watch him.

I snuggle deep into his neck and breathe in the smell of him. It's intoxicating. I kiss him on the cheek and then get up off the bed.

"Leaving so soon?" he says.

"Stay there. I'll be right back." I head back out toward the kitchen, collecting my clothes and redressing as I go.

"Give me a few minutes, okay?" I yell to him.

"Sure, I'm gonna take a shower."

I hear the water turn on in the shower as I start to unpack the grocery bags. Once all my ingredients are laid out in front of me, I start chopping the onions. I turn to the stove to start cooking the ground beef, and when I turn back around, he's standing there, wearing nothing but his jeans. Just the way I like him to be. He runs his hand through his hair and picks up his glasses off the island.

"What are you doing?" he asks slyly.

"I'm trying to surprise you," I respond with a pout.

He comes around behind me and puts his arms around my waist. "How sweet."

"Are you poking fun at me?" I try not to giggle.

"Quite the opposite. I'm flattered."

"Good, 'cause I'm making a special Mexican dish."

"What makes it so special?" he asks, releasing me.

"Claudia."

"Who's Claudia?"

"My, um, person who, you know, keeps the house. Really has kept me together since my childhood."

"I see." He smiles sincerely.

"You see what?"

"The way you smiled. When you spoke about her, it told me everything I needed to know."

"She is special to me." I reach up and stroke the necklace she gave me.

"She gave you that?"

"Yes, it's an Indalo."

"I know." He smiles.

"Of course you do, smarty-pants."

He chuckles. "What a beautiful thing to give to someone."

"Yes, I'll never take it off."

"Ah, so this is her dish."

"Yes, and it is fantastic."

He opens the cabinet and takes two glasses out.

"Wait, no wine."

"Why exactly?"

"Because," I say as I go to the refrigerator and pull out two beers. "Coronas." I laugh. "You know, to go with our Mexican dinner."

His eyes sparkle. "You've thought of everything, haven't you?"

"It's the least I could do for you for letting me crash at your place."

"Crashing, huh? Is that what you're doing?"

"Yes, and I don't usually crash at people's places."

"You are welcome here anytime."

"Thank you," I say, giving him a genuine smile.

"So, can I help?"

"Yes, you can make a fire."

He smiles wide. "That is definitely something I can do."

As I prepare our meal, I watch him as he moves about the living room with ease—making a fire, lighting candles, humming to the music. I can't help but wonder how I got so lucky, so fast.

Maybe it is too fast, but I don't care.

He takes me out of my thoughts. "Excited to ring in the New Year with me? Hard to believe it is almost 1996."

"Wildly excited," I say with a wicked grin.

"I'm sure I can make it wildly exciting for you."

"Oh, can you?" I grin.

He crosses the room toward me. His chest muscles twitch as he moves swiftly to within arm's reach of me. He stops and smiles. "If I start now, you'll most definitely ruin your dinner, and I don't want that to be your excuse."

I huff out loud. "Wow, that was one big insult. Don't you have any faith in your sous chef?"

He steps closer. "How about one kiss then?"

"Just one?" I reply, my heart beating hard within my chest.

He comes slightly closer. "One," he says almost in a whisper. He leans down, his face close to mine. He repeats, "Just one kiss."

His breath on my skin sends goose bumps up and down my frame.

"I don't know, Adam."

"If you can kiss me?" he asks as he gently caresses his cheek up my neck.

The rough stubble of his beard feels good on my soft skin.

"Yes, just once. I don't know if—" I am about to say, *I can only kiss you once*, when he shuts me up with his lips eagerly pressed hard on mine.

When he pushes his tongue deep into my mouth, I steady myself on the island as I sense my legs want to give out. He grabs me around the waist and leans me back into his arms.

I. Am. In. Heaven.

His kiss is so wonderful that I know in this moment that if 1996 is going to be anything like the last few weeks of 1995, I think I'll be okay after all. He steadies me back up and unwraps himself from me.

I still have my eyes closed when he says, "Don't burn dinner."

I burned dinner—not all of it, just the sauce I had on the stove. But I recovered most of it, and Adam ate everything I put in front of him. Well, most of it.

I laugh a little as he takes a gulp of his beer to wash it down.

"Your fault really," I say.

"I know, but it was worth it."

It sure was.

"Let me clean up, okay?"

"You sure?" he asks.

"Yes, it will only take me a minute, and then we can relax by the fire and ring in the New Year."

I grab the plates and wash them in the sink. It's good to clean up after myself. I've rarely had to do it. I like this independence more, the longer I'm away from the Hamptons. Besides, I have one more surprise for him, so I want him out of the kitchen anyway.

After I finish, I grab a tray from the top of the cabinet, and with my back turned to the living room, I take out a box of the most delicious dark chocolate–dipped strawberries in all of New York State and place them on the tray. My parents have champagne for the holidays, and my father gave me a bottle to ring in the New Year. I gladly took it along with two crystal glasses I'll return to him at a later time.

I turn with the tray in my hands. Adam is resting on one of the pillows on the floor in front of the fire. His long legs are stretched out in front of him, and his perfectly chiseled abs are curved as he leans slightly on his side. He perks up when he sees me stroll toward him.

He smiles. "What's this?"

"My last surprise for 1995."

"Wow, aren't you a beautiful sight?"

My cheeks turn rosy.

He continues, "It's every guy's dream to end the year like this."

"Is that so?"

"Here, let me take that," he says as he reaches up and takes the tray.

He puts it on the floor in front of us, close to the fire. I sit next to him, pour two glasses, and hand one to him.

"It's been fun so far, Bree," he says so sincerely.

It isn't so much what he says that makes my heart flutter; it's the tone and the direct eye contact that leads me to believe he truly means it.

"It has. It's been wonderful," I say bashfully.

We clink glasses and each take a sip.

"Wow, delicious," he says.

I laugh slightly to myself, and he notices.

"What?"

"It should be. It's three hundred dollars a bottle."

He chokes a bit. "Bree."

"Oh God, no. My dad gave it to me."

"Jesus."

"It's fine. That is, unless it makes you uncomfortable?" I've never asked anyone in my life if something expensive made them uncomfortable. It's not how I grew up; it's not who I am. Until now.

"No, well, I don't want you spending your money—"

"But it's okay if my father does?" I can't keep a straight face when I say this.

"Ha-ha, very funny. But he doesn't know you're here. You do. So, he gave it to you to celebrate. It's different."

"Does the money bother you?" I ask. Again, it's something I've never asked anyone.

"No. Why? I mean, Bree, how much money could you possibly be talking about?"

"Do you like chocolate covered strawberries?" By ignoring him, I presume it answers his question.

He gives me quizzical glance. "Yes, why?"

"Good, try these. The berries are the best."

He smiles and shakes his head. He picks up one, and I watch with pleasure as he takes a bite. I know how delicious these are, and a real food-lover like Adam will surely appreciate these.

He finishes the strawberry and then takes another sip of the champagne. "Now," he says as he picks up a strawberry, "your turn."

"Gladly," I say.

I lean in, and he feeds me a mouthwatering berry.

We feed each other almost the entire box of berries and drink most of the champagne.

While eating the last berry, he says, "You have a little chocolate on your lip."

I go to lick my lip when he responds, "Allow me."

And, before I know it, he's pounced on me, pushing me backward on the floor, while still somehow cradling my head, so it doesn't touch the floor. He's on top of me, kissing me deeply, enjoying the remnants of the chocolate on my lips.

His breathing gets harder as he, with nimble fingers, pulls my shirt off again. He unhooks my bra equally as fast and then slides my jeans off, all while still passionately kissing me. I'm now naked, lying on the floor, completely exposed to him. He runs his hands up my thighs to my hips and belly as he traces his mouth down my neck to my breasts, kissing and teasing each one with such delight.

I might erupt right here and now.

"Oh, Adam," I gasp, not even realizing the words are leaking from my lips.

My few words make him work even harder as he moves his lips down my body. As he kisses my belly, my navel, I run my hands through his hair. He hears me moan as he continues to mischievously kiss me in places I've never been kissed before. Then, as though he can't wait anymore, he leans up and unbuttons his jeans, slowly pulling them down, showing me what I believe to be mine…at least mine for now.

"My God," I whisper as the roaring fire starts to heat my body to the point where sweat starts to glisten on my skin.

He smiles a familiar sexy grin, and then with total purpose and intent, he leans back down and slowly gives me a thousand reasons to love the fact that I, Aubrey Van Tousen, chose Onondaga State University.

Seventeen

A NEW SEMESTER OF TORRID AFFAIRS

I've been afforded a lot of wonderful things in my life. So, to say the past four weeks were some of the best days I've ever had should say a lot about the time I spent with Adam in that cabin. Not only did we create what I truly believe will be a revolutionary and advanced curriculum as technology continues to change the way we function and work, but the sheer amount of intellectual and sexual time we spent together will also forever change the person I am. He came into my life when I was at a crossroads. I could have made more mistakes, like I did the night with Jason, or I could have become depressed while I angrily pushed away my friends. But, instead, I found someone that grounded me. I feel safe with Adam. I was able to develop a relationship with him enough to actually become intimate with him. I'm breaking through the darkness and I sense it.

I have spent the past three weeks back in the dorm, balancing my college life, my internship, and my relationship with Adam with flawless execution. He's expecting me to hold it together, and I plan to prove to him that he undoubtedly chose the right girl in all aspects of his life.

I am no longer a student in his class, so I don't worry as much about our relationship. But I'm still an intern in the department, working directly with him. I do have a class with Professor Gilford, however.

But today is a huge day for us. Today, Adam is presenting our plan to the marketing department at the university. Today will tell us if we have hit the mark or not.

I pace in my room all afternoon. Laura stopped by at some point to ask if I wanted to go to lunch, but I told her I couldn't eat. Not today.

I stare out my window, stroking the necklace Claudia gave me. I peek at the clock again. It's three thirty. In fifteen minutes, I can trek back across campus to the Draper building—to my fate and, hopefully, to my future.

Finally, *tick*, it's three forty-five. I grab my bag, which has been ready to go since two, and I exit my dorm and cross university grounds. As I enter the Draper building, the last class for the afternoon session is letting out. I make my way through the students and down the hallway to the offices. There is quite a bit of activity. My heart grows heavy as I notice Adam's office door closed. It's clear the light is on, so I take a seat outside his office. A few students pass me. I recognize one guy from our class. He smiles, and I simply nod in return, too nervous to speak.

It feels like forever, sitting there, waiting for the door to open. This cannot be good. Then, finally, I hear some loud voices, and the door swings open.

Adam comes out, smiling with two other faculty members. I nervously stand.

"Oh, great! Professor Webb, Professor Ty, this is Bree Van Tousen, the student who helped—"

"Oh, yes, wonderful. Well done," Professor Webb says as he reaches out to shake my hand.

"Impressive. I look forward to having you in my class," Professor Ty adds.

They continue to stroll down the hall toward, I assume, their offices.

"Miss Van Tousen," Adam says formally, "please come in."

I enter into his office.

"Have a seat," he says with a grin.

I can tell that he can barely contain his excitement.

He closes the door. "Don't sit," he whispers as he pulls me up and into him. He gives me an incredibly gratifying kiss. "We did it, Bree. We freaking did it!" His smile is electric.

I squeal as he picks me up and swings me around. I'm breathless as he puts me down.

"Oh my God, what did they say? Did they love all of it? Hate the fifth part? They hated the fifth part. I said I needed to make that better, but no—"

"Bree, did you hear me? They loved *all* of it."

"All of it?" I say as I place my hands over my mouth in disbelief.

I've worked hard in my life. School has always been important to me, and it didn't have to be. I'm set to inherit a lot of money when I turn twenty-five. But that never has meant anything to me. I want to work and earn what I have. That's why I started working so young, so I could at least say I'd made an attempt to pull my own weight.

"Yes, all of it."

I throw my arms around his neck and shriek loudly with delight.

"Shh, Bree. We can celebrate later."

I step back. He's right. I have to be careful, particularly on school property.

"I know, I know. Sorry." I release my arms.

"Trust me, we'll revel later. But, for now, go home, and enjoy the weekend."

"It sucks so bad that you won't be here. Our first Valentine's Day."

"I know, but it's only a day."

"I know, believe me. I think it is really cliché, but at least I have some girls to go out and act silly and ridiculous with. You have to go to a conference in Long Island. Ugh, boring."

"Maybe not. I'll engage some old connections of mine from the Marketing Association. Who knows where that might lead us with what just happened tonight? Could turn out to be something even bigger. One of the heads of the conference wants to meet with me about a possible symposium next year."

I smile at him. I'm so very proud of him, of us.

"Now, go, before it gets too dark to walk alone. I have a few things here I need to finish."

"Okay, okay." I laugh playfully. "I'm getting out of your hair."

Then, he grabs my hand before I can leave.

"One more kiss."

I kiss him deeply with all I have and hastily turn toward the door. I open it before I won't have the willpower to leave.

I walk out, and as I turn down the hall and toward the main entrance, I literally bump into Ashley.

"Oh, hey, Ashley."

"Hi, Bree!" she say sweetly. "Haven't seen you since last semester. Where have you been hiding?" Her tone is peculiar.

"Oh, you know, working hard, studying, and—"

She smiles wide. "I know. I hear you. Speaking of, how about that A we got on the project? Who would have figured?"

I can't place her laugh, but it sends a prickle down my spine.

"Um, well, I'm glad we did."

"I have something to take care of. I'll catch you later, Bree."

"Okay, see you," I say.

I can't help but watch her as she heads down the hallway and out of sight. She is an odd girl. There is something about her that makes me very happy I am no longer working with her.

I have to keep up the charade that I'm single. The only way I know how to do that in college is to go out and party. Tonight is the Black Hearts party. It's well known around campus as the ultimate anti-Valentine's Day party.

My floor mates don't even know that I went ahead and bought tickets for all of us to go out tonight. It's been a long time since I've had time with just the girls.

We enter the cafeteria around five o'clock. I wait for all of us to sit down before I decide to make my grand announcement about the party tonight. I know Abigail will want to spend time with Nathan, but I'm not going to let anyone opt out. I spent money on the tickets, and I'm going to insist that everyone go. If I'm going to be alone this Valentine's Day, then I'm going to make sure I'm surrounded by my friends. If I sat alone in my dorm room, I'd be so depressed, just thinking about and missing Adam.

My floor mates and I sit down at our usual table, and I wait for everyone to stop talking, but that's almost impossible when you get a group of girls together.

So, once the conversation is shifted away from what I want to talk about, I make my declaration, "So, I have a big announcement to make. Tonight, we are all going to the Black Hearts party!"

Most of the girls are excited.

"I bought tickets for all of us, and I won't take no for an answer."

"Oh, wow. Thanks, Bree. That's awesome," Jen says.

"I hear that party is a lot of fun. I'm excited to go!" Casey adds.

I wait for Abigail to respond, but I notice her eyes drifting toward the floor. I know she won't meet mine because she's too afraid that I'll demand she goes. But, surprisingly, I notice Laura squeeze her leg under the table. When she glances over at Abigail, a small smile crawls across her face.

"Yeah, I suppose that could be fun," Abigail mumbles.

Not giving her a chance to change her mind, I say, "It's settled then. We'll all meet in my room at eight o'clock."

The whole point of the Black Hearts party is that everyone dresses in all black. It's an interesting concept, and I actually kind of like it. If it wasn't for Adam, I'd probably be in a bad mood right now. But, because he is gone, I'm actually anticipating with excitement an evening of debauchery surrounded by people with an anti-love agenda.

It's been a while since I've actually had to dress up and get ready for a party. I spend extra time putting on makeup and blow drying my hair. I'm definitely not searching for anybody else, but it's still nice to get attention. I told the girls, once they are all ready, to meet me in my room. One by one, they come in. Most of them appear respectable as well, except for Casey.

"Casey, sweetheart, let me touch up your makeup a little."

"But I'm not wearing makeup."

"Exactly," I say with a chuckle.

I hear the other girls laughing, too.

"Might as well let her do it," Jen says with a sympathetic smile.

Casey glances at Jen and then bashfully adds, "Okay, Bree."

What I'm not prepared for is when Abigail enters the room, emulating a million bucks. She has completely outdone me—although I would never admit that out loud. She has a tight black shirt on with a circle in the middle, exposing her breasts. It's very risqué, and she appears to be playing the role of a sexy goddess—not exactly the part I ever saw her starring in. But, for some reason, tonight, she nailed it.

Regardless, I'm anxious to get going, so I hurry the girls out. It's a brisk stroll over to the fraternity house, and it's a little cooler tonight than it has been in the past month. I rush the girls up to the line, knowing how much I hate to wait in them. A poor fraternity pledge is standing at the door, dressed like cupid with blood on his shirt, taking tickets. It's rather embarrassing. I never glance behind me to see if the girls are close by. I'm assuming they know enough to keep up with me.

I'm not prepared for what is in front of me when I enter the room. This party is unbelievable. There are people everywhere, all dressed in black. Anyone that belongs to the fraternity is dressed as either cupid or a doctor. Some of the older brothers in the fraternity are wearing T-shirts that say *Love Stinks*. I'm actually amazed that a bunch of guys could pull this off.

We make our way to the bar and each get a cup of the sticky red punch. It probably has some kind of grain alcohol in it, which is awful, but it's the only thing here. I'd much rather be having a glass of red wine with Adam. But I know that is not possible this weekend, so I'm determined to make the best of my time with my floor mates.

The girls and I stay till about two o'clock in the morning, and at this point, I've had enough sticky red punch to last me a very long time.

As we exit the door, I realize that Abigail is not with us. Despite how beautiful she might be, to me, she simply blends into the background. So, I'm not surprised in the least that I didn't notice she wasn't with us.

"Where is Abigail?" I finally ask.

"She went home a while ago. Her foot was hurting her, and I assume she wanted to hang with Nathan," Laura says.

Abigail hurt herself about a month back. She fell down some stairs at the football house. The rumor I heard was that she was hooking up with Tank, Jessica's boyfriend, and Nathan caught her. Then, she ran out of the house and fell. I honestly find it hard to believe she'd hook up with Tank right under Nathan's nose and that Nathan would take her back. I think something else is going on. I'm just not sure what it is.

"How nice for her," I say with full sarcasm.

By the time we get back to our dorm, it's around two thirty in the morning, and I'm exhausted. There's another party tomorrow night called Cupid's Party that everyone is planning on going to, so I know I have a long weekend ahead of me.

I put the key in my door and halfheartedly say good night to the girls. I'm eager to sleep in my bed and drift off to a place where I can dream about Adam. But, unfortunately for me, I start to think about him, and now, the loneliness is setting back in. A part of me is sad that I'll be sleeping alone.

Thankfully, I sleep pretty soundly. I toss and turn only periodically throughout the night. I wake up somewhat refreshed even though I'm still disappointed that I'm alone.

I spend most of the day in my room, watching Eva's movie and reorganizing my closet. At some point before dinner, I get a call from Abigail saying that she wants to talk with me in her room around five o'clock. We usually all plan to go to dinner together anyway, so I actually don't mind meeting her in her room right before we leave. Laura usually grabs me on their way down the hall.

A few minutes before five o'clock, I can hear my other floor mates heading down the hall toward Laura and Abigail's room. I wait a minute and then stroll out of my room, wondering what the hell this is all about.

I'm not prepared, however, when I wander in and observe Abigail lying in her bed, as though she's been hit by a truck. She appears frail, bruised, and lacking her usual pinked skin. The life has been drained out of her. Considering she paralleled a goddess last night, she now appears the complete opposite and less than twenty hours later. It's rather alarming, and I can't even contemplate what the situation might be.

"I invited you all to come here because I don't want you to make the same mistake I did," she says with a hoarse voice.

My heart starts to quicken as I regard her. She appears exhausted. She's moving slowly, I can tell she's in pain.

Then, she continues, "I left the party last night alone and almost paid the price for it. I don't want anything to happen to you. The police think…"

And, as she says *police*, I can hear all the girls in the room gasp. I lean up against the wall, trying to steady myself, for fear of what she might say.

"The police believe he has done this before…to others on this campus."

Then, she hits me with a ton of bricks. "He's been going around campus, telling girls that he plays a sport at the university and that his girlfriend lives in the same dorm, which they believe. I can attest to this. Because I believed him. He makes you feel comfortable with him, and then…he attacks you."

Everyone in the room is silent. Melissa starts to tear up.

But what they don't know is that it happened to me. Exactly as she described.

My anger rises to a level that I've never encountered before. I'm so sickened and disappointed in myself that I never spoke up, that I never reported anything. I was too goddamn afraid of what others might think of me. And what happened because of that? I put a friend of mine at risk without even knowing it. I could have done something about it.

I can't meet her eyes. My heart is pounding in my chest. Disgust and shame pulse through my veins. I glance down at my arms and remember the scratches and blood that covered them. I push down my sleeve even though nothing is there. Her bruises will heal, like mine did, but this worry that she's experiencing right now might never go away. I don't know how long it will last for me, and I don't know how long it will last for her. That is what saddens me the most.

Bile rises in my throat. Queasiness rolls through my stomach, and I fear I might vomit. I place my hand near my mouth, and I swallow hard.

I want to leave so badly, but I can't draw attention to myself, so I turn my head and wait for the girls to go up and hug her. I want to so desperately, but I know, if I do, I might break down and never recover.

The only saving grace is that she thinks Tank beat up the guy who attacked her on the path after the party.

Wouldn't that be a lovely thing to happen to someone so evil?

Then again, as she tells the story, I find myself jealous of her. At least she had someone there to save her. I had no one.

"I am going to be fine, you guys. It all happened so fast, and most of my bruises are from falling on the ice. Tank got there right as he started to attack me."

As she gets up, I can see how tired and hurt she is. I'm so devastated right now that all I want to do is run and hide in my room. But, if I do, they'll all know something is wrong. Again, I find myself needing to play the part of the girl who never has anything wrong.

Gratefully, Abigail does not want to go to the cafeteria with us. I hate the idea of going with the rest of the girls and sitting there for the next two hours, discussing what they conclude might or might not have happened to her. I'm in hell right now, and I can't envision a way out. The only person I want right now is Adam. But I know it'll be at least a few days until he's back.

I painfully make it through our time in the cafeteria. However, I can barely eat. I'm so sick to my stomach, I just want to crawl in bed and pretend today never happened.

Unfortunately, we have this stupid Cupid's Party to go to tonight. No one wants to back out of going since we know the football team is going to be there. The girls all want to rally around Abigail. We want to support her and send a message to this creep that he will not win. If I back out now, everyone will ask me what's wrong, and the sound of someone asking me that might send me into a place I'm not prepared to go today. I'm going to have to suck it up and go.

At the Cupid's Party, I'm surrounded by all the football players, so I have some level of comfort. Maybe just the sheer size of them makes me feel like nothing is going to happen to me and my friends. I fixate on Tank from across the room, and I feel a little better knowing that, if a guy his size hit *him*, then in my heart, I know *he* must truly be hurt. I want so desperately to go over and hug Tank. To thank him for being there for Abigail but, more importantly, for hurting someone who has hurt many people.

But, again, I can't do that. I cannot draw attention to myself.

Act normal. Drink and smile, laugh and dance, make the world believe that Aubrey Van Tousen has no worries in the whole world.

I am so happy when all the girls decide they have had enough of the party. Abigail and Nathan left over an hour ago. I couldn't believe that she'd come to the party, all beat up as she was. But the other part of me gave her a lot of credit for not staying in her room and feeling sorry for herself. She exhibited a lot of courage, showing her face here. She, at one point, disappeared with Tank, so I'm betting they had some things to talk about. Maybe they received word about the guy and will help solve this terrible case.

Our football friends escort us home.

"You okay, Bree?" Jason asks.

He takes me out of my thoughts.

I scoff. "Totally. Never been better."

"You seem…I'm not sure…quiet maybe."

"I'm just tired. I have to get up really early tomorrow," I lie. "I have to drive to the city and meet my father."

"You do?" Casey pipes up.

"Yes, I told you that." I narrow my eyes at her.

"Oh," Jason says, sounding disappointed.

"Yeah," I say again as I fake a yawn.

"Bummer. That's a long drive, girl."

"Nah, it's a walk in the park. Easy. But, like I said, I have to get up so early. Totally sucks."

"Ladies," Marcus, who is the captain of the football team, says, "we got you home safe and sound. Take care of yourselves, and if you ever need an escort, we'll be there for you. Any friends of Abigail's are friends of ours."

"Thanks. Appreciate that," Laura says.

Before the girls can draw me in any more, as soon as we get to our floor, I say, "Good night."

"See you tomorrow," Casey replies.

"Yep," Jen adds.

Casey grabs her hand and pulls her into their room. I find this to be rather odd.

Laura whispers with a little laugh as she breezes by, "Enjoy the drive tomorrow."

I turn to her, and for the first time all night, I slightly smile. She gets me. She might be the only one on our floor who really does.

Eighteen

WE ALL FEEL WORSE

I hate the fact that I have to go through three more days without Adam. We are close enough that I can talk to him about anything related to all kinds of things about my life at the university and even in the Hamptons. I've also enjoyed hearing about his parents and his sister who live in Colorado. We have siblings who act distant toward us in common.

There is only one thing I haven't talked about with him. But I think it's time I attempt to open up. I could tell him what happened to Abigail to gauge his reaction and to get some advice from him as an employee of the institution. Maybe he knows what's going on. Knowing Adam, he'll be so sympathetic that he'll open the door wide for me to tell him about what happened to me. And, finally, I'll be able to talk about it.

I meander through my classes, my daily activities, and my social obligations with the girls.

Laura and I sit in the common area and watch television while Abigail spends some time resting in her room.

"You think she'll be okay?" Laura asks me.

I desperately fear talking about this, so I brush her off. "She'll be fine. She has people watching out for her, people who care for her."

Her eyes widen as she glances at me. I know, at this point, she knows the bitchy Bree, so it's not completely out of character for me.

"I suppose," she says slowly.

"Hey, you ski at all?"

"Since I was eight years old."

"Cool. My father likes to rent this ski house in Upstate New York. So, sometime before the end of March, we should go."

"Oh, wow. Sure, that would be great."

"I love to ski. I know, crazy, right? Grew up on a beach, yet love to ski."

"The beach is lovely, too."

"You'll get a taste this summer when you come visit. You'll love it. So beautiful."

"Yeah, I hear the Hamptons are."

"Ha-ha. I know what you're saying. The summers are remarkable."

"The Hamptons would be a far cry from Stockbridge, Massachusetts, for a bit of summer fun!" Her eyes light up.

I have gotten comfortable with Laura and have enjoyed her friendship more than I ever have enjoyed a friendship before.

She is genuinely kind and wants the best for everyone. She looks better and better each time I see her. Like she is blossoming right in front of my eyes. She is very pretty. She has this bob hairstyle that no one else has, and these amazing bright eyes. I can't quite figure out why a guy here hasn't chased her down.

She's super smart and driven. She manages her job at the radio station and her classes with total ease. She is currently taking Honors Math for teaching geometry, and from what she says, she is acing the class. But she loves it. She wants to be a teacher, and I believe she'd be fabulous at it. Then, she's got the cool position at the college radio station. I love listening to her interject her thoughts about the songs. She recently told me, they like her so much that they are adding another day to her schedule. I'm so happy for her.

And maybe, just maybe, she doesn't need a man to make her happy. She can do that fine on her own. I envy her that way, but I kind of like that she is so different from anyone I've ever known. She is nothing like Nelly or Joss, and maybe that is why I'm so drawn to her.

"Hi, Professor Gilford."

"Hello, Bree."

"I wanted you to know that I haven't seen Professor Cooper in a few days, so I haven't been able to connect with him on any of the curriculum changes that you suggested." I'm searching for information on Adam, but trying not to be obvious.

"Yes, I know. Not surprised. He's been back since Monday, but he asked for a few personal days. He mentioned that to you, correct?"

"Oh, yes, he did." *No, he did not*, I ponder as a strange sensation comes over me. I try not to react to the news that Adam has been back since

Monday. It's now Thursday, and I have not heard from him. "So, I wanted you to know I'm still working on it."

I get a worried knot in the pit of my stomach. It's unlike Adam—or at least what I know of him—not to get in touch with me when he said he would. Maybe someone in his family is sick. Oh God, I hope nothing bad happened to anyone. Or maybe the conference went horribly wrong, and he can't face me to tell me the project is dead.

I don't want to ask Professor Gilford any more questions, for fear I might give myself away.

I have a few more classes this afternoon, and then if I don't hear from Adam, I'll drive over to his house and make sure he's okay. I'm apprehensive, to say the very least.

I sit through my classes, aimlessly staring out the window, wondering, and praying that everything is all right with him. I can't concentrate. I can't do anything but think about him.

Finally, my last class lets out. I hurry across campus, and get into my car.

It's starting to get a little darker. I can almost smell the storm coming in the air. The university has warned us that a large winter storm is coming in the next few hours, so I'm anxious to get over there and make sure he's there and safe.

My heart races as I pull down his street.

From the distance, I notice that the lights on his front porch are on, so I know he's home.

I truly hope nothing is wrong with his family or his friends. It's very unlike him to, one, not be at class, and two, to not call me, particularly after he left and went to the conference specifically to talk about our project.

As I pull up to his house, there is another car parked where I usually park in front.

I drive past his house a little bit, and then I park. I'm nervous, as I don't recognize the car.

It's worse that I have to sit in my car and watch his house, as though I'm pestering him. In reality, our relationship dictates that I'm not really allowed to walk up onto the porch and knock on his door, especially since I have no idea who is in his house.

Fortunately for me, I don't have to wait long. His front door swings open, and a woman I slightly recognize comes out. Then, Adam exits behind her. He hands her a large envelope. She takes it with an unfamiliar expression on her face. She seems pleased, but not happy. Her expression is almost a bittersweet response to whatever he handed her. She says a few more words to him, and I watch as he lowers his head. He seems sad as well. She reaches up and gently touches his arm. He raises his head to gaze upon her, and only then does she give him a friendly smile, much warmer than before. He returns a slightly less happy smile, but steps closer toward her. She moves her hand down his arm to his hand and takes it in her own. She says a few more words to him, and he says something back.

I wish I could hear what they were saying.

They don't notice me, and I watch as the two of them embrace on the front porch. They hold on to each other for a long time. I'm wildly uncomfortable. Then, it hits me. I recognize her from the restaurant a few months ago. It's his friend Anna.

I am nauseated as I watch the two of them hold each other tightly. I start to get a terrible feeling that maybe she's the reason he hasn't called me.

I watch despondently as she gets in her car. She smiles and waves to him, and he does the same from the porch before she drives away. Then, he retreats back inside.

I wait a few minutes before I climb out of my car. Then, I go up and knock on his door.

He opens it and starts to say, "Did you forget some—"

I can't describe the expression on his face when he realizes it's not Anna.

I don't want to assume he's disappointed, but he isn't happy to see me. Unlike the day I drove up to the cabin to spend winter break with him, and he met me in the driveway to give me an electrically charged kiss.

I smile slightly, hoping that it's only a fleeting moment, that he has something else on his mind. That maybe something tragic has happened, and his sadness is simply a part of the state that he is in.

"Bree, hi," he finally says.

He doesn't exactly let me in either. So, I step forward with a questioning countenance on my face.

I simply respond, "Hi. I heard that you were back."

He anxiously glances outside from side to side, goggling around. It appears to me as though he is expecting someone else. I give him a pained expression.

He finally says, "Oh, yes. Sorry, please, please come in."

His demeanor is extremely unlike him. I am already starting to feel funny that I showed up at his house, which I hate even more, considering how intimate we have been.

"Is everything all right?" I ask.

He lowers his head. I can tell something is wrong. I reach for his hand, but he pulls away quickly. His reaction startles me, and I take a step back.

"Adam, you're scaring me. What's going on?"

"Nothing," he says unconvincingly. "Nothing."

"Okay, so everything is all right then? The conference go okay, too?"

"What are you doing here, Bree?"

I tip my head, confused by his question. "I came to see you. I got worried when I heard you'd been back for a few days and then needed some personal time."

"Listen," he starts.

"Does this have anything to do with the woman I saw leaving? Anna, is it?"

He stops. His eyes darken, and I suddenly am nervous.

"Listen, Bree...um..." He hesitates as he stares at the ground. This behavior is so unlike him.

"What, Adam?" I say softly.

He glances up, his face twisted with anguish. He acts like he hasn't slept in days, and I then notice how unkempt his appearance is. It's not in the sexy, rugged way he looked in the cabin; it's more like there's a disheveled darkness to him that seems almost unhealthy.

"It's over between us," he blurts out.

I almost don't comprehend what he said. I step back, attempting to steady my legs.

"What do you mean, over?" I whisper.

"Yes, over. I'm sorry, but I think it's best for you, me...*us* really."

"But I don't—"

Then, it dawns on me. Anna left his house, the warm embrace on the porch, the previous dates...

He's a serial dater, and he is going back to an old flame. He's grown tired of me already.

I glimpse at him. My mouth is dry, and my head is pounding. No matter how many different ways he could possibly say it, the story will remain the same. It's over.

My body begins to go into shock. My knees lock, and I begin to sway. I sturdy myself on the wall.

I can't believe that this is happening. I thought everything was wonderful. But maybe spending that time in the cabin was not the right answer. Too much, too soon.

"Listen, I'm dating Anna, and... we sort of got back together on a whim at the conference. She's been in and out of my life for a long time, and I think, this time, it will last with us."

She seems much older than him.

I'm closer in age, but again, it doesn't truly matter right now.

"Really? Dating Anna? Is that so? Her over me? You have got to be kidding me," I snarl.

His mouth drops open. He just got a taste of pissed off Bree.

The room begins to spin. I want to scream, run, hit, cry, laugh like a crazy woman, anything other than stand here like a total used idiot. But I can't move.

"I'm sorry if I've hurt you."

Hurt me? You've taken my beating heart out of my chest and stomped on it.

But it can all just be excuses, and I don't need an excuse, nor do I want anyone to stay with me who doesn't want to be with me.

Then, he says, "Remember, I trusted you, and I hope that trend will continue. We are—I mean, we were consenting adults, and we must continue to act accordingly at the university."

I hate that he is using my own words. The words I said to him the first night we spent together. I told him I knew how to act accordingly, so he is playing me right into this…making it impossible for me to behave any other way—not that I would. Revenge is a dangerous game, and nothing I'm interested in pursuing. I'm better than that.

I eye him and say, "Why would I do anything to jeopardize your career? If you don't care about me anymore, that's one thing, but I'm not in a position to destroy what you have here."

"Besides," he adds, "it would look bad if people thought you got special treatment from me and our curriculum program got off the ground because of our relationship."

I'm floored at what he is insinuating. "No"—I grimace—"it's such a success because I worked on it. I'd like to think the project was what the internship was about. Nothing else, Adam."

"Right," he says as a small smile creeps across his face.

For the first time in the last fifteen minutes, I actually catch a glimpse of the old Adam. The one I became infatuated with, not the one who is breaking my heart.

I'm so devastated right now, but I can't let him see me cry, so I turn and start to approach the door.

He grabs my hand. I try to pull away, but he spins me around to consider him. I note the sadness grow across his face. A tear drops onto my cheek as I close my eyes, anything to avoid staring at the face of the man I can no longer have.

He gently wipes away my tear.

"Don't do that. You don't get to touch me anymore."

He goes to speak and then swiftly lowers his head. He acts like he doesn't want me to leave, like he has something else to say, but he doesn't, and I am even more confused.

I don't say a word. I release my hand and walk toward the door. I pull it open as fast as I can, for fear I'll burst into tears.

I can't remember ever feeling so alone in my entire life—from the attacker striking again and hurting someone I know, which has reopened those wounds, to now this. I planned to tell Adam about it in the hopes that he'd be able to help me, but he doesn't care about me anymore, and I have to accept that. The man I trusted is casting me aside, like I never meant a goddamn thing to him. How easily he was able to manipulate my heart. I hate the fact that I am vulnerable again.

"Bree," he calls after me as I hurry down the porch.

I don't turn, nor do I respond. I hurriedly get into my car. My hands are trembling as I try to get the key in the ignition. I finally do, and as I pull away from his house, my body starts to heave. I can barely breathe as it truly hits me that it is over. I realize, as I watch his house fade away in the rearview mirror, that it will probably be the last time I'll ever be here.

I can barely drive through the tears clouding my eyes. But I park my car and run, not walk, into my dorm and up the flights of stairs to my room. I start to stride down the hall, but notice Jen and Casey's door open slightly. I don't even bother knocking. I push the door open.

Maybe it's the state I'm currently in, or maybe it's the fact that all I want from them right now is vodka, but the way I react to the two of them, half-naked, rolling around on Jen's bed, even alarms me.

I burst into tears as I catch the two of them making out. "One of you'd better get up and give me the bottle of vodka I know you have stashed," I cry.

I don't even shade my eyes as I see Jen practically jump out of her skin. They have been busted. I can't even handle the sex-charged happiness emanating out of this room. I want to get the hell out and into my own room to literally drown my sorrows.

Neither of them asks me what's wrong, as I know all of us are in shock for all kinds of reason. But, regardless, Jen goes over to the drawer, never even bothering to cover up, and takes out the bottle of vodka before handing it to me.

I spin on my heel, but not before barking, "You should at least lock the freaking door." And, for effect, I slam it shut.

I fumble with my keys, but finally get my door open. I don't even bother to get undressed or anything. I pull out my desk chair, sit down, and begin wasting away my thoughts, one shot at a time.

At some point around the sixth shot, I go to grab the phone to call him. To curse him out. To tell him what an unbelievable womanizing user he is. That he has torn me apart again, at my darkest hour, right when I needed someone to help me through a terrible time in my life, someone I believed actually cared about me, just me. Not Aubrey Van Tousen. Just plain old Bree.

But, instead, I take another shot and another and another. Finally, at about eleven thirty or so, I pass out on my bed.

Nineteen

THERE IS NO LIGHT

I have been locked in my room for over a day. I've been able to survive on the snacks and food I've had in my room from my last trip to the store. I only sneak out to the bathroom when I know the girls are at classes and such. So, I'm surprised when I hear a knock on my door.

"Who is it?"

"It's Brittney, your DM."

Really?

The dorm monitor has never knocked on my door, so I'm terribly intrigued as to why she is doing so now.

"Hold on," I say. I wrap my sweater tightly around my body and hide the alcohol in my desk drawer.

I unlock the door and open it. I am floored to find her standing there with Officer Murphy. The very man I ran into my first night of college. I swallow hard and feel as though the room is beginning to spin.

"Can-can I help you?" I sputter.

"May I come in?" he asks softly.

"I suppose," I say as I back up a little in my room and allow him in.

Brittney remains in the hallway, and I glower at her as her gaze draws down to the floor.

"I'll wait out here and see which person I can find next," she adds.

I quietly shut the door. My heart is beating hard within my chest. I'm incredibly nervous by his presence. I turn and face him.

"Um, sorry, I can open a blind here," I add as I reach for my window and pull the shades open. The light from the afternoon sun burns my eyes, and I have to shield them. "I was sleeping." I wasn't asleep at all actually. I was staring at the wall in the darkness.

"May I sit, Bree?"

"Sure."

He pulls out a desk chair and motions for me to sit. I reluctantly pull out the other chair and sit across from him. He removes his policeman hat and puts it on my desk.

"Bree, I wanted to talk to you about an incident that happened a few days ago to a woman on your floor."

"Yes, I know about it."

"Okay, can you tell me what you have heard about that night?"

"Yeah. Some scumbag preyed on her and said he went to school here, was an athlete and all that, and then attacked her."

"Yes, we understand he did."

"That's all I really know."

"Okay, so I wanted to ask you if you have heard of anything else like that happening on campus."

"Like what?" I swallow hard and have difficulty meeting his eyes.

"We believe he has numerous victims across several campuses in the area."

"Several?" The beat of my heart is alarmingly shallow.

"Yes, several."

"Oh."

"And I currently have two concerns. One, that he never does it again, and two, when it comes time, I will have people who can positively identify him. This will increase our chances of putting him away for life. The more crimes we can link him to, the more time he will have to serve."

"Okay, sounds like you are doing all you can."

"Am I?" he says softly.

I glance away. I take a deep breath and exhale. I don't want to repeat my mistakes, but I'm so scared to expose myself.

"Bree, I need you to understand that you can trust me."

Trust a man? No way!

"Is that why you are here?" I raise my voice slightly as I stand. I'm unsteady as I know I'm lacking nutrition and most likely dehydrated from the lack of water and the excessive consumption of vodka.

He goes to reach for me as I tip backward.

"Hold on, hold on. I'm not the enemy. I'm here solely because I care about you."

Huh, I think. *No man cares about me. Why should this guy be any different? Just because he represents the law, that means he genuinely cares about my well-being? It's a lie.*

"Why? Why care about me?" I bark.

"Because—"

"Because it's your job?" I interrupt, disdain dripping from my voice.

"No, I was going to say, from the night I ran into you outside, I have not been able to get it out of my mind. It keeps me up at night, thinking I haven't done enough to protect the students on this campus. Another young girl's life has changed because I haven't done enough." He motions for me to sit back down. "Please, Bree, I only ask that you hear me out."

I can't sit; my nerves are on high alert. "Okay," I say softly, "I'm listening."

"We have a suspect in custody. He was hurt from an altercation we believe to be with a man that another victim knows. We are confident, according to reports, that the man hit the suspect and injured him enough that he had no choice but to seek medical attention. I ask that you keep this quiet for now. We are only observing him and working with the medical professionals to ensure his injuries are consistent."

I want to scream, cry, bury my head under the covers, and never come out. I'm suddenly scared again. I have no one watching out for me, and I am terribly vulnerable.

"Before you react, can I ask you a few questions?"

My body starts to shake. So, I sit down on the edge of the chair. My voice quivers as I say, "Can I ask you *one* question, Officer?"

"Yes, of course."

I fight back my tears as I ask, "Do you know what happened to me?"

The saddest expression grows across his face, like he too might cry, and then he says softly, "Yes, Bree. I believe you were assaulted your first night on campus by a man posing as a college student. He probably told you he played lacrosse or football, was probably even wearing a team T-shirt for effect. I think he told you his girlfriend lived in the same dorm as you and that he'd walk you home from a party." He reaches over, grabs a tissue from the box, and hands it to me.

Tears start flowing down my cheeks.

I don't deny it. I don't have to say a word in fact. He knows exactly what happened to me because it's the same thing that happened to Abigail and the same thing that I am assuming happened to countless others.

I nod my head.

"So, my only question for you right now is, could you and would you be willing to identify him?"

I ponder the question for a moment. I could identify him. His face haunts my nightmares.

But will I do it? Will I go through with it?

I'm angry with myself because had I done it before, I could have saved my friend. Yes, I consider Abigail to be my friend. She is sweet, kind, beautiful, and obviously special enough to be with Nathan Ryan.

I hesitate. "I-I could identify him…"

"I understand it won't be easy. But please take these documents, and when you are ready, I hope you'll fill them out and send them back to me. When you do, I will know I can come to you and ask you for assistance." He hands me an envelope.

"Okay."

"For right now, Bree, I believe the campus is safe. But I know you work late at an internship and sometimes walk home with Professor Cooper. Please continue to do that."

His name sends blood draining from my face.

"Does he know about all of this?" I squeak out in a whisper.

"Yes, he has been made aware."

Oh God! He knows all about what is going on. Is that why he wanted to escort me home all those nights? Is that why we became close—because of a tragedy?

Awful. Simply awful. He truly never cared about me. It was all merely to watch over me and make me a nice placeholder until he got back with Anna. I feel even worse now.

"I'd like to be alone now."

He stands up and puts his hat back on. He goes over to the door. "Of course. I understand. And please consider officially reporting this. It is in your best interest and for others as well."

"Thank you."

"And please talk to a friend or someone you can trust to help you through this. You don't have to feel alone." He pulls open the door and exits, gently closing it behind him.

I pull the shades down again. Then, I go over and collapse on my bed. I cry myself to sleep and skip another full day of classes. Maybe tomorrow I'll be able to open the shades and let the light in, but for now, I see no reason to.

Tomorrow arrives, and I decide to spend most of the day in bed. At some point, while everyone is in the common area, playing some love match game with the guys in the dorm, I decide it will be a good time for me to venture out in my car.

I start to drive in one direction while I listen to Laura on the radio. I am crying uncontrollably as Laura has chosen almost all sad and depressing songs to play, like "When You're Gone" by The Cranberries, "Nothing Compares 2 U" by Sinead O'Connor, "Hurt" by Nine Inch Nails, and "Hallelujah" by Jeff Buckley.

Stab me right in the heart, why don't you, Laura?

Then, she plays "Everybody Hurts" by R.E.M., and I can't even remember where I'm driving to. I have to turn the radio off. I just have to.

I close my eyes and lean my head back.

I hear a tap on the glass window of my car. Startled, I jump in my seat. There is an officer standing next to my car. He motions for me to roll down my window, so I do.

"Miss, you can't sleep here."

"What?" I ask, realizing my voice sounds groggy and tired.

"Yes, ma'am. This is private property. You cannot stay here."

I glance up and realize I am in Dr. Leo's parking lot. My skin prickles as I shudder. "I apologize, Officer. It will not happen again."

"Okay. You all right to drive back to…"

"OSU. I'm a student there."

"Can I see your ID, please?"

"Yes." I reach into my wallet and take out my ID.

"You been drinking tonight?"

"No, sir, I have not."

"May I ask what you are doing here?"

Think, Bree, think!

"Yes, um, Officer…I…well, I'm a pa—"

He puts his hand up. "No need to explain further," he says over his shoulder, looking toward Dr. Leo's office.

I lower my head and then glance back up with appreciative eyes. "Thank you."

"Do you feel unsafe, or are you in need of medical attention?"

"No, it seemed like the safest place to come and think; that's all." I truly cannot believe I blurted that out. But it felt good. Truthful and uncensored.

"You sure you are okay?"

"Yes, Officer. I would like to go home, back to my dorm, and climb into bed."

"Okay, Miss Van Tousen, then please be on your way," he says in a formal tone.

"Yes, of course," I respond as I take my ID back from him. "Sorry to have caused an issue."

"Take care, and please be vigilant." He turns and heads back to his cruiser.

He waits for me to leave. So, I do so, keeping in mind to obey all traffic laws as I pull onto the street.

The next fifteen minutes might as well be an eternity as I drive back toward campus. It's nearly one in the morning, and I'm emotionally and physically tired. What I need right now is to shut my eyes and keep the light out of my existence. I see no reason for it at this point.

Twenty

IT'S NOT YOU; IT'S ME

I finally crawl out of bed. I glance at the calendar on my wall and can't believe it is already February 21. I've buried myself in this room, using it as a safe haven.

I got a message on my answering machine, saying that my Economics professor had called the Registrar's office, wondering if I had withdrawn from school. The school warned me to either get a doctor's note, or I would have to start showing up to classes in order to avoid being expelled. I suppose I could ask Dr. Leo for a note, but a part of me knows she'd be disappointed to find out I've been sleeping nonstop for the past few days and not attending school. School means everything to me, even though I haven't been acting like it lately.

So, I figure now is a good time to get up out of bed and be among the living.

I meet Laura in the hallway as I'm about to leave for lunch.

"Oh, hey," she says with little enthusiasm. "Want to grab lunch?"

"Hey. Sure."

Huh. By her expression, it's evident she hasn't even noticed that I have been MIA for the past few days. Not that I was up for company then. But, today, I don't want to eat alone, and Laura is about as good company as I can get.

We enter the cafeteria and grab our usual food, like mindless conformists. As I follow her to an empty table, I glance at her. She seems gloomy for some reason. As we sit down with our trays, she peeks over at me, and I can't stand the sad expression on her face. I haven't slept in days, I'm exhausted, and I feel worse than I have in a long time. I don't say a word, and neither does she. The thought of taking on her problems coupled with mine is less appetizing than what I have on my plate.

Speaking of, I have no appetite whatsoever, especially considering, every time I am around food, I think of Adam cooking for me in the cabin. I stare out into the distance as I jab my fork into the lettuce, but I never actually bring the fork up to my mouth.

She is staring at me, and I don't like it.

Finally, I ask, "So, what's your problem?"

"My problem?" she barks. "You've been sitting here for the past fifteen minutes, picking at the same piece of lettuce, all mopey and stuff."

"Yeah, well, since the second I saw you, you've had this puss on your face, like your dog just died or something."

Then, she glares at me and says, "You're the one who's acting like you just lost your dog. Not me." She huffs and then adds, "Sorry to bother you with my problems—for once."

"What's that supposed to mean?" I snip back as I put down my fork.

"Don't you want to know what's wrong with me...or Abigail or Jen or Maddie or..." Laura starts to raise her voice but swiftly lowers it again.

She abruptly stands up and grabs her tray. She glares at me and then says, "You don't care about anybody but yourself. So, forget it. I'm going to be late for class."

Ouch, the truth stings.

She storms off. She leaves me sitting there like a fool. She caused a scene, making me even more upset. But, unfortunately, she's right. I only care about myself right now. Well, to someone as kind as Laura, it probably seems like I only care about myself at all, period. No one else.

I stab a piece of lettuce again and grumble, "I am being selfish because I feel like nobody gets me."

I sit there for only a moment longer. I stand up and put on my leather coat, pulling my mane of hair to the side. I grab my bag and tray.

I'm at my lowest point. I've pissed off all my friends. Adam cast me aside like I meant nothing to him. The project that I was once so proud of feels like a distant memory, a pipe dream.

Was I kidding myself when I thought I could actually create something the university would use? Am I better off just smiling for the camera?

I want so much more, but I might have blown it by getting into a relationship with him. Then, there is my assailant out there somewhere, wreaking havoc on campuses all over the state. My parents know nothing, and I feel terrible about that, too.

However, I know where I can find some solace today. In the library. I need to find a place for me to deal with the situation I don't want to deal with.

I decided last night that I needed to fill out the damn report and send it in to Officer Murphy. The worst that can happen to me has already taken place. I hope the same applies to Abigail. I have to trust in the system and believe that, by speaking up and voicing my story, it can only make things better from here on out.

So, why am I so hesitant?

Because then my parents along with Claudia, Eva, Adam, and everyone else on this campus will know, that I, Aubrey Van Tousen, am a victim of a crime. I fear that label will be bestowed upon me forever. Dr. Leo and I have spoken at length about my fear of this. Image has always been my life—in my career and in my family's status in the Hamptons.

But I continue to have a sense of loneliness even while surrounded by people. They can't understand what I've been through and struggled with because they haven't experienced what I have.

Then again, there is this fear of reaching out to people, like Abigail, who might understand my situation because it happened to them. *What happens if she tells me what I'm feeling is wrong?* I might have to start therapy all over again as the things I thought I'd gotten over still affect me.

But, now, I have to realize this will be a part of me forever. Dr. Leo told me I'd get to choose how I wanted it to be a part of my life, and up until now, I was unable to choose.

I find a secluded section of the library and pick a cubby. I put all my belongings down, grab a pen, and open the document.

I take a deep breath, stack the papers directly in front of me, and start by writing my name at the top. I put in my address, phone number, and social security number. Then, I read the question on the top of the paper.

PLEASE WRITE A FULL DESCRIPTION OF THE INCIDENT.
PLEASE NOTE THIS IS A LEGALLY BINDING DOCUMENT.

I'm not surprised by this, but it still sends a shiver down my spine.

I put the pen down and sit back in the chair. I knew this was coming. I knew I'd eventually have to tell, no matter how many times I'd tried to avoid it. I don't want this pain anymore.

I pick up my pen, take a deep breath, and finally tell my story.

On August 31, 1995, I met a girl named Missy outside of the Student Union after I'd purchased some items in the store. She made a remark about my bag, and we struck up a conversation. A guy approached us with a flier, saying there was a back-to-school house party at 142 North Adams Street. Missy and I decided to meet at 8 p.m. in front of the Union to go over to the party together.

Around 8 p.m., we walked to the party together with two other girls from her dorm; I cannot remember either of their names. We got to the party around 8:30 p.m. and paid $5 at the door to get in.

We spent the first hour or so in the basement talking to a group of people. The music was blaring, and it was difficult to hear one another, so we decided to move upstairs to the main level. Missy and I sat on a couch in the living room with a group of kids we did not know. However, Missy recognized one guy from her hometown—I think his name was Mark—and we ended up talking to him and a few of his friends for most of the night. Missy and the guy left to get another drink from the bar in the basement. I was now alone.

I stop and put the pen down. I grab a tissue from my bag. I dab the corner of my eye. I pick up my pen again.

A guy came in the room and sat down on the couch next to me. He was bigger than average, had spiked short hair, and was wearing an Onondaga State T-shirt. He struck up a conversation with me. We talked about sports, and he said he played lacrosse at school. He said he was a junior. He asked me what year I was, where I was from, and so forth. He said his girlfriend lived in the same dorm as mine and that she was a sophomore biology major.

I waited on the couch for Missy to return. After what seemed like a half hour or so, I excused myself and went into the basement to find her. I searched the basement and never found her. I was down there, looking for her, for about twenty minutes.

Since I knew no one else at the party, I decided to leave. I went up the basement stairs and opened the door. The two guys who had been taking money when we came in were standing near the door, smoking cigarettes. I walked past them and through the backyard, toward the road. That was when I heard a male voice calling my name. It surprised me since I didn't really know anyone at school yet.

Again, I close my eyes for a moment and put down the pen. My tears leak out of the corners of my eyes and roll down my face as I attempt to force the memories away. But it is no use. I hate what he did to me. I hate what he did to my friend.

So, I pick up my pen and press down hard on the paper as I write.

Officer Murphy, you can count on me to tell the rest when it counts.

I sign my name on the bottom of the paper, fold it, and put it in the envelope Officer Murphy gave to me. On my way out of the library, I drop the letter in the mail slot. I might finally be free of that terrible night in August.

Now, I need to get others to understand that the way I've behaved these past few months has nothing to do with them; it's all about me.

Three days later, I get a call from Officer Murphy, asking for me to come to the station. My heart is in my throat as I drive to the police station. I'm about to get out of my car when I notice Abigail pulling into the station, and she is driving Tank's truck.

I knew they hung out a lot, and I knew that pissed Nathan off, but I'm surprised to see the two of them together for some reason. I'd at least think she'd have the decency to not throw it in Nathan's face. But I heard through the grapevine that there was trouble in paradise between Nathan and Abigail and that maybe their whirlwind romance was coming to an end.

She gets out of the driver's side, and I duck in the hopes that she doesn't notice me. I'm parked far enough away, but I still want to be certain that she doesn't know I'm here. I sit in my car and wait and wait for her to come back out and leave.

I wait about twenty minutes, and then she leaves the building, gets back in his truck, and starts the engine. I watch them for a moment. She appears as though she is crying. Then, suddenly, I see him throw his massive arms around her and hug her tight. They seem close. Much closer than I realized. So, maybe they are not rumors after all. Maybe she is moving on to football player number two.

Lucky her.

As soon as they are gone, I get out of my car and enter the station.

"Can I help you?" the young officer behind the counter asks me.

"Yes, Officer Murphy, please."

"Busy day for him." He laughs slightly.

I do not.

He notices and then adds, "Have a seat, and he'll be right with you."

A moment later, Officer Murphy comes down the hallway toward me. "Bree, so good to see you."

"You, too," I respond although I don't feel it's good to be seeing a policeman today.

"Please come with me."

I follow him down the hallway and to his office.

"Please have a seat."

I sit in a chair at a small table, and he does the same, sitting across from me. There are several manila folders on his table. Each has a different number and initial on the tab. He stacks them and searches for one. When he pulls it out, I note the number seventeen and the initials AVT. My heart rate picks up, and I take a huge breath in and hold it.

"Bree, thank you for filling out the letter. I have a few additional questions for you."

"Okay," I say, letting my breath go.

"Did the man you remember have any tattoos or distant markings?"

"No, not that I recall."

"Are you sure the party you went to was on North Adams?"

"Yes, positive."

"Are you positive of the date in which this incident took place?"

I regard him. He saw me that night.

Doesn't he remember the date as well? I wonder.

"Yes. Don't you remember?"

He lowers his eyes and then glances up. He says in the saddest voice, "Yes, I do remember. I remember it vividly."

Tears well in my eyes. "Yes, it was that night." I hesitate and then say, "When I ran into you, I was…I was running away from *him*."

I watch his fist clench slightly. Then, he releases it and slowly and softly touches my hand. "I'm so sorry, Bree."

I observe this distraught man. Obviously, by the stacks of folders in front of him and the revolving door of young college women coming in and out of the station today, he is truly torn up about this. I can't imagine doing this for a job—watching people in pain and knowing, at some point, you simply might be unable to help them.

"I'm sorry, too. I know you wanted to help me that night."

"I did. I still do." His eyes soften. "Bree, you should talk to those who care about you, so they can understand what you're going through. In general, people are good and want to help others. You just have to let them in—"

I stop him, "I appreciate that, but I'm managing."

"Don't go it alone; I implore you."

I think of Adam. He knows and didn't say anything to me; worse, he never asked me if I was okay. Then, there is Eva. All she knows is a man mistreated me, and I ran away from school to avoid my problems. Lastly, Laura knows I can be a real bitch; that's the only Bree she knows. But I wish she knew the real me, the Bree that Claudia and my father know. That's the Bree I like the best.

"Okay, I won't."

"Good. Now, for the hard part."

My heart thumps louder in my chest. "Hard part?"

"Yes, we believe we might have this perp under surveillance. He checked into a hospital about an hour from here, in need of medical assistance. We believe his injuries are consistent with the injures that were described to us by another woman who had an altercation with the man. He is under twenty-four-hour surveillance in the hospital."

I swallow hard. "Okay, but could he get out?"

"There is an armed police officer at his door at all times. We received some additional information, and I believe we have enough to arrest him. That is all I can share, but we plan to do that."

"Okay."

"So, I am going to place a few photographs in front of you. Please know the right answer is only the one you are one hundred percent positive about, all right?"

"Yes, I understand."

"Okay, ready?"

I nod my head. He lines up four photos in front of me. I browse each one. They all appear relatively similar. Then, I slowly go back to each picture individually. I can't describe what happens when my eyes lock on the picture of the man who stood before me and crushed my innocence, but I know that I can't move on to the next picture. As the chill runs up my spine, I know, without a doubt, that it is him.

I point at the photograph and say, "That one. That is *him*."

"You positive?"

"Yes, I am. That's him."

Officer Murphy goes over to his desk, picks up the phone, and calls someone. A few seconds later, a young man in plain street clothes enters his office. He signs a piece of paper, collects the photos, and then leaves with them.

"Bree, I can assure you, you are safe. We have this man on watch. Unfortunately, that is all I can really tell you at this moment."

"I understand."

"But please seek out someone to talk to."

"Okay, I will." I get up and head to the door. Before I leave, I turn slightly to him and say in a quiet voice, "Thanks...for all that you do."

For the first time since I have met him, he smiles. It's genuine, and it slightly warms my tired heart.

I leave the building and go to my car in the hopes that no other women from campus are coming to the station today—for many reasons.

When I get into my car, I can't even control my emotions as I burst into tears. The sight of *his* face, the stack of folders representing numerous assaults, and seeing Abigail leave the station—it is all just overwhelming. It truly overpowers me in this moment.

I hate myself for keeping this all in, and I wish more than anything that, right now, I felt better than worse.

Twenty-One

SEEKING REAL FRIENDS

I've spent the last few days back in solitude. This time, I've left my room to go to classes and for my appointments with Dr. Leo.

She has opened my eyes in many ways. She explained the process a bit more of what might happen in the coming months now that I came forward, regarding my assailant. I am better equipped to handle what might arise once he is arrested.

After listening to Officer Murphy's advice about not going through this alone, I realized with Dr. Leo's help that I need more. I need my friends. The kind and loving friends who have been right under my nose these past six months. I've just been too selfish to understand them clearly.

I haven't seen Laura at all, and I know she is completely avoiding me.

I can't blame her. I wish I could avoid myself, too. I'm ashamed of how I behaved.

I am about to go down to the common room to get a drink when I notice Jen and Casey's door slightly ajar. I take a deep breath and knock slightly.

"Come in!" I hear one of them yell.

I release my breath and step into their room. Casey is sitting on the bed, and Jen is standing in the middle of the room. Casey jumps up when she realizes it's me. My heart is beating so hard, and I know my cheeks are turning rosy.

"Hey, Bree," she says.

I watch as her cheeks turn bright red, too.

"Hey, guys. Can, um…can I talk to you, both of you?"

"Sure," Jen says more coolly.

I glance back and forth at the two of them, and then it kind of hits me smack in the face. I observe them standing before me, only inches from each other, yet I notice they are not touching, and it deeply saddens me on many levels. I should have been a better person or friend that day when I caught them lip-locked. Instead, I've built a wall between us, and that was not what I wanted to do.

"I want to apologize for the other day. For barging in here and… for the way I acted."

These two girls are my friends. And I should have done a better job of showing them. But, unfortunately, I was so self-absorbed that evening that I couldn't grasp how my reaction toward them would impact them. The heart is uncontrollable in that way. I know firsthand that, sometimes, the person you love might be unexplainable to others. You can't help whom you fall in love with. I'm living proof of that. But having people support you is all that you need in the end.

I notice Jen's shoulders relax.

I continue, "I want you both to know that I'm happy for you guys if you are happy. You are my friends, and I can see—no, I know why you like one another. And I came by to say that. I hope you can forgive my reaction and know that I support and care for you both, very much."

I turn quickly to walk out, as I might cry. Everything these days makes me cry. I'm starting to deal with all the things I chose to repress, and like a cheetah on the hunt, it's swiftly catching up to me.

But, before I can open the door, four arms wrap tightly around me and squeeze me. I can literally feel the love connecting us.

I reach up my hands and touch their arms that are wrapped over me. "Thank you," I whisper.

When they let me go, I turn back to gaze at them. Jen takes Casey's hand. My heart feels better than it has in a month.

"Oh, you guys," I begin to say as I fight back my tears, "I don't deserve your forgiveness."

"Yes, you do. This is new to me and her," Jen says as she locks eyes with Casey.

I watch Casey's eyes sparkle as she responds, "Yes, new to all of us."

"I know. I was having a really bad week, and I lashed out." *Week, month, year. Just a shitty start to college in general,* I think.

"We get it, Bree. Everyone has a bad day," Jen says sweetly.

"I can be such a jerk…and I hate that about myself," I mumble.

"Whoa, go easy on yourself," Casey says as she comes closer to me. She takes my hand.

"You out of all of them," I cry. "I was the worst to you, and you know why. 'Cause you didn't seem affected at all. You don't give a shit about what anyone thinks of you, and I admire that."

"Now, that's not true. I gave a shit when you said my outfit was bad…a few times," she mutters.

"Right. See? I'm awful." I lower my head. I can't keep my eyes on her anymore.

"Stop it, Bree. You're *you*, and that's why we all love you."

"Love me? How can you even tolerate me?"

"You take some getting used to, but we all have our flaws," Jen says.

Jen smiles at me, and I can't help but start to giggle.

"Oh, if you guys only knew, I have many flaws." I start to laugh that kind of building laugh that only happens after a good cry.

"Just one request," Casey says with a funny grin as she turns toward me.

"Sure," I say.

"Can you *not* critique my clothes anymore? You know, I'm not exactly going to dress like you." Thankfully, she laughs.

"I like the way you dress," adds Jens, staring longingly at her.

"Fair enough." I smile. "I will keep my opinions to myself."

"Ha! Unlikely!" Casey quips with a burst of laughter.

"You're right. Who am I kidding?" I start to laugh, too, as I wipe the wetness from my cheeks.

"But, seriously, thanks, Bree, for coming in and saying something. It means a lot to us, and we know it could not have been easy," Jen says.

"I should have done it sooner…but I want my friends to be happy." I pause for a moment and then say, "It makes me happy when you're happy."

"Us, too," says Casey.

"I'm working on being happier."

"Anything we can do to help?" Jen asks.

I smile slightly. "No, but I'll be sure to let you know if there is."

"Okay. You know we are here." Casey says.

"Thanks. I'll see you guys tomorrow."

"Good night, Bree," they both say.

"Good night, you two," I say with a wink as I close the door behind me.

I know Laura is surprised to hear a faint knock on her door this late in the evening. It is nearly eleven. I can hear her come close to the door, so I knock again.

"I know you're in there," I say quietly. "It's me. Can you…" My voice strains to get the rest out, but I stop mid sentence when I hear her start to unlock the door.

"Bree, hey, is everything—" Laura is barely able to get the words out.

With one glimpse from her understanding face, I suddenly burst into tears.

Dr. Leo warned me this would be hard for me, considering how much I like Laura. So, I can't even give her time to react, for fear she is still mad at me. Considering my vulnerable state, I just need to have her arms around me.

It has all come to this. Bree Van Tousen's wall is finally crumbling. I know now that I can't do this alone. Dr. Leo can't cure me. I need to begin building or leaning on my relationships to help me get through this. I have a feeling that Laura is the type of friend who holds no grudges and is willing to move forward. I need to move forward. But, before I can, I need Laura to know that I'm sorry, and more importantly, I want her to know what happened to me—all of it.

"Oh," Laura gasps as she puts her arms around my body.

I am weak, and my body shakes uncontrollably. Laura reaches up and strokes my hair. Like a mother holding a small child, I hear her hum slightly, trying to calm me.

"Oh, Laura, I'm so sorry," I start to say.

Laura gently shushes me, letting me know there is no need to apologize.

Finally, I pull away. I know my makeup is a mess, and I never let anyone lay eyes on me if I'm a mess. I'm so tired though, and I have been unable to sleep for so long that I can't care right now what I look like. I don't have the energy.

"No, you don't understand," I say as I wipe away my makeup and tears.

"Okay. Is everything all right?" Laura asks.

"I don't know. I feel like I've lost who I am. Like…" I search for the right words, but no words come to mind. So, instead, I go over to Laura's bed and lie back on her pillow.

Laura gently lowers herself next to me. I can tell she is being very sensitive to me right now, and I appreciate that about her.

She reaches over to turn on her light, slightly touching me, and I can't help but shudder.

"Bree," she says softly, "I am your friend, you know." Laura's voice is so sweet and kind.

"Thank you," I whisper. "I'm sorry I haven't been a—"

Laura cuts me off, "Would I be here if I thought for one second that you weren't my friend?"

"I guess not," I whisper as I begin to cry again.

Her expression is so soft and nonjudgmental. I'm not used to this.

"No, of course not. Now, what's going on, Bree? You can tell me anything."

I pause and take a deep breath as I try to gain some composure.

"What I am about to tell you, I ask that you keep a secret until I'm ready for it not to be."

"Yes, absolutely."

"Well, it all started on my first night at school. Before I knew any of you guys on the floor, I met a girl at the Union, and we were given this flyer to go to a party." I start to sob a little harder. "So, I went...I went to the party with her and a few other girls from another dorm."

Laura sits and listens, trying hard not to react to the horrifying account that gradually unfolds in front of her. She keeps her eyes locked on mine while I talk about my first night at college and how, up until now, I tried to go it alone. Why I left for a week and met Eva and how she made me understand that I needed someone like Dr. Leo to guide me to where I am today. But, more importantly, I explain how the events that happened changed who I once had been and how the more I was altered and provoked by that night, the more rigid I became. I make no excuses for me being bitchy—I am, and I know it—but much like others, there is another side of me that is caring and simply wants to be loved.

After about an hour of crying, my tears finally seem to dry up. I'm exhausted from talking but continue, "See? That's why I left school in the beginning. I ran away from my problems, hoping to self-heal. And I did for a little bit...until I came back and was constantly reminded of what had happened to me. That is why I wanted some big and strong guy to sweep me off my feet, to protect me, to make me feel like I wasn't just some stupid freshman girl."

"Oh, Bree. You have to know that you are so much more than that."

"Yeah, well, when you see someone who has it all and they don't even know it, it makes you wonder."

"Are you talking about Abigail?"

I hesitate and then slowly nod my head. It's hard for someone like me to admit that somebody else has what I want—a great relationship that is safe, loving, and intriguing. Or better yet, what I briefly had with Adam. The incredible sensation of meeting your match—intellectually and sexually. A person who brings out a side of you that will spend numerous weeks in a cabin, making pizza over an open flame, not in a fancy hotel room in New York City with expensive room service. Someone who pushes you because they know, in the end, they'll get the greatest you that you can be. That is what it was like to be with Adam, and that is why I miss him dearly.

"Bree, if you think she has it all, you're wrong. No one does."

"From where I'm standing, it sure seems like she has it all," I say with sadness. "I mean, she has Tank rescuing her and Nathan pining over her, and she seems like she couldn't care less."

"That is not true," Laura says softly.

"Really?"

"Yes, you'll have to trust me on this one for now."

There is silence. I can hear the clock on their wall *tick, tick, tick*, like it is haunting me. She waits for me to speak. My mind is racing as my eyes dart back and forth across the room.

"I believe they caught our attacker, you know."

"What?"

"Yes, I saw Abigail and Tank at the police station."

"Oh my God, what did Abigail say?"

"Nothing. I waited for them to leave before I went into the station."

"But you were there?"

"After hearing what happened to Abigail, I decided I should have spoken up. The night it happened to me, Laura, I ran right into a police officer as I was running from *him*. I had a chance to do something, and I panicked. I was so afraid of what others might think. So, instead, I ignored it, praying it would all go away. Maybe I cared so much that I...I don't know. You know, I can't help but believe that I could have saved Abigail."

"Hey," Laura says softly, "look at me, will you?"

I slowly raise my head.

"You are not the reason this happened. *He* is the reason this happened."

"I suppose," I respond halfheartedly.

She reaches up and gently touches my hand, squeezing it slightly. I don't pull away. In fact, I lean in closer to Laura and rest my head on her shoulder. Laura puts her chin on top of my head as she wraps her other arm around my shoulder.

I sigh.

"Is there anything I can do for you, Bree? Any way I can help you through this?" she asks.

"Being here for me and Abigail is more than I could ask of one person. I know this must be a lot for you as well."

There is silence as we sit close to one another. It is an unusual instance at best, and I sense our connection grow.

My breathing starts to steady.

"This has been a lot for me. My two dearest friends, both hurt by the same man. I am trying to absorb all of this, and I have seen the toll it has taken on both you and Abigail—with school, classes, relationships, all of it."

"I know, Laura. It has done a number on us both."

"But, Bree, can I ask you something? Something I've been trying to figure out myself these past months…"

"Sure."

"Do you believe there is someone out there for each of us? I suppose I'm asking…do you believe in fate?" Her voice quivers.

It makes me sit up, so I can question her.

I search Laura's face to make sure she is not joking around. She is serious, and she wants to know.

I have, in fact, thought a lot about fate this past year. *What made me decide to come to OSU?* I was so determined to make this my home for the next four years that I barely even glanced at the other acceptance letters. And then to think, on my very first night away from my home, my family, and my friends, I encountered him by just a slight happenstance. A flash in time, and my life suddenly changed. Then, I got the internship, and without warning, I fell for a man I knew I couldn't have, yet I did. Then, only to find out, that wasn't meant to be either, and again, my world changed. So, yes, I've thought a lot about fate, but it is much more than that.

I sit up tall, tuck my hair behind my ear, and stare directly into Laura's eyes. "Call it fate, coincidence, or even destiny, but yes, I absolutely believe that, in one moment, our lives are meant to collide with another, changing us forever. Like me and you and Abigail. All of us together." I pause, gazing deeply in her eyes. "But I've always felt that chance meetings aren't necessarily unintentional, you know. We can and should make our own good fortune in this world by opening ourselves to the possibility that possibilities happen."

Her eyes are misty, but a warm smile spreads across her beautiful face. "Wow, you really do believe. And I guess some might say a chance meeting happened to you."

"Yes, it did, and it changed me."

"It will be for the better…someday."

"I appreciate you saying that." I take her hand and squeeze it.

"But there is something else holding you back."

"What do you mean?"

"I can tell you are not saying everything that is on your mind."

I sigh again. Then, with a slight chuckle, I say, "Yeah, can you help me figure out my love life?" The words flow so hastily out of my mouth in the moment that I almost can't believe that I have said it.

"Love life?" she asks.

I lower my eyes again. "Yes, love life."

"What gives, Bree? You have a secret boyfriend?" She laughs slightly, only she doesn't know she hit the nail right on the head. "Oh my God, you do?" A smile draws across her face.

"Laura, you have to keep this between us. It's…well, it's a big deal."

"Oh, do tell!"

"Well, I...I mean, we sort of fell for each other, and now, it's over. So, not much to discuss."

"What do you mean, over? Tell me everything."

"So, the reason you can't say a word is because he could get fired from his job." I pause, watching her to gauge if she is catching on. She isn't, so I continue, "From school, here at the university."

She stares up at the ceiling, and I can tell her mind is racing.

Then, her jaw drops open slightly, and she says, "Oh my God, the hot professor who drove us home?" She gasps. "Oh, your internship professor! Holy shit, Bree, you are sleeping with your teacher?"

"Shh! Quiet, will you? It's honestly not like that. He's only twenty-four, and I'm nineteen now, so it's not like we wouldn't date had we not both been here."

"When was your birthday?" she asks.

"Last week."

"Bree, why didn't you tell us?" Laura barks.

"I was too busy sulking in my room."

"Fine, we'll deal with that later. Back to your professor. He can get in big trouble."

"I know, I know, but he called it off anyway."

"I'm so sorry."

I start to cry again. "Me, too. Everything was going so well. I mean, really well. We spent the whole winter break living in his cabin. It was incredible."

"Wow, that sounds totally hot."

I blush as I daydream about us over the winter break. "It was, Laura. He's kind and a genius and gorgeous and sexy and knows how to cook and treat me like a normal girl. It was never about my money or anything fake like that. It was real, and I totally fell for him. And I thought he fell for me, but...I was so wrong."

"When did he break up with you?"

"He went away over Valentine's Day to a conference, and when he came back, he said he got together with—oh, wait, you saw her. The woman at the restaurant."

"The older woman with the wedding ring on? That woman? No way."

"What?"

"No way. Not buying it. She was much older. Not that it really matters, but a hot guy like him, who would be interested in a girl like you, would not run to a woman who was married. Not buying it one bit." She gives me such a serious expression that I actually start to question what the heck is going on.

"This is not exactly making me feel better."

My mind is racing with all kinds of wild thoughts. *Is she married? Is he having an affair with her? Was he lying to me just to get rid of me? Is she the woman who called in the cabin? Is that why he was weird when he answered the phone? Was it her, begging him to come back? Did he feel trapped with me in the cabin that he had to wait until the winter break was over to dump me?*

"It has to be something else," Laura says with confidence.

"Like what?"

"If he spent all those weeks with you in his cabin and then came back to school and everything was cool for a few more weeks, something else had to have happened. It's only an assumption, but…"

It did seem wildly out of the blue, I think. "Regardless, it's over. I haven't heard from him in two weeks."

"And how has he been acting?"

"What do you mean?" I tip my head to the side and stare at her.

"Has he been showing up to class, to your internship, and all that? Have things with him been normal?"

"No, not exactly, but maybe he's worried about me blowing the whistle, so to speak."

"No way. You're too mature not to be trusted," she says so matter-of-factly that I can't help but start to question the whole situation.

"I suppose, but I don't want him to trust me. I want him to love me." I almost can't believe I said what I said.

Laura's eyes light up. My heart thumps stiff in my chest, and I burst into tears.

"Oh, Bree. Then, go tell him that!"

"I can't," I respond through my sobs as I lower my head. "I can't, Laura. I am *so* hurt."

"Yes, you *can*." She waits for me to meet her eyes. Then, she continues, "In my opinion and what I'm assuming would be most people's opinions, you two have already done what you were not supposed to do, so what difference does it make at this point? Love is love, and if you believe he loves you, too, then don't let him get away." She pushes on my leg. "Don't let him."

"I don't know. A part of me thinks he felt sorry for me because of the attack."

"What the hell are you talking about?" she barks.

"Office Murphy told me he knew about me, and I believe that is why he paid attention to me."

"So, he invites you to his cabin because he felt sorry for you? He put his job on the line because he felt sorry for you? Think about what you are saying. It doesn't make sense."

She is right. Maybe that doesn't make sense, but I can't deny that he told me he was back with Anna. *How can I dispute that?*

"I know. I have been so sad, Laura. Like I know I had something special, and it didn't last long enough."

"Oh, Bree, I'm so sorry. This has been a terrible start to university life. I wish I could help more or do something. Ugh."

She too starts to cry. She grabs a tissue and dabs the corner of her eye.

"You are helping, Laura. Thank you for being my friend all this time, despite my bitchy behavior. It's just sort of who I was at home and how I became here. I'm not proud of it, but please know I do mean well."

"I know you do."

My God, she actually gets me.

"I'm sure Abigail hates me, but I guess I was so jealous of her and Nathan. That was, until I found Adam. Then, when I found out she was attacked, I hated myself for not being stronger. I shut down."

"Abigail does not hate you. She doesn't hate anyone."

"Ugh, God, is she really that perfect?" I say, unable to control the smile as it spreads across my face. I wipe the remaining tears off my cheek.

"Ha! I know, right? Beautiful, smart, caring—she has it all. And so do you, Bree."

"Funny."

"No, I'm not kidding. You both are so lovely. You're more alike than you know."

I don't even hesitate as I lean over and embrace Laura. I squeeze her tightly and whisper, "It's you who is lovely, Laura. Abigail and I are both so very lucky to call you our friend. You are the rock on this floor. You keep us all together."

"Oh, thank you, Bree. I try. You guys sure do make things interesting." She laughs.

I release my embrace and sit back. "I know, right? Never a dull moment around here."

"Yes, so keep the roller coaster moving, and go talk to him. Even if it's merely to get final closure. He'll appreciate that you did. He wants to know you're okay, Bree."

"I'll think about it, okay? But I'm not making any promises."

"Well, someone had better bring the love back to this floor. I'm counting on you."

I smile slightly and then say, "Speaking of love, you hear about Jen and Casey?"

Laura smiles so genuinely that it nearly melts my heart. "Yes, and it's the best thing to happen to our friends this year. So, all is not lost."

"All is not lost," I repeat.

Twenty-Two

AIMING TO DESTROY

I walk out of my class and head down the hallway of the Draper building. I am sort of hoping to catch Adam in his office. At least if we meet in his office, I can keep it to business, and he won't feel as though I am going to make it about us even though I'd like it to be. But Professor Gilford scolded me for not completing some of the adjustments to the project's outline, and he more or less indicated to me that Adam and I had better get our act together. People are waiting on this project, much to my surprise. I assumed, at this point, that Adam had been making the changes, and I was to be left out of the picture, but that doesn't seem to be the case.

I approach his office. The door is closed, and the light seems to be off. I sit down in the chair in the hallway across from his room. I pull out my notebook. At least I can leave him a note and tell him to make the changes before Professor Gilford gets even more pissed.

I rummage through my bag and finally find a pen. I write *Adam* but hastily scratch that out and begin a new sheet that says *Professor Cooper* on the top.

I peek up and try to find the right words to say. I don't want to seem bitchy, and I don't want to seem like I don't care. *Ugh, this is too hard.*

Then, suddenly, out of nowhere, I hear, "Writing a love letter?"

I whip my head around and notice Ashley standing there, hands digging into her hips.

"Excuse me?" I say as my eyes narrow.

What is your freaking problem? I think. *Are you that bent because you didn't get the freaking internship? You can have it! And, by the way, learn to take rejection like I have from Adam. Shit, we both have! Move on with your life, girl, like I plan to. We both don't have a choice.*

I wish I had the energy right now to say all of that, but instead, I mutter, "You say something?"

"Never mind," she says as she twirls her blonde hair to the side. "See you later, *Bree*." The way she says my name with a laugh makes my skin crawl.

God, I have got to pick a new major, I think.

I watch as she starts to exit the door. But before she does, she turns ever so slightly to me and then gives me a cruel smile before pushing open the door and stepping outside.

What is her problem?

I pull up in front of Adam's house and see his car in the driveway. I park in my usual spot, get out, and then hurry up the stairs. I knock with authority on the door.

I observe him through the glass as he approaches.

Damn it, I think.

He is absolutely gorgeous. My heart flutters, and my stomach starts flipping over and over.

He pulls open the door a crack. "Bree, what are you doing here?"

"Professor Gilford sent me. We need to talk about the project."

"I know," he says. "Tell him I'm fixing it."

"Can I please see it? I'd like to think my name is still on this?"

His face softens, and he reluctantly opens the door completely in order to let me in.

"Yes, of course. We could go to my office? I can meet you there in twenty."

Shit, Bree, think fast.

My shoulders drop, as I know he's right to say that, but still, I need some time alone with him.

"Listen, Adam," I say as I step in and close the door behind me.

He twitches slightly at the sound of his name, and I hate it. He never did that before. He got so used to me calling him Adam that, naturally, it became a regular thing.

"I know I haven't seen you in a while, and I understand why…"

He studies me, cocking his head to the side. His eyes soften, and I can tell something is off.

"How is Anna by the way? You two happy?" I use a little sarcasm, just to be honest and true to me.

He hesitates and then says, "Yeah, sure, we are."

"See her much? Doesn't she live far away?"

"Just a few hours, but, Bree, it's not really your business anymore."

Ouch, that hurts.

"I know. I thought we were friends, but I assume I was wrong about that, too." *Was I ever your friend?* I wonder.

"We were friends. But we can't be now."

"Why is that? Does Anna know about me?"

"Yes, I told her."

"Why?"

"I needed her, um—" He stops and observes me. "What's all this about, Bree?"

I can tell he's getting frustrated, but I continue, "So, you chose to tell her about me, but no one else. Why not pretend it never happened?"

"Because I couldn't, Bree. Is that what you want to hear?" He runs his hand through his hair.

His cheeks pink. I can tell I've hit a nerve.

"Only if that is the truth."

He stares down at the ground now, awkwardly shifting from foot to foot, unable to stand still. "Yes, it is."

"So, you told your past/current girlfriend about me because you had to? Seems odd." I decide to continue, "Is it odd perhaps because she is married?"

He whips his head up at me and stares at me. I'm getting a gnawing impression in my gut that I have caught him in a lie.

I aspire to channel Laura as I take a deep breath. She said I could do this. She picked up on the fact that Anna was married. *So, is she?* If nothing else, I want to know.

"She is married, right? Or does she wear that massive diamond on her ring finger to make others jealous?"

"When did you see that?" he asks, not realizing that he admitted at minimum that there is a ring on her finger.

"At the restaurant, the night you drove Laura and I home. In fact, even then, you never said she was your girlfriend. You said nothing."

"That is because I wouldn't have labeled it to the two of you. It was none of your business."

"But we were just two girls, out at an off-campus dinner, who happened to run into a professor at a location far from school. What would have been the harm then?" He stares at me, so I continue, "I mean, you are allowed to date older women. Just not women closer to your age, say, at the university, right?"

"Bree," he says, peering past me toward the door, as though he is expecting someone to be outside. "You should leave. We can continue this conversation at school, okay?"

"Boy, you truly don't care for me, do you?" I whisper. It hurts to even say the words.

"Bree, please…"

The tears begin to well in my eyes. "Please what? Try to understand how you could dump me so hastily? How am I not supposed to think it's odd that you're dating a married woman and so fast?" My voice quivers.

"Like I said, I've known her a long time."

My hands are shaking. I squeeze my fists tight, trying to steady myself. "I see. Boy, do I feel better now, Adam. I'm glad I was a placeholder for you, someone you could watch out for because, in the end, you merely felt sorry for me. Is that what you told Anna? That you were sympathetic to my situation? Another stupid freshman victim? So, what? You'd walk me home to keep me safe, be the hero, and then decide to lure me into your bed…" My lip starts to quiver as I choke out, "Only to cast me aside once they caught the asshole who has been terrorizing the campus." My heart rate speeds up as my words come pouring out of me.

His eyes grow painfully wide. But he says nothing.

He takes a step toward me, but I move away.

"What did you just say, Bree?" he whispers as he comes closer again.

"Stop, Adam." I hold up my hand.

"Why do you know about that?" he asks through gritted teeth.

"Know about what?"

"That *asshole*."

"Officer Murphy." I pause, searching his face.

He appears like he's going to be sick to his stomach. But I can almost guarantee he doesn't feel as bad as I do.

"He said you knew about…me," I whisper, lowering my head.

He comes closer. My back is now up against the wall.

"Oh my God…no, Bree."

I peer up at him, barely able to meet his eyes. "What, Adam?" My voice is trembling badly, and I hate it.

"Are you telling me you were attacked by that man on campus? Is that what you are saying to me?" His eyes flash with anger and deep concern.

"Yes, but I thought you already knew that." A tear rolls down my cheek.

"I-I had…what I'm trying to say is Officer Murphy and I have become friends over the year, and he let me know there was a major issue on our campus…but no names were ever exchanged." Then, in a whisper, he adds, "Now, I know why you scream at night."

"What did you say?"

"Nothing. I mean, I wondered why, sometimes, at night in the cabin, you wouldn't sometimes sleep well."

"I'm sorry."

"Don't be. I thought it was maybe how you slept, and I loved having you next to me that…I didn't care."

I have to glaze over his comment about sleeping beside me because it hurts too much to think about those days in the cabin. I long for them and hate him for giving me such a wonderful taste of how good our relationship could be.

"Why then…why would you insist on escorting me home all the time?"

"At first, I wanted to, um…talk to you, get to know you better."

"I see. Of course…until—"

"Bree, listen to me. Are you okay? Is there anything I can do to help you or find you help? I want you to be okay. Are you sleeping at all?"

"I'm fine."

"How can you be fine?"

"I'm not your concern anymore, Adam, so let me handle my life, and you do the same." Only I don't mean it. I'm not fine. I don't want him to leave me alone.

"I'm sorry it has to be this way…"

Boom. Another blow to my heart. I can't take it anymore.

"So am I, but I don't want to be with someone who doesn't want to be with me. So, you can stop feeling sorry for me, and quite honestly, I'd appreciate it if you acted like you never knew me." I have thought long and hard about what I'm about to say to him. "You can take my name off the project and do as you wish with it. I'll tell Gilford that you and I had creative differences and that I'd like to end my internship." It's too hard to continue to work with him.

"You can't mean that."

"Yes, I can, and I do. Being around you, after all we have been through and now you knowing about what happened to me…well, I'm better off cutting my ties and finding something new to occupy my time."

"I believe you're giving up on a fantastic opportunity."

"Why—and be honest, Adam—do you even care?"

"Because I do, okay?" He takes a step back and again seems wildly agitated.

He is confusing me even more, but I'm too tired to argue.

"You can save it for Anna, okay?" I say with deep sarcasm.

"Listen, it's just that…"

"That what?"

He doesn't speak, so I turn deliberately toward the door and say, "Thanks for clarifying your feelings, and don't worry; I won't tell a soul about us—ever."

I start to open the door when his hand reaches over the top of me and pushes the door back shut.

"Bree, look at me, please."

I can barely get my words out. "I can't."

"Please, I…I have to tell you something."

"Then say it, Adam."

I still can't turn to him, as I know the tears are filling my eyes. He's probably going to give me one final parting gesture, like, *It was fun while it lasted,* or, *Sorry it didn't work out,* or worse, *It's not you; it's me.* And that alone makes me want to run out the door.

I reach for the knob when he doesn't speak. "Let me go, please," I plead.

"That's just it, Bree. I *had* to let you go."

I lower my head, thinking, *I know. We've already gone through this. Because of Anna—as unbelievable as I think that reason is.*

"I know…Anna."

"No, it's not Anna."

My skin prickles as he gently places his hand on my shoulder.

I turn to face him. "What do you mean?"

"I had to end it in order to keep my job and your reputation."

"Why do you say that?"

"Because…I can't tell you exactly. You just have to trust me."

"Trust you? All you're doing is speaking in codes. The bottom line is that you have someone new. You don't want to or can't—whatever it is— be with me. So, the situation for me remains the same."

"I know, and I'm sorry. Truly."

"I don't believe that, not even for a second." I blink back my tears.

"Please, Bree, I can't have you leaving here, believing I'm some monster who doesn't care about you. Who doesn't think about you all the time? Sleepless nights, wanting so badly for things to be different."

"Why can't they be different?"

"Because they can't."

I wipe away a tear on my cheek. I give Adam one final glance, knowing it might be the last. "Good-bye, Adam."

I open the door and head out onto his porch. I know he is standing there, watching me.

Then, without warning, he utters, "It's Ashley."

My heart can only be broken so many times in one day, month, year, and I think I have hit my quota for all of them. It aches so badly in my chest that I want to curl up in a ball and forget the world.

I stop on the porch, and then it dawns on me—her smug expression the other day, seeing her in his office again, seeing her leaving here. All the little snide remarks she's said to me. Sticking close to me on the project. It was never going to just be him and me. He plays the field, like he played me—and quite well, I might add.

I spin back around. Now, I'm angrier than sad. "I get it. So, you told me it was Anna, so I wouldn't find out you were back to screwing another one of your students. Very clever, Adam. I give you props for that slick move."

"Please come back inside." His voice is dark.

I narrow my eyes at him and don't budge.

"Please, Bree. You will want to hear what I have to say."

"Oh, really? Now, you're going to tell me the truth? Let me guess. I'm not the first student you took to the cabin. I'm not the first girl you chose for the internship. I'm—"

He gasps. "*Bree….*" His eyes are so sad and lost.

I might have gone too far.

When I don't move, he says again, "Please, I beg you."

I cross my arms and enter back into the foyer.

He closes the door, locks it, and then says, "Follow me." He leads me into the kitchen.

"Adam, you're scaring me. What the hell is this all about?"

He turns, and I notice sheer sadness on his otherwise handsome face.

"I need you to hear me out before you react, okay?"

"Adam, please."

"Say you'll promise me, Bree?"

"I promise," I say through clenched teeth.

He stops in front of the sink and turns to me. "You're right. Anna and I are just friends. In fact, she and her husband are both close friends of mine. I was his student for several years, and I have written and published two papers with him. So, yes, we are very close, and no, I am not dating her."

A huge sigh of relief comes over me although I'm still sick to my stomach.

"So, you've never had a romantic relationship with her?"

"Never, Bree. That would be like dating my aunt. Never even crossed my mind. They are happily married. The only reason I said it was her is because you met her and saw her leave my house. So, I knew it could make a plausible story."

I raise my eyes at him.

He adds, "At least it worked for a little bit. But I should have known you'd catch on. You're too smart not to see through me." He smiles slightly.

"But I never saw this coming. I thought we were just starting. I thought our time spent together was genuine. I didn't think I was some fling who would be so easily dropped. I still don't get why, Adam. Why do you think you are going to lose…" Then, my skin pricks at attention, and my heart races with anger. My eyes grow wide. I gasp and place my hand over my mouth.

He stands there, shaking his head, like he's already lost.

I slowly release my hand, and I can't help but hiss, "That little bitch."

"Bree, please hear me out. I have no idea how Ashley found out, but she did. She would occasionally come to my office to ask me questions about class, but one day, she showed up, and I knew something was different. I don't know how long she has known, but she knows."

"What *exactly* did she say?" I can't tell if I want to cry or knock a hole in the wall.

"Honestly, she started in with me at first. Asking me all kinds of questions about why I stopped seeing her. I'd thought it was water under the bridge. Then, she started in on you. She said that there was no way you deserved the internship, that I gave it to you because I wanted to sleep with you. She also said that because you got the highest grade on the final that I must have given you the answers."

"Now, wait a minute. I aced that test because it was easy!" My voice rises about ten octaves.

"Shh, Bree. Now, listen to me. Twenty-three people in the class out of eighty failed it. Didn't even pass. It was not meant to be easy. She barely passed herself."

"But you didn't give me even a clue about the test. And the internship, you didn't even want me to begin with. I barely knew I had the internship until the day you randomly announced it in class!"

"I know, but listen, she plans to go to the school board, and that could prevent me from teaching. She wants to report that you got special treatment during class, in the internship, and on the final exam. It will ultimately smear your name, and you, too, could be asked to leave the university. You could be expelled. After all you've been through this year...enough is enough, Bree. I know this is the right decision—for both of us."

"But you didn't even ask me or talk to me. You cast me aside, like I meant nothing to you."

"I had to react. She gave me no time. She told me, if I told you anything, she'd come forward. Once the rumors are out there, Bree, they might as well be true because people will believe the gossip over fact any day. She gave me no time and no choice. It was either do as she said or both my career and your education would be gone."

"So, that's it?"

"Yes, I'm afraid so."

"Didn't you deny it to her?"

"I tried…" He goes over to his cabinet near the refrigerator and takes something out. He approaches and hands me a picture. "But she showed me this."

I feel like I'm going into shock.

It is a clear photograph of Adam and me locked in a passionate kiss. No mistaking it; it's us. And there is definitely no mistaking that we aren't just friends.

"Oh my God." I slowly lower my body down and sit at the table.

"She says she has more."

"She is stalking you?" I whisper.

"I'm not sure if she doesn't want me to be with you or if it really is about her and me."

"But you said you only dated briefly."

"We did. It was only a few weeks, and I broke it off. It wasn't the right chemistry between us. But, again, she said she could prove that we dated."

I can't help but think about our chemistry and how it just seemed to be *so* right.

"That was why Anna was here that night. I needed her legal advice. She is not only my friend, but she is also my lawyer, and I trust her. So, she said I should appease Ashley until we can find out what the ramifications might be, should I come forward." Exhausted, he runs his hand through his hair, and with the saddest expression, he adds, "Bree, I need you to know I had to do what I had to do. And I'm so sorry for that."

"So, you were going to let me go on thinking that you never cared about me?" I hate that I have to say it, and I hate even more that we are so far apart from where we were just weeks ago…when we were so happy.

"No, I was hoping, eventually, I could find you again and tell you the truth."

"Find me again? Why? Are you leaving?"

He lowers his head.

"Adam, please, what is it?"

"The reason Anna was here is that, with Professor Gilford's permission, I will be taking a sabbatical for the next year. I'm going to go out and teach our curriculum to other universities. It's a huge opportunity for us—me and you, Bree—to get our work out there."

"But you're leaving? For a whole year?"

"Yes, I have to separate myself from this situation and Ashley. She agreed that, if I leave and break it off with you, she'd drop all of this."

"How the hell am I supposed to go on here, knowing that she could destroy me or you at anytime?"

"Because she says she won't, Bree. As long as I leave and you're here, then this all goes away."

"I see. So, you just leave, and everything will be fine. That is your plan?"

"Yes, for now, it is. I can't ruin your life or mine—or anyone's, for that matter. Sooner or later, we all need to move on, and I suppose this is simply forcing us to."

I stand up and step back from him. A thousand knives are jammed inside my chest. I'm speechless. This scenario keeps getting worse.

Finally, I find my words again. "Wow. Okay. I guess I'll leave you then. And if I run into Ashley?"

"You must ignore her, please. Do your work, and you'll be fine, Bree. I know you will."

Fine. I'll be fine. Has anything that has happened to me this year been fine? The attack wasn't fine. Going to the police station wasn't fine. Being rejected by Nathan wasn't fine. The only things at school that have been fine had to do with you, Assistant Professor Adam Cooper.

And, now, here I stand, brokenhearted and alone, yet again.

I turn without saying a word and walk down the hallway to the front door. I can't even set my eyes on him. I yank open the door and step out.

As I slam the door, I hear a faint cry, "Bree, wait."

I get into my car and drive straight home.

Twenty-Three

HARD-NOSED ADVICE

"Daddy, it's me," I say, shaking him slightly.

It's three in the morning. Good thing my mother sleeps with an eye mask on and earplugs in; she always has.

"Bree, darling, what are you doing home?" My dad's eyes grow wide.

"I'm fine, Dad, but I need to talk to you," I whisper.

"Okay, let me get dressed. I'll meet you in my study." My father is used to being woken up late at night. He was once a lawyer, and he'd get calls at all hours from clients needing his services.

"Thank you, Dad," I whisper.

I pace his study, back and forth and back and forth, until I finally hear the creak of the door as he opens it.

"Bree, you all right?" he asks, eyeing me up and down. "Why are you not at school?" He's panicked.

Before I can even get one word out, I burst into tears. "Oh, Dad, I need your help."

"My God, Bree," he says, rushing over.

He hugs me tightly as I begin to sob uncontrollably. His big arms around me is something that can never be replaced or duplicated, and I realize unequivocally that I should have come to him from the beginning.

He sits us down on the couch. "Shh, darling, everything will be okay. I promise, honey. Tell me how to help you." He strokes my hair like he used to when I was a child and was crying from a bump or scrape.

I can't take my arms off of him. Feeling the warm embrace of my father is enough to begin to thaw my heart.

He continues to rub my head and waits for me to move.

I finally sit up. I wipe the wetness from my cheeks as my father hands me his handkerchief.

"Dad, I didn't know where else to go."

"Did you drive all night?"

"Yes. I know what you're going to say, and I'm sorry. Next time, I won't. But I needed to see you, face-to-face."

"Bree, you can't be reckless like that, okay? You should have called me. I would have come to you."

"No, Daddy. I wanted to leave."

"Leave? Why? Please tell me, sweetheart."

I blink back my tears. I think long and hard before I speak. My father is not naive, nor does he think that I am, but I'm still his little girl. I know everything I'm about to tell him will hurt him, the same way it hurts me.

I start from the beginning by telling him about my first night at college. I cry my way through my night and through the next few weeks of my life, the pain and suffering that I went through alone. I do, however, confess that I didn't leave school to do a reshoot for Miguel, but rather I left school to try to get away from the living nightmare I was circling in. I tell him about Eva, Dr. Leo, my friend Abigail and what happened to her…and all the other girls. I watch as my father, for maybe the first time, cries in front of me.

"Dad, please don't cry. Please."

"But you are my Bree." He places his hand over his heart.

I reach up and take it. "Dad, I will get through this. But I need you now. I need you."

My father knows exactly what I am talking about, and I watch as he gathers himself, collecting his thoughts and his breath.

Then, in true lawyer fashion, he flips the switch.

He asks me about the police report, which will be made available to my father—or should I say, whichever lawyer he hires.

My father, being a lawyer and strict businessman, never overreacts to situations, which is why I am comfortable with talking to him. I know, deep inside, he is devastated, but showing it to me right now would only make what happened worse. I love that about him. He is being calm and composed and trying to think ahead. I need him to think ahead.

Without warning, my father hangs his head. I take his hand.

"Dad, please forgive me for not coming to you sooner. I know it sounds so cliché, but the more I tried to hide it from all of you, the darker my heart got."

"My sweet darling, I wish I had known. But I can't even imagine the internal turmoil you must have battled each and every day."

"I had to in order to come to this moment. No matter how many times Dr. Leo asked me if I'd told you, I was never ready until now. When I was sitting in the police station and I noticed all the files of other girls, I couldn't help but wonder, what if some of those girls didn't have anyone to turn to, no one to help or support them? Then, it dawned on me. I'd be one of them until I told someone."

My dad exhales.

"For starters, I'm glad that you did."

"I knew then that I could not do this alone. None of us can."

"You let Abigail know, if she needs any help, I'm here for her as well."

"I will, Dad." My eyes start to well again as I think of her.

My father pats my arm. "I'll call my lawyer in the morning, and we will get ahead of this and make sure you are taken care of during the process. But, Bree, I'm so proud of you for stepping forward. It's a brave thing to do, and you should feel good about that. No matter how or when you did it, it's the fact that you did."

"Thank you, but I have more to tell you."

"Okay, go on."

I take a deep breath in and search my father's face. My eyes dart back and forth. I breathe out and say, "I fell in love with someone I shouldn't have, and now, his career is on the line all because of me."

I'm surprised when a slight smile grows across my father's face.

"You fell in love?" he whispers.

I've never told my dad that I even liked someone enough to bring them to the house, let alone be in love.

"Yes, Dad. He's brilliant, sweet, engaging, wildly interesting, active, and a hell of a cook."

"You don't say. Who is this mystery guy?" he says with an enormous smile.

It fills my heart to see him happy for me.

"Herein lies the problem. He is a professor."

My father sits back and feverishly rubs his face. He went from happy to contemplative.

"But, before I say anything else, he is only twenty-four, only a year out of graduate school. He's so brilliant, Dad—"

"You mentioned that," he says dryly.

"I mean it. We are working on creating this amazing program that other universities want to use, but now, all of that might be gone. Well, I just—"

He holds up his hand toward me. "Slow down, Bree. Tell me what the problem is."

"He's being blackmailed—at least I think he is—by a former girlfriend. Although it's doubtful you can even classify her as that, but still, she made him break up with me. She threatened to tell the school that I received preferential treatment and was given the internship and answers on the final because of my relationship with him."

"You—"

"No, Dad. Of course not. I would never do that." It hurts that he asked me.

"I know, sweetie. I have to ask. It's the lawyer in me."

"I know, but nothing she is saying is true."

"Who else knows?"

"Only me, him, her—er, Ashley is her name—and my floor mate Laura."

"That is all?"

"Yes."

"So, it is her word against yours?"

"Yes, but she told him she would drop it if he broke up with me and left school. So, he did. I mean, he is."

"He is leaving the university?"

"Yes, and…" I start to cry.

"What kind of man would let you go over a threat?" His voice is surprisingly irritated.

"That is not fair. We are talking about his career. He is on track to take over for the head of the department. He can't jeopardize that for me."

"So, he's too driven by his job?" My father seems strangely angry on my behalf.

"You, of all people, can't say that. Think of all the sacrifices you made to get ahead, to make sure that, in the end, you got to where you knew you needed to be."

"I know, honey, but I don't like to think of someone breaking your heart."

"I've had my heart broken a lot this year, and I'm still standing. I might wobble from time to time, but I'm on my own two feet."

He reaches over and touches my hand. "I know you are. You are a Van Tousen, and we stand tall."

"Thank you for understanding."

"I understand some of it. But why not fight back a little? Tell her none of this is true and force her to prove it?"

"She already did."

"How so?"

I reach into my pocket and pull out the photo I took from Adam's house—without him knowing. I knew, if I asked him for it, it might tip him off, so I was hoping he'd forget I had it. And it worked.

"She gave him this."

I watch my father's eyes scan over the picture and am embarrassed that he has to see me kissing someone. It must be so weird.

"Hold on a second. She is taking pictures of you both, without your knowledge?"

"So bizarre, right? I have no idea when this was taken, and she said, at least to him, that she has more."

"She is a student at the school?"

"Yes. She was in my class last semester. Introduced herself to me once and asked me how I got the internship. She said that she had applied twice and never gotten it. Then, we worked on a project all semester together, and I thought she was a little short with me. There was something about her that rubbed me the wrong way."

"Okay. And what did she say to him?"

"She told him he had to break up with me and leave the school."

"Leave the school?"

"Yes, he is taking a sabbatical for now. He plans to spend the next year teaching the curriculum that he and I spent over three months working on. So, not only is he doing that, but it also leaves me out of the process. I can't blame him. That is not the issue. I was the intern on the project, but Adam and I know I contributed much more than that."

"Adam?"

"Yes, his name is Adam Cooper."

"Has he already left?"

"No, he will in the next few days."

"Does the professor he is set to replace know of this, dare I say, blackmail? Or does he think Adam's simply going off for a year?"

"I'm assuming the latter. I don't think he'd tell Professor Gilford all of this."

"Do you trust Gilford? Could you talk to him?"

"What is your advice, Dad? What would you do?"

He thoughtfully looks at me. His eyes flash with the intelligence and the heart that I need right now. He squeezes my hand again and gives me the same expression he has given me my whole life. The face that lets me know he'll stand beside me, by hook or by crook, but that he also expects me to stand with him.

He releases my hand and then brushes his fingers on my face, gently touching my cheek.

With sadness, he says, "I'll tell your mother that you got home around eleven and that you had called me at the last minute to let me know you were coming home for a long weekend."

"Thank you."

"This, of course, means you'll have to stay."

"Oh, I don't mind. It will be a welcomed break for me."

"Good. It will give me some time to iron out my thoughts and make some calls."

"I love you," I say as I stand before him and try to give him a smile.

He gets up, too, and gives me a big hug. He then whispers to me, "I love you, too. And I'm so terribly sorry, my sweet Bree."

I pull back as I can hear the pain in his voice. He glances at me, and I can see the tears in his eyes.

He chokes them back as he says, "I hate the thought of anyone hurting you, and I'm so sorry that you went through such a terrible time."

I, too, start to cry. I should have known I could count on my father. I should have known he would help me, but better yet, I should have known his love for me was unconditional.

I bury my head deep into his chest. "I know, Daddy. But please know, I always knew I'd have you to come to when I was ready."

"Every time, my love."

We stand in his study, my favorite room in the house, and hold each other like we are the only two people in the world. My father, the first man I ever loved and will always love, is holding me tightly, and I am finally safe again.

Finally.

We release our embrace and walk toward the door to his office and into the foyer.

As we make our way up the flight of stairs, he whispers, "Boy, Claudia is going to be so happy to see you tomorrow. She'll get to lay out your clothes all weekend." He playfully jabs me in the ribs.

"Ha-ha. I can honestly say, I've probably missed her more than she has missed me."

"We have all missed you."

I work quietly alongside my father in his study for most of the weekend.

Thankfully, my mother had plans at the club with her friends that she was unable to change. Charity work in my mom's circle of friends is an important part of their lives and is taken very seriously. So, she is gone most of the day and night on Saturday.

I speak with my father's lawyer, Brandon Piper, about the case on campus and how I know there are other victims and so forth. He tells me he will call the station and get a full report.

Mr. Piper tells me he will handle everything from here on out and that I no longer need to speak with the police or anyone else for that matter. I am so relieved to hear this.

These situations can be so complicated that I'm glad I finally decided to tell my father. I had to get comfortable saying it, so I might be able to make him comfortable hearing it. I was not ready until last night; this much, I know. It won't change what happened, but it will make things easier on me going forward. Less lying and having a shoulder to cry on sure sounds like a welcome win-win to me.

My father convinces me that, before I leave to go back to school, I should, out of respect, tell my mother, face-to-face, about what happened. We agree, however, that I can keep the situation with Adam and the school between my father, Mr. Piper, and myself until she needs to know. I'm grateful I don't have to tell her all of this at once. I don't think she could take it. One major issue at a time. My father learned that throughout the years as they raised a teenage son. One crisis at a time. Don't pile on everything at once.

Before I leave this afternoon, I sit down my mother and tell her what happened. My father sits next to me, holding my hand, as I let my mother know about my first night at college. I watch as Claudia moves around the kitchen as I speak. We are all so used to her being wherever we are that it doesn't faze my parents in the least. When Claudia realizes what I am saying, she stops in front of the large window near the sink and lowers her head.

My mother, on the other hand, unexpectedly cries during most of our conversation. Once I'm finished telling her, my father reassures her that Mr. Piper will take good care of me, and I will be well represented.

I watch as my mother smooths down her hair and then observes me, differently than she used to. For once, she regards me like a mother should—not inspecting me for beauty, but seeing me for who I truly am. That I'm vulnerable, and I can't be protected in the real world by money or fancy cars. To the outside world, I'm just a freshman at college, like thousands of others, trying to start my life. And, sometimes, life can be painful and scary.

"That cut on your lip, over Thanksgiving," she asks, her voice trembling.

I lower my head. She knows I don't need to answer her question.

"Oh, honey," she gasps as she takes my father's other hand. "We will get through this. We will."

"I know, Mom, because I have all of *you*." I project my voice to get Claudia to turn toward me, and she does.

I smile slightly at her. She nods her head at me. Then, she kisses her fingers and makes the sign of the cross. She smiles ever so slightly back.

"Yes, you do," my father says.

He motions for Claudia to join us. She comes over.

"Please be good to yourself," Claudia says.

"I will."

"We love you, Aubrey." My mother then leans over and hugs me with such deepness that I sense her love pulse through me.

Little does she know she's just solidified that coming home last night was the best decision I've made in a long time.

Twenty-Four

THE TRUTH SHALL SET YOU FREE

I knock on Professor Gilford's door.

"Come in," I hear him say.

I turn the knob, take a deep breath, and enter his office.

"Bree, nice to see you."

I doubt you'll feel that way in a few minutes.

I close the door behind me and sit on the edge of the chair across from him. My heart is beating in overtime as I glance up at him.

"Great job on the changes to the outline. I think you and Professor Cooper made the right adjustments. Very proud that this is coming out of our department. You should be, too."

"I am, Professor Gilford, and thank you," I say, trying to mask the sadness in my voice, but I can't.

"I have a feeling that is not why you are here." He searches my eyes, and I have to briefly turn away. "How can I help you this evening, Bree?"

Help me? I bet you're going to wish I'd never enrolled here.

I start to talk, but a wave of nausea washes over me, and I think I might throw up. I shake my nerves by breathing deeply, but it does nothing but make me slightly light-headed.

I finally slow my breath and then begin, "I wanted to talk to you." I nervously play with my hands. This is so unlike me, and I know it. I've typically been confident, except for now. "It's about Professor Cooper," I blurt out.

"Yes?" he says with an apprehensive face. "What about him?"

"There is a situation that I need to make you aware of."

"Okay." His face is twisted with concern.

I think of my father and the encouraging words he left me with. *"You only have one chance to tell the truth, so take the opportunity to do it right. There are no second chances."*

"Professor Cooper is being threatened by one of your former students."

"What? Bree, this is news to me."

I try to remain calm, like my father told me to. "I understand, and that is why I'm coming to you. It is very serious, and I'd like to discuss it with you before it goes any further."

He leans forward on his desk and rummages through some papers until he finds a pen and clean sheet of paper. "Go on."

This makes me nervous, but I have to press on. If I tell the truth, I'll have nothing to worry about, right? "There is a student, Ashley Duncan. Do you know who she is?"

"Yes, I do, of course."

"She has threatened Professor Cooper—"

"Threatened him how?" His eyes get wide.

"She is forcing him to leave the university."

"Professor Cooper is taking a sabbatical to promote this program you two created, no?"

"Yes, but his original plan was not to leave the university," I respond sadly.

"I'm not following."

"He planned to stay here, learn as much under you as possible, so he could, you know, take over for you whenever you retire."

"Who said I'm retiring?" he asks with a bit of an edge.

"He did. He confided in me that it was the agreement the two of you had." I am laying out all my cards.

"Oh, did he now?" he says. It's obvious that he is even more irritated.

"Yes, but please understand that is why I'm here. I am the only one he told that to, so that is why you must know that his leaving is only a product of him being forced to do so." My heart rate increases, and the temperature in the room just skyrocketed.

"Forced?"

"Yes, Ashley told him she would expose him if he didn't leave the school, and…"

"And what exactly?"

"He is trying to protect…me."

"Protect you?"

"Yes." I lower my head, unable to meet his eyes.

"Are you in danger?"

"I'm not positive, Professor Gilford. I'm unclear of her motive."

"Motive?"

"Yes, she said she would go to the school and tell them that I received preferential treatment, was given answers on the final, and only got the internship because of Professor Cooper's bias toward me."

"Bree, I must ask, are any of those things true?"

"No, not at all. In fact, it is just the opposite. I've had to work harder these past two semesters. I needed to prove that I was the right choice for the internship, despite my relationship with Professor Cooper—"

"Relationship?" he scoffs.

I swallow hard. I know my cheeks are burning hot pink. "Yes, sir. Please understand…" I slide a little closer to the edge of my seat.

"Understand what?" he says in a disapproving tone.

"My relationship with him evolved over time. It wasn't something that happened overnight. It organically developed. I'm not proud of the fact that I might be the reason he gets fired, and worse, I hate the idea that she might be able to ruin my hard work by simply opening her mouth. So, I wanted to come to you first."

"Bree, I must say, I'm both surprised and displeased to hear that my assistant professor has been having relations with his student. That is against the code of conduct."

My face flushes again. "I understand. I do."

"Do you? There might be severe consequences for both your actions."

"Yes, I do. And I am prepared for the consequences." I lower my head and then whisper, "I think."

He doesn't respond, so I continue, "But I believe that harassing a professor and a student should trump an indiscretion that happened between two consenting adults." Now, I see his face flush.

He glares at me and then responds, "It is hard to argue with that point, Bree."

"I'd like to believe that a university would much rather be dealing with an inappropriate relationship than a student stalking, harassing, and threatening a professor and a student."

"They both leave little to be desired."

I know he's right about this.

My head spins as he finally says, "So, tell me why you think I should let Professor Cooper return and eventually take over the department I've spent the last thirty years developing?"

I try not to smile slightly to myself as the past few months flash through my mind like a movie being played backward. I'm drawn to only the good memories. I believe truly that, despite why I am here today, we had many more good times than we had bad ones.

I clear my throat and soften my eyes as I watch Professor Gilford anxiously wait for my response. I channel my father, as I want to get my point across clearly and concisely. However, I have to think of Mother and how she looked at me. As though she saw, and maybe for the first time, that I, too, am just a girl, vulnerable and scared, who is trying to move on and do the right thing.

"I can remember the day he told me that teaching was all he ever wanted to do. I almost didn't believe him. He is so young, at only twenty-four, to know, so unmistakably, what he wants to do for the rest of his life. It's what attracted me to him." His eyes get wide. "See, I grew up being around people who didn't necessarily have dreams that required them to work hard for them. I grew up where your name made you; you didn't have to make a name for yourself. But Adam is different. He knows how to work hard, to stay focused, and to push his life aside to advance his career, for his dream of taking over for you."

A slight smile creeps onto his face, but swiftly fades.

"But then again, he is simply a man, and despite our attempts to keep our relationship neutral, we couldn't. We have chemistry, and that showed wholeheartedly in the work that we produced. When two people can work side by side with mutual respect, then I see no harm in that. No one knew about us. I wasn't doing it to get ahead. Like I said, I could leave school today and be taken care of for the rest of my existence, but I don't want that. I want to grow and be challenged, to feel like I have some purpose. Adam gave me purpose. He made me understand that I belong here. Despite some tough times in the beginning, I finally was happy. And, now, the thought of him not being here because a young woman is too unstable to know that you can't force someone to love you…well that is exactly why I'm here today. People either love you, or they don't. But she *cannot* go around threatening people to get what she wants. Adam is an asset to this school. You know it, and I know it. You can't let him walk away from his dream because of me."

"That might be too late," he says sadly.

"No, I am telling you, Professor Gilford, you have my word that I will walk away. I came to officially resign from my internship. I will also ask that my name be removed from the curriculum project."

"What about the situation with Ashley?"

"Well"—I reach into my bag and pull out the photo—"she is, I believe, stalking Adam, and someone should do something about it." I hand the picture to him.

"Oh my, this is serious."

"Yes, and I don't think Adam should be threatened to leave something he loves…because of me or her or anyone."

He hands me back the photo. "But, like I said, it's too late."

"How can it—"

"He's gone, Bree. I thought you knew that?"

"He's leaving, yes, but he's not gone."

My throat tightens as I watch him shake his head. He appears sad, and I'm not sure I understand why.

"He left today. Dropped off his keys to me this morning, and gave me a copy of the final project."

The heavy feeling in my heart is one I've become all too familiar with. The sting of tears in my eyes blinds me, but I fight them back.

"I-I didn't know he left," I choke out.

"I'm sorry, Bree. I thought you knew."

"No, we don't talk anymore."

"That certainly seems like a shame."

I draw my head up and stare at him.

"Maybe it's none of my business, Bree, but it sounds like it's you who should be with him. You should be out there, talking about this project, just as much as him. You say he gave you purpose and that you know how to work side by side, so perhaps it's you who can one day take over for him."

"Me?"

"Yes, you. You're brilliant, Bree. Professor Coop—I mean, Adam told me what you said to him when you applied for the internship. I knew then, if we didn't choose you, we would be making a huge mistake. It was ultimately my decision, Bree, as to whom we chose for the internship."

"Oh, I didn't know that."

"I recognize a lot of the qualities that I have always admired in Adam in you."

"Oh, thank you, Professor Gilford. I appreciate that, and I'm sorry I have caused these issues. It was never my intention. I just…" *Fell in love with a man I knew I shouldn't have fallen in love with.*

"I understand. But, for now, if you'll excuse me, Bree, I should attend to the matter of Miss Duncan."

We leave his office together.

"Thank you," I say.

"I'll be in touch. There will be consequences for both your actions, you do realize this?"

For the first time in the last half hour, Professor Gilford truly is disappointed in me, and a part of me is glad that he is. Although I can't quite put my finger on exactly why.

"I know." I prepared myself for such a thing.

I know, in my heart I did the right thing, irrespective of the punishment. I should have to pay the price for my actions. Here, at OSU, I'm treated like everybody else, and it is oddly refreshing. I, Bree Van Tousen, am full of flaws, both externally and internally. And something about that feels right…for once.

But, as I step out of the Draper building and watch as Professor Gilford hurries off toward the Dean's Office, I can't help but feel a sense of relief because I know the truth had to come out even if that meant it would set me free…from everything.

Twenty-Five

NO REGRETS

With me being at my parents' over the last weekend, I have undoubtedly been out of the loop. But I won't be able to move forward unless I know. I need to see for myself that Adam is gone. Something in my heart tells me he is. Long gone, away from here and off on his new adventure.

I pull down his street, and a sadness I cannot explain comes over me. I get closer to his house, and there is a For Rent sign out in front of the old Victorian.

I pull in my usual spot and park the car. I check my surroundings before getting out to make sure Ashley is not watching me. The road is empty…much like me.

I get out of the car and march up the stairs to the front door. The Adirondack chairs are gone, but the swing is still hanging there. I go over to the big window in the front and peer in. Although most of the furniture is still in there, his personal items are gone. I'm crushed.

I approach the swing, realizing that I never once sat in it, but always wanted to. I was too afraid to be hanging out in front of his place, for fear of being caught. Little did I know, it would happen regardless.

I sit in the swing and take out the picture of him and me. Although this picture very well could be the sole reason we are no longer together, I can't help but gaze longingly at him. When I do, it reminds me of better days. The emotions I'd have when he touched me, kissed me, and sometimes, just observed me. One look was all I needed from him to make me feel remarkable.

The wind picks up slightly, and a chill runs down my body. I zip up my leather jacket as I continue to swing back and forth. It's getting darker now, and as I sway, I ponder my next move.

I know I should call my father and mother and tell them what happened. I should also probably call Mr. Piper, and lastly, at some point, I'd like to talk to Abigail. I want her to know how sorry I am that all of this happened to both of us, and maybe, as the process continues, we can find a way to support each other. We could have a painful and long road ahead of us, one I am not eagerly awaiting. Even if the outcome is favorable to us, it will still suck to go through it.

I'm about to get up and continue on with my life when I detect headlights coming down the street. I duck slightly on the swing to wait for the car to pass before I get up. My heart rate picks up and wildly beats in my chest as I realize the car is pulling into Adam's driveway. I won't be able to get off the porch in time, so I steady the swing and pray whoever it is goes away.

No such luck.

I hear the car engine cease, followed by the opening and closing of a door. I hold my breath and wait, hoping the person will not notice me and praying it is not Ashley.

Please don't be Ashley.

I hear footsteps on the stairs.

And then a whispered, "Bree?"

I briefly close my eyes and then open them and sit back straight. Adam is standing before me, only feet away, and it's as though he's not real. I blink hard as I'm unable to find words.

"Bree, is that you?"

Finally, I whisper back, "Adam, what are you doing here?"

"I could ask the same of you."

"I-I heard that you were gone."

"I forgot something; that's all. I had to come back."

"Oh," I say as I stand, "I see. So, you *are* gone then."

I want to leave so badly as the mere sight of him makes me want to cry, but in order to leave, I'd have to brush past him. The thought of being that close to him is too hard.

The wind howls past us, and a light flurry of snow begins to fall. He is not wearing a coat.

"Come in for a minute," he says as he turns to unlock the door.

"I can't. I'm sorry. I have to go."

"Okay, I understand." He turns to put the key in and pushes open the door.

I walk toward him to pass him, and as I do, he grabs my wrist.

"Please come in, for a moment. I'd like to say good-bye."

"That's just it, Adam. I don't know if I can say good-bye again."

"Please, Bree." His tone is almost bordering on desperate.

With a slight nod of my head, I finally agree to go inside with him.

"Thank you," he adds tenderly as he allows me in first.

"So, only back for a minute?" I ask as he switches on the light.

I have my answer as I glance around. The house is bare and unwelcoming. The warmth I used to feel when I'd come in here is clearly gone.

"Yeah, I forgot some of my papers and my passport."

"Oh, going somewhere special?" I cringe, waiting for him to answer. It's hard enough, imagining him gone from OSU, but knowing he might be in another country is horrific.

"No, but you never know when I might need it. Besides, I didn't want to leave it in the house in case it gets rented."

"Understood. I guess I'll leave you to it."

"Bree, wait. I have something I want to say to you."

"What, Adam?" I am trying hard to keep my tone neutral.

"I'm sorry if you believe I gave in too easily."

"I do. I think you did give up on me, on us, too easily," I say sadly.

"I was cornered. I didn't have a choice."

"But you didn't even talk to me."

He's heard this all before, and nothing changed. I am defeated yet again.

"I know, and I feel terrible about that. But, deep down, you have to know, it was not what I wanted. My back was against the wall. She had proof. I had no choice."

"I did, Adam."

"What?"

"Well, since you never actually came to me and asked me what we should do, then you left it in my hands to do what I needed to do...so I did."

"Bree, what did you do?" he says with a disapproving expression.

"I'm taking care of me. For once this year, I'm taking care of things my way."

He crosses his arms over his chest. "Bree?"

"What, Adam? Do you even want to know? As of three hours ago, you were long gone. Off somewhere. I have no idea even where."

He uncrosses his arms and sits on the stairs leading up to the second level. "I am going to stay with Anna and Harrison. They are letting me live with them. They live in Brookline, Massachusetts."

When I don't respond, he says, "What did you do, Bree? Please tell me." His tone is much softer now.

I watch his eyes move back and forth. My heart flutters as he watches me.

I take a deep breath. "Adam, I went to talk to Professor Gilford today."

"Oh, Bree, what did you do?"

"I did what I had to do. I told him that I was ending my internship. I told him that I wanted my name off the project. More importantly, I told him that you are a good man who should not be forced out of what you love to do because some girl thinks she can blackmail you into leaving." *And worse breaking up with me.*

"Bree, you told him that?"

"Of course I did."

"You told him I dated you?"

"I had to. I can't let her run you out of the university. You once told me that being here, working under Gilford, was all you ever wanted. Sure, I believe this opportunity you are working toward is great, but doing that is one thing. Giving up a year of your job, only to come back and have her still here—haunting you, watching you—it's not fair, Adam. Simply not fair."

"But, Bree, it's not only about me. Your reputation is at stake, too." He exhaustedly runs his hand through his hair.

"I know. And what would have happened when you came back and saw me? Were you planning to ignore me and expect that I do the same? Just to make *her* happy?"

"No, I didn't think that far ahead, unfortunately. God, I feel so foolish, Bree."

"Can I be honest?"

"Please do," he says with a smirk.

He knows I can be brutally honest—sometimes, to a fault.

"You underestimated me."

"I doubt that," he says with a smile.

"When I spoke to Gilford, I knew he would understand that you and I are a separate entity. But blackmail—someone taking pictures of us, watching us, and threatening our reputations and jobs at the university—is not okay with me. And I know you feel the same."

He stands. "I do. You know I do. I made the choices I did because I had to. Something told me I had to."

"I know."

"But do you, Bree? Do you know how difficult it would be to go to my mentor and tell him I was sleeping with the woman he picked for his internship?" He steps closer to me. "The woman he knew was the right choice before I even did. He knew, after what I told him you said, that you were the top choice. And there was no more discussion."

"I knew you didn't want me."

"No, don't misunderstand that. I was attracted to you the minute you entered my office. So full of life. However, there was a darkness in you." He looks down for a second and then adds, "But you also had a savviness that I knew I could appreciate, that I wanted to work with. But I was clouded by your beauty. I was so torn, and I needed him to decide."

I swallow hard. He's said a lot of things to me, but these compliments are deeper than the other surface compliments I've become so accustomed to.

"You had to toe the line."

"Exactly, and I should have done a hell of a better job with that…but, Jesus, Bree, it's *you*. How could I ignore a girl like you? So striking, so smart. I could not stay away."

"But, Adam, despite all that we had…here we *are*."

"I know, and I'm leaving."

"I know. But Gilford doesn't want you to go…and neither do I. You belong here."

"But what about you? What will the school say?"

"You said it yourself. Gilford believed in me long before any of this happened. So, why would that change?"

"Because of the rumors, the destruction of our respective reputations." He comes even closer to me.

"I can take my punishment, whatever it might be." I smile slightly.

"So, you told him everything?"

"Yes, and I even showed him this." I pull out the photo.

"I went crazy, searching for that," he says as he takes it from me.

"I took it because I knew I could use it to further our cause."

"What? Did you get a lawyer or something?"

"My father was a lawyer, and my brother is a lawyer. I know the law. At least, I have an understanding, and I knew I needed to have that to show my lawyer that stalking is not okay. Blackmail is not okay."

"But, Bree, just because Gilford understands doesn't mean the school board will. Sleeping with my students is not the kind of controversy they want surrounding the potential future head of the department."

"I know this. But, Adam, what she has been doing is far worse."

"I understand, but…"

"But what?"

"I'm still leaving, Bree." He lowers his head.

I fight back the tears in my eyes. "I did this before I knew you had packed up and were leaving. I thought I had more time."

He steps closer to me. He takes my hand. It is so good to feel his skin on mine again, however short-lived it might be.

"You stood up for me, and I can't thank you enough."

"I didn't do it for a thank-you. I did it because I thought it might get you to stay, regardless of how you feel about me."

"Do you honestly believe that I no longer have feelings for you? That some girl could come along and force me not to feel the way I've felt about you since the moment I laid eyes on you?" When I don't respond, he says, "Now, you have underestimated me."

"Adam, please don't. I can't take another heartbreak. I've had a terrible year—well, that is, for most of it."

"I know, and I'm sorry I wasn't there for you. On so many levels, Bree."

"But you were. I found you right when I thought I'd never be able to trust or be with anyone again. I soon realized I wasn't meant to be with some college guy only wanting a good time. I need someone I can connect with intellectually. That was the only way I was going to feel safe physically. And that is what you did for me. I didn't think I'd have to articulate that. I thought it was unspoken between us."

"Oh, Bree, I'm such an idiot for giving you up."

"Yeah, you kind of are," I say, slightly smiling, as a tear drops on my cheek.

He comes closer, our bodies only inches apart. He whispers, "I have missed you so badly, Bree."

I swallow hard and gaze up into his beautiful eyes. "I have a feeling, I've missed you more."

"Impossible," he says.

He puts his arms around me, and I lean in and rest my head on his chest. I can hear his heart beating, and it reminds me of being back in the cabin when I used to rest my head on his bare chest and listen to the life inside him, wishing and hoping I'd never *not* hear that sound. Tears start falling from my eyes, and I don't aim to hold them back. I've missed him so much that I almost can't believe he is holding me again. I convinced myself we would never touch again.

He pulls me back. He gently takes his thumbs and wipes the tears from my cheeks. Then, he rests both hands on my face, his fingertips gently caressing the back of my neck. "Say you'll forgive me, Bree."

"There is nothing to forgive. We did what we thought we had to."

"Say you'll forgive me, Bree," he repeats. "Please."

"I know, in time, I will. I have so much going on right now that I guess, in many ways, I am having a hard time determining which end is up."

"I completely understand. I haven't earned your trust back, so I shouldn't be asking for your forgiveness. It's just…I-I have missed you so much, and knowing about what happened to you and now with your academics…it is too much for one person. I feel like I've failed you as a boyfriend."

"Boyfriend?"

"Of course. Can you imagine for a second what it would have been like if we hadn't had to sneak around? That going to the cabin was by choice, not a necessity? That I could hold your hand whenever I wanted to? That I didn't have to tell my family to keep it a secret that I'd found the most amazing girl?"

Amazing girl?

My heart flutters.

"You told your family?"

"Of course, Bree. Besides, during the holidays, it was hard to keep it a secret. I was floating. The first thing my mom said to me was, 'Who's the girl, Adam?' She knows me too well."

"Why didn't you tell me any of this?"

"Because I didn't think I'd have to in order to save our relationship. I thought it was simply banter between me and my mom, but I was wrong about that, too."

"Did you tell them what happened?"

"No, not yet. I've only told Anna and Harrison. I can trust them with my career, undoubtedly. I needed people who could give me advice. My mom is not the one for that. Particularly after the holidays. She was dying to meet you and even said she'd stop by at the cabin, unannounced." He pauses, and then a sly smile grows across his face.

"What?"

"Nothing."

"What?"

"Well, you know, I told her that would not be a good idea."

My cheeks blush.

"You're blushing," he adds.

"Adam, stop it."

"Sorry."

"No. I mean, it's okay. It's just…I have so desperately wanted for one thing to be normal since I started school. But nothing has been." I draw back from him.

He smiles slightly. "I know, Bree. God, you know I hate it when you are unhappy. Please don't be sad anymore."

"I'm only sad because you are leaving."

"So am I. But Harrison has made some major connections for me for the summer, and I can't break those commitments now. Not without further discussion. If I get suspended from the university, I'll need something…"

I don't want him to feel like he needs to explain any more. He looks deep into my eyes. I know the answer has not changed. He is leaving. This is a lot for him, and there are no guarantees he won't be fired from OSU, and I won't be expelled.

So, I simply say, "Don't go…"

He reaches forward and tucks a strand of hair behind my ear. I close my eyes. I breathe in deep, and immediately, I'm brought back to the beach in front of my house. Such peaceful thoughts as the sun touches my skin. I move my toes in the sand and welcome the therapeutic sensation it gives me. The waves lap against the shore. I smile. For the first time in a very long time, I smile.

I open my eyes.

He is softly caressing my cheek. "Can I kiss you?" he asks softly.

I don't need to answer him, and besides, I'm afraid, if I do, my words will be contrary to how my body feels. My eyes lower as he leans in and softly brushes his lips onto mine. He releases his hand from my face and wraps it around my body, pulling me in close. I can't help but place my arms around him. I've missed this feeling of us being so close. It was so natural, and I've desperately wished to be with him again.

He starts to kiss me harder, and I am overwhelmed with emotions. He grabs on to me firmer and with desperation. I kiss him back, deeper, as I run my fingers through his thick hair.

"Bree," he whispers as he starts kissing my neck and cheek. "I want to hold you like I should have when you were hurting. Let me be that person for you. Let me make you feel safe again."

I wish I could say no, but I can't. I long to be with him again, and I can't contemplate him leaving. I can only think about this moment. He reaches over and turns off the light. The house is now dark. He gently scoops me up into his arms. He carries me up the stairs, all while keeping his eyes locked with mine.

He pushes open the door to his bedroom. "Stay with me, Bree. That's all I want."

All I want is to be near him, too.

"Okay, Adam," I whisper.

He sets me down on the floor in front of his bed. I unzip my jacket and pull my arms out. I toss it on the floor. With nimble fingers, he unbuttons my blouse and eases it off my shoulders. His eyes widen as he caresses my shoulders. He pulls his sweater over his head and tosses it aside. As he bends down and slides out of his pants, I do the same. He goes over to his dresser and takes one of his T-shirts out of his drawer. He moves back toward me and eases the shirt over my head. This reminds me of the first night I spent in his house, and I can't help but smile slightly.

He brushes back my hair over my shoulder and smiles sweetly at me. "Oh, Bree," he sighs, "I've never regretted the day you walked into my office. I knew, even then, that my life would change." He leans in and brushes his lips softly on my ear. "And, boy, did it ever."

A tingle runs down my skin. I reach my hand up and run my fingertips through his hair as he pulls me in closer. Then, swiftly, he picks me up and then lays me right on the bed. He slowly crawls next to me, pulling a blanket up with him as he does.

I sigh quietly to myself. I am surprisingly content. No expectations, no pressure.

He takes my hand and gazes into my eyes. Our bodies are intertwined, his long legs over mine.

"I'm so glad you came to the house, Bree." He locks eyes with me and smiles sincerely.

"Me, too, Adam."

He leans down, and with soft lips, he kisses me with such passion that I can sense my body melting into the bed. I sigh as our lips part.

No regrets, I think.

That is how I want to live my life moving forward. Have no regrets for my actions and live in each moment because I'll never know when someone in my life might just have to leave me.

Twenty-Six

WE ALL NEED SOME PROTECTION

The next morning, I wake, and Adam is gone. The sheets where he was lying are now cool to the touch, and I have no idea how long it has been since he slipped away.

He left me a note with a copy of the final curriculum and project outline on top. This is what he'll be out promoting, and I can see that he still has my name on the document as a secondary contributor, right under his name. Somehow seeing my name next to his does not make me sad; it makes me happy. The two of us accomplished something together. I actually did something great my first year of school.

I dress in a hurry, as I hate being in this house alone. I grab the documents and note and start to hurry down the stairs to the front door. As I take the final step onto the main floor, I hear a female voice mumbling. I can hear keys in the door and another woman's voice. I slip into the dining room and hold my breath.

"So, this home is for rent now, but you said you were hoping for something for next year?"

"Yes," I hear a young female voice say.

"The thing is, Ashley, I'm not certain he wants to wait to rent it until the next school year. He's trying to rent it now."

My skin prickles, and I lean forward, so I can see her. *This girl is absolutely insane. Why is she in the house? She knew enough to contact the relator? On top of that, she actually went through with making an appointment to get into the house.* I'm more afraid than I was twenty-four hours ago.

"So, the person renting the home is gone?" she asks coolly.

"Yes, left a day or so ago. But most of the furniture is still here. He is renting it furnished."

"Great. Can I take a peek upstairs first?"

"Um, okay. I don't see why not."

"Great. Lead the way," she says cheerily.

I hear the creak of the stairs as they make their way upstairs.

"Show me the master bedroom first," I hear Ashley say.

I take this as my cue to run and run fast as they will probably see the unmade bed. I sneak back into the foyer and slowly open the door. Then, two steps at a time, I bound down the stairs, hurry up the street to my car, and peel out down the road.

There is only one person that I know who can truly help protect Adam from this psycho girl. And, well, now that Adam is gone, I might need a little protection from her as well.

"Can I help you?" the young officer asks.

"Yes, I'd like to speak with Officer Murphy, please. It's important."

"Okay, let me see if he is available."

"Tell him it's Bree Van Tousen."

"Yes, ma'am."

I nervously pick at my nail polish, waiting for him to come around the corner.

"Miss Van Tousen," Officer Murphy finally says.

I glance up and say, "Can we speak privately?"

"Yes, of course. This way."

He leads me back to his office and sits down at the table. I take the seat across from him.

"How can I help you?"

I close my eyes for a moment and think about what my father told me about making sure the right people knew the right information. I told Professor Gilford about Ashley because of Adam's role at the university. But, now that she is going into this home and continuing her quest for him, she needs to be told to stop.

"It's about Adam."

"Adam?"

"Yes, Professor Cooper."

"I see."

"I'm worried about his safety and…well, possibly mine."

"How so, Bree?"

"We believe, um…Adam and I, that is—that Ashley Duncan is stalking him."

"Okay. And what makes you say that?"

"She photographed him without him knowing, she made him leave the school with the threat that she would expose his relationship with me, and lastly, she was in his home this morning, pretending to a realtor that she was interested in renting it." I exhale deeply as I spilled my guts in one long sentence.

I continue, "She took this without us knowing and tried to blackmail him." I take the picture out from my pocket and slide it across to him. "I heard her in the house today. There was something about her tone and the questions she was asking that gave me the creeps."

"She was in his house?" He pauses and takes out his notebook. He gives me a questioning expression and then says, "Adam was here this morning."

"He was?"

"Yes, he said he wanted me to watch out for you. That he felt there was a situation on campus with a young lady that would require my attention. I planned to call you, Bree."

I'm shocked into silence. My jaw drops open slightly. "Oh," I barely whisper.

"Yes, he's worried about all that you have going on right now with the other potential case pending and then this."

"I-I see." I want to cry.

"Yes, so can I take this picture as evidence?"

Even though I don't want to give it up, I have to. "Yes, you can," I whisper.

"Good. I will add it to the others. Hopefully, we can get to the bottom of this."

"The others?"

"Yes, Adam dropped off a few other photos she has allegedly sent him."

Again, my jaw drops open. "There are more?"

"Yes, and some letters, too." He pulls out a large file. "Can I ask you to look at these and see if you recognize anything in the photos? Where they were taken?"

He hands me the pile of photos, and I begin sifting through them. Most of the photos were taken at Adam's house on campus, not in the cabin. There are some of him, but others are of him and me. A complete chill runs up and down my spine as I look through these. Knowing I was being watched is more than I can handle.

"He said he didn't know who they were coming from at first, and you know, sometimes, students, girls, at school can get a little starstruck, if you will, about their professors."

He locks eyes with me, but I narrow my stare back.

"I am not easily starstruck, Officer Murphy."

"I get the sense you are not."

My expression softens. I continue sifting through the stack of photos. Then, suddenly, a wave of fear rushes over me as I am now looking directly at the picture of my grandmother on the beach, holding my mother as a child. The one I thought had fallen behind the dresser. I gasp, and my body starts to tremble.

"Bree? Bree, what is it?" he says with panic.

"It's a picture…of my grandma. It's mine…from…" I peer up at him.

"Bree, slow down, and tell me."

"*She* was in my room," I blurt out. I slide the picture over to him.

I hear him whisper, "Jesus Christ."

"Someone stole the master keys in my dorm weeks back, and I had a sense…a feeling that something wasn't right and—holy shit, she was in my freaking room!"

He abruptly gets up and strides over to his phone. "Yeah, I need you and Captain Frankel in the team room. Now," he barks. "Stay here, Bree. I'll be right back." He walks out of the room and shuts the door.

My hands are trembling as I pick up the picture again. I start to cry. I'm in way too deep now.

He returns about ten minutes later. "So sorry, Bree, to keep you waiting in here. The school has been notified, and we are taking precautionary measures as we speak. I ask that you don't speak about the photos with anyone. We want to make certain we do this right and make zero mistakes."

He fills me in on as many details that he can without compromising the case. He assures me that I am safe and that Ashley will be nowhere near me.

I nod my head and try to compose myself. *Stop crying, Bree.*

"Adam only learned yesterday that the school was aware of what was happening, so we got these prints this morning. In some ways, we have you to thank for that."

"Ha, lucky me…twice."

His massive hand overtakes mine. "Bree, this is a lot to handle for one young lady. Do you have anyone, a friend, who you can talk to? Maybe even stay with for a few days?"

"I have my floor mates." I pause and glance up. "Abigail Price is one of my friends," I say quietly. I can see him react. "You know her, right?"

"Unfortunately, yes, I do."

"You know what they say. Misery loves company."

He pats my hand again and smiles. "You girls be good to one another. You need each other now more than ever."

"I know," I whisper.

I pull up to my dorm. After what Officer Murphy told me about Ashley being under surveillance and how they know not to allow her near my dormitory, I deduct that I'm relatively safe while moving about campus. At this point, with all I've endured this year on university grounds, if there is no one watching out for me now, I've seriously misjudged the police and my friends, including Adam.

I enter my building and two campus security guards are sitting at a table in the lobby, checking student IDs.

"What's this all about?" the kid in front of me asks.

"New security protocol. Nothing to be concerned about."

I know the guard is lying.

I show him my ID, and he nods sympathetically at me. I take the elevator up to our floor. I stride down the hallway, passing my room and going straight toward Abigail and Laura's room. I take a deep breath and then let it out before I knock.

"Come in!" I hear Laura yell.

I open the door with hesitation and then finally say, "It's me, Bree."

"Hey, Bree," Laura says.

I step into the room and see Abigail and Laura on the floor, sitting cross-legged and reading magazines. Abigail is as beautiful as ever as she peers up at me and smiles slightly.

"Hi, Bree," she says softly.

I try not to burst into tears at the sight of her.

"Hello. Mind if I sit?"

They both seem surprised, but rapidly respond in unison, "No, please."

They slide over, and I take a seat on the floor, facing them.

"What's up?" Laura asks.

"I was hoping I could talk to you…both…for a minute." I clasp my hands on my lap to keep them from shaking.

"Of course." Abigail sits up straighter.

"I'll start by saying, I'm sorry, Abigail."

"For what?"

I close my eyes, breathe in deeply, and hold it for a moment. I open my eyes, and recognize that there are two strong women sitting before me. I realize that I owe it to them and to me to speak it all.

"I have not been kind to you, Abigail. I could tell you all my reasons, but none of them are worth your time. Plain and simple, I'm sorry. I should have been nicer to you."

She looks shocked at my omission. "It's okay, Bree. Laura, here, told me there was a good side to you, and I believed her," she says with a slight chuckle. "I'm kidding really, but I appreciate you saying that."

"Thank you. I had every intention of coming to school and finding real friends. Then on my first day of school, before I knew any of you guys, I went to a party and left alone. I, too, was approached by someone I'd met at the party, and unfortunately, the same thing you told us all the other day…happened to me." I swallow hard.

She is no longer smiling. Her big blue eyes grow increasingly wide as she stares at me.

I continue so I can get it over with, "He said he was a student athlete and that his girlfriend lived in my dorm, and…well, you know how the rest of the story goes. It doesn't end great, so…" I can't get myself to say what happened to me, particularly as I gaze upon the face of another one of his victims. It is too close to home.

She reaches over and touches my hand. "Oh, Bree, I am so sorry. Are you okay?"

"I think I'll be. I left school after it happened. I didn't want anyone to see my face." I motion over my lip and eye.

She starts to cry.

"But I'm okay, Abigail. You see me. I'm okay. I've healed on the outside. I might need a little help on the inside."

Laura smiles slightly and says, "I believe you're doing better than you think. Both of you."

"Thank you, Laura. But, unfortunately, I have another issue on my hands." I nervously play with my fingers.

"What?" Laura's voices rises about ten octaves.

I peer up at her. "Yes, but I'll get to that."

She shakes her head. "All right."

I continue, "But, Abigail, I wanted to let you know that I have gotten a lawyer and plan to proceed with trying to put this guy away, and I'd understand if you—"

"Me, too. I plan to be there as well."

"Oh, good. It's good for all of us to stick together and make sure he never steps outside of four concrete walls again."

"Agree wholeheartedly," she says with conviction.

"Do your parents know?"

"Yes, and they plan to be there during the process."

"Mine, too," I say thankfully.

"I'm glad you decided to tell someone," Laura adds.

"I am, too. I'm sorry it took me so long to come forward."

"I'm not positive I would have either, Bree. The only reason anyone found out is because of Tank and Nathan," Abigail replies.

"I know. I got so angry because I was jealous you had someone, and I didn't."

She inhales sharply. "Oh, Bree, I'm so sorry. I had no idea."

"I know, but what was worse is that it happened to you. Maybe…had I said something"—I start to cry—"I could have prevented others from going through what I did. What we did."

She puts her hand on my leg. "Please don't cry, Bree. I, more than anyone, completely understand. I got very lucky. I was fortunate in that moment to have someone watching over me that night. I know it could have been a lot worse. But, thankfully, Tank has this way of knowing when I need something. Hard to explain really, but we have this connection."

I can't help but glance up at her when she mentions Tank.

"Believe me," she continues, "I know the rumors out there, and everyone thinks it's a love triangle of some kind. But, really, Tank and I truly care about each other—as friends. He is an *incredible* friend. And he proved it to me that night for sure. Risking himself the way he did…he's amazing."

"He *is* amazing, and I can't wait to tell him that myself when I see him."

He's the reason the jerk finally got caught.

"Yeah, he's been through a lot himself this past year. So, I know he'll appreciate it."

Laura's voice is calming when she adds, "And what matters now is that you are both safe and can rely on each other for support during what I know will be a hard time. For you, your parents, and those who love you the most."

Those who love me the most, I think. *I only wish I had him by my side.*

I stare at my hands in my lap and ponder over the past year as it flashes before me like a beautiful nightmare.

"Bree, is something else bothering you?" Abigail asks.

I gaze at her. Her voice so tender and welcoming, and it's in this moment I know that, despite all I've done this year, she still thinks of me as her friend. I had a sense the day I met her that she was a good person, and in many ways, I spent too much time trying to convince myself that she wasn't.

"Yeah, I have another situation that has become more problematic than I originally anticipated."

"Really?" Laura says with obvious concern.

"Yes, see, I told Laura the other day that I met someone, and well, I thought it was a bit risqué at the time, but lo and behold, I totally fell for him. He's everything I never knew I wanted. He's so intelligent. Brilliant, some might say."

"That sounds wonderful," Abigail interjects.

She knows I was interested in Nathan; I made it pretty clear. I feel badly about that now. He was meant for Abigail, not for me.

"Yes, it was until it became a school issue."

"What do you mean, school issue?" she says with furrowed brows.

"He is a professor here, but before you react, he's young, only twenty-four. Yes, I know it's not the right thing to do, but it was only supposed to be between the two of us. Eventually, we were going to find a way to make it work, and no one would have been the wiser." I let out an exasperated sigh.

"So, it is a secret?" she asks.

"It was. That is, until he was blackmailed into leaving the university."

Laura gasps. "I had no idea, Bree."

"I know. I found out all of this over the course of a few days. It wasn't about Anna at all."

"Who is Anna?" Abigail asks, looking back and forth between us.

"A woman he pretended to be seeing, so he could appease the blackmailer and leave without causing any of us trouble."

"Wow, Bree. This is insane."

"I know, and I'm trying to digest all of it still. Do you remember that girl I worked with on my project, Ashley?"

"Yes, the rude girl," Laura says.

"It's her. She is obsessed with him and is hell bent on keeping us apart. But anyways, for now, I wanted you guys to know, so I could have a safe place to go."

"Safe place?"

"Yes, not in a scary way, but a place where I can go to lean on my friends and not tell one of you one thing and then another something else."

"Completely understand. Oh, Bree, this is simply too much." Laura takes my hand.

"I'm starting to feel it, too, like it's holding me down, and I don't like the way it makes me feel."

"So, the school knows about all of this?" Laura asks.

"As far as I know, things are in place to stop her from stalking him, and..." My tears start to form in my eyes, but I fight them back. "She knows about me, and she told him to stop seeing me, or she'd tell the school I cheated and got special treatment."

"What a bitch!"

I am shocked to hear Abigail swear, and I can't help but crack a smile. Laura starts to laugh, too.

"What?" Abigail says.

"It's just, you know, a swear word coming out of your mouth doesn't seem to fit," I say with a chuckle.

She glances at Laura, who is still laughing.

"Yeah, it's not you."

"Well, I call it like I see it," she says with a huff. Then, she breaks into a smile. "I know; I get it. Little Miss Perfect doesn't even swear. Ugh, I can't wait to shake this image."

"Image? You keep screwing the football team, and you will!" I say with a full smile.

"Ha-ha. I'm only screwing one." She playfully punches me in the arm.

"That we know of." Laura snickers.

"Wow. How did this become about me, you two? Huh? Tell me," she says, pinching Laura's arm.

"Okay then, back to Bree," Laura says. Then, she smiles. "Because Lord knows it's never about me!"

Abigail starts to laugh and then says with a sly smile, "Laura, you were telling me a pretty juicy story about the guy at the radio station."

My eyes grow wide. "Excuse me? What is this all about?"

For the first time since I've known her, Laura's cheeks glow a beautiful pink hue. She can't even control the smile that is spreading across her face.

"Juicy? Hardly!" she scoffs. "Complicated and interesting? Yes, most definitely."

"What? Spill it!" I screech.

"I...well, you know, I've met someone." She fumbles with the magazine in her hand and won't look at me, which tells me it *is* juicy.

"Someone?" I probe.

"Yeah, he works with me...at the radio station."

"Get out!" I bellow as I push her shoulder back with my hand. "I knew there was a reason you were spending so much time at the station!"

A shy smile spreads across her pretty face. "I mean, yes, I've taken on more shifts, and it hasn't hurt that he is there." She tucks a strand of hair behind her ear, and her eyes remain gazing at the ground. "It has kind of a long story, you know. So, I haven't even had time to tell you guys."

"Oh, Laura, I know it's always about someone else," I say as I put my arm around her shoulder and pull her close. "Abigail and I are both so lucky to have you."

"I know you guys are," she says with a smirk.

I release her and blow her a kiss. "You're the best."

She glances up at me. "I know, I know." She smiles wide. "I'm all right." She chuckles again as she rolls her eyes.

I can't help but smile at her. She warms my tired heart, more than she probably is aware.

"So, does this mystery guy have a name? What's the story?" I ask her.

"*Colin* has worked with me at the station, and he had a girlfriend, but I'm gathering that she cheated on him or something. So, for a while there...we were just friends really."

"And now?" Abigail nudges her with her elbow.

Laura playfully giggles as she leans back. "We are hanging out more. I'm not certain it is something I can label. You know, we work together, so we are trying to keep it quiet in case it doesn't work out, and...well, it can be somewhat awkward, I suppose."

"Don't I know that!" I pipe in.

"I know. You've gone through something similar. Well, sort of..." She pauses and then says thoughtfully, "If you two have taught me anything this year, it's that relationships are complex and hard, and more times than not, they involve some sort of baggage."

"Don't I know it," Abigail mumbles.

Laura reaches over and reassuringly pats her hand. Then, she turns to me. "But, seriously, Bree, now what?"

Laura is clearly not ready to talk about whatever is going on with Colin, so I take the hint.

"They are keeping an eye on Ashley, making sure she won't come near me, and the police plan to file charges on her for stalking. But this is all new to me. I found this out at the station this morning. Adam went there before he left to file a complaint. She needs some serious help."

"Adam left?" Laura asked.

"Adam is the professor?" Abigail asks.

"Yes, he planned to take a year off to keep his job intact. He got approval to take a sabbatical and promote the project we'd worked on at other campuses. He created this tour on the fly in order to not draw suspicion to the fact that he needed to take a hiatus. So, at least I know he'll be doing that. But I don't know what any of this will mean for him, here at the university."

"And what about for you?"

"For now, I plan to get through the semester and hope for the best."

"Hope for the best?" Laura responds.

"Yes, I need to get through the next two months. I need to make it until May, and then hopefully, I'll have some kind of answer about what disciplinary action the school may or may not take before I leave for the summer. I'd love nothing more than to have this behind me. But, until then, I have to stay focused on school and prove that I'm a good student. But, more importantly, I know I'll need to rely on my friends for support so that I don't go crazy in this place!" I laugh slightly.

"You can count on us," Laura says with a smile.

"I know I can. And I hope you both know that you can count on me during all of this. Abigail, I'll be there right alongside you."

I start to stand and am surprised when the two of them rise with me. Without much warning, the two of them envelop me in a bear hug. I groan slightly and am about to protest when it dawns on me that these beautiful, caring, and selfless women are my friends, my dear friends, thrown together by the sheer drawing of a residential roommate lottery.

And I can't help but feel like, no matter what happens tomorrow or the next day or the day after, I'll somehow have this crazy, confused, and messed up time called freshman year to look back on with them...and, boy, will it be some fucking story to tell.

Twenty-Seven

HAS IT REALLY BEEN TWO MONTHS?

The campus is beautiful in May. The trees are blooming light pink and white flowers along the brick pathways. The last of the snow finally melted a few weeks ago after a long and arduous winter. Then, almost unbelievably and in the flash of an eye, spring is here, and so is the end of my first year of college. I'm going to miss the campus when I'm gone. That, I am sure of.

I hustle slightly across the sidewalk as the track team comes jogging by on a routine run. I hear someone whistle at me as I hurry past. I smile to myself, but continue on, never glancing back.

I practice my speech again as I get further and further away from my dorm.

My heart is in my throat as I pull open the door to Rounds Hall, where the Office of the Dean of Students resides. I fussed over my outfit for way too long, and now, in typical me fashion, I'm a few minutes late. I approach the room I was instructed to arrive at via my conversation with the dean's administrative assistant a few weeks back. I exhale sharply as I pull open the door.

Everyone turns to observe me, and I want to crawl into a deep hole and never be seen again. But I channel my father yet again and head toward the front of the room where I take a seat at a small table and try to compose myself.

In the room is a representative of the Academic Council, a representative of the Student Council, and the dean of the school.

She smiles at me.

I extend my hand. "Dean Barrymore, pleasure to see you again."

"You as well."

I smile at the others and say hello.

Dean Barrymore begins, "We wanted to talk to you about a few things."

"Okay," I say. *Thump, thump, thump* goes my heart.

"We wanted to speak with you before you leave for the summer. The process, as you know, is laborious, but necessary. We've had to take into consideration the entire academic year and what transpired in addition to the harassment situation."

"Yes, I understand."

I understand this because, during the last two months of the semester, I was summoned to speak in front of a few committees as it pertained to my interactions with Ashley, my relationship with Adam, and my academic involvement and participation within the marketing department.

"We have officially expelled Ashley Duncan from the university, effective yesterday. The hearing went well. Her parents were both in attendance, and without getting into details, they have acknowledged there is a need to get Ashley some mental help. She has been released into her parents' custody in Arizona. They left with her this morning."

"Okay," I respond. *Good. Arizona is far away from here.*

"I know you've been in contact with the police regarding this situation. We, the school administration, and the authorities have agreed we have this situation under control. We feel her actions were a result of a fantasy rather than a reality."

"Yes, Dean, I understand."

"We have notified her other teachers and her roommates that she, under any circumstances, should not be within a mile of this school. She is not welcome back on this campus."

I swallow hard and try to decipher how I got in the middle of all this. I am calmed by her words, but frightened all the same that there is someone who once walked among us at this school that is now expelled and not welcome. That the girl was so unstable that she is no longer allowed on the campus in which I inhabit.

Immediately, I want to know if Adam knows. *What was his reaction to all of this?* I want to ask the dean about Adam, but I'm too scared to hear what she might have to say.

"Yes, I'm sad to hear that about her, but it is comforting that she will no longer be here."

"It is in her best interest as well. You must know that. You did the right thing coming forward because, now, she can get the help she needs."

The representative for the Student Council nods her head in agreement, but the room still remains somber.

Dean Barrymore peers over at the Academic Council representative and gestures.

He speaks for the first time since I entered the room, "As for you, Miss Van Tousen"—he clears his throat while his expression tells me he is not pleased with what he has to say—"the board has decided that the grade of an A-plus you received first semester will be revoked and removed from your transcripts. You will need to repeat your Advanced Marketing class. As much as we understand that there was no favoritism, we have to abide by the code of conduct put forth for all our students. Do you understand?"

I sigh deeply. "Yes, I understand."

I knew this was coming, and with some convincing by my father, I agree that I'm getting off pretty lightly. I accepted this in many ways to help Adam. Being agreeable in the process allowed us both to seem rational, accepting that what we did is and will remain frowned upon by the university.

"Good," Dean Barrymore adds.

I think the dean had some sympathy for me, considering she found out that I was included on the list of women attacked who had come forward at OSU.

"I will also ask that you complete your Marketing class with Professor Ty. The schedule will be posted this summer."

Professor Ty is the toughest in the department. I know this is no mistake that she is telling me I have to retake the class with him. But, all in all, I have accepted this and know I'll do as well in his class.

"Yes, of course."

"All right then. Do you have anything further for us?"

"No, thank you, Dean, and thank you all for your time," I say as I lock eyes with the other members of the Council in the room. "I appreciate it," I say as I stand and now face the Dean.

She rises before me, as do the others.

She is an attractive woman, slight with dark hair. She is intimidating, to say the least. She reaches forward and touches my arm. This shocks me.

"Bree, I know you have had a tough first year at OSU, and I'm sorry your experiences and time here have been unfavorable," she whispers. "But please know we are taking stronger safety measures and researching better ways to support our students on campus. We are continuously trying to improve the ways in which we, as an institution, can make it more conducive for students to report a crime. We plan to form a campus task force of faculty, staff, and students. If you are interested in joining next year, please come see me."

Her words hit me hard as this subject is now near and dear to my heart.

But I'm able to choke out, "Thank you, Dean Barrymore. I appreciate it."

"Our institute considers its students and their safety as a top priority. I want you to know that." She turns toward the others as they nod.

"Yes, we all do," the Student Council representative adds with sad eyes.

"Thank you all for your time." I leave the room and gently close the door behind me.

Once I'm out of the building, I exhale intensely and then glance at my watch. Now, on to the next part of my afternoon. I have a meeting with Professor Gilford before I leave for the summer as well. As I near the Draper building, I'm both excited and frightened as I pull open the door.

"Bree, please come on in," Professor Gilford says with a straight face.

"Thank you."

"Have a seat." He motions to the chair across from him.

I sit down in the chair. "Thank you, Professor, for taking this time to speak with me."

"Of course. Now, how can I help you?"

"I wanted you to know that my grade from your class will be revoked and that I will be repeating Advanced Marketing."

"And how do you feel about that?"

"I believe it is more than fair."

"As do I, Bree." He shows me little emotion.

"Understood," I say as I lower my eyes.

I know he is disappointed in me, and I can't blame him. This whole situation got way out of control and shed negative light on the department.

"Bree, how have you been doing with all of this? Should I be concerned?"

"No. I mean…I think I'm doing fine. I'm sorry the department was brought into all of this. I will do my best to help rebuild the reputation you've worked hard on developing. But what I want to know is, how has Professor Cooper fared in all of this?"

"Bree, I cannot be discussing this with you."

I lower my eyes and glance at the ground. I know he's right, but I can't help myself. "I understand, but I have to know. I've been through so much that I need to know if he will be okay after the dust settles."

"I think he will be okay, Bree."

"Have you spoken to him?"

"Yes. And you know that is all I can say for the moment. It is between him, me, and the university."

My heart drops. "Oh."

"Listen, I want you to be able to put this behind you, like he has."

He has? He's put this all behind him? I wish it were that easy for me, I think. *Maybe he has forgiven Ashley, but I'm not so sure I have.*

"Put it behind me…" I say softly to myself. "I understand, Professor, and I will try to do that."

His eyes soften. "You know what I mean, Bree."

"I'm trying to understand all of this, but yes, Professor Gilford, I do."

"Good."

"I should probably get going."

"Yes," he responds as he glances at his watch. "Have a safe drive, okay? And a productive summer. Keep me posted. I am eager to see you back next year. It's sure to be a bigger and better year for all of us."

"I look forward to it as well. And thank you, Professor, for becoming an unofficial mentor of mine this past semester. I know I burdened you with a lot of information, some," I add with a slight smile, "that you probably did *not* want to know, but thank you all the same for hearing me out and supporting me."

He blushes slightly. "Miss Van Tousen, you are an easy young lady to stand up for and support. Your willingness to stick your neck out, despite the potential consequences, is a quality I admire."

Now, it is my turn to blush. "Thank you."

"Now, you have my number, so check in over the summer."

"I will."

"Good luck, Bree. You'll do great; I know it."

I smile at him and then turn and head out of the building and to my car. I climb in, shut the door, and let out the longest sigh. For maybe the first time all year, I'm finally safe...free...connected...focused...energized...and most importantly, back to being me.

As I get on the highway, I'm thankful that, before I left for my meetings, I was able to see everyone. I said all my tearful good-byes already to Laura, Abigail, Maddie, Melissa, Jen, and Casey, wishing them a wonderful summer. But what made it even more exciting was that we had all decided to keep our rooms, on the same floor, in the same dormitory, for next year. We will all be floor mates again, and I'm elated about the fact that I met these wonderful girls I can now call my true friends.

But, like most people I know, I hate saying good-bye. So, a quick exit is best for me. Saying good-bye can be so final, as though it might be the *last* time you say *good-bye*.

I prefer the hellos.

Three hours later, I rummage through my bag, tossing aside the papers and documents, making sure not to ruin any of them. I pull out the note Adam left me to double-check the address, but I can't help but read it again.

Dear Bree,

I didn't wake you this morning because I knew you hated saying good-bye. And, besides, after last night, I could not run the risk of you opening your eyes and possibly changing your mind about giving me another chance. But I am so glad that you have. I plan to spend the rest of my time making up for leaving you when you needed me the most. But what that time apart did teach me was that I need you so much more, Bree. You are my inspiration and my reason for doing what I do.

I am looking forward to putting my arms around you and holding you, knowing all of this will be behind us. Then, we can go back to doing what we do best—being us.

Anna and Harrison will be thrilled to have you. Anna, in particular. She knows how much you mean to me.

In merely two short months, we will not only have an incredible summer together, but we are also going to blow the minds of all the universities from Boston to Chapel Hill. I'm thrilled to be sharing this experience with you and so very proud of what you have envisioned for our university and, hopefully, others as well.

Please be safe while I'm not around. Stick close to your friends; you're going to need them. From here, I'll be sure to stay connected to Officer Murphy and Professor Gilford. I hope you'll lean on them as well.

Longing to be with you,

Adam

There is one hello I've been eagerly anticipating more than anything else, I think as I fervently climb out of my car and close the door. I smile wide. The wait is finally over.

Epilogue

I stand in front of the full-length mirror and fidget with the cuffs on my silk blouse. *Roll them up or roll them down?* If I do it too many times, they'll wrinkle, so I decide to leave them down and buttoned.

I pull my hair back in a ponytail and touch up my makeup again. My fingers are trembling as I apply more mascara.

"Relax, Bree," I mumble. "You've got this. Professor Gilford told you that you could do this." I put down my makeup wand and slip on my high heels.

I hear my name being called from downstairs.

"I'm coming!" I respond. I take one final glance and gather my bag and papers, and then I dash for the door.

"Coming, coming," I say sweetly.

I hear Adam whistle as I make my way down the stairs toward him.

"My God, Bree, you are stunning."

"Don't make me more nervous," I say. My cheeks fill with heat as my eyes catch his.

"There is nothing to be nervous about." He is standing in the foyer, wearing a navy-blue sports coat, a button-down shirt, and tan pants. He could be a model with the way he is standing there with one hand in his pocket and the other one running through his hair.

"Easy for you to say. You're used to being up in front of people." I step in front of him and force a smile, but inside, I am more nervous than I ever was at a modeling job.

"I know, but you've got this. You're a natural, and you know the material inside and out." He smiles warmly at me.

"But it's Boston College. This is no joke," I respond with a furrowed brow.

"Bree," he says as he takes me in his arms and gazes longingly in my eyes. "You are beautiful, smart, and always a little late." He smirks. "So, we need to get going."

He softly kisses me on the lips.

"I know, I know. Sorry." I laugh, rolling my eyes.

"Good news is, I like you and see past all your flaws."

"Hey," I scoff as I pass in front of him, toward the door. He pinches my behind. "Ouch, hey!"

"More of that to come later, babe," he says with a wicked grin.

"I hope so." I smile as I exit out the door.

Once we are at Boston College and check in for our meeting, the butterflies begin swirling unmercifully in my stomach. Adam tightens his grip on my hand and then releases it.

I gaze up at him and can't help but smile.

A few minutes later, a tall man in his mid-fifties or so steps into the common room and says, "We are ready for you."

We both get up. I take a deep breath and smile wide as I enter and take my place at the front of the room.

He runs his hand slightly through his thick hair and then says, "Hello, and thank you for having us. I am Professor Adam Cooper, Assistant Chair of the Marketing Department at Onondaga State University, and this is Aubrey Van Tousen, creator of our marketing initiative for the twenty-first century."

I nod slightly to the room filled with professors from Boston College's pristine Marketing Department.

"I'll turn it over to Aubrey to start us off."

"Thank you, Professor," I say even though it's so strange to call him that. In some ways, I get a charge out of it, and I know he does as well.

"Thank you for having us here today and for allowing us to share our ideas with you." I take a deep breath in and then begin, "Emerging and implementing an effective marketing program, one that leaves a student with the ability to connect to our changing technology, is the most important job any professor has, especially as we approach a new century. Failure to change with the times will ultimately leave your institution giving the impression to your students, alumni, and donors that you are unable to build on the momentum of our changing environment.

"Marketing is a lot like life to a college student; it's ever-changing and unpredictable, and if it doesn't interest us, we won't bother with it. But, if it does, if it grabs our attention, *really* grabs our attention," I say as I slyly divert my eyes toward Adam, "then it becomes more than an academic exercise; it becomes a passion."

A passion indeed.

I've found my passion in Adam and my ability to accept that I cannot change the past, nor can I change whom I have fallen in love with. Meeting him has given me so much more than I think even he knows.

Now that I've decided to minor in education so that I, too, can become a professor of marketing, I have finally found my place in this world. A place no one would have ever predicted for me. I want to be a professor and maybe, someday, if I'm lucky enough, be employed at a prestigious school like Onondaga State.

I laugh to myself as I envision it. The model, the stuck-up girl from the Hamptons, the victim, and the girl who fell for her professor has finally found her calling *and* her equal.

Unfortunately, I knew our infatuation with one another might cost him his job and me, my enrollment at the university.

Ashley forced me to make a decision.

Should I walk away before anyone got hurt more, or should I risk it all?

In the end, I risked it all.

About The Author

Laurel (Kupillas) Ostiguy was born in Queensbury, a town sandwiched between Lake George and Saratoga Springs in Upstate New York, where she still visits with friends and family.

She attended Plymouth State University and graduated in 1997. She also received her master's degree from Northeastern University in 2003.

She is now married to her college sweetheart, Jeff, and they have two sons. She currently lives outside of Boston, Massachusetts. When she is not working, she loves to spend time with her children, ski, skate, swim, write, or just enjoy the beautiful New England seasons.

What's Next From The Author?

Abigail and Bree made it through their freshman year with the help of one dedicated friend, Laura Chase. But what they could not see through their own struggles was the confusion, pain, and heartache that Laura endured while watching her friends suffer. To try and help them, she auditioned for a job at the college radio station.

Now, she wants to be the eyes and ears of this institution if they are ever going to heal from the chaos the Campus Creeper bestowed upon the otherwise sleepy college community.

What Laura doesn't know is that, while she has been faithfully watching out for others, someone has finally noticed her. Will Laura's new romance be the root cause of a divided campus, or will she be able to bring together a university that has lived in fear for over a year?

Join Laura and her friends at Onondaga State University as they wash their hands of their unforgettable freshman year and enter their sophomore year a bit wiser and with something to prove.

www.ingramcontent.com/pod-product-compliance
Lightning Source LLC
Chambersburg PA
CBHW051958240626
47153CB00005B/1801

* 9 7 8 0 6 9 2 8 3 3 4 8 3 *